WHISPERS

FROM THE ASHES

ISBN: 0984561609
ISBN-13: 9780984561605

Disclaimer: This is a work of fiction. While, as in fiction, the literary perceptions and insights are based on experience, all names, characters, places, and incidents are either products of the author's imagination or are used fictitiously. No reference to any real person is intended or should be inferred.

WHISPERS *from the* ASHES

ACKNOWLEDGMENTS

I am indebted to my ancestors, who came to these shores not only with the desire for freedom but also with the perseverance and will to fine-tune their dreams.

To my family of origin: my deceased parents Dan and Burneatta Hester, who allowed me an unfettered childhood filled with unconditional love; my deceased siblings Gail Karazia and Danny Hester, whose memories of the coal fields made this book possible; and to my living sisters Sharon Tobin and Linda Jones, who have waited too many years for this story to be told.

To my offspring, Brad, Brandy, and Ben Wiggins, for showing me that creative energy continues to fuel Hester dreams.

To my supportive best friends Elaine Miller and Nancy Anderson, who never doubted my ability to bring this book forward.

To my editor Todd Manza, whose attention to detail from first to finished drafts took this story to a higher level.

To Teresa Janssen, my critique partner, for her weekly feedback and advice.

To members of writing groups in Tacoma and Port Townsend, Washington, who considered each new version of the same scenes with enthusiasm.

And to Moe.

CHAPTER ONE

They say my great-grandmother had the gift. That she could speak with spirits from the other side. I don't know the truth of that, but I do know this: if she could speak with the dead, Sue Ellen Beckerman certainly earned that right. And if there were any place on this green earth where spirits gathered, it was at her home along the road called Giant's Despair in the Valley of Wyoming in eastern Pennsylvania.

Sue Ellen and her husband Charlie—always known to me as Granny Sue and Old Charlie—settled their farmhouse squarely on one side of Wilkes-Barre Mountain, where its porches captured the mountain's cooling summer breezes and its black slate roof drew in the pale winter sun. They never gave directions as north or south, east or west, but used the sun and the Susquehanna River as their compass. East was where the sun rose over the mountains behind the house. West was where it set over the Appalachians, off the broad front porch. North was where the river entered the valley, behind the steeple of the Catholic monastery. About a mile in that direction the railroad cut a swath as it reached for the mountaintop in a roundabout way. Empty coal cars always headed north up the slope, toward the active mines. Fully loaded cars, heavy with black gold, screeched and smoked their way back down the steep grade to empty their loads at the valley breakers. The river headed that way, too, carrying its own load of human waste and mine tailings toward the Chesapeake Bay. And that was south. For much of my life these would be my directions too.

The house reclined on a foundation of glacier rocks on land Sue's grandfather had willed to her. The property was just large enough to fit the house, a small barn, a good-sized garden, an orchard with apple, plum, and cherry trees, and one hayfield for their horse and cow. Early on, Old Charlie planted native hickory trees to mark the property's four corners and a boxwood hedge to keep road dust from blowing into the open windows of the house.

On the far edge of the orchard, a sturdy grove of sassafras trees provided roots for poultices and teas, and several tall elderberries, their feet cooled by a small spring, sacrificed their heavy heads for tonic wine. Native mountain laurel grew wild in the shade of a hardwood forest that stretched from just beyond the orchard to the heart of the Pocono Mountains.

Best of all, an unnamed mountain stream curved and pulsed like a grass-walled vein through the roots of ancient oaks to give life to the garden and orchard. Where once the horse and cow had drunk their fill, the stream dropped into a small ravine to join a larger creek that cut the village of Giant's Despair in half on its race to meet the river. Eventually I would follow that creek from its source, where it percolated from the mountainside a mile above the house, to a point a few miles downstream where it fell over a steep waterfall.

In later years, when sleep came reluctantly, I could follow its clear waters in my mind's eye and allow its cool peacefulness to lull me into a deep and dreamless rest. But when we first came to live in the big house, I was not allowed to teeter over the creek's inviting edges or tiptoe alone past the wooden cover of the well off the back porch. I was almost five years old and had no knowledge of the drowning deaths that caused Mom's entire family to be skittish about deep waters.

By the time we came to live in the house, much of the old forest had been sacrificed for mine timbers, slag heaps littered the mountainside beyond the creek, and an underground mine fire steamed from cracks along the mountain's middle ridges. But the hickory trees continued to stand guard and the boxwood hedges, overgrown and flowering, were twice as tall as Pop.

Before that year, 1947, we had lived in Back Mountain in a house that had no plumbing. Pop drew our water from an open well where an abundance of snakes lurked in the walls of natural rock and kept us kids away. I remember that the doors inside that house had latches but no doorknobs. When a door was closed, the pointed end of a file was used to twist open the latch. Because I was often in need of the file, I learned to keep close watch on its whereabouts. Pop said that's how I taught my brain to remember so well.

When we came to live in Sue's gingerbread house, I had free reign to explore every cubbyhole, crawl into any hiding place, or close any door. I liked to pull myself up on tippy-toes and peer out the broad front windows to the valley below, where the ribbon of river slithered between the mountain ranges like the well snakes at the house with no doorknobs.

There were spirits in the house even then. It creaked and groaned some nights as if it were old and aching, yet when the morning sun warmed its steep slate roof, it awakened like a young child, full of energy and expectation. Sometimes I thought I saw a horse in the shadows of the decrepit barn. Mom said it was probably Old Charlie's black workhorse back to haunt the place. When a bulldozer came in to knock down the tilting barn, I cried for days because I was sure they had run over that horse. I had no inkling that there were more ghosts in the big house than ever occupied the barn.

Mom brought us with her when she was summoned to care for failing Granny Sue. She was the only female of her generation willing to do the job.

One early morning that autumn, I ran into my parents' bedroom and found Mom sobbing. She'd cried often since we moved into the house where she'd grown up, but this time, instead of waving me away, she pulled me to her.

"You'll have to be on you very best behavior today, Molly," she said. "A lot of company will be coming in to say good-bye to Granny Sue."

"Where's the old lady going?" I asked.

"She's flying up to heaven to be with Jesus."

I nodded before pushing hard against her to get away. This news was just too good to hold back. I ran to the front bedroom, where my older sister Sally was sitting before an antique dressing table, trying to pull her thick brown hair into two barrettes. Her face, a tiny heart framed by cascades of thick curls, looked back at me from three mirrors. Her green eyes flashed.

"Go away," she said. "I'm busy."

"Granny Sue's flying up to heaven," I announced.

"Mom told me." She dropped her arms as a barrette fell to the floor. "If you don't get out of here, I'll send you to heaven too."

I didn't wait to be told again. I liked living in this big house and had no intention of going anywhere with the old woman. I ran to the other front bedroom, where my big brother Marty was sitting on the floor tying his shoes. His sleep-tossed blond hair stood up in several cowlicks. He glanced up at me with eyes the same warm brown as Pop's.

"Granny Sue's flying up to heaven. Sally says she's sending me with her," I whined.

"I heard." He tied his final knot. "But don't worry. No one can go to heaven unless they're dead. You don't look dead to me."

"Is Granny Sue dead?"

"Not yet. But Mom says she's giving up the ghost. That means she might as well be." He wrinkled his nose and sent a shade of summer freckles wriggling across his cheeks. "All the old relatives will be coming to watch."

"Can I watch?"

"Nope. Only old people can watch. They sit around and cry. When they get tired of crying, they drink all the whiskey and start telling stories."

Armed with that knowledge, I sat in the darkness at the top of the stairs and waited for the stories to begin.

By midmorning I could wait no longer. While many of the visitors were having drinks in the main parlor or smoking cigarettes in the overgrown yard, I tiptoed down the stairs, through the second parlor where all the draperies had been drawn, to the library. The French doors were partially ajar. Beyond their glass-filled panels, deeper darkness waited. The murmuring hum of many adult conversations filled the heavy space. I peeked into the room.

There, in a narrow bed that had been pushed against the nearest wall, with an enameled bedpan on a stool nearby and a ceramic covered potty just visible where the fringe of white chenille bedspread ended, my great-grandmother lay dying. It was not possible for me to reconcile the old crone who crooked her pointer finger toward me and twisted her toothless mouth into what could have been a smile with the Granny Sue I had heard about all morning—the young Sue Ellen who had cooked and cleaned and birthed and sewed and mourned and celebrated in her big house.

On that day of death, Granny Sue's pale face, propped up with thick white pillows and surrounded by a wild halo of silver hair, startled me. I stepped back into the second parlor, caught my breath, and waited until my child's curiosity made me look again.

The old woman continued to beckon with one bony finger, but it was not me she wanted at her side. She whispered softly to a dark shadow that filled the book-lined corner on the other side of the door. I watched her mesmerizing movements and listened to her one-sided conversation with the shadow until I heard my mother say, "Can you see what she needs, Sean?"

Pop stepped into a wedge of light near the open door. He placed one hand on the headboard of the bed and leaned toward Granny Sue. The old woman's arms reached up and pulled him down. Right into her bed. Then she was kissing him—covering his entire face with feathery kisses.

"I've prayed to God for your forgiveness, Sean," she murmured. "Thank you. Thank you."

I heard gasps from the family members who sat unseen against the shelves of books.

From the dark interior of the room, an old aunt said, "She doesn't know what she's doing."

Another said, "He's not even family. She must think he's someone else."

As Pop struggled to gently disentangle his shirt from Granny's grasping fingers, Mom slipped under his arm to help him escape. He stumbled backward and disappeared into the darkness.

The old crone's arms flailed the air above her bed. When her hands came up empty, she began to cry.

And so did I.

Pop scooped me up. "You shouldn't be spying, you little bum. How did you sneak in here?"

I wrapped my arms around his neck and held on tight. I had heard what Granny Sue whispered to that dark shadow in her room before she started kissing Pop. She had said, "Come here to me, Bernie. I've missed you, Son. Come take me with you."

~

On the day of the wake that same week when I was almost five, I knew nothing about spirits. I was kept in an upstairs bedroom with Aunt Iris's twins, Lenny and Larry, who were five like me, while the undertaker laid out Granny Sue's bony old body in a polished box in the front parlor. When Mom led us downstairs, the rooms were filled with bouquets of garden flowers that clouded the air with an overwhelming sweetness.

The undertaker waited for everyone to be still before he raised the wooden lid of the coffin.

A collective moan escaped from the crowded room. It was the same sound Mom made when I made a mess or broke something. I looked around to see what had gone wrong but saw only old women dabbing at their powdered faces with lacy handkerchiefs. I raised myself up and peered into the box. The old woman was sleeping there. She had curled her silver hair and rubbed round spots of red rouge over each thin cheek.

"Seven," I heard someone wail. "She's the seventh one to be laid out in this room."

"And so many in their prime. Such a shame."

"Broke Old Charlie's heart, it did. Losing all his boys."

"And sweet, sweet Faye. Oh, she was such a beauty."

Heads wagged and shook.

"And Sue Ellen. Poor Sue Ellen, all alone in this big house. Not even her dear brother to comfort her."

"All in heaven. Praise the Lord. All in heaven."

When the room settled down, I climbed onto the arm of an overstuffed chair and leaned comfortably against Mom. One of the old aunts began discussing Sue Ellen's last hours and how she had tried to pull Pop into her narrow bed.

"What do you think she was doing?" she asked. "She certainly didn't recognize Sean. Who do you think she was talking to?"

I knew, and I couldn't wait to tell.

"She was talking to Bernie," I said. "She wanted to go with him."

The room became stunningly quiet.

An old aunt looked toward heaven and exclaimed, "She has it! She has the gift! Sue Ellen gave her the gift!"

The woman pulled me from my perch and pressed me to her skinny bosom. She smelled like a closed-up chest of winter clothing, a cloying mixture of lavender, mothballs, and Granny Sue's covered chamber pot. Her hands caressed my skull. Her fingers tangled in my hair.

"She does!" she shouted. "Feel!"

She handed me off to another woman, who exclaimed, "She has the knowledge bump. She has it!"

"She said some stuff to Pop too," I shouted as I pushed away.

"What? What did she say to your pop?"

I was about to tell them how Granny Sue had whispered, "I've prayed to God for your forgiveness, Sean," but there was Pop again, scooping me up, weaving between chairs and family, holding me tight as we headed toward the hallway door.

"Leave her be," he said. "She's just a kid."

~

A giant of a man, nearly six foot two, with hammer like hands and feet too big for normal shoes, Pop wore steel-toed boots and flannel shirts that pulled across shoulders broad enough to hold up any child's world. He kept his chestnut hair neatly trimmed so silver strands showed along the temples of his clean-shaven face. Despite his size, he spoke and walked as quietly as the monks who inhabited Saint John's Monastery.

He had been a hobo—one of those railroad boys you see on the old newsreels of the Great Depression. He never carried a stick and bundle, as some might expect, but he did have some baggage. He carried along his younger brother Mike, who was palsied from birth and unable to utter an intelligible word.

Pop rarely discussed those years, but he did say that he and Mike were the luckiest kids to ever ride the rails. That's because they found Magee, who was older and wiser, in the very first boxcar. Magee had lost his own family in a California earthquake, so he understood boys who were suddenly alone. He was willing to share what little he had.

"He taught the boys survival. How to recognize the good that often opens hearts in the worst of times," Mom told me. "If not for Magee, life on the road would have blackened Pop's soul."

My first memory of Magee is of a fresh spring morning when the air had a chill and the cool grass beneath my bare feet was slick with dew. I had crept out to the garden without waking anyone in the house. As I headed toward the orchard, Magee rose up from a bed of hay behind the tool shed. Wrapped in his long canvas coat he looked like a big brown cocoon straight from the pages of *Alice in Wonderland*.

"Good morning, Molly," he said. "Is your daddy home?"

I giggled and nodded.

He unraveled himself from his wrap and winked. "Go and get him for me, would you? Tell him it's Magee what's here."

I scampered into the house and burst into my parent's room. "Magee's here," I announced.

Pop awakened instantly, with Mom not far behind. They stumbled over each other in their efforts to be first out. I beat them to the back porch.

"Where?" Pop asked.

I pointed to the garden, where skinny, brown, bald Magee stood grinning up at us. He was nearly as tall as Pop, and when he laughed his toothless gums showed shamelessly from a Santa Claus beard. I learned right then that it was impossible not to laugh with Magee.

And that's exactly what Pop did. He laughed out loud, ran headlong down the stairs, whooped like a young boy, and did a small jig on the garden path. He threw Magee's canvas-and-wood backpack over one shoulder and led him into our new home.

I clapped my hands together and copied Pop's jig. The joy the two men shared was catching.

I remember that visit like it was yesterday. How that beanpole of a man could eat more than anyone I'd ever known. How after supper we gathered on the back porch, where Magee produced a small box from his pocket. He handed it to Pop.

"I'll be darned." Pop shook a shiny harmonica into his big hand.

"I saw you needed a new one last time I came through." Magee pulled his own harmonica from his breast pocket. "Hoped we could play a few tunes."

"Hell, yes." Pop pulled his chair opposite Magee's. He wet the new mouth organ with his spit.

They warmed up with some polkas, playing together without missing many beats. Then Magee made the sound of a whistle way far off. That set a train to moving. Suddenly a steam engine was pulling a load of boxcars out of nowhere. Each man played a part, bodies bent and folded, chug-a-chugging, whistle blowing, steam a-belching, rails clacking, feet a-stomping, fingers snapping to make a noise so loud I had to step away to avoid being run over by that train. It ran full tilt past the house before it disappeared down a lonely line of track.

"Do it again," I begged. And they did.

I can still feel my disappointment when I woke the next day. The hobo named Magee had gone on his way.

~

Because of his silence on the matter, I did not become fully aware of Pop's history until eight years later.

Before that year, 1955, I had likened him to the Jesus who graced the front window of the Giant's Despair Unity Church. In a spotlight of sun, the white folds of that stained-glass Jesus' robe glowed with a loving heart wrapped in a golden ribbon. Pop's heart was like that. I knew, because as he stood by my bed some nights I would hear him whisper, "You have my heart," and I could feel the golden ribbon that held his heart to mine. So it was that I shared his heartache when his friend Magee was late for his visit that spring.

CHAPTER TWO

The scrape of Pop's hoe caught my attention as I came into the kitchen.

"You'd better leave your pop alone, Molly," Mom warned. "He starts the swing shift at the wire plant tomorrow. He's going to be working the copper annealer—a dangerous job and one he hates. And he's worried about Magee."

"What if the railroad cops caught up with Magee and threw him in jail?"

"Then we'll have to look on the bright side: at least he'll have three square meals and a bed off the ground." She curved her generous lips into a smile, but I could see the wrinkles in her brow as she turned back to her cooking.

The determined rhythm of Pop's hoe stopped.

I ran to the screen door. A locomotive came into view on the eastern curve of the mountain a mile away. Pop dropped the hoe and strode off toward the tracks.

I caught up to him as he climbed onto the pile of rubble that had once been the boiler house of the defunct Red Ash Colliery. The train, pulled by a locomotive of our Pennsylvania line, was already passing. I leaned against the pile of crumbling bricks and began to count boxcars and tankers as they rumbled by. Too soon, the caboose disappeared through a cut of layered rock.

I looked up at Pop. His hopeful smile had changed back to the worried frown he'd worn for weeks. He shoved his hands into his workpants and jingled his pocket change.

"One hundred seven," I said. "Not one of them the Reading." Magee usually arrived in a boxcar from the Reading line.

"Not one," Pop sighed. He gave me a hand up so I could join him on his perch. "Wait for me here," he said. He stepped down to the backside of the rubble pile, where a small door opened into a cavelike room.

I didn't follow. I had witnessed his weekly ritual for the seven years we'd lived in Giant's Despair. He always did it the same way: climbed into the bunker, pulled from one wall a brick marked with a faint X, retrieved the tin box that held safety matches and dry paper, replaced any missing supplies with those he carried in his pockets, placed his carefully folded messages to Magee on top, dropped in his pocket change, replaced the box, replaced the brick, then checked each dark corner to be sure there was enough dry wood to start a fire. His careful restocking ensured that bums who knew of the bunker could quickly start a fire in the rusted boiler that had once powered the colliery. They would have enough coins to buy some food. Pop knew how cold and hungry a man could get riding on an open train.

I turned to study the mine fire clearly visible at our back. Its smoke had changed from the steamy white blackdamp that covered the valley on rainy days to waves of translucent blue with a sharper, hotter, sulfur smell.

Pop climbed up and stood beside me.

I pointed to the mountain. "Why'd the smoke turn blue?"

"The fire is probably moving up to more coal seams on the surface. The old burn is getting hotter."

"If I got up close, would I see flames?"

"You won't see anything more than you can see from here."

When I didn't comment, he took my hand and stooped so he could look into my eyes.

"That thing's been burning for forty years. There's nothing new about it. Understand? You stay away from it."

"I bet you can see flames," I persisted.

"Do you want to end up in the damned fire?"

"I wouldn't go that close."

"There are no flames. You want to see what it looks like, look in the kitchen stove. All coal burns up exactly the same."

"That fire's a lot bigger than the kitchen stove."

"Stay away. Do you hear me? Solid rock weakens and sinks before you can see fire. There's no solid ground up there."

I remembered Mom's warning not to rile Pop, so I touched my free hand to my heart. "I won't go close. I promise." We kids knew that a promise made to or from him could never be broken.

"Come on, then." He walked off the rubble pile in two steps and lifted me down. "That's the last train for today. They'll be no Magee at the supper table tonight. Maybe tomorrow."

I stayed quiet on our walk back to the house. My eyes were on the mountain and the hot blue smoke that marked the fire's hungry path.

After supper, strains of opera from the old Victrola filtered through the parlor from the closed library doors. I knew that meant Pop was working hard not to let sadness come into his heart. Sometimes those ladies and men, singing in a language I couldn't understand, gave him the lift he needed to outrun the blues. If they couldn't help and Magee didn't show up, I feared a bad drinking binge would take him away.

In my upstairs front bedroom, I got on my knees and prayed that the singers would lighten Pop's heart. I prayed that Magee would show up the very next day and relieve his worry. I prayed that, if neither of those two things happened, the drinking binge would be short and sweet, so as not to upset Mom the way it could. Not that Pop was ever mean when he drank. Sober or drunk, he was always kind and gentle. It was that his binges kept him away from work at the wire plant, so no money came in. Sometimes he did foolish things like climbing the ladder to work on the slate of our steep gambrel roof or setting fire to the field on a windy day. At times like those, Mom had to step in. That made her nervous in a way that put all three of us kids on edge.

And there was another, more serious problem with Pop and the booze: if he got into too much hard liquor his asthma flared up and felled him. During those attacks, he sat hunched forward on a kitchen chair, head down, feet wide apart, hands clasped together so tightly that blue veins popped out on his fingers. His chest heaved in his struggle to take in air.

"That damned mine fire," he would say as Mom fretted.

"It's not the blackdamp, Sean," she often answered as she gave him quick sips of sassafras-and-willow tea provided by John Hale, the town healer. "You know darn well it's the booze."

When he raised the cup of bitter liquid to his lips with both hands, his forearms shook.

Seeing him like that made me understand why Mom was so against the booze. That asthma and the mine fire had me worried as I climbed into my big brass bed. I tried to get comfortable. Something wasn't right. I had gone about my prayers all wrong. It would be best to concentrate on Magee's well-being, since that was the root of the problem. I got back on my knees to start over.

My prayers worked a little bit: Magee didn't show up that spring, but neither did Pop go on any binges.

CHAPTER THREE

As I climbed the path from the schoolyard toward the big house, the heavenly scent of purple lilacs competed with the sweetness of mock orange to blot out the acridness of the mine fire.

Mom was in the backyard. She had dragged every large carpet from the main floors, hung them over the clotheslines, and was beating them to death with a handled wire loop.

"What are you doing?" I asked.

"Housecleaning." She didn't interrupt her swings. "Getting all the critters out."

Something more than carpet dirt was in the wind. "Is everything okay? Did you hear from Marty?"

My brother Marty had graduated the previous year and had taken a job in upstate New York. Calls from him always cheered her.

"No," she answered, "everything is not okay. I've been hearing a bulldozer working behind the culm banks all day. I'm just sure that damned Ald Coal Company is working on the Red Ash Road." She could get pretty riled up where coal companies were concerned.

"Let's go up and see," I said. If that bulldozer had turned up slate chunks, I might find some good fossils.

We crossed steppingstones in the shallowest spot of the creek and followed an overgrown path that led to the banks. As we began to climb the mountain of slag, Mom stopped and lifted a handful of black sand.

"Every crime against the little guy has been committed by some big shot coal company." She opened her small hand and allowed the wind to take the dirt. "They let all this mess lay here.

Never bothered to clean it up. They treated the old-time miners the same way."

I had heard this rant before, but had learned to listen with one ear while my mind moved elsewhere.

"In the old days, if a man died in the mines, they carried his body home and laid it out on his back porch. When his family woke up they would find their dead father or brother or uncle there on the wood planks, stone cold dead. Right there on the porch. Treated no better than slaves."

She took my arm as we neared the steepest part of the bank. Loosened gravel gave way under our feet and sent small avalanches down the hill behind us. At the peak of the bank she stopped to catch her breath and then pointed toward the ridge of mine fire on the mountain above.

"There used to be a patch over there where the Red Ash miners lived. Right next to the mule pits."

I knew about the patches—rows of squalid houses with a common outhouse shared by several families. They were named for the immigrants who occupied them or the coal company that owned them. Some patches remained in the valley. Irish Patch clung to a steep hill just beyond the borehole while Scranton Patch's brown shacks darkened the eastern corner of Wilkes-Barre. Diamond Patch lay down the main road, along an abandoned railroad spur that once carried coal to the Empire Colliery. Aunt Iris, her hard-drinking husband, and their eight children lived in a three-room shanty in Diamond Patch.

"Now the only things left are the house foundations that serve as chimneys for poisonous gases. And these ugly banks," she continued.

I wondered what might be buried beneath the bank where we stood.

"If the mine fire hadn't forced them to stop, these banks would be across the creek by now." She pulled herself to her full five-foot height and pointed.

"I knew it." A fragment of new road, shining with hard black shale, lay below us. "They're up to something." She stiffened her knees and launched headlong down the bank.

I had to hustle to keep up.

At the edge of the new road, forward momentum threw her over a jagged chunk of slate. "Damn it." Blood oozed from a tear on her shin. She lowered herself onto a boulder and used the hem of her cotton dress to staunch the bleeding.

I lifted a manageable slab of multilayered slate and smashed it against the solid roadbed. It split into layers filled with fossilized leaves.

"Look," I said. "An evergreen piece."

She took the fossil, smoothed it, and handed it back.

I stuffed three good specimens into my skirt pocket. The next slab was more solid. It didn't shatter when I dropped it.

"This stuff looks like coal. Why doesn't it burn?"

"Oh, it will, if a fire is hot enough."

I followed her gaze to the wasteland where the mine fire's heat had turned solid rock to ash and its sulfurous smoke had painted a line of skeleton trees brilliant yellow. The ravaged trees stood like rigid warriors, their maimed limbs pointing righteously toward the sky.

"Pop says some drunken miner started the fire," I said.

"That's true. He forked a bunch of extra hay into the underground mule pit so the animals could have a Christmas feast." She reached down and retrieved a sliver of slate. "Oh! A bird." She smoothed her hand over the petrified remains. "It's so strange that a living thing could be trapped like this and become perfectly preserved for eternity. It's like a scar in the rock. Painful to look at, in a way."

I had to keep her still so I could look for more. "Tell me about the miner."

She was always good for a history lesson about the valley. "His lantern must have fallen into the hay. All the mules burned up."

I smashed another hunk of slate but found nothing.

"By the time the foreman reopened the pit, the burning timbers had turned the coal seam into a blast furnace. They drilled big pipes into the shafts and tried to douse it with chemicals and clay."

One of those pipes, twenty inches around and welded shut, protruded from the ground along the edge of our orchard.

"If they had stopped mining, it might have gone out on its own. But the coal barons were too greedy to stop. When it started to smoke again, they had your great-grandfather Charlie blast all the shafts closed."

"When was that?"

"I don't know exactly. I think around 1921."

I smashed another chunk. "Why him?" Not one trapped bit of life.

"He was the foreman at the powder mill and an expert on explosives. He placed all the charges."

Sharp edges poked through my stuffed pockets as I lifted another slab.

"Cutting off the air supply dampened off the fire, but anthracite burns long and hot with only a little oxygen," she said. "It will still be here when we're all dead and gone." Her leg had stopped bleeding.

"It can't get to us, can it?"

She limped onto the hard-packed road. "I'm afraid a good draft might get it roaring like a lion."

I followed her along the curved base of the bank until a bright yellow bulldozer came into view. A logo on its side announced that it belonged to Ald Coal.

Her jaw tightened. "They only push in new roads when they mean to haul out coal. I hope they're not planning to go after more of that Red Ash vein."

We followed some crumbling Loki runs back toward the house. The mounds had once been topped with narrow mule wagon tracks to carry slag from the mine to the culm banks. Now they curved like stretch marks across the mountain's belly and provided the only safe passage through the spreading mine fire. Along one edge, where the new road began, tiny drifts of steam seeped from exposed cracks.

"Oh, look what they've done. They've gone and stirred up the damned fire."

If only I had known then, that destructive fires also burned beneath the surface of our lives. Had I known, I might have let them be.

CHAPTER FOUR

I was in my last year at Giant's Despair School. In the fall I would begin taking a bus to Wilkes-Barre High School, where Sally would be a senior. Now sixteen, she was allowed to work part time in one of the small shoe factories along Empire Street.

When Pop's swing shift at the wire plant ended, he often stopped at the Empire Tavern for a beer with the other men. Sally's shift at the shoe factory ended at the same time. On work nights, she walked up the street to the tavern and waited in his car for the three-mile ride up the mountain.

On his arrival home, Pop joined Mom on the front porch swing. Even with both my bedroom windows open I could not make out the content of their murmured conversations, but I learned to gauge the difficulty of their days by the tone of their voices in the night. When times were good, they laughed a lot and their voices rose like the warm hum of a barbershop quartet. When times were bad, their voices cut through the darkness like the warning buzz of the spring sewing bugs that split the mountain air into tiny pieces.

On a warm night in May, I climbed through my bedroom window onto the wide porch roof to hear better. A white moon cast tree shadows on the grass below, where tiny swaying ghosts of Sue Ellen's daffodils crept along the edges of the yard.

"I got caught behind one of those new buses at the tight curve near the monastery," Pop said. "The damned thing had to slow to a crawl to make the hill and stunk worse than blackdamp. They're too slow and too big for the road." His voice was louder than usual, a sure sign that he'd had a shot of whiskey with his beer. "What was wrong with the electric Laurel Line, anyway? It was quiet and came up that hill rain or snow. Never got in anybody's way."

Mom allowed the swing to take several sighing passes before she commented. "Things always change when you least expect. You should know that better than anyone." I was sure she meant changes in our family—like Marty's move out of state—but she had coal companies on her mind. "I was suspicious enough when Ald Coal began widening the Red Ash Road, but all day today dump trucks have been moving up and down the mountain. Those huge things would not have fit under the trolley lines. No one can tell me it's not been planned."

"Can't trust big shots," Pop said.

"Never!" Mom's small feet thumped against the floor of the porch. "They've always wanted that vein of coal under us. They'll move the whole damn mountain, and us, to get to it."

"That fire is getting too close for comfort."

"Oh, Sean, it could take this house and everything in it."

I loved our house and my town. The thought of both burning caused my heart to rise up in my chest and begin racing.

"I'd like to think they'd not allow that to happen."

"We both know that money talks louder than reason."

"Someone's getting paid under the table." Not much riled Pop.

"But Sean, this house is all we've got."

A long silence intervened before Pop spoke again. "There's trouble brewing at the mill, too."

"What kind of trouble?"

"They're saying that the factory might be moving."

I heard Mom's quick intake of breath. "Moving? Moving where?"

"Nobody knows. But they say it's probably going out of state. That's why the layoffs have started and why the union is talking strike again. They say that if it doesn't move, it may close down for good."

"You'll be able to find something else, won't you?"

"I don't know. Jobs are short. I've got enough seniority. I don't think they can just let me go." He lowered his voice and added, "But they can make me move."

I wanted to go to the roof edge and shout that we couldn't go anywhere, that we belonged here, that nothing would ever be the same if we moved, but I knew my eavesdropping would make them think less of me. With deep feelings of guilt for my untrustworthiness and fear of the mine fire burning in my soul, I crept back into my room.

~

Intense summer heat came early. We threw open every window. One night, as I waited in my bed for the sound of Pop's car, I listened to our nearest neighbor, Mrs. Donal, play a quiet tune on her guitar. Her only son, Tom, had been killed in the mines the previous fall. Her music held sadness in every long note. I closed my eyes and dozed a little. A car, taking the Devil's Elbow curve too sharply, jarred me awake with screeching tires and squealing brakes. Dogs barked. Newly hatched katydids screed an ancient song that matched the rhythm of their night-borne mates. Mrs. Donal's music stopped. The town was almost asleep. Pop was late.

Downstairs, the telephone rang. Mom answered it. Her voice took on a frantic tone. The fear I heard in her voice pulled me from my bed. I ran down the stairs and stood next to her. She hung up quickly, dialed, spoke, hung up, dialed, and spoke. She was asking for a ride. Could so-and-so give her a ride? She didn't seem to know that I was there.

After she finally found a cousin's husband who could pick her up, she stopped long enough to say, "Your pop's been hurt. There was an accident at the plant. They've taken him to the hospital.

You stay here. Oh, I hope Sally gets home safely. Your pop was supposed to pick her up. I'll watch for her on the way down the mountain. You'll be okay. I'll call you."

She was gone.

I had never been alone in the big house.

The house creaked, window curtains swayed with a gentle breeze, the back screen door rattled on its hinges. I sat wide-eyed on the parlor couch, waited for my sister, and prayed for Pop.

I thought of Mom saying that Granny Sue's spirits were nothing to worry about—that they only came around when the house was empty. I turned on every light.

I thought of Sally walking up the hill in the dark. I shivered with fear for her. An hour passed. I decided Mom must have picked Sally up. When the phone finally rang, I nearly fell over the buffet to get to it.

"Your pop's okay," Mom said. "He's still in the emergency room, but they'll be putting him in a bed soon. He'll have to stay here for an awfully long time." Her voice trailed off. I knew she was crying.

"What happened?"

"He slipped on a wet floor in the plant. He fell into boiling water. He burned his legs so badly he can't even walk." She paused. Her voice became stronger. "Are you okay?"

"Yes." But I wasn't. I was scared to death.

"I'll stay with Pop until they get him settled. Did Sally make it home okay?"

My heart began to beat faster. Sally wasn't home. "She's coming up the stairs right now," I fibbed.

"Good. Do you want me to tell her?"

"No. I can tell her."

"You girls take care of everything. I'll be home as soon as I can." She hung up.

I had never felt more alone. I ran to the front windows and looked off down the hill. A lone figure was moving quickly up the street. I ran to the porch and yelled, "Sally?"

"I'm coming," she shouted.

I bolted down the stairs to meet her at the hedges.

"I couldn't find Pop," she sobbed. "I walked up and down all of Empire Street but his car wasn't there."

"He got burned," I said. "Mom's at the hospital. She said he's okay but he has to stay for a really long time."

"Nobody gets to stay in the hospital unless they're almost dead. Is he going to die?"

"Mom didn't say a word about him dying." I hugged her as we started up the steps. "I was worried about you, but I thought Mom must have seen you and picked you up."

"It was so dark." She paused at the top of the stairs to catch her breath. "The buses stopped running. There was not one other person out. Whenever I heard a car coming, I ducked into bushes or between houses. Do you think we could call the hospital and talk to Mom? I should let her know that I'm home, so she doesn't worry." She started to open the screen door.

"I fibbed. I told her you were home so she wouldn't worry. She was crying."

"Oh." She moved to the swing. "I have to sit down. My knees are weak."

"Do you think Pop is worse off than she let on?"

"She'd fib. Just like you."

I felt helpless. I sat beside her and gently rocked the swing. On the railroad tracks below, one of the new diesel trains glided down the mountain. The carloads of coal clacked and clicked as they moved through the night.

"I keep thinking I've been to that hospital," I said.

"You were born there. I was born in a house down near the tracks. So was Marty. Granny Sue birthed us."

"It couldn't have been when I was only a tiny baby."

"We did go there once, when Marty was sick."

"Was it a brick building with wide steps out front?"

"Yes. We couldn't go in. We were too young."

I pictured riding on a narrow road between farms and fields held together with walls of loosely piled stones. "There were houses close together on a city street."

She nodded. "Pop parked on the street that faced the building."

"And we were supposed to stay in the car."

"Yes. I'm surprised you can remember that. You must have been about three, because I was in second grade. I was sick like Marty and stayed home from school. You got in trouble."

"I did?"

"Pop pointed out a window and said he'd wave from it. We were supposed to stay right where we were, not to get out of the car for anything. You didn't listen."

"What did I do?"

"After Pop waved from the window, you got out of the car and went to look for a dog."

"I think I remember you reading me funny books."

"Until that darned dog started barking."

I remembered a long, hedge-lined driveway and a black dog.

Sally took on a big-sister tone. "I told you not to go, but you never listened."

"My shoes didn't fit right. They flip-flopped when I ran."

"They were my old shoes. We didn't have any money then."

I remembered the coolness of the shade behind the house, the scent of peppermint, a white frame garage with double doors, and a doghouse with a red roof.

"The dog was chained up."

"Behind a house."

"I lost my shoe."

She nodded. "The dog picked it up."

"I started to cry, didn't I?" I remembered Sally shouting from an open car door.

"Well, I told you not to go. I screamed for you to come back."

I remembered that the people who lived in the house had stepped out through a side door and asked who I was and where did I come from. I don't remember that I answered, but I'm sure I did. I was Molly Branigan. I was proud that I could say my name.

"And Pop came after me?"

Sally kicked the floor of the porch to keep the swing moving. "He saw you from the hospital window and came running."

I remembered him bending over, picking up my shoe, and saying something to the people who owned the dog.

"I made those people mad."

"Yep. Really mad. They started yelling at Pop."

I closed my eyes and let the rhythm of the swing take me back. I could remember Pop holding my hand. He had my shoe in his other hand and was patting it against his leg in a nervous way, as if he was beating the dust from a rag. The lady yelled at him, "You're a goddamned Branigan, that's who you are! Get out of here! Get away!"

I remembered falling into Mom's outstretched arms, Pop putting us in the car, and Mom saying something like "Drive away, Sean. Just drive away." That's what he did. And that's all that I could remember.

"Were those people mad about the Molly Maguires?"

"I don't know. Pop was so mad, he didn't say a word all the way home." She stopped the swing with both feet and started into the house. "Do you think Mom will call again?"

I followed her. "She said they were going to put him in a room. She left some dinner in the warming oven."

"I can't eat. I'm really tired. Can I sleep in your room?"

She didn't have to ask twice.

The next morning Mom rode the bus home. Every day thereafter she went to Wilkes-Barre to sit beside Pop and force him to get well. I was too old to be babysat, but kids had to be fourteen to go inside the hospital. I tried to convince Mom that since I looked fourteen we could lie, but she would have none of it, so I had a lot of time to think about the memory that now plagued me. Something about the Branigan name had set those people off. I wondered what that something was.

Three weeks later, before breakfast, Mom announced that she was going to bring Pop home. "He's signing papers to get out of that place."

"He's all better?" Sally asked.

"No, he's getting worse. His burns are infected. I can give him better care at home. John Hale said he'd help, and Doc Rosen will come by and check on him."

John Hale had served Giant's Despair as both policeman and healer for nearly forty years. He didn't wear a policeman's uniform or have a license for his healing services. In the last years of Granny Sue's life, when she did not welcome visitors, only John Hale had been allowed into her kitchen. They consulted about the plants that grew on our mountain and how to get the healing parts out of them. He had been a good friend of her oldest daughter, Faye, who had died of tuberculosis and thereby orphaned Fern, the other girl who was raised with Mom and Iris.

He had learned both his healing and his policing skills in the trenches of the First World War. But, as the town's paid policeman, he had become more of a teacher than a punisher. The eye-stinging vapor of a fresh-cut onion as he soothed a bee sting, or his thick knuckled fingers running a sewing needle through the yellow flame of a safety match to sterilize it before digging out a splinter, or the sight of his thick white hair gleaming in the light as he diagnosed an ankle sprain—all said John Hale to me. I was captivated by the contents of his leather drawstring bag and the mysterious scents that rose from jars containing black tar, Numotizine, Epsom salts, boric acid powder, fish oil, rubbing alcohol, and any number of dried herbs. He had once shown me how to dig tender sassafras roots from the grove beyond the house to brew Pop's asthma tea. I trusted John Hale, but still I worried.

"Isn't it dangerous to bring Pop home before he's better?" I asked.

"It's more dangerous to have the bills adding up. The hospital keeps sending people to his room to talk about money. I told them not to, but they won't listen to me. If your pop starts worrying about money, he'll never get better."

Despite having a union that was good at calling strikes and agitating management, the men at the wire plant had no workmen's compensation, no health insurance, and no pay if they weren't able to work, even if the injury happened on the job. The factory did provide the care of a company doctor, Doc Rosen.

"Who's going to drive him home?" Sally asked.

"John Hale. He'll take the bus to the factory, pick up the car, and help me bail out your pop. Now I need you girls to help me set up the sick room in the library."

~

Two hours later the car pulled up at the bottom of the porch steps. I was used to seeing Pop hop out, long legs first, head close behind, arms wired with energy. But this time, Mom climbed out and opened the back door. She reached in, bent her knees, straightened her back, and pulled until I could see Pop's pale, freckled hands clearing the open door.

She couldn't leverage him out. She lost her hold and sent both of them tumbling onto the seat. She came back out.

Pop's two scuffed slippers appeared, searched until they found solid ground, and planted themselves. His hands reappeared, grasped firmly on the sides of the door, and pulled his head through the opening. John stepped up, took Pop's hands, and pulled hard.

He came out, head down, arms crooked at the elbows, his back so bent that he seemed like one of the praying mantises that loitered in the garden—all arms and legs and oversized head—silent, swaying, stick-hard.

I had to see his face. I had to know that he wasn't burned red or scarred. I ran down the stairs.

His skin was different, not red and peeling, but pearly gray and pulled tightly over his cheeks and brow. His mouth was a grim slash almost buried beneath a grizzle of beard.

"Pop?"

His faded eyes fell on me. They lighted up for a few seconds before the starch went out of him and he began to fold slowly toward the ground. I ducked beneath his left arm and took his weight on my shoulders. I was taller than Mom and stronger. He didn't have to stoop to be held up.

"Go slow, Pop," I said. He placed his other arm over John's shoulder. A small noise escaped from his chest, a short outtake of breath combined with a primal groan that in later years I would instantly recognize as the sound of a man holding back excruciating pain.

"Watch his legs," Mom said as she moved aside. "Don't touch his legs."

I watched his legs. They wobbled.

"Sean," John said, "can you move?"

Pop's fingers dug into my upper arm. He nodded, grunted, filled his lungs with air, and shuffled forward one step. We inched him toward the concrete step at the bottom of the stairs. His feet dragged in protest of every movement. Mom hovered anxiously. Sally waited on the porch.

At the concrete stoop he stopped stock-still and let out another funny noise. There was no rail at that wide step, only boxwood hedges carefully sheared on both sides and a very big step up.

"Home," he said. "Thank God. I'm home." The funny noise turned into a small laugh. "Damn it. Somebody moved the ground. Look how big that step is."

"He must be drugged," John murmured.

"No. He's right," I said. "It is higher." The earth had settled beneath us. The stair was at least an inch higher.

He made the step up and reached for the handrail on the wooden stairs. Mom stood behind him. All of us lifted and heaved as he advanced one painful step at a time.

At the top of the stairs, he stopped to hug Sally and then turned toward the swing. "I want to sit here for a minute," he said.

"No, Sean," Mom said. "We made a bed for you in the sickroom. You need to lay down."

He moved toward the swing. Mom's face pulled into a tight mask but she held the swing still while we settled him onto its oak seat. He leaned back gratefully, stretched out his legs, and seemed to go into a swoon.

"Sean?"

He opened his eyes, took in a deep draught of mountain air, and patted the seat beside him. "Come sit by me, Toots." He only called her Toots when he felt the need to calm her.

"Don't be silly," she answered. "You need to be in bed. We need to get to work on those legs. John has other things to do."

"Come sit by me, Toots."

"Sean." She resisted.

"Come sit by me, Toots." He reached out and pulled her in.

Her short legs cleared the deck. Her skirt wrapped around her hips in disarray. She tucked herself against his side, careful not to touch his legs.

John tapped my back lightly and pushed us girls toward the front door. As I entered the hallway I heard Mom let out a sob and then Pop's comforting voice.

All was well in our world again. Pop was home. I wanted him to never leave again.

~

Later, as Pop shuffled from the porch to the narrow bed, I heard the wheeze of asthma in his heavy breathing. He dropped onto the bed with a deep grunt. Mom propped him up with pillows, but his breathing didn't quiet. I began to feel sick.

"Molly, get a dose of that sassafras brew we made last year," John said.

Mom shooed Sally out after me. "Don't come back until we call you." She closed the door that connected the library to the kitchen.

Sally found a jar of asthma medicine and began to dig out its paraffin plug with studious concentration. I leaned against the nickel plate of the stove. Goose bumps prickled my arms with each muffled moan that came from behind the closed door.

After what seemed an eternity, Mom opened the door and ushered us back in. The closed-up room was filled with a sweet, putrid odor that clotted the air. I swallowed hard to keep from gagging.

Beneath Pop's weeping legs, a red rubber sheet had been formed into a tube that funneled into a bucket on the floor. Next to the bucket, a paper bag overflowed with putrid, reddish-yellow bandages. My knees became weak. I forced myself to stay upright.

Sally offered Pop the cup of sassafras tea. He waved her away with an upright hand. His face glistened beneath sheens of moisture.

"Drink it," John ordered.

Pop's mouth tightened into a scowl. "They started giving me that penicillin stuff day before yesterday," he whispered between wheezes. "It must be working; the feeling's coming back."

"Looks like your boots saved your feet." John's voice was matter of fact.

Sally again offered the cup to Pop. He raised his hand. Mom stepped in and tipped the cup to his lips. He gagged but gulped some of the liquid. She used her apron to wipe his chin.

"I never heard of anybody falling into a copper annealer," John said.

"Damned if anyone did," Pop gasped. "We had just finished pulling a bunch of wire through. My work buddy forgot to close the grates. I got out of it pretty damned quick."

"You're a lucky man."

"Could have been worse. Could have been I didn't grab hold and all of me went in."

Mom held the cup to his lips again. "Drink."

His eyes begged her to take it away. She would not be put off.

"Drink," she repeated.

He gulped more of the potion. She handed him a clean workman's handkerchief from the stack of linens on the table. His hand shook as he drew it over his sweating face.

"I was in a hurry. I slipped and went right into the boiling water. It could have been worse, Toots. It really could have been worse."

Mom nodded, but from the look on her face I knew she didn't agree. She turned away to set the empty cup on the table.

John laid his fingers across the leaking flesh of Pop's legs in the same way Mom laid her hand across my forehead to check for fever. "Good circulation," he said, "but bad infection. You're losing too much fluid. We've got to get the old flesh cleaned out."

Pop managed a grin. "Here I thought I had sprung leaks from all the shots those nurses gave me."

My heart filled with gratitude for his good nature.

John lifted an enamel pitcher and slowly poured liquid over the burns. It drained into the bucket on the floor. He looked to Mom. "Keep the boric acid solution weak, Bessie. Don't touch anything to the burns. Do you think you can find some aloe vera plants?"

Mom turned to the table to write a list. "I'll get some somewhere. Anything else?"

"You'll want to get his resistance up. He'll need fruit juice and fresh apples and some good protein—eggs, beef."

Mom put her pencil down and stared out the window. When she turned back she wore a look of determination.

"I've got more bed sheets baking in the oven."

"Good. After you rinse his legs, slide dry ones under them."

"I'm feeling better already," Pop said with a smile. His wheezing had softened.

John removed the rubber sheet. "Let the legs air dry." He placed a rolled towel under Pop's heels. "That'll keep them from rubbing against the bed. You girls listening?"

We nodded soberly.

"Keep the room warm and don't cover his legs. Close the windows every night before the sun goes down and don't open them again until the sun hits this side of the house. Keep the window screens in." He turned to Pop and patted his shoulder. "You going to let these girls of yours take care of you?"

Pop flashed another grin. "You betcha."

While John burned the bandages in the backyard barrel, Mom got on the phone and started rounding up aloe plants from neighbors and friends. Within an hour they began arriving on the front porch. I helped her line them up where they would get the most sun. We carried two plants inside. John split some stems of one and dripped the juices over the raw flesh of Pop's legs.

~

Night was on us when he gave his final instructions. "Your pop can't ever have anything touch the burns. You'll have to be his policeman."

I hung back as everyone left the room. Pop beckoned me to his bedside.

"You're too quiet," he said. "What's on your mind?"

"You aren't going to die, are you?"

"A big tough guy like me? Never."

"Do you promise?"

"Yes. I promise."

"Then touch your heart and say it."

He touched his heart. "I promise. I'm going to get better in a few weeks. I'll walk out of this room like nothing ever happened. How's that?"

"Good."

"Now I have to ask you for a favor."

"What?"

"Will you to go to the boiler house once a week and look for that message from Magee."

I nodded.

"But I never want you to go alone."

"Why not?"

"Because it's a new time and not all the bums who use the place can be trusted."

"I'm not afraid of any bums."

"Do you see how big I am?"

"Yes."

"Big as I am, I'm still afraid of some bums."

"If I tell any of my friends, they'll spread the word and the boiler house won't be a secret anymore."

"Ask your cousin Lenny. I bet he can keep a secret."

"He won't walk all the way up here, just for that."

"Promise him some of Mom's great homemade bread and he'll run the whole way."

"You aren't going to ever leave, are you?"

"Never. Absolutely never."

I felt hope returning. "I'll ask Lenny."

CHAPTER FIVE

Lenny and I strolled through the hottest part of the day, kicking dust from the road with our sneakers, turning now and then to walk backward and study the blue smoke of the mine fire. As we shuffled along, I practiced the whistle he had already mastered. He could force a piercing squeal between his fingers when he laid them on his tongue and blew. Mom said it was unladylike. She wouldn't let me practice in the house.

As we neared the railroad tracks, I could see a figure sitting on the rubble of the boiler house. I recognized the rounded shoulders of Ronald Miller. Ronald was Sally's age and a bit wild. He lived across the tracks in Irish Patch in a house that was never painted. His father was rough and careless with his sons, cuffing them in public, reportedly beating them in private.

He was hunched over, cigarette in hand, the barrel of a rifle showing above his shoulder, its butt resting on the ground between his feet. He killed dogs. That's what everyone said. If someone wanted their dog put away, he would take it into the woods and shoot it once, right behind the ear. He didn't bury carcasses but let them lie along the path or tossed them into a stripping hole. He eyed us up as we came close, but didn't move.

"Got a smoke?" Lenny asked.

"Not for a kid like you," Ronald answered. He took a big drag and flicked the butt into the dirt of the road.

Lenny chased after it. He tried to take a drag but yelped when it burned his fingers.

Ronald laughed. "You want one?" He held his open pack toward me.

I shook my head.

He stood, shouldered his rifle, and stepped down to stand beside me. He was as tall as my brother, but wiry. I craned my neck to look into his face. His eyelids slid halfway over faded blue eyes.

"Your shorts are ripped," he said.

Before I could move he shoved one finger into a small tear near my pocket. His finger caressed my skin.

I jerked away.

He laughed and stepped onto the road. "I'll see you around." He headed down the tracks.

"Nice guy," Lenny said.

"Yeah, if you like snakes."

I climbed onto the pile of rubble and watched Ronald until he disappeared into the cut of rock. Pop was right. I'd never want to come here alone.

I showed Lenny how to find the box. At first he wanted to take the coins, but I said I'd tell Pop, so he put them back. There was no message from Magee.

###

After the first week, when Pop took a turn for the worse, lost his appetite, and started having some stomach problems, Mom stopped giving him the penicillin. She smiled for Doc Rosen as she agreed that the drug truly was a modern miracle. She didn't tell him what she was using to treat the burns.

After the second week, she made Pop, who tried to protest in a manly way, come to the table for all his meals.

"You're a taskmaster," he joked as he moved slowly into the room. "I thought nurses were supposed to be gentle and kind."

"Never mind the gentle and kind. Get your Irish rear in here if you want to eat."

Fresh from her afternoon bath, Mom had washed and pinned her hair. Soft black ringlets circled her heart-shaped face. Her bibbed, knee-length apron was starched and spotless. I laughed when Pop patted the soft roundness of her backside as he moved past her. That's when, through the open window, I heard voices coming up the hill.

The factory where Sally worked lay near the Empire Colliery in an area that was owned by the Diamond Mining Company. The building was one story, swaybacked, brick-faced, and blackened with a century's worth of coal dust. Sally had begun cutting through the dirt parking lots that backed onto Diamond Patch to visit Aunt Iris and our cousins when her Saturday day shifts were done. Now she was climbing the steepest part of Fitch Lane with all eight of Iris's kids in tow.

I followed Mom into the street.

The smallest boy took hold of Mom's skirt. "I'm thirsty. I'm so thirsty."

Mom used her apron to wipe his face. It left round white clean spots on his nose and cheeks.

"Well, come on. We'll get you to the house and find you some water." She lifted him and began the climb back up the hill.

"Nobody was there," Sally said. "I decided it would be okay to bring everybody up here."

"Of course it's okay." Mom turned to Cousin Janet, who was sixteen like Sally and went to the same school. "Where's your mom?"

"She's in the workhouse again. She called this morning to the pay phone at the gas station."

Workhouse was a polite name for the women's jail, before it became widely known that women could do deeds as bad as men.

"Where's your pop?" Mom asked.

"I don't know. He went to do his shift on the railroad last Friday and he didn't come home."

"Did you call the company?"

"I didn't have money for the phone. I was afraid to leave the kids alone."

"Did you have anything to eat?"

"We had some bread and jam. Last night it ran out. I kept hoping that Pop would show up. Friday was his payday."

"You all must be starving," Mom said as we reached the house. "Let's take care of that first. Then we'll figure out the rest. Sally, you and Janet take the children upstairs and wash their hands and faces. I've got stew for supper and some baked bread. I've got to see to it."

I followed her into the kitchen, where she added more water to the stew to make it a soup.

"Molly, go open up the dining table and add both leaves."

She goaded Pop from the kitchen into the dining room and handed him the phone. "You'll need to talk to Jake's boss," she ordered.

He kept his voice low as he spoke to the Diamond Mining Company foreman.

The boys came down the stairs one at a time. They were all very thin. Their clothes were soiled and held the odors of a closed, damp house. I started to help the youngest ones into chairs, but the twins, Lenny and Larry, took over to settle their brothers. When I smiled at one of the younger boys, he shrieked, "Don't look at me!" Everyone laughed. That broke the ice. We all started talking at once.

Mom brought in the pot of soup. "I think everybody will feel better with full stomachs."

She began to ladle garden vegetables, broth, and shreds of beef into bowls. Sally passed around slices of bread spread with jam. I worried that the soup would run out before Mom got to me, but it lasted. Everyone quieted and began to eat. The twins picked up their bowls to drink the broth. Pop, who would have quickly corrected me for those kinds of manners, didn't say a word. I noticed that he took only a half a bowl of soup and refused the bread, so I didn't ask for seconds when Mom offered them around. The last piece of bread disappeared between the twins.

"Lenny, you and Larry take the boys outside. Help them play in the oak trees. Be careful no one falls," Mom ordered.

When they cleared the room, she turned to Janet. "Now, tell me exactly what happened on Friday."

"They had a fight. They were drinking. Neither of them had any money left. Iris kept saying that Pop had to have some coins in his pocket. He kept saying, What did she expect? It was payday. Before he left for work, Mom got dressed up. She said she was going to the tavern to find somebody who could buy her a drink. Pop said, 'Fine, I hope you get real lucky because I don't intend to ever buy you a drink again.' When he left for work, he took some extra clothes with him. Neither one of them came back. That's all I know."

Mom looked to Pop. He raised his hands in a gesture of futility. "The shop said he came to work on Friday, was supposed to work on Saturday, but didn't show up. He hasn't been back."

"He said he was going to Pittsburgh to find work in the steel mills," Janet offered. "He has a cousin who can get him a job. He always says that."

"That's what he told a buddy at the shop, too," Pop said. "The buddy took him to the bus station."

"Well, you'll all want to stay here while we get this sorted out," Mom said. "I'll ask you girls to go back down to the house and get all the clothes you can find so I can wash what's on the boys' backs. While you're gone, I'll figure out where everybody will sleep."

That night, while Sally and Janet slept peacefully in my big brass bed, I crept to the open windows to listen as Mom aired her concerns on the front porch swing.

"There will be no welfare money for the kids," she said. "They don't provide support for kids of jailbirds unless they're in foster care. We'll have to make do."

Pop didn't hesitate. "We'll figure something out. Iris and Jake just had another falling out. He'll be back. He's probably gone off on a toot."

"I'll ask Lillian if she can help. With only Sally working, eight more kids will be a lot of mouths to feed. We won't be able to do it for very long."

Lillian and Iris were sisters with twenty years' age difference between them, but they were more like twins than just plain sisters. They dressed alike, in sequined blouses, pencil-slim skirts, and high-heeled alligator shoes. Peroxide had turned their hair to nearly colorless white-blond and neither would be caught dead carrying a purse that didn't match her shoes. They had husky voices that Mom said were made gravelly from too many nights spent in smoke-filled beer joints. When she stood close to the two blonds, Mom looked like a brown paper bag beside two crystal chandeliers. But if there were children in the room, they gravitated naturally to my mother.

Lillian didn't want to be called "grandmother" because she was too young for the role. That's why we called her Lillian. Pop called her Lily. Her boyfriends called her Lil.

When I was younger, I believed that Lillian was rich, because she slipped each of us kids, even the cousins, one dollar each time she visited and because she brought beautifully wrapped presents for birthdays and holidays—entire celebrations in shopping bags from the best department stores in Scranton. In truth, she earned good tips from a waitress job, supplemented with rents from operating a boardinghouse on the second floor of the Scranton Hotel. She'd been working at that same job since she left Mom to be raised by Granny Sue.

"Let's take it a week at a time," Pop said. "We're okay this week. You can see Iris at the workhouse next visiting day. We'll go from there."

Mom was silent for a while. "I hate going to that place."

"I know. You've done it an awful lot. If they would let men in, I'd go. You know that."

"She'd listen better to you."

"I don't think Iris listens to anyone."

"Well, she'd better this time. They'll take those kids away if she doesn't wise up."

They lowered their voices. I couldn't hear anything more.

The next Saturday morning John Hale and I waited in the car as Mom knocked loudly on the workhouse door. She ignored the women shouting from the windows above. When the door opened, she stepped quickly inside. She stayed for a very long time. When the door opened the second time, I could tell from her face that she'd been crying. She stopped suddenly, shook her fist at one of the girls screaming through the bars above her head, and climbed into the car.

She did not speak until we reached the traffic light at the corner.

"Jake filed for divorce. Now, that witch won't agree to have the kids stay with us. She told the matron we're as poor as church mice."

"So what's next?" John asked.

"A social worker is coming to the house tomorrow."

"No." He braked for a red light.

Mom pounded her small fist on the dashboard, sat forward, and leaned her head on her folded arms. Her shoulders shook.

John kept both hands on the wheel and stared straight ahead.

Through the window, I saw smoke billowing up from the gas plant that changed stone-hard coal to gas.

"Could we go look at the gas plant?" I begged. "Could we?"

John didn't answer, but he turned into the parking lot and pulled against a barrier.

I could see the river flowing darkly into the turbines of the plant. I rolled down my window. The car filled with the rotten egg stench of sulfur mixed with the musty dampness of the Susquehanna. I touched Mom's back and pointed twice, but she wasn't interested. My eyes burned from the acrid air.

"Let's go," I said. "This stink is terrible."

"It's about as bad as a stink can get," John agreed.

Mom leaned against the seat back and closed her eyes. She didn't speak the rest of the way up the mountain.

The next morning, Iris's family was taken away in two cars.

~

There were no miracles to supply an income. Mom asked Sally and me to answer the phone so she wouldn't have to speak to bill collectors.

While she managed to get foods Pop needed by using some of Sally's wages, we girls ate oatmeal cooked with different spices, fried up with a little sugar caramelized on top, or baked into crunchy loaves of bread. John Hale delivered the grain in tall burlap sacks, along with fresh vegetables he collected on his rounds of Giant's Despair. Pop's garden supplied some additional greens and carrots, but mostly it had gone to weeds. For everything else, Mom relied on our tick at Harry's store.

We owed so much on that tick that I dreaded placing Mom's carefully drawn lists on the store's scarred counter. She wouldn't let me out of it. A month after Pop came home, she nudged me out the door. I plodded down the hill to Harry's.

"Have your mom come in." Harry clenched his jaw and slid the list back toward me.

I was afraid he wouldn't fill the order. "She can't." I avoided his eyes by moving to the candy case and ogling black licorice babies, red jawbreakers, and penny squares of rich, Grade A chocolate. I couldn't back down. "Pop's real sick."

"It will only take a few minutes," he persisted. "I need to talk to her."

I knew that talking wouldn't help. Mom had been able to borrow from Lillian to help with Iris's kids and to get needed supplies during the first weeks Pop was out of work, but now Lillian could not stretch her waitressing tips any further.

I looked into Harry's eyes. "Mom's not feeling good today. I'll tell her you want to see her—as soon as I carry the order home."

He put everything into a bag, took out his tick book, and pulled a pencil from behind his ear. As he added up two long pages of sums he ticked off each number with a heavy mark.

"Tell her she owes me ninety-nine dollars and fifty-two cents. Until she pays some of it, I can't give her any more credit."

Neighbors in the store turned away to study cans on the shelves or to read the headlines of the newspapers on the stacks. My face grew hot. I started toward the door, remembered the precious bag on the counter, turned back, snatched it up, and ran home.

The look on Mom's face when I burst through the door, my cheeks wet with tears, told me that she understood.

"Next time, I'll go myself," she said.

~

But the very next morning she came brightly into the library where Pop and me were reading the morning paper. She placed two fried eggs, some toasted oatmeal bread, and a small glass of fruit juice on the table and announced, "We're going to the city today, Molly. I need to do some shopping."

I put the newspaper down.

"Get cleaned up. Wear a skirt. Comb your hair. I'm in a hurry."

We didn't walk down the main road past Harry's store to catch the bus but took a footpath over the railroad tracks near the boiler house. At an iron cross with the name Beckerman in raised letters, Mom stopped.

"Let's rest for a minute," she said. "I'd like to pay my respects."

"Who died here?"

"Silas. He was run over by a train."

"Silas? Who was he?"

"He was Granny Sue and Old Charlie's second son."

"And he was killed too? Like Bernie?"

I was anxious to catch the bus but death had become a new interest of mine. I sat on a rocky outcrop and listened as she pulled weeds from around the marker.

"The engine crew saw him standing in the darkness by the tracks. He was holding Iris by the hand. The engineer rang his bell, but Silas must have tripped. He fell under the tender. It's a miracle that Iris wasn't hurt. Her guardian angel was looking out for her that night."

I could not imagine Aunt Iris ever having a guardian angel. "How old was she?"

"Four."

"Where were you?"

"I was still living with my mom and dad down in Wilkes-Barre."

I didn't want to hear the story of her parent's divorce again. I stood and brushed dust from the back of my skirt. "Let's go, Mom. We're going to miss the bus."

"We're not taking the bus." She turned and strode across the tracks. "We're walking."

I followed her around the tall banks of the borehole that had been drilled a century before to test the thickness of rock covering the Red Ash Mine. The hole, about twenty feet in diameter, was filled with brackish water. As we passed the cattails that grew on its shallow edge, Mom pointed to the bloated carcass of a dog floating on the surface. "It looks like Ronald Miller's been here," she said.

We descended to the Empire Colliery and passed Diamond Patch and the Empire Tavern before we started to climb again.

"I'm hot," I whined. "I can't go another step."

"You're doing fine. We're almost there. See." She pointed to the city below, where a sluggish curve of the Susquehanna pressed against the public square. "You should be ashamed to complain," Mom lectured. "Your ancestors survived a bloody Indian massacre and climbed over these hills on a day hotter than today. One of the women was so far along she delivered a baby up near Prospect Rock. Still she walked all the way to the New York line with four small children and that newborn girl. If she had been as puny as you, none of us would be alive today."

I had heard it all before. "And it was her that named Giant's Despair," I finished in my best sarcastic voice, "after the villain in *Pilgrim's Progress.* Because she thought the hill such a torture."

"You watch your tone," she said.

I wadded up the center front of my blouse and pulled it through the neckline to form a halter. "I bet she was smart enough to fill up on water before she set out walking."

She reached out and tugged the halter free. "Tuck that in. You're too young to show so much skin."

"I'm hungry."

"When we get to Wilkes-Barre I'll buy you a soda."

"You don't have any money."

"But I will soon." Her smile made me wonder what she had up her sleeve.

When we reached the flat streets of the city, I tried to rest under a shade tree in the public square, but she continued walking. I ran to catch up. On South Main Street, she pulled open a heavy glass door stenciled with the words HOMEWARD FINANCE. LOANS. NO COLLATERAL. NO QUESTIONS ASKED.

We walked into a narrow room lit only by uncovered store-front windows. A dark-suited man lounged behind a desk, flanked by two army green file cabinets. He stood as Mom approached.

"Hello," she trilled into the cavernous space. "I'm Bess Branigan. I called earlier in the week? About a loan?"

He bowed and swept his hand over the only other chair. "Please. Sit."

She settled on the chair's edge.

"And this must be your lovely daughter." He bowed toward me. His smile was as false as his teeth.

"Molly, say hello to Mr. Reid."

"Hiya," I said.

"Molly. What a sweet name. Let me find you a chair."

"That's okay. I'd rather stand." I turned away and peered out between the two Ls in COLLATERAL. Across the street, a line of men in work clothes waited to enter the unemployment office. I had heard Pop talk about the growing number of laid-off workers, but I hadn't paid much attention. There were an awful lot of men in that line.

Mr. Reid laughed. I turned to see him place a sheaf of papers on the desk. He pulled a pen from his shirt pocket and tapped the first sheet in the stack. Mom bowed her head and began to sign. As she completed each page he lifted it away and tapped the next. When she reached the bottom he tapped them together and placed them to one side.

Mom smiled as he unlocked a drawer and counted paper money onto the desktop. She tucked the bills into her purse, snapped the bag shut, and draped it over one arm before she propelled me out the door. Once on the sidewalk, she backed me up until the bricks of the building bit into my shoulder blades.

"Don't you ever tell your pop about this," she warned.

There was something wrong with all of it.

"Why not?"

Some of the men from the unemployment line looked over.

"Lower your voice," she whispered. "You have to understand. It will make Pop sicker if he learns I was forced to borrow money. If you tell him, he'll climb out of bed and go back to work."

I knew she was right about Pop. He would pull his pants over those boiled legs and go to work, no matter what anybody said—even Mom.

"But you have to pay loans back, don't you?"

"I'll cross that bridge when I come to it. Right now, it's either borrow or lose everything." She glanced at the men across the street, took a deep breath, and offered me a bribe. "If you promise you won't tell, I'll take you to the Woolworth's counter and buy you whatever you'd like for dinner."

I had the best ham sandwich I ever tasted, on toasted bread, with mustard and sour pickles, washed down with an orange soda in an iced glass. We stopped at the Planters Peanut store and bought fifteen cents worth of fresh roasted cashew nuts to share on the bus ride home. I was ashamed of how easily, and for what a low price, I could be bought.

We waited for the bus in the shade of the Paramount Theater marquee. Mom smiled more genuinely than she had in weeks. The bus pulled in. I stood aside to let her go first.

"Now I can pay off the bills so the hospital will stop calling every day." She let me take the window seat.

"Wasn't Marty in the hospital once?" The question popped into my head. I was pressed to ask it before the subject changed again. You had to be quick with Mom.

"Yes. He had pneumonia."

"And didn't I get out of the car when I wasn't supposed to and a dog took my shoe?"

"Yes."

I took a deep breath. "And didn't the people with the dog get mad and call us dirty Branigans?"

She turned her face to me and answered innocently as a lamb. "Yes. I'm surprised you can remember that."

"Why did they do that?"

"Do what?"

"Call us names."

"Sticks and stones can break your bones, but names can never hurt you."

"But why?"

"It's old news."

I shrugged as if it didn't matter to me at all. "I'll ask Pop."

"Don't you bother him with that. It involved his brother. It happened a long time ago." She looked at me sideways, as if she hoped I would lose interest.

I held her gaze.

"Everybody believes his brother did a really bad thing."

I waited.

"He didn't, but you can't change people's minds once they're made up."

"Did Pop do anything bad?"

"No. But people like to make broad strokes with the tarring brush."

I had no idea what she meant but I wasn't about to get off the question at hand.

"What did his brother do?"

"He died in jail." Her voice took on an impatient tone. "Why are you so interested in all this?"

"If the kids at the high school are going to call me names, I should at least know why."

"I don't think anyone at the high school will call you names. Neither Marty or Sally were bothered."

"But they might."

"Might counts for nothing. It's nothing."

I studied her face. She was keeping secrets.

Back at home, Pop asked how she had managed to buy fresh hamburger for dinner. She said that she had borrowed money from Lily, which was technically true because she didn't say "*the* money." She added that Sally had done really well at the factory the previous week and had received a nice paycheck. That was also a fact. She didn't bother to tell him that she had stopped at Harry's store to settle our tick, or that the hamburger was the start of a new one. He believed her, which goes to show how sick he was. She was not a good liar.

Two miracles near the end of July. First, Lenny came loping up the hill with the news that Larry, Janet, and he were back with their mom in Diamond Patch. The other boys remained in an orphanage downriver.

Second, at the boiler house we found an envelope, dirty and wilted from passing through many hands, addressed to Pop. My legs pumped so fast on the hill that Lenny had to run to keep up. When we reached the side yard he stuck out his foot and sent me flying into the grass. The envelope fluttered from my hand. He snatched it and ran toward the house. I leaped on his back and pummeled him. He dropped to knock me off. We rolled down the small knoll into Mom's row of roses. That got us to our feet.

"Give it to me," I yelled.

He screwed up his face and spit.

"It's mine," I said. "Give it to me and get out of my yard!"

"It's not your yard."

"Is too."

"Nothing here belongs to you! Your pop stole this place. You're the one who should get out of here."

"Oh, yeah? Who says?"

"Everybody says. Everybody knows you shouldn't live here. The whole family says we should throw you out."

"Lillian owns this house! She says we can stay!"

"They just tell you that! Your old man stole this house from Old Charlie and someday we're gonna take it back!"

"I'm gonna tell him what you said. He doesn't like kids who lie."

"He's the liar. He's scared to death that we're gonna throw you out. Why do you think he lets all of us come and stay here? My mom says that as soon as she gets herself together she's gonna throw you out on your bare asses. She says you ain't never had a pot to piss in before you stole the house."

His sureness frightened me, but I was my mother's daughter and not one to take anything sitting down. "I'm going to break your scrawny ass."

Our shouts brought Mom onto the porch. "What are you kids doing?"

"Nothing," Lenny shouted.

Mom looked to me. "Come in here and get ready for supper."

"Not before he gives me my letter."

"What letter?"

"From Magee. I found it at the boiler house."

She was off that porch so fast Lenny hardly knew what happened. She snatched the letter and went running up the steps.

I wish I had seen Pop's eyes when she handed him that letter. By the time Lenny and I sorted out our differences with a few good punches by the back door, Pop was reading it to Mom.

"S and B, Sorry that I couldn't make my usual visits. Hear you've been looking for me. Not enough trains and too many schedule changes shot me off in the wrong direction. I'm in Oregon and won't get back that way until fall. See you then. Magee"

Mom sat on the side of the bed and smiled broadly. "So, he's okay. That's good. He's okay."

"Yep," Pop said. "He sounds fine."

"We worried for nothing."

"Yep," Pop repeated. His voice wasn't right—like he'd gotten a completely different message than the words he'd read.

"Can I see it?" I asked.

He handed me the note. Sure enough, he'd read it word for word. When I met his eyes, he repeated again, "He's fine. Magee's fine."

"When was it written?" Mom asked.

"No date," Pop said. "Could have been a week ago, could have been last March."

"Well," Mom stood and moved toward the kitchen, "that's one less thing we'll have to worry about."

I went out to the creek. It had rained during the night. The water was running fast. After I whispered a thank you prayer, I dangled my feet into the icy stream.

In the seven years we'd lived on Giant's Despair, no one had ever actually said that Lillian owned the house. What if we could be put out on the street? What if Iris moved in? I couldn't bear the thought of that. I loved everything about the house. I wanted to live in it forever.

CHAPTER SIX

Mom believed that all things come in threes: good things, bad things, deaths, births, and big life changes. Iris losing her children to the foster care system was number one. Pop's accident was number two. Now she was waiting for number three.

Pop's skin was healing as a piece—without the cracks or fissures that John Hale had warned us would be bad. The new, bluish flesh didn't match the old, but as it grew confidently over the raw areas, it wiped out the distinctive odor that had fouled the air. Pop no longer clenched his jaw and turned his head away when Mom did his daily treatments. When John Hale made his Saturday rounds he found no black bits of scab to trim away with boiled scissors. When nothing more happened, I decided the number three was no threat.

It was in August, when the tomatoes first showed color, that he began to show signs of worried impatience. I had heard his visiting coworkers tell of big announcements to be made at the factory outing. I decided he was as afraid as I that we would miss the annual clambake along the Lehigh River. Unlike the Susquehanna, the streams in the Pocono Mountains ran clear and were thick with native trout. The picnic allowed the men to drop their fishing lines into the river while their wives gossiped and we kids played and swam. I bet if someone were to count, the beer kegs tapped far outnumbered the fish caught. But I never heard a man complain about free ale.

We had never missed a picnic. Mom said we wouldn't go without Pop and it would be up to John Hale and Doc Rosen to say that he could make the trip.

A week before the event, Doc Rosen pronounced Pop well enough to attend. He was to be extra careful not to bump his legs or sit in one position for too long, and he definitely could not drive.

On the day of the outing, Mom placed steamed comfrey leaves over his remaining burns and wrapped his legs in a good layer of bandages. He looked normal sitting in the front seat of the car, chatting away about the weather and the upcoming fall elections with John Hale, who had volunteered to drive.

As we came out of the thicker trees of Bear Creek and approached the bridge that separated the fishing from the swimming areas, a cloud of smoke, thick with the scent of grilling hamburgers, wafted through the open car windows. The river ran high and swift beneath the car as its tires clattered over the loose planks of the old bridge. After the hot sun of the high mountain roads, the sudden chill of the river and the dark shade of the overhanging trees cooled my face and shoulders as if I had dived headfirst into the flowing water. And that's exactly what I intended to do.

John pulled a folding chair from the trunk of the car and helped Pop to a strategic spot where he could view the river and easily reach the line of ice-filled tubs topped with kegs of beer for the men and bottles of soda for us kids.

The picnic tables groaned with the weight of potato and macaroni salads and mounds of yeast rolls covered with sheets of waxed paper. Kettles of fresh corn on the cob, steamer clams, and pots of drawn butter simmered away on charcoal stoves. Mom placed a glass of beer into Pop's hand then left him with his male friends while she went off to visit with the women.

I pushed my hands through the icy slush in a galvanized tub, pulled a misted bottle from its nest, and watched as the warmth of my hand cleared the fogged glass. The orange color of the drink became bright and enticing. That cold clearing was nearly as refreshing as the first taste of its cool sweetness. I carried the bottle with me to the swimming area. I planned to spend all my time in the water, before everyone was sated with food and flush with drink and before the big shots stood with their backs to the river to make their long-winded speeches about how the company had done and what they expected in the next year.

The river widened below the bridge, and like most of the ancient streams in the Appalachians, its deep middle channel ran icy cold over sharp outcrops of submerged rock. I found several girlfriends splashing about in the shallows. On the side opposite the picnic the boys played rough games of shoving and dunking. Most were drinking beer openly. They screeched as they swung out over the stream on a high-flying swing and whooped as they hit the water.

A group of older girls giggled and pranced in their one-piece bathing suits to catch the boys' attention. I made my way through them and moved carefully into the water, taking time to absorb the shock of its coldness. I began a slow stroke against the current toward the bridge, staying in the shallows so my folks wouldn't worry. When I was well into the shadow of the bridge, I flipped onto my back and allowed the river to float me silently back to the girls' beach.

The bell for the first lunch sounded as I reached the bridge for the twelfth time. I treaded water and listened as the bare feet of forty boys thumped across the bridge above. When the noise ceased, I turned to float downstream. I remember looking up toward the cooking area and seeing Mom and Pop standing together on the edge of the picnic grounds.

As I raised my hand to wave, slightly off balance in the water, I felt hands grabbing onto my shoulders and I went under. I thought one of my friends had sneaked up to dunk me, but when I tried to duck away, the arms wrapped tightly around my neck. I kicked hard and tried to show that I wanted to be let go. The hold became tighter.

I felt the temperature of the water change and sensed the strength of the current pulling me. I panicked as I realized that I was moving rapidly downstream in the deepest part of the river. I struggled, forced my head above water, glimpsed bright sunlight, but wasn't able to take a breath. I kicked hard against the surging water as it threw me against rocks, sometimes bashing my head, sometimes battering my softer parts.

I fought the cold rush of the river until my arms became weak and my legs slowed to a sluggish paddle. The stream became warmer, less hostile, and gave up some of its downward pull.

I felt the person clinging to me jerk against my neck and let go. All sound disappeared except the gentle gurgle of water and the thud of my slowing heart. Comfortable warmth buoyed me as a sense of expectancy centered itself in my brain. I opened my eyes as I was lifted, light as a feather, toward a kind, smiling face.

The face hovered in front of mine, small when far away but expanding as it moved closer. Two hands reached out through a haze of blue and beckoned me from thick robed sleeves. The vision filled my entire field of sight and every inch of space around me. I could see its face behind me, to the sides of me, as well as in front. I could see all of it, and all at once. I was floating with it, in it, on it. I raised my arms slowly and rose into its shining softness.

Somewhere, far off, I heard Pop call my name. He shouted in a tone of voice I had never heard before. I tried to tell him to hush, to leave me be, that we were in the presence of someone very important, but I couldn't remember how to speak. I knew that I should hold my finger to my mouth and shush him, but my arms no longer belonged to me. I needed him to stop his infernal noise.

"Breathe!" I heard him shout. "Damn it, Molly, breathe!"

I turned my attention toward him and opened my mouth to tell him to hush. Orange soda erupted from my stomach, seared the raw linings of my throat, and splattered on rocks beneath my face. The rushing river rattled the gravel beneath my cheek in an angry way as I struggled against a heavy weight on my back.

"Now look what you've done," I wanted to say, but I couldn't form the words. I wanted the weightlessness of that lovely place, yet even as I had the thought, I knew with certainty that Pop wouldn't allow me to go.

The pressure increased on my back. Another gush of water and soda filled my mouth and nose. It hurt to breathe, and when I did my lungs made a funny noise. I struggled against the painful pressure on my rib cage. A high, rough squeal of air forced its way out of my chest. I heard the sound of many voices gasping in unison, much as they had on the day my great-grandmother's casket was opened. As I slowly returned to the land of the living, I felt the wonderful place slip silently out of reach.

Pop pulled me to a sitting position, but my backbone wouldn't hold me up, so he held me against his chest. I threw up on him. He laughed. I turned my head to see why my vomiting had made him so happy. I saw the bare legs and feet of many swimmers. A shiver ran through me. Icy cold seemed to enter the very center of my spine.

I found my voice and squeaked, "I'm so damned cold!" Everyone laughed. Someone threw a beach towel over my shoulders. Pop stood and tried to lift me to my feet.

My legs gave way. I reached for him and saw that his burned knees were bleeding through his pants. I struggled to my feet.

"I can walk," I said. My voice was tiny. It hurt to speak. A spasm of coughing doubled me over. He placed one hand flat against my forehead, another around my waist, and supported me as I emptied my stomach of the remaining soda. His warm hand burned through my skull as the wet gravel turned a pretty orange color.

Together we hobbled up the river toward the place where a bigger crowd of people lined the riverbank. It seemed a very long walk. Mom met us on the path.

"I couldn't come any closer," she cried. "I couldn't watch." The crowd surrounded us as we came into the picnic area.

Someone handed Mom a blanket. She wrapped it around me, hugged me close, and sat with me on a picnic bench. She began to rub my limbs and back through the blanket. I shivered uncontrollably.

Pop pulled a reluctant teenage boy from the crowd. "This is the boy who saved her," he announced. "This is the guy who dove off the bridge and saved both the girls."

I recognized him. His name was Chuck and he was a little older than Sally. His eyes were the same shining greenish blue as the river. His smile was shy and slack. He stood before the crowd sheepishly. I wasn't sure if he'd had too much beer or if he was embarrassed by all the attention focused on him. He struggled to catch his breath as his body jerked with congratulatory smacks from people in the crowd.

His eyes met mine. In that moment he seemed to know what I had seen, where I had been. Something passed between us—an exchange of spirit energy, a melding of life forces, or maybe the knowledge of a broader connection.

I remembered a story Pop had told about a man who'd saved his friend's life in a flood. He said that when someone saved a life he became responsible for that life for eternity. I thought of that as everyone marveled at how Chuck had saved two lives—mine and that of the girl who had nearly drowned me. He had become a hero, but he didn't want any part of it. He turned on his heel and hurried back to his friends. The older girl—the one who had panicked, grabbed me around the neck to save herself, and had been punched, pulled off my back, and dragged to shore by Chuck—raced after him.

We couldn't stay for the speeches or the picnic. Doc Rosen told Mom she'd better take Pop and me home. I'd breathed in enough water to catch pneumonia, he said, and Pop was going to get his knees infected again if he didn't get the dirt cleaned out of them. That's why we weren't there when the big shots made the announcement. The factory was selling out to a big company and moving the operation to New Jersey. When a guy called and told Pop the news, Pop's face became as pale as that day he had come home from the hospital.

"New Jersey," he said to Mom. "I hoped I'd never have to see that place again."

~

Two days later, drowning pneumonia announced itself with a fever that was hot enough to make the round brass joints on my bed rails spin so fast that I became dizzy and threw up again. In my delirium I railed wildly against my sister and brother, who I believed had climbed up on the highboy to throw smothering pillows over me. My back and chest hurt when I shouted at them to stop. Mom frantically applied Numotizine poultices to my chest and bathed me with an ice-cold cloth that raised goose bumps on my superheated skin. She rarely left my bedside.

John Hale offered me bitter tea. I spit it over the mound of covers on my bed. The smell of it smothered the room. Despite the damaged skin on his knees, Pop climbed the stairs to persuade me to take the medicine. I wouldn't do it. I fought them when they tried repeatedly to hold me down so they could spoon the stuff into my mouth.

It was then that they called Doc Rosen.

He laid his ear against my chest for a very long time before he shook his head. Through a fog of sweat and heat I heard him tell Mom that, if I wasn't any better by the next morning, he would put me in the hospital. There it was again—that *hospital* word. I determined that I would make myself better by morning.

Doc left a big brown bottle of liquid penicillin, and this time when the spoon came to my mouth I swallowed. It might have been that banana-flavored chemical or my dread of those people near the hospital who hated us or my mother's constant vigilance and cooling cloths—whatever it was, my fever miraculously broke that night.

Mom celebrated with music. Her own. She hummed as she bathed my face and hummed as she changed the tea-stained sheets and hummed as she carried the dirty bed linens away. I could hear her steady rhythm all that day. It comforted me in a way I could not explain. It was as if she sang a celebratory aria from somewhere deep within her soul, for me, for my survival, for my future.

The pneumonia left me puny and out of sorts. I was to be confined to bed for six whole weeks so as not to overtax my lungs and heart. Mom promised pineapple juice and boiled eggs. That was what I craved and that was what she would conjure up. Sally brought me a sketchpad and colored pencils and John Hale brought me a loose-leaf notebook and a pen, but I looked around my room as night fell that first day of the doctor's sentence and wondered how I could possibly survive within those four walls for six whole weeks.

As evening fell, Pop came slowly up the stairs and settled himself in the overstuffed chair by my double windows.

"I can see Pleiades tonight." He pointed high in the sky through the window.

I remembered how he used to shake all three of us from our beds in the middle of the night to watch the falling stars of August.

"Isn't it time for the meteor showers?" I asked.

"Yep."

"Remember how you used to tell us those silly stories?"

He laughed. "What? That the seven sisters of Pleiades were our family?"

"Yeah, and Cassiopeia's chair was Mom's throne, and the Big and Little Dippers spilled milk and honey to make the Milky Way. And when Orion the mighty hunter showed up it was because he was going out to find deer and bear meat for our winter meals."

"What about the North Star?"

"If we could find the North Star, we could follow it all the way to Alaska."

"That one is true," he said. "You could do that someday."

"What?"

"Follow the North Star to Alaska. You don't want to stay in this valley your whole life, do you?"

I had never thought of leaving. I believed that travel was for boys and men. Mom had been out of the valley only once, on a school train trip to Washington, DC. Pop had come and gone many times.

"You can find the way to almost anywhere if you learn the stars," Pop was saying. "Magee gave Mike and me lessons every night when we were boys."

"Did you and your brother always sleep outside?" I asked.

"Mostly. Unless we were lucky enough to find an empty boxcar."

"Did you like sleeping outside?"

"In good weather there was nothing to compare. We liked the open prairies best—lying in the grass, listening to the trains whistling toward us from way, far away, and watching the stars."

Pop had a dreamy, faraway tone in his voice that made me think he might like to find those open places again and that he might forget to take us with him. I decided that he must have been more like Orion the hunter than the no-good bum that Aunt Iris said he was.

"Aunt Iris says that Mom had to call you back one time when you were living by the railroad tracks and already had two kids. She said that you took off running after a passing train."

"Iris would say that."

"Did you do that?"

"Probably. I was a little wilder in those days. After a few beers I was liable to do about anything."

"Even leave Mom all alone with kids?"

"Am I still here?"

That made me laugh. It hurt my chest. I decided his yearning for those times had once made Mom a little nervous. When I was younger and we stayed out under the stars too long she would call out the window, "Sean, you bring those kids in before you all catch your death of a cold."

He would rise to his feet, shake us out of the quilt, and chase us into the house, pretending that he was a pinching bug.

"There!" He brought me back from my memories. "A shooting star!"

"I'm not going to be able to see even one of them," I whined.

"We can fix that. I'll get Mom and Sally and we'll move your bed over here to the windows. That's where Old Charlie liked it after he had his stroke."

I wasn't much interested in having a conversation about my great-grandfather. He had been dead for seventeen years. I was alive and I wanted to see out that window.

Pop limped to the hall banister. "Toots," he called.

"What?" Mom answered from below.

"How about bringing Sally up here and help me move this bed for Molly."

"Don't you touch that bed, Sean Branigan," she scolded as she started up the stairs. "You're not to do any more lifting or pushing until those legs are completely healed. Do you hear me?"

Pop came back, grinning. "That moved her," he said with a wink.

I sat in the chair in one corner while they took the bed apart. It was too big to turn as a whole. In the end, Pop did have to lift the heavy steel springs, but he was careful and didn't bump his legs. When the bed was reassembled next to the windows I stood to walk the few steps to it. I became lightheaded and dizzy. Mom caught me in the nick of time.

"That proves that Doc Rosen is right," she said. "I don't want those legs to come over the side of the bed unless someone is here."

They left the room together. From the head of the bed I had a view of Giant's Despair Road. Halfway up the mountain, two steam shovels worked in the night. As their headlights rotated across the newly exposed seam of coal, they caused the wet sheet of anthracite to glisten like the black silk dresses Lillian and Iris sometimes wore. Chains covered with twists of lights formed necklaces from crane to crane. I wondered how a machine of iron and steel bent on destruction could appear so beautiful. Then I moved to the foot of the bed to view the lights of the city far below. I lay flat on my back and watched several shooting stars arc across the sky. It was enough. I would be entertained.

In the light of day, the shovels lost their mystery. Like sad old workhorses, they bent their heads under heavy loads of stone. As they emptied their buckets into waiting trucks, their chains rattled and shook black dust from their necks. I had to pull the blinds. I couldn't bear to watch them chew away my mountain.

CHAPTER SEVEN

It was September, and all my friends and Sally returned to school. Missing the first weeks of high school meant that I would be behind from the start. Pop was granted his freedom, but not for work. The factory would not allow him back until Doc Rosen cleared him. Every afternoon he headed off on foot to have a few beers with his friends at the Empire Tavern.

One morning, after I had finished breakfast, I turned onto my stomach and traced the wallpaper design with one finger. I was thinking about sketching a similar basket of flowers when I noticed a long-unused vent that had been part of the original heating system. In all the years we had lived in the house, the old brass bed had covered that fancy plate. I used my butter knife to remove the screws that held it to the wall. What I saw when I pulled the grating free caused me to pull up on all fours.

A small book was wedged into metal louvers at the back of the vent cover. My heart raced as I removed it. Its torn leather cover was thick with dust.

I sat up to the screened window and blew hard against the book edges. It hurt my chest to blow so hard. Mom's footsteps clicked up the stairs.

I was not a secretive person, but the book was someone else's secret and I was not yet ready to share it. I tucked it under my pillow, sat up straight, and bundled my sheets and blanket to hide the open square in the wall. She bustled into the room, stacked my dirty dishes on the dresser, and turned to straighten my bed.

"I'd like to make my own bed for once," I said. "I'm feeling better and I'm bored."

She stood for a minute and studied me, then turned away. "Okay. But I want it neat and I don't want you to stand to do it. You have to stay in that bed. Your feet are not to touch the floor."

I waited until I could hear her clinking dishes together in the kitchen. She had taken my knife. It was difficult to replace the plate screws with my bare fingers. By the time I did the repair and neatened my bed, I was exhausted. I closed my eyes and slept. The book lay unopened beneath my head.

~

When I awoke the house was quiet. I removed the screen from my window and listened to the voices of my parents, who had taken to the front porch swing. I pulled back my pillow and lifted the book. A gray shadow remained on the sheet where it had lain. I laid the book on my lap and allowed its pages to fall open.

Inside the front cover, in fading formal penmanship, my great-grandfather had written his name: Charles Leonard Beckerman. I turned the pages slowly. The first few contained lists of groceries and their cost. The amounts purchased were so large, I decided, they must be for the mess hall at the powder mill where Old Charlie had been foreman. Next came observations that a grown man would make: the temperature at the farm, the weather, and snippets of home and neighborhood news. Some of the more interesting entries described a series of explosions at the mill. He had carefully listed the names and towns of men who were injured and how the accidents had happened.

Then came a list I recognized: the names of Old Charlie's departed children whose stories were common themes in Mom's historical ramblings.

Burton, July 10, 1915, drowned in Crystal Lake/Ira

Silas, September 20, 1920, run over by 11 pm train/Ira
Faye, November 8, 1931, consumption/POISON?/Ira
Arlie, November 17, 1931, wasted away/POISON?/Ira

A fifth entry in large letters—MIKE IRA—had been penciled in by a shaking hand.

Burton was Old Charlie's firstborn son—the Bernie whose name Granny Sue had uttered on the day of her death. I knew about Silas and his death by train. But what did that questioning word *poison* have to do with Arlie or Faye? Arlie had died of leukemia. Faye had died of tuberculosis following years of slow decline. The story of how Mom and Fern had done most of Faye's care was one I'd heard many times.

I laid open the last two pages to reveal "CRYSTAL LAKE CABIN MY CAR GO" in scrawled, uneven letters. The words had been pressed into the pages with such anger that the writer had partially torn the last page and the cover.

I studied those last entries. The first four names were written in faded strokes of different colored fountain ink. The slash and Ira after each appeared to have been added later, and with the same pen. The fifth, Mike, was scrawled hastily in pencil, and that same pencil had made a heavy mark after each of the first four names in the same way Harry the storeowner ticked off the sums on Mom's bill. It was also that pencil that had thrust through the last pages in its angry need to be heard.

Who was Ira? What did he have to do with the deaths of Charlie and Granny Sue's children? I had never heard a whisper of the word *Ira* in our house. And why would Old Charlie include Mike in his list? They were not related, except by marriage. And who had made those last angry notations? Certainly not Charles Leonard Beckerman. His writing was precise. The last scrawls were large and printed in the block letters of a child.

Old Charlie had died in the brass bed in 1939, three years after he'd had a stroke that left him paralyzed on one side. I thought of asking Mom what the entry meant, but the secret was too good to share.

Maybe the diary was a big joke from Sally, who had first claimed this room. She would love to see me fall into solving a mystery that was no mystery. But no, the book was so encrusted with dust it couldn't have been handled recently.

I decided to think about it some more and so, confined to my bed with no talent for drawing or interest in the daily workings of the house, I carefully copied the secret entry into my notebook and slid the diary under my mattress. All I had to do was find the right people and ask the right questions.

Mom, worried about getting me ready for high school, had started letting down the hems on Sally's skirts. She insisted on sitting in the overstuffed chair in the corner of my room, where the light from the windows was good. She had skillful, graceful hands, and like most of her people, she was small in stature and fine-boned. Even though they tended toward roundness, the women of her line could wear high-heeled, sling-back shoes and still move with efficient, purposeful strides. They mostly had dark hair, like my sister, and green eyes. As I watched her make perfect stitches in the hems of those skirts, I wished that they could transform me into as pretty a teenager as Sally.

In truth, I had inherited more of Pop's genes than Mom's. I had his eyes, plain brown hair that frizzed and curled like Little Orphan Annie's in the funny papers, and an Irish curse of freckles that ran across the pale skin of my nose and cheeks. But the worst was that, in this small town surrounded by Mom's short-statured relatives, I had already grown taller than any girl or boy my age. I was big, awkward, and had my father's square hands, with long fingers that were perfect for hard work, not for fashion. To my mother's dismay, I had no interest in fashion and, according to her, much too much interest in reading or wandering through the woods on my own.

I could tell by the way she suddenly bunched one finished skirt into a ball and scrunched her face into a worried frown that she had something important on her mind and that she didn't know where to begin.

"You know, Molly," she finally said, "you're getting to the age where boys will want to do it with you." She blushed.

I nearly fell off my bed. "Doing it" was all that girls my age talked about. The problem was, not one of us had any idea what "it" was.

I ducked my head. I could think of nothing to say. When the silence lengthened to an uncomfortable pause, she smoothed the skirt onto the upholstered arm of her chair and walked slowly from the room.

Just my luck that, while I was stuck in that room, gazing out windows to a world dominated by culm banks and coal trucks, and dying to be alone so I could study that diary, Mom had decided it was time for me to grow up. She came back upstairs carrying two of her Aunt Faye's ancient nursing books. She placed both volumes on the dresser next to my bed and walked out. Until that day those volumes, showing human anatomy in side views and veiled shadows, had been completely forbidden. I opened one as soon as Mom left the room—and closed it when I heard her footsteps on the stairs an hour later.

Without commenting, she settled back into her chair and to her sewing.

After an appropriate interval, I asked, "Mom, do you think you could bring me something different to read?

"You don't like Aunt Faye's books?"

"They're boring. And the pictures are gross."

"Oh. What would you like?" She picked up the nursing tomes.

"The family Bible."

"What do you want with that big old thing?"

"I want to see what kind of people I came from. You know, where I fit in and all."

She raised her eyebrows and let out a low exhalation but soon had Pop carrying the Bible up the stairs. She picked up her sewing again.

I read slowly, running my finger down each page of births, marriages, and deaths registered in different shades of fountain ink until there it was: the name Ira, written with jet-black ink and blotted carelessly.

Ira Raymond Reece
Born June 5, 1898
Died July 21, 1937/self-removal

I looked to Mom, "What does 'self-removal' mean?"

Her head jerked up from her sewing. "What? Why are you asking that?"

"It says here that someone named Ira Reece died of self-removal."

She ducked her head back to her work and mumbled, "It means suicide. Ira committed suicide."

"Why?"

"Why? How in the world would I know why? He died without telling me why."

"Did you know him?"

"Of course I knew him. He was my uncle."

"How come you never talk about him?"

"Because he's dead. Why should I talk about him?"

"I'd talk about my uncle if he committed suicide.

"You have no uncles."

"But if I had one, I'd talk about him."

"There's nothing to say. He was Granny Sue's half-brother, but he was much younger than her. Her father started a second family after her mother died. Ira lived with us in this house, off and on, for years. You know, Molly, sometimes it's best to let sleeping dogs lie."

"Did he die here? In this house?"

"No. He drowned in Crystal Lake."

"Maybe it was an accident, like Bernie."

"He left a note."

"Oh. Did Old Charlie like him?"

She broke the thread with her teeth and jabbed the needle into the top of the spool.

"No. Charlie did not like him. And neither did I. There was no love lost between Ira and most members of this family."

"How come?"

"He wasn't very nice. He was mean. He didn't care about anyone but himself."

"Why did Old Charlie let him live here?"

"Why wouldn't he? He was family."

"I wouldn't let anybody live here if I didn't like them. Not even if they were family."

"You wouldn't turn them away if they asked. You would never live it down if you did."

"Pop wouldn't put up with someone he didn't like."

"He would if I asked. He's always helped with my family."

"How come Pop doesn't have any family?"

"He has Aunt Mary Margaret."

"What happened to the rest of them?"

"Aren't you in a questioning mood." She stood, gathered in her arms the three finished skirts, and strode toward the door. Over her shoulder she said, "All of that is Pop's business. Ask him."

~

When Doc Rosen next visited, he laid his ear on my chest and said, "Still some fluid in those lungs, but she can start to do a little more. Get her outside in the fresh air on clear days when there's no blackdamp. But no strenuous activities, no climbing stairs."

When they left to walk him to the door, I slipped quickly out of the bed and shoved the diary into the side of the overstuffed chair, way down below the cushion. I thought it would be accessible yet safe there, but when they came back to my room, Pop slung me in his arms and carried me downstairs. I was to take up residence in the library sickroom so I could be closer to Mom and get my own books. Pop was moving back upstairs. I looked over his shoulder to be sure Mom had my notebook. My notes now filled six pages.

The good news was that after less than one year of independent life, my brother Marty was moving back from New York. He had found a job as a mechanic at a car dealership across the river. The bad news was that cousins Lenny and Larry were moving into my vacant room and Janet would be sharing Sally's room. Iris had finished her probation and was allowed to have her children back, but divorce now forced the family from their Diamond Patch home. She and her youngest sons would stay with Lillian in Scranton.

"Why doesn't Aunt Iris come here and take care of all the kids?" I asked.

Mom stowed my belongings on an empty library shelf. "She can't accept living with me under the same roof."

"She seems determined to get her life together this time," Pop said. "Maybe she'll do better without Jake."

"I'm glad she's allowing the boys and Janet to stay with us. I suppose she has decided to trust you, Sean. Heaven knows you'll be good for the boys."

"I wish Iris would mind her own business," I said. I did not want long-term boarders in my room.

Pop pulled me into a warm hug. "You've got everything you need," he said. "The twins have nothing. You can share for a while, can't you?"

It wasn't that I minded sharing, even though I had become used to having a good lot of attention. It was that all I could think about was Old Charlie's diary and how the twins' nervous fingers might come across it in the chair upstairs.

"You'll mind your manners, Molly, and make them feel welcome. Do you understand?" Mom scolded.

Two hours later I felt a pang of shame as the twins hesitated in the entry hall. Their sandy hair was long and shapeless, their green eyes downcast, and their fingers nervously twisted the tops of brown paper bags that contained every item of clothing they owned. The bags were nowhere near full. Even though they weren't identical twins, Mom said they could read each other's thoughts and often acted out each other's problems. Now, the way they carried themselves, awkwardly with a slight bend of their heads toward one another, made me think they could do just that. Lenny was the taller of the two and tended toward sullen ways. Larry was the best looking, with a sunnier disposition.

Mom softened them both with big hugs. "Come on, boys," she said. "I've changed over Molly's room for you. Now don't worry. It looks like a boy's room. I've used some of Marty's things to fix it up." They followed her slowly past the library and up the stairs.

The next day Mom enrolled all three cousins in the city high school. That did make me jealous. The boys would be in the same grade as me and would have a leg up. I had two more weeks of recovery before I could join them.

When Lenny and Larry came back from school, they came into the library. Lenny pulled a can of marbles from the shelf.

"We're going to live in a big house like this soon," Larry said.

"Yeah, and we're going to the moon, too." Lenny dumped the marbles onto the puzzle board. They rolled quickly off the table, across the floor, and under my bed. "Man, would you look at that. This house is really leaning."

"Settling," I corrected him. "It's because of the mines. It's happening all over town."

"How come?"

"Because the mine fire's burning every slab of coal it can find. When it turns to ash, the ground on top falls in."

"Could it swallow a house?" Larry asked.

"I think so. I saw a picture in the newspaper last year that showed a car disappearing in a big hole in a street on the East End."

Larry crawled under my bed and began handing marbles to Lenny, who plunked them into the can.

"Pretty soon this place will slide right into the mines and you won't have anywhere to live either," he said.

I shrugged. "It doesn't matter anyway. We're going to move to New Jersey when Pop's factory goes."

Mom heard that from the kitchen. She wiped her hands on her apron as she entered the room. "We are not moving to New Jersey."

"Pop said we are." He hadn't really said that, but it was what I prayed would happen. I couldn't imagine life without him, and it looked like he would have to go.

"He's looking for work. I'm sure he'll find something."

I had heard him say that he was too old for anyone to hire him, what with all the younger guys out searching and his damaged legs. Not one company had called back.

"We won't be going anywhere. I've spent my entire life in this valley and I intend to die here."

"If the house keeps settling, we won't be able to live here anyway."

"It's not settling."

I sat up straighter in my bed, took a handful of marbles from the can, lined them up against a book on my bedside table, and lifted the book. The marbles rolled rapidly over the edge.

"Hey!" Larry cried. "This time you pick them up."

"I'll have to have Pop take a look at that table," Mom said. "It seems to be getting a wobbly leg." She walked back into the kitchen.

A week later I was cleared to begin walking and Pop was cleared for work. I was a week ahead of schedule. Pop was a month behind.

I bounded up the stairs, retrieved the diary, and carried it, covered with some clothing, into the sickroom, where I stashed it in a deep drawer full of blueprints and rolls of Red Ash Mine schematics.

CHAPTER EIGHT

The next week, on one of those hot, clear days of Indian summer that are so awash with color they make a person joyful just to be alive, Pop said I could take Lenny and Larry up beyond the mine fire to see Squirrel Hollow.

We laughed as we splashed across the creek. Larry found a few small fossils as we climbed the culm banks. Once clear of the banks we made our way around the soft edges of the mine fire. When we reached the crumbled house foundations of the Red Ash Patch, Lenny balanced on the smoking edges of the broken rocks and pretended to be a seer, breathing in the smoke and rolling his eyes at the blue sky.

"You will marry a man ten feet tall and have thirteen children," he prophesied. I had to pull him away. At the edge of the hollow a stand of yellow oaks, orange witch hazels, and crimson maples paraded down the slope of native rock that led toward my favorite place on the mountain.

"When will we see some squirrels?" Larry asked.

"We won't. They're all gone. Mom says they disappeared when the native chestnut trees caught blight and died out. That's what they ate. Chestnuts."

"Probably starved to death," Lenny said.

"Or got shot by hunters," Larry said.

"I think I'd rather be shot than starve again," Lenny said.

Near the center of the bowl-shaped ravine, a small spring flowed over moss-covered stones until it collected in a basin of translucent green. All the trees on the hollow's sides marched downhill toward that small basin. Their yearly contribution of leaves formed a spongy mat that gave way in silence under our feet.

On the far side of the spring, an old trail climbed steeply through rocky outcrops and glacier-smoothed stones until it reached Prospect Rock, where the entire valley could be taken in with one smooth sweep of the eye. Mom said that the Indians had used the monolithic rock formation as a lookout and had once hidden there in order to ambush some men of General Sullivan's party as they marched through the wilderness. I told the twins that story as we walked—how Sullivan's army had surged through the great swamp of the Delaware Water Gap, braved the canals and woods of the Shades of Death, and marched across the Endless Mountains to avenge the Wyoming Massacre. How, as they marched, Sullivan's men widened the game trails that led from New York and opened the overland route to our valley. The twins lost interest when I got to the part about farmers, loggers, and millers taming the valley. They were more interested in the Six Nations tribes that had hunted the rich lands along the Susquehanna. Larry showed us how to walk pigeon-toed-Indian style so as not to make noise as we strolled down the ancient path.

We rested and watered at the spring then started up the overgrown trail toward the mountaintop. I knew where to find symbols carved in stone that marked the way. They were all that remained of the natives' claims to the land and had been preserved in the glacier-smoothed rocks only because they shared hiding places with Diamond-backed rattlers. The dangerous snakes grew long and fat among the rocks and kept most of the curious away.

My longer legs carried me ahead of the boys. They paused frequently to overturn rocks and beat at bushes with their sticks in hope of finding some snakes. When I found myself far ahead, I began to take short side paths to give them time to catch up.

One of the old trails dead-ended at a huge boulder balanced at the ragged base of a high ridge. I felt a downdraft as I drew closer to the rock. Curiosity propelled me up a stone path. There were rumors of an Indian cave, said to have been an escape route for marauding savages, in the area. I hoped that I had stumbled onto it. I decided that with a toehold to push myself up I would be able to look into the dark space beneath the rock. I hesitated, scanned the area for snakes, found crevices for my fingers and toes, and stretched up to peer into the shadows. In the musty darkness I looked into a pair of very tiny eyes.

I lost my balance and fell backward, skinning my knees as I went. I backed up, shaded my eyes with one hand, and tried to see what was lurking there.

It was late in the day. Angled rays of the lowering sun brightened the crack under the boulder. The creature hadn't moved. I tossed a small stone that clunked under the face of the cliff, yet the eyes remained on guard. There was something strange about that animal.

I found a long curved stick and probed the crack delicately. Still the creature did not move. I waved the stick enticingly back and forth waiting for a snake to strike. It didn't take the bait. I began to stack rocks far enough from the entrance to give me safety but high enough for me to see into the dim space.

The twins came slowly up the trail, calling my name, complaining of the heat and wanting to go home.

I said, "Look, there's something in there."

"Where?"

"In that crack. Under that rock."

Even though they were the same age as me, they were too short to see.

"Help me make this pile of rocks bigger. I want to see what it is."

In unison they dropped to the ground and refused to move.

"Too tired," Lenny said.

"And thirsty," Larry added. "I want some more of that spring water."

I continued to increase the size of the stack until I could stand at eye level with the crack. I convinced the boys to help me onto the precarious pyramid of stones. They stood on each side and allowed me to use their shoulders for balance. At last I could peer into the space.

There was a doll in there. A tiny stone doll, dressed in rotting leather and staring at me from a faded face. Yellow lines marked a warlike mask, and some kind of hair had been fastened onto its head. I again checked carefully for snakes, then stretched one arm out to its full length. I was not well balanced. My touch pushed the doll backward and I could hear it plunk, plunk, plunk into the empty spaces of a void. I stretched up again, could feel the cold breeze of the underground and smell the dankness of a closed space.

The clanking sound raised the boys' interest. "What is it?"

"A doll. An Indian doll. It fell down the crack." We probed with a stick for an hour and pushed at the huge rock with all our might but we couldn't widen the opening or see any other dolls. Defeated, with the sun dropping low on the horizon, we turned and walked back down the mountain.

I will remember this place, I thought. I'll know it by my pile of stones. I'll come back and find that cave.

~

As that fall of 1955 became colder, the needs of our extended family grew. Mr. Reid, the man who had lent Mom money in the summer, began to call and demand payment. Lenny had no coat. We all needed shoes. Lillian promised to bring new clothing for the boys on Thanksgiving. Iris was working at the Globe department store and looking for an apartment big enough for all the kids.

Sally and Janet's friends began to hang out at our house. The girls exchanged cancan slips, cinched-waist skirts, and wide elastic belts. They flirted outrageously with boys, sometimes riding off in their cars or holding hands and going off into the woods. The house became so full and noisy that I had to keep the library doors shut tight while I worked on my diary list.

One evening, Pop tapped lightly on the French doors. "Why aren't you out here with the rest of the kids?" he asked.

"I'm busy," I said.

"Doing what?"

"Looking at stuff."

He came into the room and glanced at the stack of books piled on the table. "What kind of stuff?"

"These old books."

"Why would you be interested in those?"

I shrugged. "I don't know, but I am."

"What are you looking for?"

"Stuff about the people in the stories that Mom tells. You know—about the Indian massacre and the mine fire, family stuff."

"Don't look too deep," he said. "You may not like what you find."

As I watched him walk with slow deliberation toward the door, I hoped his words wouldn't come back to haunt me.

He paused and motioned for me to follow him. "Come on," he said. "It isn't normal for a girl your age to sit in here alone."

"I like it here," I said. "I like the quiet."

"Are you sure you're okay?"

I laughed at his concern. "Of course I am. Why wouldn't I be?"

"If something was wrong, you'd tell me, wouldn't you?"

"You're the first person I'd tell, Pop. I'm reading about stuff. I like to read."

He shrugged, smiled, and ambled off. The scent of beer stayed behind in the room.

That night, in a picture book of the 1937 Susquehanna River flood, I found a stash of folded newspaper clippings so creased that I had to weigh them down with a few books to hold them open. Someone had scrawled "1921" on the side margin of the first one.

Mine Fire Threatens the Town of Giant's Despair
A mine fire on Wilkes-Barre Mountain, long believed extinguished by the valiant efforts of the Red Ash Coal Company, has been discovered to be a stronger foe than anyone previously realized. Mr. Charles Beckerman, whose spacious home lies less than a mile from the abandoned main shaft of the mine, reported that he has discovered a smoking crevasse along the old Loki runs behind culm banks near his home on Giant's Despair hill.

Alas, the fire has proved a difficult adversary and it will now be necessary to implement newer methods to snuff out the monster. Work will begin this week on the Beckerman property. Drilling rigs will penetrate the rock roofs of the underground tunnels and install piping to allow a mixture of fire-stopping chemicals, clay, and water to be pumped into their blackest depths. This will wall off the blazing inferno and allow the Red Ash Coal Company to continue operations in the rich vein of anthracite that lies under Wilkes-Barre Mountain.

A second clipping was dated 1928.

Underground Blast Furnace to Be Snuffed Out

> Crews headed by Charles Beckerman of Oliver's Powder Mill are again preparing to do battle against the mine fire that spews its noxious smoke across the face of the mountain along the ridge above the old workings of the Red Ash Coal Company and can be seen from most parts of Wilkes-Barre. Today, Mr. Beckerman will enter a back shaft of the mine below the Devil's Elbow curve of Giant's Despair hill and will place charges to close off all related tunnels. Experts believe that completely blocking those tunnels will deprive the conflagration of oxygen and will entomb forever that portion of the seam of anthracite that runs beneath the community of Giant's Despair. The Diamond Coal Company has purchased the mine and its workings and expects to continue operations in viable shafts along the southern ridges of Wilkes-Barre Mountain.
>
> Mr. Charles Beckerman is no stranger to the Red Ash holdings. His home is perched precariously near the very shafts he will enter today. This brave man, with stamina belying his sixty-one years, will take on this project with the same exacting dedication he has exhibited in his past efforts to extinguish the blaze. We wish him good and safe success.

As I removed some pages from my notebook and carefully taped each article onto a clean sheet, all of Mom's history lessons became relevant. I had not fully understood that the pipe in our orchard was a doorway to another world where poison gases lurked and men had sometimes died in complete darkness. Now our house was sinking into that same abyss. When she had told me that most people paid more attention to the world at large than the things right under their noses, she was absolutely right. I wondered if anyone or anything would be able to stop the coal company's folly.

~

Some men from the neighborhood who knew how to properly place jacks under the beams of structures to raise them as a whole began to lift the neighborhood back to normal. Mom finally agreed that the house needed work and put us on their waiting list. She said she would borrow money from her mother, but instead we visited Mr. Reid again. I was sure he wouldn't advance her another loan, but he seemed awfully eager to help as she signed more papers. This time, I couldn't be bought off with a visit to Woolworth's, but neither did I tell Pop. The ability to keep secrets ran deep in my Branigan veins.

A truck delivered the concrete blocks that would replace the glacier rock of the house foundation. Pop and Marty began pulling out the tongue-and-groove oak walls of the cellar rooms. The door to the outside was on the listing side of the house, and since Marty had grown to be as tall as Pop, they both had to crouch like coal miners to get through the low space and pull the boards out. Mom fretted so much about Pop's legs that he made her stay in the house while the rest of us worked.

Marty did most of the hauling through the low cellarway while the twins and I stacked everything on the front lawn. A century's worth of clutter began to pile up: dust-covered bottles labeled birch and root beer; a capping device; empty wine barrels; a foot-operated sharpening stone; a complete set of shoemaker's tools, including the bench and chair that went with them; a belt-operated sawmill; a pie safe on tall legs; several pairs of crutches, a powder horn, and water carrier from the Civil War; and a piece of the American flag from the Battle of Gettysburg. All but the Civil War stuff, the sharpening stone, and the sawmill was hauled off to the dump. Pop carried the historic things to the top of the inside cellar stairs and hung them on nails near Mom's cast-iron pancake grill and frying pans.

Pop and Marty set up the sawmill on the driveway side of the house. The gigantic steel blade needed sharpening, but with a good hosing off and some grease on the axle, the pulley turned and the carriage slid forward and backward like new. Pop said he could use the saw to get in a supply of wood for winter. The price of coal had skyrocketed.

We worked every day until Pop left for the plant. He still limped and walked slowly but he was able to drive a forklift four hours a day. The factory was winding down operations. One day a dump truck delivered several loads of wooden spools used for transporting wire. Pop jacked up the back of his car, removed the tire, and looped a wide belt over the wheel of the saw and the rim of the tire. When he put the car in gear, the saw whirled at an amazing speed. Without safety equipment—not even gloves—he began to cut the spools into chunks of firewood. His head was so close to the spinning blade that, from a distance, it seemed that it would cut his face in half right down the center. Nails in the spools caught on the spinning blade and were sent zinging through the air like lethal darts.

Mom came to the rail of the back porch and called for Pop to stop.

I could tell by his slack smile that he'd had a few beers too many. He pretended not to hear her.

I stood in the driveway, afraid to gesture because I might break his concentration but afraid to look away, as if my not paying attention could put him in greater danger. While I tried to think of what to do, Mom strode off the porch, climbed into the car, and cut the engine.

Pop jumped back as a partially cut reel bucked and caught on the blade. "Hey! What'd you do that for?"

"I hoped it would break the blade," she shouted from the car, "so you would have to wait until you were sober enough to find a new one." She shook her head. "I didn't work so hard to get you better to have you cut your hand off with that darned thing."

"I know what I'm doing." His voice held a sharp edge that I had never heard before.

I would have been on his side, but I shared Mom's fear. I stepped forward.

"I hate watching you do that, Pop. Can't you wait for another day?"

"Well aren't *you* getting too big for your britches." He dropped the partially cut reel to the ground.

I looked to Mom. She turned away and strode into the house.

He pulled the belt off the wheel and tossed it carelessly onto the drive. I helped him pull a musty canvas sheet over the pile of cut wood. We worked in complete silence. He didn't wave good-bye when he walked down the hill toward the tavern. For the first time in my life, I felt true anger toward him.

The carpenters finally arrived. As their jacks broke through calcified joints, the house filled with the painful sound of its own breaking bones. The foundation stones that had been hand-mortared in place by Old Charlie were hauled to the creek and laid side-by-side until they looked like a pox of stone above the slow water. With gray concrete blocks, square and stern, filling the gaps between the weathered stones, the cellar wall became a jigsaw puzzle with many pieces missing.

The jacks were removed and the house stood straight, as if the weight of a century had been lifted from its shoulders. I stood in the new cellar doorway that opened into the lower yard and watched Pop pat insulation over the water pipes between the rafters. His upturned face soon became a Frankenstein mask of wet asbestos. Lenny and Larry began pelting each other with balls of the paste from Pop's bucket. I escaped into the house.

Mom was in the library, wiping plaster dust off the shelves and books. She handed me her rag and pulled the step stool to the wall.

"You're taller, Molly. Can you climb up there and dust that picture?"

I stepped up and began to wipe the bubble of glass that covered a photograph of Sue Ellen's family hung high on the wall.

"Be real careful," she said. "The glass is cracked."

Up close I could see small fracture lines across the entire curve of convex glass. The image of Granny Sue's young family came into clearer view.

"How'd it get smashed all the way up here?"

"Granny Sue did it."

"Why?"

"I don't know. She was a bit out of her mind in later years."

"How'd she get up here?"

"She didn't. She took a broom to it. I heard her in here when she was sick. I came to look and there she was, swatting the picture with her broom."

"Was she mad?"

"I don't know."

"Well, how'd she look?"

"Sad. She looked sad. She was crying."

"Did you ask her why she did it?"

"You're going to fall. Come on, that's good enough. Get down."

"Well, did you?"

"It wouldn't have done any good. I told you, she was out of her mind by then."

I backed down the small steps and moved into the middle of the room. I studied the picture. A smiling family looked down on me. The girls were pretty and slim, with ruffles at their necks and bows in their curled hair. The boys were young, blond, and handsome. The tallest boy wore glasses and a serious frown as he held down the shoulders of a young brother, as if to keep him still. Granny Sue and Old Charlie were dressed in gray worsted and each also held restraining hands on a young boy.

"When was that taken?" I asked.

"Right before Bernie drowned," Mom said. "I think that's why she was hitting it. They said she grieved horribly when he died."

"Why aren't you in the picture?"

"I wasn't even a glimmer in my father's eye. That's your grandmother Lillian next to Bernie, the tallest boy." She laughed and took the dust rag from my hand.

"Which one is Iris?"

"She wasn't born yet either."

"Lillian was pretty."

"A real heartbreaker, according to John Hale."

"Did John do clinic then, too?"

Mom laughed again. "John Hale was a boy like Bernie. They were great pals. He had a crush on Aunt Faye. After Bernie drowned, John went off to the military and Faye married someone else."

"How do you know all this, if you weren't born yet?"

"John told me himself. He says he has two regrets in his life: one, that he wasn't with Bernie the day that he drowned, and two, that he went off to the army before he could marry Faye."

"It's hard to imagine John Hale being young," I said.

"I know," she sighed. "He's always seemed old to me too. But," she said in a false cheery way, "we were all young once."

"Do you have regrets? Like John Hale?"

"Heavens, no!" She hurried toward the kitchen a little too quickly. "And I doubt he has any now. He's been happily married for more than thirty years."

I stood for a long time and studied that fractured picture high on the wall. I had pushed it a bit off center. A bright yellow line of wallpaper showed where it had lain. It reminded me of ancient fossils pressed in their beds of slate.

That fall the mines were almost finished and the good jobs on the railroad disappeared with the passengers, who preferred to drive cars. More men became unemployed. Those who could find work accepted menial wages; others found an age-old way to escape. By three each afternoon, every stool in the Empire Tavern was filled. A private rod and gun club, more for boozing than for holding turkey shoots, sprang up behind Harry's store.

Thanksgiving arrived, accompanied by a cold rain that flooded the roadways and left deep polio puddles at the top of the driveway. We kids had received the new vaccine that should have freed Mom of worry about the disease rumored to lurk in stagnant pools, but still she hesitated before allowing us to play under the newly elevated front porch, where Lenny had diverted the downspout to form a series of ponds from one side to the other.

Through the fretwork skirting I watched a taxi pull up to the concrete stair. Lillian pushed her head through the open door, unfurled a black umbrella, and stepped from the cab. She gathered her coat about her and leaned back into the cab to pull out a shopping bag. Janet and Sally danced down the stairs to help Iris's three youngest boys from the car. Iris climbed out of the front. She laughed at something the cab driver said as she handed a shopping bag to Janet, who then climbed the porch stairs with the excited younger boys.

The twins heard their mother's laugh, dropped their Matchbox cars, and ran into the downpour. Iris shot them a look before she stepped to the open trunk. With nervous, rapid movements, she handed bags and boxes to Sally and the twins. As the kids ran up the stairs to the shelter of the porch, Iris turned back to the driver and laughed loudly. Lillian patiently held the umbrella while Iris lit a cigarette and inhaled deeply. Lillian paid the driver. As the two women turned toward the porch, I could see that Iris clutched a bottle wrapped in plain brown paper.

I watched matching red skirts and high-heeled black patent leather pumps take the first step up as Mom's scuffed penny loafers and bare legs scampered down. The three women climbed the stairs. Neither Mom nor Lillian saw Iris turn back to wave and smile at the cabbie.

Above, on the porch, Lenny and Larry's voices were filled with excitement. "Shoes! And coats!"

I stood between the artificial mountains and ponds and studied my worn shoes. A wave of unholy envy washed over me. I moved from under the porch and slowly made my way up to join my family.

Not once that afternoon did Iris offer to lift a finger to help. When the meal was done, she stayed in her chair and sipped vodka while the rest of us, including Lillian, picked up the dishes. She leaned across the table and poured the dregs of her bottle into Pop's glass, then stood, cigarette case in hand, and leaned toward him for a light. She staggered slightly as she straightened, and laughed too loudly as she reached out to steady herself against Pop. He upended his glass, stood, and moved upstairs. When he came back down he was in work clothes.

"I promised Marty I'd help him with his car," he said. He ducked his head against the rain and ran for the protective tarp that hung over Marty's jacked-up car.

Iris paced between the front windows, clicking the heels of her shoes on the wooden strip that edged the carpet and trailing clouds of cigarette smoke. Suddenly, she marched into the kitchen.

"I'm bored to death," she announced. "I'm going to walk down to that new club."

Lillian turned. "The cab will be here at seven. Will you be back by then?"

"Oh, definitely."

"I didn't think the club would be open today," Mom said.

"Well, it isn't, legally, but the cab driver said I could knock on the back door and they'd let me in."

"Iris," Mom said, "it's only an hour until you have to head back. Can't you stay and spend some time with your kids?"

"They won't mind," Iris shot back. "They won't even notice that I've left."

Janet stepped forward. "I'll mind, Mom. I wanted to tell you about school."

"I went to that school. I know everything I need to know about it. I'll only be gone a while." She pulled on her coat.

"You're going to get awfully cold and wet in this rain," Lillian warned.

"Don't worry. I'll be here."

Mom turned back to drying dishes. For a minute I thought Lillian would stop Iris, but she was already running down the porch stairs.

Neither Iris nor the cab driver returned.

Lillian called the company to order another car but was told it would be a long wait because of the holiday. She went into the library, threw open the window, and shouted to Pop. "Sean, Iris has gone to the rod and gun club and she's not back. I've got to get these kids home."

"Don't ask me to go looking," he answered. "It's a losing proposition. The rod and gun club is closed for the holiday."

"She said she could knock on the door and they'd let her in."

Pop said a few words to Marty, and then, "Marty says he'll try that."

"Thank you," Lillian slammed the window.

The crowded room had overheated from the oven being used all day. Mom pulled her damp hair away from her face before she sat at the table.

"She's gone off with the cab driver, Lillian. We won't find her tonight. I doubt that the gun club was ever going to be where they'd meet."

"What will I do with the little boys? I can't handle them and work. I can't leave them alone."

"Janet can go back with you and watch the boys for the weekend. Sally too, if you'd like," Mom said. She poured two glasses of wine and handed one across the table to Lillian.

"You don't expect her back tonight?"

Mom sipped her wine and shrugged. "Best for everybody to plan ahead."

"Why in the world would she do this now?"

"She's never been able to go very long without a man."

"Well, you can't blame her for that," Lillian snapped.

"I'm not casting blame. She found an available man. She'll be back in the morning."

"Oh, Bess, I've done everything possible to help her. I didn't expect this kind of payback."

"We never do." Mom upended her glass and poured another.

That surprised me. She rarely drank.

When Marty came back, he had no news. "The gun club is closed up tight. Looks like I'll have to drive you to Scranton."

That night, as the first winds of winter came up from the valley floor, the off-kilter doors and windows allowed cold air to squeal through openings that were no longer plumb. A hum of gathered voices rose above the doorframes, under the eaves, and down through the cellar. A softly crying woman crept into the library. The hallway keened with the deeper, pain-filled groan of a man. The front door frame emitted the high-pitched persistent wail of a young child. I pulled my bed covers tightly over my head to block out their dead voices. When I could bear no more, I crept into my parents' room. Mom said I had too active an imagination, but she allowed me to sleep against her back.

And then came the next big thing. Early that Sunday morning another sound broke the quiet. A constant thumping drumbeat, clumsy and unsynchronized, accompanied by the nervous shouts of men and the rattling of many chains. I hurried from my room and onto the back porch, where I had a clear view of the commotion. A line of trucks streamed along the new stripping road. Behind them, visible over the tops of the culm banks, moved a giant swinging bucket suspended from the top of a massive crane.

I had never seen a machine so big. It moved forward with a determination that caused a flutter of fear to clutch my heart. As I watched, the crane tipped and leaned dangerously, but the men on its high box pulled a series of levers and the machine righted itself. When it lumbered across the wooden troughs that had carried mountain runoff away from the town for a century, it splintered the solid wood and sent spring water cascading over the field of mine fire crevasses. As it reached the ridge beyond, it paused and settled itself like a huge cat, feet tucked beneath its yellow body, its head moving slowing left to right as if scanning the valley beyond for prey. While it lurked above Squirrel Hollow, purring with apparent satisfaction, dump trucks began to cozy up to its massive underbelly.

I ran back into the house and up the stairs to my room. This was too much. They were going to dig up Squirrel Hollow and no one could stop them. The screen door slammed as Lenny and Larry shouted and headed out across the field. Pop and Marty, just as determined to marvel at the new machine, raced after.

Breakfast was full of it.

"It takes three men to keep it moving." Lenny said. "One for the shovel operation, one for the body operation, and one to keep feeding it oil so its hydraulic parts keep going."

"Sixty cubic yards," my brother said, his eyes as big as the pancakes Mom placed in front of him. "That bucket can hold sixty cubic yards!"

"And the shovel alone weighs almost five thousand tons!" Larry said.

I knew how much a ton was from the loads of coal delivered to the bin in the cellar in good years, but I had to ask about the other part. "What's a cubic yard?"

Marty, Lenny, and Larry all shrugged.

Pop sipped his coffee and looked down the long table. "One cubic yard is a box three feet wide, three feet long, and three feet deep. Like that yardstick you gals use for cutting material for your skirts. That's three feet, or one yard. Picture a box like that and multiply it by sixty and that's how much coal that damned machine can haul out in one drag."

"That's a big steam shovel," I said.

"Not a shovel," Larry said. "It's a dragline."

"And it's not steam either. It's electric and hydraulic," Lenny added.

"And it walks instead of rolls. On two big feet that are taller than me and Pop combined." Marty said.

"They call it the Mountaineer." Pop was not excited.

"Why? Because it's going to take down our mountain?" Bitter bile rose up in my throat.

There was a short silence broken only by Mom flipping pancakes on the cast-iron griddle.

"There's nothing we can do about it," she said, with her back to us.

"Unless we want to go up there and blow the thing up," Lenny said.

"Pop's family already tried that once." Mom placed another plate of pancakes on the table. "Look what it got them."

"What?" Lenny asked.

"Got them hanged." She turned away as if it were as normal as eating to be hanged.

"By who?" Larry said.

"The government and the great Pinkerton detectives from Philadelphia," she answered.

"Who?" Lenny asked.

I looked toward Pop and for once he seemed ready to spill his guts.

"The coal companies hired a detective," he said. "A guy came in and said the Irish was all Mollies."

"So who was hanged?" Lenny persisted.

"It was years ago. It's nothing to talk about now," Pop answered.

"History repeats itself—too easily, if you ask me," Mom said.

Pop studied her as he stood and moved toward the door. "I think I'll have a smoke." He let the screen door slam behind him.

"What history?" Lenny asked.

"Coal mining history. The big shots always win. Can't take them on. Can't win."

"But who was hanged?"

"Pop's great-grandfather," I answered, so he'd shut up.

"And there isn't a soul in this valley that doesn't hang on to that," Mom said. "Dirty Irish they call them still. Molly Maguires. The Mollies tried to organize the miners, to get them out from under the thumbs of the mine owners. But instead they got accused of a string of murders and some good men were hanged."

"How could that happen?" Larry scoffed.

"Oh, it happened. And it could happen again. So don't any of you boys get your blood up and think you can do something to stop them." She slid the iron griddle to the cool side of the cook stove with the lifter, peered into the box of hot coals, added three small shovels of fuel, tilted the lids over the pot holes, and slammed the top vent open with a loud clang.

"You can't," she said, as if she could dampen off our young fires as easily as she regulated the stove. "So don't even think of trying."

Before the sun set, the side of the mountain where I had lost the Indian doll was savagely cut away. In the days that followed, Squirrel Hollow completely disappeared. Cold anger grew thicker and more solid each time I thought of that doll lying deep within a culm bank under a thousand pounds of slate. I had read about voodoo dolls and hoped that it was one. And then I began to worry that it actually was.

Iris did not return. On Monday morning the twins and I went to school without Janet and Sally. As we jumped off the bus, a social worker waited with the school principal. They escorted Lenny and Larry to a state car. The principal took me to the office and allowed me to listen as he called Mom. Iris had been taken into custody and the children would be placed back into foster care. Mom must have asked what Iris had done because the principal said, "Public drunkenness, indecent exposure, and resisting arrest." He paused for a few seconds and added, "She was with a man in a cab parked along Main Street."

A secretary walked me to my classroom. Everybody turned to stare. If I'd been given the chance, I would have left right then.

That night Lillian called to ask if she could keep Janet and Sally.

"I'll send more clothes," Mom said. "But if they're going to be longer than three days, I'd like them to not miss school. You'll need to register them. And Lillian, you'll need to watch both those girls around boys."

When she hung up, she began to cry. "They've split up the twins," she said. "Larry was sent to live with a family across the river and Lenny was sent all the way to Philadelphia to a center for troubled kids."

"Why?"

"Lenny got mad when they told him he would have to leave us and his brother. He hit the social worker."

That night the house seemed awfully empty. I even missed Lenny.

⁓

Mom began another rash of housecleaning and room adjustments. I helped her fold up the rollaway bed and move it back into the closet. When I tried to fit it into its space I found an old suitcase blocking the way. I pulled out the suitcase and shoved the bed in.

"This thing is heavy," I said. "I can barely lift it. What's in it?"

"Pictures," Mom answered. She placed her stack of blankets on top of the metal bed frame and took the suitcase from my hand.

"I want to see. Can I look?"

She placed the case between us. "It's old family pictures," she said. "You can look, but make sure you don't put your fingers all over them."

"Can I take it upstairs?"

"No. It stays here. When you're done looking, put it back where it belongs. It's not ours. It belongs to the whole family."

"Kind of like this house," I said.

"Who said anything about the house?"

"Lenny. He said that the whole family knew we shouldn't be here and that Iris is going to throw us out on our asses as soon as she gets straight."

Mom laughed. "Well, I guess we'll never have to worry about that, will we?"

I turned the suitcase on its side and sifted through photographs, bits of lace, high-button booties, and yellowing documents with increasing excitement. It might take weeks, but I was determined to put names with every picture in that case.

The first one was easy. Cased in hard cardboard that opened like a book, an easily recognizable young Lillian, replete with lacy wedding gown and veil, smiled beside a mustachioed man, dapper in a vested suit and cocked black hat. Folded neatly into the crease was another newspaper clipping, yellow with age. I unfolded the paper onto the library table.

Wilkes-Barre Leader, September 20, 1921

Ralph Marcy "Is a Man Who Is Not Satisfied With One Woman"
That Ralph Marcy, this city, "is a man who is not satisfied with one woman" was sworn to by his pretty little wife, Lillian.

Lillian has had an unhappy career since she approached the holy state of matrimony. The way for her has been hard, and the testimony that she gave at a hearing held recently before a master in divorce corroborated these facts.

"He's now living with a young woman at our home to whom he is not married and there is no one else at home at night except a small child."

Ralph was not so bad, when murderers and the like are considered in the same thought. As his wife swore, she is now in the decline as a result of his treatment and his failure to abide by the vows he sacredly made. Ralph did not stop with the common young women who would be satisfied with a nice tête-à-tête. He chose the kind that they rave about on Broadway, the kind that the whole world loves and adores, the "actress."

Lillian said that her husband fell desperately in love with an actress who played in Wilkes-Barre for some time. His infatuation with this girl in the spotlight was so passionate that he blinded himself to any devotion that was due his wife. He went as far as destroying a will he had made, in which his wife was the chief legatee. The actress, it seems, had not been long in Wilkes-Barre when she was forced to make a jump to Scranton. Ralph followed her to the Electric City, but his wife was wise to what he did and followed. As Ralph and his actress friend were leaving the stage door, Lillian insisted on her husband accompanying her. Fearing a scene, he took her advice, abandoned his actress-lover, and escorted his wife to their home in this city. When they reached their home, the "will scene from the infuriated husband" was enacted. Thus it was that Lillian was eliminated from the will of her husband. All on account of her interference with his love play with an actress.

> Lillian and Ralph were married October 9, 1914, and had one child, a little girl, who at the time of the hearing was stated to be seven years of age. At the time of the ceremony, Lillian's home was at Giant's Despair while Ralph lived at 16 South Street, Wilkes-Barre. During their married life they resided at South Washington Street. April 6, last, Mrs. Marcy was forced to vacate the home due to his cruel and barbarous treatment.
>
> Ralph is a husky and his poor little wife had very little chance with him in an argument. However, at times, despite his strength, she through sheer determination gained her point. One time in particular, it appears that it was very fortunate that she did, for her uncle testified that Ralph tried to pour Lysol down her throat. Were it not for his assistance, she may have never brought this action for divorce. The court last week granted the petition that was substantiated by the above information and issued papers for divorce to the little woman.

My head was nearly bursting with questions. Was the uncle who testified for Lillian the one and only Ira? Had he been present at more of the stressful situations family members had experienced? I had to find the right people to ask those questions, without arousing their interest in my search for answers about the series of deaths in the diary and why Ira was the common denominator in each of them. I slid the article into my notebook and replaced it in the large drawer under the blueprints and rolls. I closed the suitcase and slid it under the library table. With all the relatives gone from the house, I would now be free to take lots of time with my research.

~

I began to visit the city library after school, even though it meant I had to walk home for lack of bus fare. In short time I found one book about the Molly Maguires and another about the Ancient Order of Hibernians. When I told the librarian that I was doing a paper about the coal industry, she led me to the newspaper files in the basement. The earliest files had been converted to microfilm; later ones were stacked by month and year on rollers, waiting processing.

I took the diary with me and began with Bernie. I found him on a July 1915 microfilm roll.

Burton Lewis Beckerman Dead From Drowning
Burton Beckerman, of Giant's Despair, died at the age of eighteen on Tuesday during an outing on Crystal Lake. He would have reached his natal day in one week. Deceased was the son of Mr. and Mrs. Charles Beckerman of 42 Fitch Lane, Giant's Despair. He was the beloved brother of two sisters, Faye and Lillian, and two younger brothers, Silas and Arlen, all of the home. He graduated from Giant's Despair School one month before his accident and had been hired as a driver for Oliver's Powder Mill. He was a member of the Giant's Despair United Church. The funeral will be held from the home, Friday at 2 o'clock.

I carefully copied the obituary into my notebook, then dug deeper. The drowning had been front-page news.

Young Man Drowns in Crystal Lake
Despite Best Efforts of the Community, Body Not Found Until Late Last Night
Uncle Reports Morning Swim in Cold Water Resulted in Death

> The body of Burton Beckerman of Giant's Despair was discovered late last night in the shallows of Crystal Lake near his family summer cabin. The young man had been on an outing with his uncle and two younger brothers when he disappeared while swimming. Mr. Ira Reece, uncle of the man, had been on an early morning swim with his nephew when he lost sight of the boy. He searched the lake and the shore, but could find no trace of his ward. He summoned help from neighbors along the lake. An all-day search resulted in discovery of the body late last night. His unexpected death is a severe and sad blow to his family.

On my next visit I discovered a second page of the article on Lillian's divorce. Despite the granted petition for divorce, the custody rights of their daughter were in dispute. I knew that was Mom.

Ira Reece testified to the good character of Lillian and accompanied her from the courthouse when the proceedings were done.

For all of his service in times of trouble, his family sure had forgotten Ira pretty quickly. Maybe that's why he removed himself. He must have felt awfully bad about not taking better care of his nephew. Maybe he was trying to make up for that.

Two weeks before Christmas vacation began, I tried to find Silas. Cold air seeped through the stone rooms of the library and into my hands and feet. My neck began to ache and my eyes seemed to pull from their sockets with the strain of reading in the poor light. I was about to give up for the day when the librarian came down and said they were closing early. It had begun to snow.

I gathered my books and stepped out into a fierce wind. The thermometer on the Miners Bank building read five degrees above zero. Snow was falling steadily and night seemed to be arriving earlier than usual. The bitter cold made me painfully aware of my lack of boots and gloves. I hugged my books, pulled my fingers into my coat sleeves, ducked my head into the biting wind, and walked as Mom would have—fast, unthinking, and humming a monotonous tune.

On the twisting turn below Saint John's Monastery, I came upon a mess of cars stacked up in disarray on the sidewalks and wedged against the monastery cliffs. I was forced to weave between cars and their surprised drivers, who had gathered in protective groups, heads together, trying to decide how to clear the roadway. One car spun its tires and swayed dangerously back and forth across the road. I moved to the side, pressed one shoulder against the concrete wall of the shoe repair shop, and hurried on. My breath came in short icy gasps. At the next side street, I slipped and began to fall. A hand came out of the darkness. Chuck, the kid who had saved me from drowning, steadied me with a firm grasp on my elbow.

"Whoa! You should have better shoes," he said. "Aren't you cold?"

"It's okay." I was overtaken with shyness. "As long as I keep moving."

"Well, let's go then."

His arm in mine felt wonderful, his body radiated heat. I suddenly understood why my older sister and girl cousins so liked the company of the boys. I leaned against his wool coat, head ducked, face turned away.

"I'll help you as far as the railroad," he said. His breath was warm on my ear.

It would have been difficult to carry on a conversation with the wind and snow in our faces, but I don't think either of us would have spoken anyway. He seemed as shy as I. When we reached the bus stop at the tracks he let go of my arm, turned, and strode back down the hill.

"Hey! Thanks!" I shouted after him. The howling storm took the words away. With a surge of energy, I crossed the railroad tracks and ran the rest of the way home.

The house was completely dark. I could see Mom standing at the front window. Something was wrong. I hurried up the stairs and into the front hallway.

"Lenny has run away," she said. "He's been gone nearly a week and they just now decided to tell us. I've called everyone I can think of and nobody's heard from him. I don't know how he's going to survive in this storm."

I looked back into the blowing snow. It was impossible to see past the porch. Even with his new coat and shoes, he would freeze to death in the bitter cold.

Mom led the way to the kitchen. "The power is out. I saved your dinner. Come in where it's warm."

"He'll find somewhere to stay, won't he?"

"He's a runaway. Who's going to take in a runaway?"

"Maybe somebody will. He's only a kid."

"We told them that they should never have separated those brothers. Your pop is going to be furious."

"Pop always took care of his brother, didn't he?"

"Yes, he did. Until the end, he and Mike were always together."

In the kitchen she added a shovel of coal to the already roaring fire, propped my shoes against the ash box, hung my socks over the open oven door, and placed my coat on a hook on the cellar door where the heat from the stove would dry it.

I leaned my cold backside against the polished chrome above the oven. "When the storm lets up, Marty can get someone to go with him and start looking for Lenny."

"Marty couldn't make it up the hill. He's staying the night in town with friends," Mom said. She turned and studied the fire. "If Lenny is heading this way, Marty would never be able to find him between here and Philadelphia anyway." She placed a kerosene lantern on the table. "It's a hundred miles away and there are at least ten different roads to get here. I don't know what we can do." She paused to gaze out the side window toward the dark valley below. "This is going to be a dilly of a storm."

I took my plate from the shelf above the stove and carried it to the table. Each forkful of meatloaf and mashed potatoes warmed me from the inside out. I hoped that, wherever Lenny was, he had food.

"Somebody should punish Iris," I said.

Mom remained with her back to me. "What did Aunt Iris ever do to you?"

"Nothing to me. But she sure doesn't care about her kids."

"She's too pretty," Mom said. "Pretty girls have too many choices in this world."

"She might be pretty but she stinks like cigarettes."

"So does your pop."

"She smells like booze too."

"So does your pop."

"Then if she's so much like Pop, she should love her kids like he does."

"She does love her kids. She doesn't know how to show it. She tries. She really tries."

"She hardly even talked to them when she was here."

Mom shrugged and changed the subject. "There isn't a light on in the valley. The power must be out all over."

The meatloaf stuck in my throat. Lenny would have nothing to eat. I pushed my plate aside.

"We'll have to think about how to find Lenny in the morning. I need to dampen down the fires and the house will get pretty cold. It's best that we go to bed early. If you're finished eating, I'd like you to go down and throw more wood on the furnace and close it down."

I dreaded going into the dark cellar. For years, Pop had teased that family spirits hid in the shadows behind the ancient furnace. He would grin and add, "But don't you worry. Turn on the light so they can see your face. Not one of them is looking for you. It's me they're after."

That night there was no light in the cellar. I followed the glow from the front dampers of the fire until I stood before the pile of wood left by Pop. I opened the upper door and tossed a chunk of cable reel onto coals that had burned low. Sparks flashed and popped. I tossed another chunk. The warmth from the open door settled comfortably onto my face and forearms. One more chunk. I stood mesmerized and watched the black Os, Ks, and Es of the company name painted on the reels catch fire, turn red, then yellow, and finally white. I raised my eyes and studied the space behind the furnace. Shadows danced in the darkest corner.

"Charlie," I whispered. "Please. If you're here, could you look out for Lenny? Could you bring him home?"The fire crackled and blazed with new life.

I closed the dampers and felt my way back to the stairs. As I placed each foot into the grooves worn into the wooden steps by kin who'd climbed before me, I heard the ring of the telephone.

"That was Pop," Mom said. "He's staying the night at the Empire Tavern." Worry lines deepened on her face. "The storm has turned into a blizzard. No cars are making it up the mountain.

It's best he stays put, but I don't know . . . The tavern is not a good place for your father to wait out any storm."

We closed up the kitchen and found some old coats in the downstairs closet to spread over our blankets for added warmth. When Mom walked away with the kerosene lantern, I pulled the covers over my head to deafen the wind's keening cries, but all those layers of protection couldn't block out my worry for Lenny and Pop.

~

Morning was almost as gray and dark as evening had been. Clouds hung low over the gambrel roof. Windblown snow stung the windows, crackled under the eaves, and settled in spaces behind the clapboard siding. Heaped drifts lay against the tops of the hedges. The hill where the driveway climbed beside the house disappeared into a smooth plain of white. In the bathroom, water would not fill the flush tank or flow from the faucets. Tiny icicles hung from the radiator.

Grateful that Mom was up, I hurried to the warm kitchen.

"Power is still out," she said.

"I've been thinking about Lenny all night. He'll never survive in a storm like this."

"Your pop and his brother made it through worse. He could tell you stories that would make your heart stop. They were young and determined, and so is Lenny. We have to believe he'll be okay."

She was as scared as I was, no matter how strong she pretended to be.

We sat at the table, ate warm oatmeal, and pretended that everything was fine and would continue to be fine.

Around noon the wind finally stopped. I pulled on two pairs of jeans, a sweatshirt, another sweater, and an old coat of Marty's. I found unmatched wool socks to use as gloves and pushed open the back door. The snow cast a white coverlet over the dark and dirty parts of the land. The scorched earth of the sulfur mines lay hidden under a mantle of sharp ice. The mountains loomed large and white above the silent dragline, steam shovels, and dump trucks. I stood still, looked past the devastation on the mountainside, and pretended Squirrel Hollow was over the ridge—and beyond it, the trail that led to the Indian cave.

I plowed through the snow to the lower yard. Domed drifts curved over the lawn, rolled up the small hill, and nearly covered the new foundation of the house. I climbed a big drift lodged against the front porch and tumbled into the dim protected space where the boys and I had played all fall. I could use this as a fort, I thought. I could shovel more snow and leave a small door to come in and out. The light from the open stairs would be enough to see by. I was about to go back into the house to get a shovel when a movement deep in the shadows caught my eye.

I moved slowly toward the farthest corner, where a formless lump shifted slightly. The musty odor of cellar filled my nostrils. It was the canvas tarp that Pop had used to cover the woodpile and then had lumped up and shoved under the porch when he tossed the firewood into the coal bin.

The mound shook as if hit by a sharp wind. One edge peeled open and, like a plaster of Paris dwarf peering out from one of the rubber molds we kept in the downstairs cupboard, a face, slick and shining with pasty light, unfolded from the darkness.

I shrieked.

The ghost lifted a dark stick and pointed it toward me. "Stay away!" its gravelly voice warned. "Don't come any closer."

"Lenny?" It didn't look like Lenny, but if it wasn't him in the flesh, it was for sure his ghost.

"I'll shoot," he said. I recognized his living voice. "Go away." He didn't recognize me.

"Lenny, it's me. Molly. What are you doing out here? Come into the house."

He raised the dark stick higher. "I'm telling you. Go away."

He was holding a gun. A huge, dark, heavy, real gun and it was pointed right at me. He didn't have to warn me again.

I threw myself over the drift of snow, tumbled into the side yard, and began to stumble toward the back door—toward Mom.

But then I knew clearly that I shouldn't get Mom. Mom would demand that Lenny drop the gun. She wouldn't go slow. She would tell him in no uncertain terms that he should give her that damned thing. She would scare him and he would shoot her. He wasn't in his right mind. When someone not in his right mind needed to be talked to, it was Pop who should do the talking.

I turned in my tracks and pushed my way to Mrs. Donal's house. Her visiting granddaughter opened the door.

"Your phone," I said. "I need to use your phone."

"My grandma's not here," she said. "She's at the church, cleaning the rectory."

"Do you know where the phone book is?"

She brought it to me and watched as I dialed the Empire Tavern. A man answered.

"I need to speak to Sean Branigan," I said.

"There's no Sean Branigan here."

I took on my mother's most demanding voice, low and sure and half smiling. "I know he is," I said. "And this is his daughter. And this is an emergency. Tell him that."

I could hear him yelling into a cavernous room. "Hey, Sean. There's a young gal on the phone. Says she's your daughter. Says it's an emergency."

After what seemed a very long time, Pop's voice came on the line. It was thick with booze, but clear enough. "Yup?" he said.

"I found Lenny. He's under the porch and he has a gun. You've got to come home."

Silence hung thickly between us. I waited. It seemed another very long time before he reacted. "Don't go near him. Stay away. I'll have to hoof it up the hill. Wait for me. Does your mother know?"

"I'm at Mrs. Donal's house. I didn't tell Mom."

"Good girl. Whatever you do, don't tell her." He hung up without waiting to see if I'd understood.

I went back to the lower yard and tried to roll the dry snow into a ball. It wouldn't stick together. I dropped into the thick powder and made snow angels. I kept one eye on the fretwork under the porch. The wind picked up again. I was becoming rigid with fear and cold. I wanted to go into the house, but I knew that Mom would recognize that I was upset. If she asked, I would tell her everything. I stamped my feet, danced around the mulberry bush, and sang "Here We Go 'Round the Mulberry Bush" in my loudest voice. The wind forced me to find shelter behind one of the remaining ash trees. I began to shiver, so I made myself sing one of Mom's crazy war songs:

Whistle while you work.
Hitler is a jerk.
Mussolini bit his weenie,
Now it doesn't work.

And when I had calmed some, I sang the one she liked, about having babies:

Bear down, Mrs. Brown, bear down.
We have three fingers on the crown,
On the cro-wwww-nn,
And soon we'll pull the little bugger out.
Bear down, Mrs. Brown, bear down.

I realized that Mom couldn't see me from the kitchen window, so I moved back into the open yard. I was too late.

She came onto the back porch and shouted, "Are you cold? Where have you been? I looked for you."

"Why?"

"Because I don't want you to get sick. I saw you go over to Mrs. Donal's house. Is she okay?"

"Yes," I tried to shout, but my voice quivered and broke.

She cast her eyes on me like one of the house cats leaning over the rail to watch a mouse.

"Molly, I think it's time for you to come in here. Now."

"I'm coming in pretty soon. I like it out here. I like feeling the wind."

She raised her face into that wind she had known her entire life and agreed.

"Okay," she said. "Five minutes more."

"The wind uncovered Pop's saw," I said. "I should cover it."

"Fine. You do that and then you get in here where it's warm." She disappeared into the house.

I made my way around the lower yard and began to cross in front of the house as slowly as I could. When I glanced down Fitch Lane, Pop had turned the corner. His breath steamed into the cold air. His legs pumped through the snow like the pistons connecting the wheels of the old locomotives. He kept his eyes on me as he climbed the hill and motioned for me to meet him. I bounded through the drifts to join him behind the hedges.

"He's under the porch," I whispered. "He has a really big gun. There's something wrong with him. He doesn't know who I am. He was going to shoot me."

"Where under the porch?"

"On the top side, a little bit in. He's under that dirty old tarp you used for the wood. The snow is all the way up to the floor-boards, so you can't get in that way."

"Where did you go in?"

"At the bottom end. There's a big drift there too, but not all the way up. He'll probably shoot us if we go near the stairs."

He leaned against the hedge, shivered a little, and said the thing that scared me the most.

"I want you to go and stand in that drift at the bottom. Stay to the side of the new concrete pillar. I want you to try to talk some sense into him. Don't go close and don't move out of the shadow of the house. I'm going to dig through that drift at the top and get behind him."

I grasped his sleeve and begged, "No, Pop, please. Don't go in there."

"I have to," he said. "He's freezing to death. We've got to get him warmed up. If we can get him into the house, we can help him."

"He'll shoot you."

"Not if you keep him busy."

I knew I had to do it, but my legs didn't want to move.

"I'm too cold," I whined.

"He's a hell of a lot colder than you are. I'm going up to the top. You get moving." He moved away without another word.

I made a lot of noise moving up the small slope to the porch, so as not to surprise Lenny. When I showed myself on the snow-drift, the huddled form did not move.

"Lenny?" My voice squeaked above the mass of cotton that had thickened my tongue.

The dwarf mold unfolded and there was that pasty white face and that big black gun. "Git!"

"It's me. Molly. I want to take you into the house. You need to get warm."

"Git!"

The snowdrift behind him moved. I took a deep breath. "Mom has oatmeal bread in the oven and she's making your favorite raisin cakes."

"Git!"

"You can have my bedroom again. Come inside and I'll show you some pictures of you and Larry when you were babies. I found them in a suitcase in the closet."

"Git out of here!"

Pop's hands let in a circle of light. The peak of his hat moved in jerks as he dug at the snow.

"Come on out and we'll make some snow angels."

There was no answer this time, but the gun moved a little. I leaned deeper into the shadow. "Lenny?"

It all happened at once. Pop came crawling up behind the tarp. The gun went off. A porch beam above my head splintered and showered slivers of wood into the dark space. I fell to my knees.

Pop came toward me, holding Lenny tightly against him and shouting, "Are you hit? Are you okay?" His face was as pasty white as Lenny's.

I couldn't speak. I nodded and stood up.

"That damned gun is still in there. And it's loaded. Don't go near it! Come with me."

I hurried after him. His longer legs plowed a narrow path to the back door. Mom let out a distraught groan as she took Lenny from Pop and began to remove his clothing. He fought weakly against her as the room filled with the sickening stench of stale urine and something rotten. I fled to the frigid dining room.

Pop followed and gathered me to him. He patted my arms, my back, my chest, and looked over my face and skull. "You sure you're okay?"

I collapsed against him and nodded. "It hit the porch." I began to cry. "I was so scared."

"Me too," he said. "I don't remember when I've ever been that scared." He sat on a dining room chair and rocked me against his chest. "That was too close," he said. "Too, too close."

"I need some towels," Mom called. "And some flannel sheets. Strip them off the beds if you have to."

We scrambled to obey. I found flannels on Mom and Pop's bed and pulled them behind me down the stairs. Pop was more organized. He carried a neatly folded stack of towels and blankets on one bent arm. As he held the door for me, the stench was overpowering.

"Close the door," Mom ordered. "Sean, put your stack in the warming oven. Molly, hang those sheets over the boiler. Then both of you move the small couch from the hall close to the fire." We did not hesitate. Pop wanted out of that stinking room as much as I.

By the time we pushed the small couch to the front of the stove, Mom had wrapped naked and delirious Lenny into a mummy of warm sheets. She sat on the couch and pulled him onto her lap.

"Sean, go find that big dropper thing we used to feed the puppies. I think it's in the medicine cabinet. Molly, pour some milk in a pan with some sugar. Put it on the warm side of the stove. Then throw those stinking clothes onto the back porch."

She continued to rock Lenny as she gave orders. He was an overgrown baby in her arms. He no longer struggled. His face was as translucent and white as the paraffin wax Mom used to seal her jelly jars—like Granny Sue's face when she was dying, before they put the cheek color on her.

I had to ask. "Is he dying?"

She didn't look up. "No, but he's sure close to it. Once I get him warm enough, I'll need to get sugar milk into him. If I were to try now he'd choke and end up with pneumonia like you did." She began to hum.

I listened for a few minutes before I hooked one end of the broom handle on Lenny's filthy coat.

"Don't fool around with that stuff. Pick it up with your hands and get it out of here," Mom said.

As I lifted the coat, metal clinked onto the floor. I reached out quickly to scoop up scattering bullets. I was too slow.

"What is that?" she demanded.

"Bullets," I mumbled.

"I knew it! I was sure I heard a gunshot. I was coming out to check when you came running in. Where did they come from?" She looked toward Pop, who had returned with the dropper. "Sean?"

"He had a gun," Pop said as if it were as normal as breathing. "He doesn't have it anymore." He reached out. "Give those to me, Molly."

I dropped the bullets into his hand.

"Where is it?" Mom said.

"You take care of him and let me worry about that."

Her eyes opened wide. "Where do you think he got a gun? Do you think he used it?"

"We'll have to ask him that when he can answer." Pop reached out one hand and propped himself against the nearest wall.

"Sean, you'd better get to bed. Did you drink all night?'

"Played a couple hands of five card stud."

"Did you sleep?"

"Nah."

"Go to bed. There's nothing you can do here and you'll have to work this afternoon."

"I don't think they'll operate. Most of the foremen stopped at the tavern too. They were going to fold up shop early for the holidays anyway."

"Then go to bed and sleep it off. Molly, take one of the sheets off the boiler and go up with him. Help him get his wet boots off and wrap him in the sheet. Cover him up good, will you?"

I followed him up the drafty staircase. He dropped onto the bare mattress fully clothed.

"You'll have to sit up, Pop," I said, "so I can get your boots untied."

"Leave them be," he said. "They won't hurt anything."

"They're wet and dirty. They're making a mess of the mattress."

"Who the hell cares?"

"Mom does."

He closed his eyes and didn't answer.

"Pop, sit up. Here, I'll help you."

He took my hand, pulled himself up, and swung his legs over the side of the bed.

As I knelt by his feet and struggled to loosen his wet rawhide laces, he placed a gentle hand on my head. "Sometimes, Molly, things get so damned mixed up that you wonder where the hell to go next."

I thought he was talking about New Jersey. But, as I tugged his steel-toed work boots off, he mumbled, "They make slaves of us. It always comes back to that. Wear us down, use us up until we have no fight left."

"It'll be okay, Pop," I said. I had no idea who "they" were, but I felt sad for him. My eyes welled up with tears. I loved my pop, drunk or not drunk. There was no one else I trusted more.

"You're the best pop in the world," I said. "And no one can wear us out. Not when we have such a good family."

He smiled, lay back down, and pulled the warmed flannel sheet around his ears. "That we do. Don't ever forget that. We'll always have our family."

I covered him, first with the blankets, and then with some extra coats. "It'll be okay, Pop," I said.

I wasn't sure anything would ever be okay again, but Lenny had made his way back, and even though Pop had had too much to drink he'd kept his head, so no one had been hurt with the gun. I closed his door and sat at the top of the stairs until I got the rest of my tears out. I was still wearing all my added clothes and Marty's wet coat was becoming awfully heavy.

Finally, I went back to the kitchen. As I opened the door I was greeted by that horrible stench and remembered Lenny's soiled clothes. I held my breath and tossed the whole mess out the back door. The wind blew the door wide open and scattered a layer of newspaper Mom had laid open on the floor so she could empty the ash pit of the stove. One page caught a thermal from the overheated stove, lofted high above Mom's head, hovered for a second, and dropped.

With her arms full she couldn't avoid the page as it covered her head. She peeked out from beneath one corner and began to laugh. I slammed the door and fell onto the couch beside her. Together we vented the tight emotions stored up since the storm began. We laughed until my tears again began to flow.

CHAPTER NINE

Three days later, when the last of the storm passed, Lenny was practically back to normal, except that his fingers and toes had turned numb. He was asleep when I found Pop in the library. He had opened the chamber of the revolver and was checking for lodged bullets.

"Did you keep any out, Molly?"

"No."

"Not a one?"

"Not one."

"You're sure?"

"Positive."

He fitted the gun into his peacoat pocket. "Do you want to climb the mountain with me and see how that damned dragline has fared in the storm?"

Like the factory, the stripping operation had closed down early for Christmas. I hoped he was going to let me shoot the gun. I grabbed my coat and beat him out the door.

The snow had melted over the land that covered the underground fire. In places, dark holes spewed steam though the cracked crust of the earth. Pop led the way, carefully winding through hot spots until we reached the newly deposited culm banks that ringed the most recent stripping. The hole was already partially filled with water thickened with tree parts and castoff bits of metal machinery. A few truck tires were frozen into the water's edge. The center was not yet solid. On the opposite side of the pit, a black wall of anthracite waited to be mined. They were not nearly done with their destruction.

We passed the snow-covered Mountaineer and three dump trucks parked against the newest culm bank. Pop stopped me with a touch on my arm.

"Do you see any workers or hunters around? Look carefully."

I scanned the woods on the mountainside and let my gaze glide over the entire length of the stripping operation. Nothing moved. The snow was pristine, untouched, and shining with diamonds in the afternoon sun.

"Do you see anyone?" he repeated.

"Nope."

"Good. Stay here and keep your eyes peeled. Whistle if anything moves."

He made his way another three feet, to the very edge of the precipice, and pulled the gun from his pocket. He wound his arm back and flung the gun, grip first, with all the power he could muster. I watched it sail through the open air. It hit the water in the very center of the stripping pit fifty feet below. He reached into his pocket twice more and flung the bullets. I watched them plunk, plunk, plunk over the collected water before churning tiny ripples as they sank. Pop turned and came back. He was smiling.

"Why'd you do that?" I asked. "Couldn't you have sold it?"

"Can't hurt anybody now."

"Shouldn't you have given it to John Hale?"

"Don't ever want anyone to link up Lenny and that gun. That big Mountaineer machine will fill in that hole and no one will ever be the wiser."

I thought about the buried Indian doll and began to chuckle to think that thousands of years from now some kid like me would break a piece of slate to bits and wonder at the imprint of the doll or the outline of a gun.

"What's so funny?" Pop asked.

"Some kid will find its fossil one day."

He laughed. "She'll probably think the bullets were scat from the gun." I could imagine that.

"Lenny probably stole it."

"Doesn't matter. Put a name with a gun and all kinds of problems can come out of it. Every bad deal from here to Philadelphia for the last week could be tied to him. I don't believe he hurt anyone, but if the gun was used for anything bad everybody will want him hanged."

"Like your great-grandpa. The one who was a Mollie?"

"Yes, like him."

"Did your grandpa really kill a guy?"

"Nobody will ever know. That's the problem with the government and the law. Anything can be pinned on anybody if you get the right people to swear to it. Some folks are better believed than others. You always want to be on the side that looks the best." He turned and began to walk back down the trail we had broken through the snow.

"Lenny almost shot me."

"He wasn't in his right mind. We're all damn lucky that that bullet went up in the air and didn't hit the house foundation. It might have ricocheted and hit you. It gives me butterflies in my stomach if I think of that too much. I wasn't fast enough and his hand was nearly frozen to the trigger. We'd best not dwell on that."

"He might have shot you."

"But he didn't."

"I was scared."

"I was too. As a matter of fact, I'm still shaking in my boots." He laughed and ruffled my hair.

I had seen him feeling sad, but I couldn't imagine him ever being afraid. I took his hand and swung it as we shuffled through the deep snow.

"If he did something wrong, he might never own up to it," Pop said. He looked off into the distance.

"He'll have to tell us sometime."

"No, he doesn't. Some things are best kept inside. Telling somebody else makes them need to keep a secret, too. That's a lot of work. Not everybody is good at keeping secrets."

"I am," I said.

"I bet you are," he smiled. "I bet you're a Branigan through and through."

I skipped through the snow, sending showers of dry powder into the still air. His compliment warmed me from the inside out. I felt that I was somehow special, maybe more special than anybody knew. He wanted me to keep the secret of the gun. He had trusted me with the knowledge of its resting place. And yet he had never come right out and asked. I wondered how he could not ask and ask at the very same time.

As soon as we got back to the house, I had Lenny help me drag out the suitcase of photographs. I hoped to get the goods on him. I liked using that turn of words: "get the goods on him." I had read it in the book about the Molly Maguires from the city library. The author had used those terms when he wrote about Pinkerton detective McParlan, who brought down the Mollies and caused Pop's great-grandfather to be hanged. According to the book, McParlan pretended to be an Irish immigrant, gained the confidence of the Mollies, and learned the coded hand signals that they called "the goods." Once he had the goods he was privy to all the goings-on in the closed organization.

Because I'd read about the Mollies, I understood what Pop meant when he said that sometimes hiding the truth was the best thing to do, especially when it involved big shots. McParlan, who had pursued Irish daughters and hung out in Irish taverns, including the one owned by Pat Branigan—who was himself a drunkard and philanderer but maybe not a murderer—had betrayed Branigan to the coal barons. The detective had been hired by Asa Packer, who owned the railroad, and by several absentee mine owners who stayed in their mansions while McParlan did their dirty work.

When I asked Mom about the book's version of the truth, she said, "Well now, Molly, there's another side to that story."

For once I had been interested. "So tell me."

"It started when the Irishmen got tired of being in debt to the companies. They began to ask for more pay."

"And they didn't get it?"

"No. And worse, the mine owners started importing cheaper labor by the boatload—Slovaks and Welshmen mainly. They took over the jobs of the already poor Irishmen."

"Couldn't the government stop them?"

"Hah! The big shots in government never can be trusted. They go where the money goes. And in this case they went with the coal companies."

"What about the newspapers?"

"When the Irishmen began to fight back, the newspapers told some of the truth, or maybe what was nearly true, but they painted a nasty picture of the organizers among the Mollies."

"Why did everyone believe them?"

"People like a good story, and that dirty McParlan was a master at storytelling."

"So he lied through his teeth?"

"Yes. And in the end they hanged every Irish guy the detective tagged."

"Could that happen now?"

"Of course it can. And with a name like Molly, you'll need to be careful in the world or you could end up hanged too."

She had laughed when she said that, so I knew she was teasing me. Just the same, I had given it some long thought.

Lenny and I settled the suitcase on the floor of the library, out of the way of Mom, Pop, and Marty, who were pulling Christmas decorations from the storage closet. We sat cross-legged with the open suitcase between us. I took a long cardboard envelope with "Sean" written on it, put it aside, and spilled a handful of other pictures into my lap.

Lenny lined up all the pictures that he thought might be his family and rifled through the suitcase looking for more. None of the photos were labeled, so I should have had no idea who most of those people were. But the strangest thing was that when I looked at the pictures I knew who they were. It felt like someone whispered names into my ear, though I had yet to confirm their identities.

Lenny didn't know if most faces belonged to his part of the family, either—except for his mother. He could hardly miss Iris, because she posed like a vamp even when she held a baby in her arms. Most of the pictures of Iris were with babies.

I desperately wanted him to talk about the gun, but he changed the subject whenever I got close to asking. I wasn't so sure that Pop's way was the right way. Waiting for someone to tell me the stuff that I was dying to hear was not my style.

"Do you think this is Larry and me?" He lifted a photograph of two babies lying side by side on a light-colored blanket.

I leaned across the suitcase and studied it. "It must be. You're the only twins that I know of, and they look like boys."

He smiled. "Yeah. I think that's us."

"Mom went to see Larry while you were missing. She said he's with a nice family. They bought him new clothes."

"I ruined my shoes."

"That's what happens when you walk a hundred miles through the snow."

"I didn't walk the whole way. I stuck out my thumb and caught a couple of rides."

"Weren't you a-scared?"

"Yeah, but I got so tired and so cold that I figured hitching a ride with a stranger was better than freezing to death."

"Did you get anything to eat?"

"Yeah. The guy who gave me the gun got me breakfast in a real restaurant. Eggs and bacon and toast. I ain't never been in a real restaurant before."

"Musta been a nice guy."

"Nah. He was the most scary." He lowered his voice to a whisper. "Promise me you won't tell."

Promises were not lightly made in my family. We were taught early on to think long and hard before we said the words because, once a promise was made, it had to be honored—unless we wanted to be shunned forever. I thought about the gun and Pop's need to know and my own curiosity and I decided that I could probably find a loophole in the words once I said them.

"Crisscross my heart, my right hand up to God." I made the motions with my hand.

Lenny seemed relieved to spill his guts. Once he started, he hardly took a breath.

"He said he killed two people in Philly. Said traveling with a kid would make him look innocent. Said I had to stay with him or he'd shoot me with that gun."

I tried not to look too surprised but I felt my eyes open wide and I know I gasped. He seemed to like that he had shocked me. He rocked back a little and leaned on his hands.

"He had blood on his shirt. I saw it when he was reaching for the check from the waitress."

"Real blood?"

"Yeah. And a lot of it."

"Was he shot?"

"Nope. When we got back in the car I asked him if he was shot. He said, 'Hell, no. Why'd you ask that?' I said, ''Cause you got blood all over your shirt.' He said, 'Ain't none of your business. You keep your mouth shut or it'll be your blood next.' I didn't say another word after that."

"Did you have to shoot him to get the gun?"

"Nah. He left me in the car when he went into this store up in the mountains. He came out with some money and he made me get out of the car. He said he'd shot somebody in that store and now he was goin' to get the hell out of the area. He put all the bullets in my coat pockets. Asked me my name. Said if I told anybody about him he'd come find me and shoot me full of holes. Then he handed me the gun and told me to start walking. Said if the cops asked me about the gun to tell them it was mine.

"It was damned cold and I heard a train, so I ran into the woods toward the sound. I thought I could hop on a freight and get down here. That was a laugh. Wasn't another train the whole night. I kept following the tracks downhill and damned if I didn't see the old boiler house. I crawled in and slept for a long time. Once I got a fire going, it stayed pretty warm—until the wind started filling it up with snow."

"You were lucky none of the bums came. Or Ronald Miller."

"I felt pretty safe with that old gun in my lap."

"Did you tell that mean guy your name?'

"Not my real one."

"What'd you tell him?"

"I said I was Marty Branigan. It's the only name I could think of."

That seemed a reasonable thing to do to me. "You're a fast thinker," I said.

He smiled, lay back on the floor, and held the picture of the two babies at arms length in front of his face. He seemed very innocent and young. I had hoped he could stay with us, especially since Marty would be leaving for the army after the holidays, but Mom had lost every argument with the social worker. Even though Pop said he would not allow the court to place Lenny, I knew everybody was taking a short holiday from the mess.

Behind us, Marty and Pop carried the platform for the Lionel train from the storage closet while Mom tried to lift out the heavy Christmas tree holder. Its thick round base supported an upright tube that fit snugly through a hole in the platform. Once gravel was packed around the trunk of the tree it would stand firmly above a miniature village and railroad pathways.

"I wish you kids would come here and help," she said. "Put that suitcase away and carry this to the parlor."

Lenny headed for the parlor with the holder. I slipped the envelope into the drawer with the blueprints. I knew I shouldn't be sticking my nose into Pop's business, but once done, I wanted to keep it only my business. I picked up all the other photographs and pushed the suitcase under the library table. As I neatened the room, a loud commotion started in the parlor. I hurried into the room.

Pop was jumping up and down, alternately hugging Mom and waving a folded newspaper in the air.

"Christmas is a-coming and the goose is getting fat!" he sang.

Mom disengaged herself and smiled so broadly that I thought her face might split.

"He won," she said. "The treasury numbers. He won!"

"What's a treasury number?" Lenny asked.

She took the newspaper from Pop and pointed to a tiny square on the front page. A series of numbers preceded by a dollar sign was all I could see.

"It's the United States Treasury report. The men at the factory run a contest on it every week. Each man puts in a dollar and writes a number. Pop guessed it right."

"Yeah, but the best thing is, no one has won for months. It's over five hundred dollars! And the money's right there now, at the union house, waiting for me to pick it up."

Pop snatched the paper from Mom's hands, took her in his arms again, and began to dance her around the table.

"We'll pay off bills," Mom sang.

"Hell, no, we won't. We'll have a great Christmas first and use what's left for bills. I've had enough worrying for a while. It's time to celebrate."

Mom broke away. "I'll only be a minute," she shouted as she dashed for the stairs. "I'm going to change into shopping clothes. We'll need to get a really big tree. Marty, you take Lenny over by the creek and cut some green bread-and-butter vines for the banisters." They obeyed.

Pop carried the newspaper into the kitchen, leaned his backside against the nickel trim of the stove, and began to read. I stood in the doorway and tried to decide how much I could tell him of Lenny's story without breaking my promise.

He read the paper backward because he liked to check out the end of each article to see if it was worth reading.

I studied headlines that hung between us. "Man Arrested in Murder of Liquor Store Owner." I moved closer.

A man and his wife had been shot in Philadelphia. A grocery store clerk near Blakeslee Corners was believed shot by the same gunman. The man had attempted to rob a liquor store in Harrisburg and had been shot by police. He said he had a teenage accomplice from Wilkes-Barre who had carried out the previous robberies and shootings. The police were looking for a boy who lived in our area, and the gun used in the Philadelphia killings. The grocery store clerk had survived.

I looked at Pop as he read contentedly and was sorry that I had to say it. "Pop?"

"Yeah?"

"There's a story on the front page."

"Yeah?"

"It's the story Lenny told me about the gun."

He turned the paper and began to read. As his eyes moved over the words, his face grew pale. He took my hand and led me to the library.

I began to cry.

"Don't cry," he said. "You've got to be calm. I need you to tell me everything he told you."

"I promised I wouldn't tell."

"This is an emergency. I'm afraid you'll have to tell me."

When I finished, Pop took in a deep gulp of air. "Do you believe him?"

"Yes. If he'd done anything bad he would have bragged about it, don't you think?"

He nodded with awful slowness. "I'll have to talk to him and he'll know who squealed."

I shook my head. "He'll be mad at me."

"Yes, for a while. But he'll get over it."

My tears became loud sobs.

"I don't have any other choice. I have to make sure he's telling the truth."

"He couldn't shoot anybody. He didn't even shoot me when he was out of his mind."

"People sometimes do things they wouldn't ordinarily do when they can't see any other way."

"I believe what he told me."

"I believe it too, but I still have to hear it from his mouth."

"What are you going to do? Are you going to tell John Hale?"

"I don't know."

"Lenny's going to hate me. I promised him I wouldn't tell."

"If I could see any other way, I'd do it."

"But I promised him."

"A promise has to be broken if you know that keeping it will hurt somebody really bad. Lenny trusted you, but saving him from jail is more important than a promise. Don't you think?"

I didn't have time to think about that. I heard Lenny's and Marty's voices racketing in through the back door. I bolted through the front hallway and up the stairs. As I closed my bedroom door I heard Pop say, "Lenny, come in here would you? I think we have something to talk about."

Forty-five minutes later the car drove away. I crept down the stairs, sure they had taken Lenny with them. But he was on the floor trying to fit the round Christmas tree stand through the hole in the platform as Marty guided him from above.

I waited under the archway. Lenny wriggled out from under the low platform. He smiled.

"So you're not mad?" I asked.

"Nah. He said he made you tell."

"What's he gonna do?"

"Dunno."

"Where'd they go?"

"Shopping."

Marty emptied the contents of the platform parts into the center of the nailed-down Lionel train tracks. "You two can finish up here," he ordered. "I'm going to go buy presents."

We worked in silence. By the time we had made the room look like Christmas, I had forgotten all about the guy who gave Lenny the gun and who had got himself shot.

We went into the kitchen, spread homemade bread slices with peanut butter and gooseberry jam, and sat side by side on the small sofa.

We would throw caution to the wind and have a crazy good Christmas. Who cared if Mr. Reid came knocking on the front door? That old bill collector wasn't going to change his stripes, no matter how much Mom paid him. It seemed a long time since Pop's accident. Even though I knew how far in debt Mom was to Mr. Reid, I decided to put all of it out of my mind. I was with Pop on this one.

"Your pop said I could work on his jigsaw puzzle—the one with the fall scene," Lenny said.

"You want some help?"

"Yep. Never did a puzzle before. Never had a train or a platform either."

"No platform?"

"Nope. Do you think they'll really buy a big tree?"

"That's what Mom said. You can help decorate it."

"Nah. That's girl stuff."

We went into the library, where Pop had placed the thin puzzle board and boxed puzzle on the table. It had been a long time since the room hadn't been used as a sickroom or extra bedroom. Seeing the table set up made me believe that things were getting back to normal. Now we could go on happily and have no more problems. Then I remembered New Jersey. I was beginning to hate that place as much as Pop did.

Lenny took the chair opposite me and opened the box. He withdrew a few pieces, studied them carefully, and tried to snap them together.

I showed him how to dump the whole thing out, find the end pieces, and sort the pieces into piles by color. I tapped the board in front of him. "First decide where the top and bottom are."

He was slow and methodical. I was impatient.

"Look at the picture on the box and you can see where the sky is and where that fence post goes," I said.

"Huh! That's kind of what your pop was saying."

"What? To look at the picture?"

"Nah! He said that sometimes we can't see the whole picture until we put all the pieces together, and that sometimes the pieces are hard to find, so you have to be patient."

"Pop said that?"

"Yeah. He said that life is sometimes like that. It's hard to find the right pieces because we don't have the finished picture to know what goes where."

"My pop's pretty smart."

"Yeah. He said I should think about that the whole time I'm putting this damn thing together. You know, he's not actually scary at all."

"Did you useta think he was scary?"

He nodded as he placed the four corner pieces in their proper places.

I began collecting the blue sky and white clouds. "Why'd you ever think he was scary?"

"'Cause my mom always says he's from the Mollies and that he's Catholic. Everybody knows you can never trust a Catholic."

"I like Catholics. My Aunt Mary Margaret's a Catholic. She was going to be nun, but she got married instead. She's Pop's only sister."

"Iris says that your pop put old Charlie under a spell and got him to sign over this house to him."

Now, that made me mad. My pop would never put anybody under a spell to steal something.

"Old Charlie *had* spells. After he had that stroke thing. My mom told me that. She says that sometimes he wasn't in his right mind and that he couldn't talk good enough for people to understand him. I told you, this house is Lillian's, not my pop's."

"Then how come you get to live here all the time?"

"Because Lillian is Mom's mother. And she wants to be nice. Because my mom's her only daughter."

"That's not what Iris says. She says that after Granny Sue's funeral, your pop beat up my pop with one of those spokes from the banister upstairs, and that sent him to the hospital, and that's why he's never set foot in this house again."

In my opinion, his mom and pop were a couple of liars, but I wasn't going to start fighting again. "He would never do that."

"He did. That's why that spoke is missing from the upstairs banister."

There *was* a spindle missing. It had always been missing. I had a fleeting vision of that spindle swinging through the air, attached to a man's arm, followed by a horrible scream. Had that happened? Had I seen that happen? I leaned over the board, my arms straight and stiff.

"That's not true," I said in my meanest voice.

"Lillian said it too." He didn't look up.

I snatched one of his puzzle pieces and snapped it into the picture in front of him. "If you don't know what you're talking about, then you shouldn't say a word."

"Don't get mad at me. I'm only saying what I heard."

"Well, you heard wrong. Pop would never hurt another person like that. Iris must be telling fibs, and that's a sin."

"Lillian was there, too, and they'd all had lots of whiskey and pretty soon they were telling all kinds of stories about your pop."

"Oh, yeah? Like what?"

"Like he was a bum and he had a brother who had fits and was crazy. Lillian said that your mom had to look out the window every time she heard the trains, because she was sure your pop was gonna hop a freight out of town. Lillian said it wouldn't surprise her if he did that, first chance he got."

"I heard that story before. He said it isn't true. Besides, Mom never even notices the trains." I was getting madder with every spoken word.

"Nope. Not anymore. 'Cause she's got him tamed now. That's what Iris says. She says that your mom has your pop under her thumb and ain't nobody ever gonna get him out from under it."

"Well, if that's true, why's she gonna make him go to New Jersey all by himself?"

He had no answer, and since I had nothing else to say we worked in angry silence until the outside edges were almost together. That's when I heard Pop's car turn around in the driveway. Lenny heard it too. We nearly overturned the table in our hurry to get to the door to see what they had bought.

CHAPTER TEN

The Christmas platform and its overhanging tree took up half of the living room. The dining room table, extended to its full length and surrounded by sixteen chairs, took up most of the dining room. Marty and Pop moved the small couch from the kitchen into the front hall. The doors to the library and the second parlor were locked up tight. When Lillian arrived she would use the rollaway bed for her stay and keep the secret presents safe. At the sight of those locked doors, Lenny and I were overcome with excitement. We turned the handles and pushed our weight against their curtained panels whenever we passed.

On the day of Christmas Eve, Lillian arrived with Iris's younger boys. I breathed a sigh of relief when Iris failed to step onto the driveway. Instead, Sally, wearing makeup and high heels, with her shining hair piled high on her head, stepped out of the front seat. Janet, as brassy and blond as Iris, followed closely behind. She spoke to the cabbie in the same raspy, throaty voice that usually announced her mother's presence, and she carried a brown wrapped bottle, as Iris would have. Against Mom's wishes, both girls had found jobs at the Globe department store and Janet had dropped out of school.

The cab driver placed a whole case of wine and several bottles of vodka on the concrete stair between the hedges. I could see the set of Mom's jaw tighten as she watched Pop carry the liquor into the house. As soon as he left the kitchen, she carried half the bottles down the cellar steps.

Lillian laughed at her daughter's retreating back. "Can't change human nature," she called out.

"No, but you can slow it down a little," Mom shot back.

After supper, as the house began to fill with family and neighbors, Lenny and I sat with our backs against the dining room wall, next to the buffet where the open wine bottles waited. With so many people crowded into the rooms, no one took notice of us folded below the staircase.

Lenny was quick on his feet. He poured two glasses of wine and brought them down to our corner. I had never tasted wine before. I liked its rich red sweetness. We emptied our glasses and Lenny poured us another. My head started to feel funny. I relinquished the third glass to my cousin.

He soon began laughing so loud and often that he caught Lillian's attention. She made her way toward us. I stood up. A sudden spinning overtook my brain. I couldn't move. My stomach rose up into my throat and, to my surprise, I had to hold on to the buffet to stay on my feet.

Lillian caught me as my knees were giving way. "I can see that your eyes are bigger than your belly," she said. "We'd better get you to bed before your mother notices." She took Lenny's glass and smacked him gently on the head. "You too," she said. "Get up." She guided us up the stairs, cackling like a hen that had found a juicy worm in its scratchings.

Lenny's room was at the top left of the hall. As she helped him get undressed, I leaned against the inside wall of the rail-protected opening of the stairwell. As I tried to slow the spinning hallway, I vowed silently to never touch another glass of wine. My eyes focused on the gaping missing-spindle space on the banister. Behind the wall at my back I could hear Lillian getting Lenny settled. She seemed to be taking an awfully long time.

I could no longer hold myself upright. I slid down the wall until I lay supine. The light from the party cast long shadows on the adjacent wall. Voices, disembodied and full of excitement, floated up the stairs.

Janet called into the open stairwell, "Lillian, come look at this! Lillian? Where are you?"

From Lenny's doorway Lillian shouted back, "I'm getting these kids settled. I'll be down in a minute."

"You need to come now. Hurry up!" Her voice, so much like Iris's, triggered a memory, a wisp of a thought, dreamlike and vague.

I had seen it here in this hallway. I had seen a man rip out that spindle and swing it with all his might over the shoulder of another man. I had heard that voice, Iris's voice, shouting, loud and screechy.

"Bastard. You lousy Irish bastard. You're all alike. Shysters. Murderers. Liars."

Her brassy head had cleared the upper floor, where the light shining on her scrunched-up face made her look like the raging witch in *The Wizard of Oz*. Mom had been there too. She had come up beside Iris and pulled her down, away from the two wrestling men.

I felt Lillian's touch on my shoulder. Her hand urged me to stand. I allowed myself to be tucked into bed. The ceiling of the room spun uncontrollably. My open bedroom door allowed shadows and voices from below to invade the recesses of my reeling brain. I turned around in the bed so that my head was at the foot. When I opened my eyes I could see down the long hall, past the missing spindle, and into the open door of the bathroom.

Some time, long ago, I had lain in this bed with my sister, my brother, and the twins. Two up and three down, my head exactly here, where I could see the open bathroom door and the shadows in that long stairwell hall. I had been sleepless because I was worried about Granny Sue sleeping in that box in the parlor where the Christmas platform now stood. The room had been filled with people, like tonight. I remembered that: Mom saying that there were too many people in one room as she carried me up to this bed.

I remembered a rumble of men's voices running up the stairs and women's voices coming quickly behind. And then shouts from below, rising shrilly like the air raid siren they sometimes tested down in the valley. I could not remember more. I tried to visualize the two men who fought, but their faces would not become clear. The room slowly stopped spinning. I closed my eyes and slept.

Sometime in the night Sally and Janet climbed into the big brass bed, but I didn't hear them. It was the odor of stale alcohol from our breathing and a pounding in my head that awakened me before first light. I pulled a sweater over my nightgown and tiptoed down the stairs.

Mom and Lillian were already at work in the kitchen. The door was partially closed. When I peeked in through the narrow opening, I could see the freshly washed turkey in a pan in the middle of the table. Mom had her back to me. She was cleaning vegetables under running water in the sink. Her mother worked at the stove, stirring a pan of stuffing that emitted the most wonderful scent: wilting celery, onions, and sage. They talked loudly to one another over the noise of running water and the scratch of the spatula on the cast-iron pot.

I lowered myself onto a chair in the dining room. Brightly wrapped presents were stacked neatly down the center of the table. I reached out and picked up a package.

The voices in the kitchen took on an angry tone. I turned my aching head to hear what they were saying.

"Well, he's awfully quiet. He didn't say two words at supper."

"I'm telling you, Lillian, it's the job worries. He doesn't want to move to Jersey. That's all it is."

"Seems like a lot to worry about, to me." Lillian's voice trailed off as she stepped away from the stove.

"Somebody will hire him," Mom said. "He's still putting in applications."

The package had my name on it. I shook it softly. It didn't rattle but was very heavy.

"Well, he's not so young anymore, you know," Lillian said. "There are at least one hundred younger men with the same experience out looking. Everyone knows that."

"Mother! I'm not going to worry about it. Sean will take care of it."

I had never received a gift this heavy before.

"Maybe you should talk to him about it. Maybe you should at least consider moving."

"Talking won't help. Sean doesn't like chatter. It makes him nervous."

I held the present on my lap and turned it over. Maybe a bit of tape might loosen.

"You take him for granted," Lillian said.

It was sealed tight. I put the package back on the table and picked up another.

In the kitchen, the water stopped running.

"Don't get me started, Lillian." Mom lowered her voice to a near whisper. "You and this whole damn family were against Sean from the start. Why do you suddenly think you know him better than I do?"

Lillian continued on loudly. "I'm not saying I know him better. I just think he could use a little more of your support. That's how marriages are supposed to work."

"Lillian, shush. You'll wake the whole house."

For a few minutes they worked in silence.

"Since when do you know so much about how marriages work?" Mom hissed.

The package was for Lenny. I put it back on the table and stood up. The kitchen was silent for another long moment.

"I may not have been married long," Lillian said more quietly, "but I've seen many a marriage fall apart when people don't support each other."

"I cook his meals, clean his house, take care of his kids, wash his clothes, and lots of other things. You don't know anything about what I do."

I started to open the kitchen door. Neither woman was facing me.

Lillian took a big breath in and then let it out in a rush. "I wish that you weren't so damned pigheaded!"

Mom slammed the colander of vegetable peelings onto the drainboard. She ducked her head as she lifted two handfuls of cut potatoes from the sink. When she looked for something to put them in, she dropped most of them on the floor. She stooped, picked them up, and tossed them carelessly back into the sink.

Neither of them noticed me standing in the doorway.

"After all, he could have been here and gone," Lillian persisted. "He could have left you pregnant and alone. He could still be running."

I stepped back out and carefully pushed the door until it was almost closed. No way was I going to miss this one.

"He stayed."

"But he didn't have to."

"Neither did I."

Upstairs, someone stirred and padded down the hall to the bathroom.

Lillian glanced up at the ceiling and lowered her voice. "You were a baby. Where would you have gone?"

"With him. On the road."

I couldn't imagine Mom hiking along some road in her cotton housedress and flowered apron.

"That would have been stupid. What would you have done? Hopped freights with him? Slept in hobo camps along the tracks?"

"If it came to that, I would have." Mom sounded like she was crying. "He's the only person who's ever made me feel loved."

"Bess! That's a terrible thing to say to your own mother. You have a whole big family that loves you."

"And never shows it." She definitely was crying.

"You still blame me for not raising you, don't you? You'll never understand that I had no way to support you? You still believe that I ran off—like your father? That I took the easy way out?"

"Well, didn't you? You're so used to people running off, you believe Sean would have."

Another pan slammed against a hard surface. "I never said that. I said he *could* have. And as for me, I had no choice! The best thing I could do for you was have you live here with my mom and dad. The city was no place to raise a little girl. I sent you things. Money. Toys."

"But you hardly ever sent yourself."

"I came whenever I could. I still do. I always hoped that you would live with me when you graduated—like Sally and Janet are now. Before I had a chance to say anything, you and Sean were married."

"I was starting to show. We had to hurry. I couldn't wait."

"Why do we have to go over this again? It's Christmas. Why can't we just this once be happy for a change?"

"You started it," Mom said.

"You started it years ago. Did you think anyone would be fooled when you ran off in such a hurry to get married?"

"What would you have done? Sent me off to one of those places where they make you give the baby up? Tell everybody I was spending the year with Aunt Penny in Reading? And when I came back, thin and sad like Iris did, what would you have said? 'She's been a little under the weather'? We did the right thing. I would do the very same today."

Upstairs, the toilet flushed. Feet padded quietly back to one of the front bedrooms. I moved to the crack in the door on the hinge side and peered into the room.

"You run off, live hand to mouth, never have a dime in your pocket, birth three kids that constantly need things that you can't give them, alienate yourself from your church and most of your family, and you call that right?" Lillian had moved with the heavy pan of stuffing to the table where the turkey waited.

"Right for me! Don't you come here for Christmas and start moralizing and telling me how to run my life! We're doing fine! And don't tell me that I alienated my family! It's them who stay away! Not one of them will ever get over Sean having this house!"

That brought me up short. So Pop did own the house.

Lillian turned and studied Mom. "Well, you're right about that. Even you have to admit, Bess, that having someone who's not even blood related get a house in a will when there are plenty of blood relatives who could've used a roof over their heads . . . Well, that would stick in your craw too."

Mom seemed to soften a little, as if she could see Lillian's point. "I admit it would. But I know Sean and I knew Old Charlie and I know that whatever caused it, it wasn't Sean and it wasn't because Charlie was crazy. He put it in writing before a lawyer and no one can say he didn't."

"That doesn't make it right."

"It's not a question of right, Lillian. It's a question of the law. The law says the house is Sean's. It doesn't say he asked for it. It doesn't say he cheated to get it. He doesn't say he ever even wanted it. It simply says it's his. And as far as I can see, that's that."

That wasn't that, as far as I was concerned. Something was not right about the entire thing. Why didn't Pop ever talk about the house as his? Was Granny Sue forgiving him for getting the house, on the day that she died, or was she speaking of something else? Why did Charlie give the house to Pop? Did it have something to do with the five deaths listed in the diary? Did he do something bad to get it?

None of it seemed to fit. Now I was more determined than ever to find the pieces that fit Charlie, Granny Sue, and Pop together in this house.

Mom began to root through the cupboards, banging pans as she looked for something. When she finally found the big pot for boiling potatoes, she slammed it onto the drainboard so hard that Lillian startled. Lillian turned back and began spooning hot stuffing into the cold turkey. They continued to work in silence.

When the silence deepened and the cold seeping into my bones began to make me shiver, I decided I should go back to bed.

I climbed the stairs, whispering this new knowledge to myself. Mom had to get married. She was in the family way before she stood in the church and said her vows. She and Pop had sinned. Their hearts were as black as the coal being dug out of the ground by that big machine.

I could hardly wait to get my sister alone so I could tell her that Marty was the reason Mom and Pop got married in the first place. And Iris had sinned too and had been sent away to have a baby. And Pop did own this house, after all.

I sneaked up the stairs and crawled back into the warm bed beside Sally and Janet.

Two hours later we all began to gather in the chairs and on the floor of the parlor. The bottle of aspirin in the bathroom medicine cabinet was almost empty by the time I got to it. Almost everyone who entered the dim room exclaimed first about actually having a white Christmas and then about the big pile of presents that had materialized to cover the entire center of the room. Mom passed out sweet rolls and said "Get some coffee from the buffet" at least every five minutes. She was so jittery with excitement that she kept patting Pop's broad shoulders or standing behind him, resting both hands against his back.

Finally, everyone was up and Pop took his seat near the lighted tree. He smiled and whispered, "Well how should we give out these presents? Who should be first?"

Mom answered, "Youngest first."

We all shouted our disagreements. Pop pretended not to hear, picked up three boxes, and handed them to Iris's smallest boys. While they were tearing their's open, he handed the big heavy one to me. I tore into the wrapping and struggled with tape until I finally pushed aside a layer of tissue paper. A pair of ice skates, pure white with shining blades and blue laces, lay within my reach.

I had learned to skate wearing a pair of antique hockey skates that had belonged to my grandmother's brothers. They were brown leather with molded iron blades pitted with rust from hanging in the cellar. Despite the coarseness of the blades and the lack of toe picks to stop and start, I was a good skater. I could go backward and do crossovers, but I fell a lot when the awkward blades tangled up, and I had to wear several pairs of socks to make the skates fit. I never minded the sock part because the extras kept my feet warm.

The new skates were insulated with a thin layer of foam and soft blue plaid flannel. Their black, polished soles and heels added to their beauty. I had never dreamed of a pair of modern skates. My heart filled with so much love for my parents that I couldn't speak.

They smiled at my speechlessness.

Lenny protested when Sally began opening a box. "Hey," he said, "I'm younger than her."

Pop pretended not to hear.

"Hey!"

Janet exclaimed over a pair of silk pajamas.

Marty looked like he might fall over when Pop unlocked the door to the second parlor and brought out a pair of skis. "For Colorado," Pop said, and returned to the second parlor.

When he came back out, he carried a very long sled, brand new, painted with high gloss varnish, with shining steel runners. When he held it up so we could see its underside, Lenny jumped up from where he was sitting on the floor and climbed over everybody to reach the sled. Across the boards on the bottom, Pop had used a wood-burning tool to engrave in fanciful script "This sled is the property of Lenny and Larry Lukash."

Lenny burst into tears. Mom made her way to him, took him in her arms, and hid his face so we couldn't see.

Pop hurriedly continued on with the presents. Matching hats and mittens for each of us. Coats. Boots. The promised paint-by-number sets. A wagon for the smallest boys. Puzzles. Makeup kits and perfumes for the older girls. A dress coat with a fur collar for Sally. Brand-new board games.

And then all of us kids put on those new hats and gloves and boots and coats and went out and pulled our sleds to the top of Mrs. Donal's hill. Lenny gave everybody rides on his American Flyer, belly-flopping onto the long boards with the ease of a high-board diver. His rider stretched out on top of him or knelt on the very back of the sled after giving a hefty running push, then both owner and rider screamed with delight as they flew down the hill.

Marty fell so many times on his skis he began to limp. But he continued to mound higher hills of snow to use as jumps. He never tired. When his legs went out from under him, he landed in a heap against Mrs. Donal's fence. He laughed so hard he couldn't stand up.

Janet and Sally walked down the hill in their new coats and boots, toward the teenage gathering place, their faces snug in furry hats, wafting streams of Evening in Paris behind them.

As the women set the long table in the dining room, Pop sat in the parlor making the Lionel train go round and round the tracks, stopping it at times to squeeze a few drops of liquid into its smokestack so he could watch it huff and puff as it climbed papier mâché mountains. He kept his constantly filled glass of whiskey balanced near the miniature church. By the time we kids came in for dinner, we had to help him to his place at the head of the table. We all snickered as he mumbled a grace that started with "Now you listen to me, Lord."

The day drew into evening. We cleared the clutter from the table and set up new board games. Pop played scrabble against a variety of opponents. He always won. Mom played pick-up sticks. She repeatedly uncovered the black stick early in her turn and used it to such an advantage that sometimes other players never got to take their turns. I proved that I was still the champ by besting her whenever I could get a turn. Lillian sat in an easy chair and watched. Her argument with Mom seemed to be forgotten.

It was Marty and Lenny who caused the sudden uproar. Marty had been treated like an adult all evening. We understood that he would be taking on a man's job with this move into the military. Everybody agreed that if he was old enough to fight for his country, he was also old enough to drink whiskey and smoke cigarettes. He overdid the whiskey a bit. When he and Lenny became bored with the games, they began wrestling boisterously through the crowded rooms.

Mom jumped up from the table and attempted to intervene. She was too late. Marty fell backward over an arm of the small sofa in the front hall and landed with his full weight on the small boys' new wagon, which had been parked out of harm's way. The wagon collapsed into a twisted heap of metal.

The boys' anguished cries filled the rooms. Mom's murmured reassurances developed a higher pitch as she tried to calm them. Marty suddenly bolted through the dining room and, unable to get past the crowded table, used the newel post at the bottom of the stairs to launch himself upward. He took the steps two at a time.

Pop pushed his chair aside and followed closely behind. Lenny tried to pull the bent metal of the wagon into some semblance of a movable toy.

I wasn't sure what to do. I looked to Lillian for direction, but she seemed to find the entire scene too hilarious for words. Her cackling laughter, out of place in the tense room, raised my ire. I stood and followed Pop up the stairs and into Marty's room. I expected to find both Marty and Pop in that room, but instead there was an open window sash and the room was empty. I crept to the window, shivering—not from the draft of frigid air that cascaded into the warm room but from the overwhelming fear that Marty had gone right out and jumped off the back roof. I held tightly to the wooden frame and leaned out.

Marty was standing against the gingerbread siding of the second floor in the small snow less space where the jutting gambrel roof provided protection from the weather. Pop had maneuvered to the far side of him and was pressuring him to sit. Marty finally bent his knees, drew them up, and wedged himself securely against the house. His feet sank into the thick layer of snow that covered most of the roof. Pop took the same position next to him.

Marty began to sob into his uplifted knees. "I ruined it. I ruined the best Christmas we've ever had!"

"No. No, you didn't," Pop soothed. "It's not even half over yet."

"I made the boys cry."

"Small boys cry at the drop of a dime," Pop countered. "It's a phase. You all went through it."

"But they're still wailing."

"They'll calm down. Your mother will take care of them."

"I ruined their new wagon."

Pop laughed. "That you did. There's no denying that. Flattened it like a pancake."

"It's not funny."

"Your grandmother thought it was. And it was. You should have seen your face!"

Marty shook his head violently from side to side and placed his closed fists into his eyes. His feet slid a little farther down the roof.

Mom squeezed in next to me and thrust her head through the open window. "Sean! You get him off that roof! He'll kill himself if he falls!"

I could see Pop turn his face toward her, but it was too dark to see his eyes. "It's okay, Toots. It's okay."

"Sean! Please!"

I felt the weight of Lenny leaning between Mom and me.

"There's too much snow on the ground for him to hurt himself," Pop said with authority. "Look for yourself. It's almost six feet deep from shoveling the path. He's okay. You are okay aren't you, Marty?"

Marty continued to cry into his hands.

"Marty, you tell your mother you're okay. Hear me?"

Marty's words were muffled, but he said it. "I'm okay, Mom. I'm okay."

"Then you get in here!"

Pop patted Marty's knees. "We'll sit here awhile, Toots. You go ahead and give the kids and Lily some of that pumpkin pie you made. They're probably ready for that now. You go ahead. We're okay."

"Sean." Mom's voice had a worried, warning tone in it. "It's freezing out there."

"We're going to sit here for a while, Toots. Then we'll come in and have some pie too. Won't we, Marty?"

Marty nodded without looking up.

"See that, Toots? He's ready for some of that pie too."

I could tell that Mom wasn't going to be distracted with talk of pie. She suddenly thrust one bare leg through the window and pushed herself out onto the roof. She wobbled for a few seconds before she found her footing on the narrow snow less strip of shingles. I shivered for her as I felt the cold air against my bare arms and saw her cotton dress catch a draft of air. She sat down on the nearest side of Marty. Now he was sandwiched between the two of them.

"Molly," Pop called out. "Throw out that blanket from the bed for your mother. Before she catches her death of pneumonia."

I turned and pulled the wool blanket from the bed, but instead of throwing it out the window, I crawled out too. I sat down very carefully next to Mom. She placed an arm around me as I pressed my back against the house. We snuggled into the blanket. She stretched the blanket out and covered some of Marty.

At my back I heard Lenny whisper, "Hey, are you all going to be staying out there?"

"For the time being," Mom said.

"Well, heck, I'm coming out too."

"Bring another blanket if you're coming," Pop called.

Next thing I knew, Lenny was being handed off through the snow to Pop. He sat close up to Pop so they could share that other blanket and put some of theirs over Marty too. Lillian came to the window with a small boy under each arm.

"What are you doing out there?" she asked.

"Just sitting, Mother," Mom answered. "And don't you dare come out here!"

"I wouldn't dream of it," Lillian cackled. "You're all a little crazy, if you ask me. What are you going to do out there?"

"I told you. We're going to sit here. Is there something odd about that?" Mom began to giggle.

"You are crazy," Lillian repeated. "This whole family belongs in Retreat State Hospital."

Now, even Marty had to laugh.

"Oh," Mom said, to take advantage of the momentary pause in Marty's tears. "Look at the stars. What a sight."

I looked up and away from the black strip of shingles and the precipitous edge of the white roof. The stars were so clear and close that I wished I could reach right out and grab hold of one of them. I felt very small and was suddenly grateful that I could snuggle against my mother and be safe.

I turned my face into the wind so that I could see past the school building gleaming grayly against the white snow. I watched the car lights on Route 309 stream steadily to a vanishing point behind the ridge of mountains. It didn't seem possible that one small line of pavement could connect our small valley to the big cities in New Jersey and New York.

I followed the path of a train, probably much like the one that had brought Pop here to meet Mom, as it made its way slowly along a parallel course toward the mountain summit. Those were the tracks that had led Lenny safely to us all the way from Philadelphia.

On the valley floor I could see the city full of tiny dots of colored Christmas lights. The bright lights flickered, dimmed, and sometimes doubled along the reflective ribbon of black that I knew was the Susquehanna.

I seemed at once to be in my own little world of steely gray and black and white and yet part of some stark master scene, wide and limitless and moving as slowly as the Milky Way that cut the sky of ink in half.

My attention was diverted by twin beams of yellow light that levered over the hill in front of Mrs. Donal's house. They glimmered past the frozen mulberry bush and shined first against, and then past, our house. We all turned our heads to watch their progress as they illuminated the driveway in a swaying arc then winked out behind our hedges.

I expected to hear Lillian call out that there were visitors, but instead I heard the crunch of footsteps climbing up the drive on the frozen snow. A male voice called out "Halloo?" as a shadow lumbered around the corner of the porch.

"Up here," Pop answered.

"Everything okay?"

"What the heck are you doing out here on a Christmas night?" Pop asked.

I hadn't seen John Hale in his policeman's uniform in years, yet there he stood, a deer-spotting light in his right hand and a worried frown on his usually calm face.

"Mrs. Donal called. Said there were strange noises at your house. Said I should come and have a look."

"Nothing strange about the noises," Pop joked, "unless you might think it strange that the whole damn family's gathered on the back porch roof in the middle of winter with sixteen inches of snow on the ground."

"I'd consider that a little odd."

"Had a bit of family trouble. Came out here to clear the cobwebs out of our turkey-stuffed brains."

"And nothing bad is going on?"

"Nah."

He shined his light across all of us and stopped it at Pop.

"Funny thing. I had you on my mind anyways, or else I wouldn't have bothered coming out on a holiday. Had a call from the police in the city. Said they heard a funny story from the Harrisburg department. A crook was caught there, trying to rob a liquor store. When he started talking, he named a Branigan boy as an accomplice in two Philadelphia murders and the shooting of a grocery clerk near Blakeslee. Serious crimes."

"Oh, yeah?"

I tensed involuntarily and Mom felt it. She hugged me closer.

"Yeah. This robber wasn't so lucky in the liquor store. The owner shot him back. When they questioned him about the other shootings, he said that a kid had done those. Said the kid's name was Marty Branigan."

"Ain't that something? Marty Branigan, eh? Like my Marty?"

"Yeah." He moved his light to shine on Marty. "Marty, you haven't been out of town lately, have you?"

"No, sir." Marty's tone was so genuinely honest no one could have doubted him. "I've been working over at Ben's car service all week. And the roads have been so bad, I haven't even been able to go see my gal up at Mountaintop, let alone go to Blakeslee Corners."

Pop managed a big grin. "The boy's become a man," he said. "Leaving at the end of the week for basic training. The army is taking him to Colorado."

"Is that right?"

"That's right."

"So he ain't never been to Blakeslee this past week?"

"Hell, no. Been right here getting snockered with his old man."

John thought about that for a few minutes and then moved his beam of light to Mom. "Hey, Bess."

"Hey, John. How's the wife and kids?"

"Fine. Had us a nice Christmas. You know Dorothy's expecting again. Due in April."

"She having any trouble?"

"No. Strong girl. She sure gives us beautiful grandchildren."

"She should. She always was a beauty herself."

"Speaking of beauties. Didn't Iris get herself in trouble again?"

"Sorry to say, she did."

"And didn't one of her boys recently run away from Philadelphia and come high-tailin' it up this way?"

Pop threw his left arm over Lenny's shoulder, and then with his right hand he patted Lenny's chest. He didn't let go. Under cover of that blanket, he grabbed good holds on Lenny's shirt.

"Yeah, John. This here's Lenny, one of Iris's twins. He's staying with us for a while. Now isn't he a good-looking boy, if you ever saw one?"

The light turned on Lenny. "Good to see you, Lenny. Come up the turnpike, did you?"

Pop answered for him. "Nah. Like his Uncle Sean, he followed those old reliable railroad tracks. Got him right here to the boiler house. That old boiler house saved his life."

"How's that?"

"There's still the old stash of firewood and the matches that the bums keep there. He came in the night before that big storm, more than a week ago. If he hadn't come upon that old boiler house he'd likely have frozen to death."

"Is that where you found him?"

"No. He got a little confused from the cold and he ended up sleeping under the front porch. Molly here found him."

Now he shined light of that big flashlight full on me. I had to squint to see. I ducked my face into Mom's armpit.

"You didn't find him with a gun, by any chance?"

"A gun?" I mumbled.

Pop cut right in. "No gun, John, just a kid nearly out of his mind with cold. Bess nursed him back to right."

"Seems like a big coincidence doesn't it? I mean a coincidence that the man in Harrisburg could give a Branigan name and at the same time Iris's boy is on the road from Philly?"

"Sure does. A big coincidence."

Neither man said another word for a long time. Pop kept his hands intertwined solidly in Lenny's shirt while I tried to keep my eyes averted from the piercing gaze of John. I watched Pop carefully. He allowed the time to pass without a twinge on his face or a movement of his body. Finally, he spoke up.

"Well, John, what's happened to the guy in Harrisburg?"

John scuffed a boot in the deep snow, twirled a miniature whirl of snow, and stamped his foot hard on the frozen ground. He shined the light back on Pop. "He died."

I could see Pop relax a bit. "Died? Well, I guess that ends that. Man shoots that many people deserves to die, don't you think? Man like that can only cause more trouble. Wouldn't ever do anybody innocent any good, would he?"

John grunted and made more swirls with his boot. With slow intention he moved the light back to me.

"So, young lady, you say you didn't see a gun?"

"I'm afraid of guns," I answered. Mom squeezed my shoulder.

"But you never saw one with your cousin there?"

I looked toward my mother's face. "He was darned cold under that porch," I said. "He could have froze to death."

John shined the light toward Pop. "She sure takes after you, Sean, doesn't she? Chip off the old block."

"That she is," Pop answered. "Almost as smart as me, too, don't you think?"

"And with the Irish gift of the gab. I can tell that right away."

"It's a good gift to have, if I do say so myself."

"Never knew a true Branigan who didn't have it."

"So, what do you say, John? Got time to come into the house and have a piece of pumpkin pie with my family? Bess here was talking about that pie and how she'd already whipped the cream to go on top. And Lily is putting the coffee on. Will you come in and have some with us?"

John hiked up his pants a little and smiled. "Sure. I'm not one to turn down pie any time."

And that was the end of that. The gun and that Indian doll, resting under a thousand tons of slag. And me, learning to talk like Pop and seeing how to be prepared in case someone's about to jump and run.

And then Lenny, pale and still scared, but sitting in the library, putting one piece after another of Autumn Farmhouse into its rightful place. And both of us scooping up big forkfuls of pumpkin pie nearly drowning in sweet whipped cream.

CHAPTER ELEVEN

First thing in the morning, Lillian, Janet, and the younger boys took a cab home. Sally would be allowed to follow after the New Year. Mom wanted her home to see Marty off to the army.

Mom, Sally, Lenny, and I were finishing breakfast when Pop came downstairs. He took a quart of beer from the refrigerator; murmured apologies to Mom for not wanting breakfast, turned to us with an impish grin and said, "Nothing like a little hair of the dog to get you started on a cold morning."

"That beer isn't going to help your hangover any," Mom protested. "It will just get you started on another full day of drinking." She stood and began to clear the table.

"Only one glass," he said. He took the seat next to Lenny. "Today's the day. Won't be any serious drinking. We've gotta go across the river and talk to Larry. I mean you and me, Lenny."

Lenny sat up straighter, his spoon of oatmeal stopped halfway to his mouth. "Is this a trap?"

"In a way, it is," Pop answered. "And in another way it isn't. Larry wants to see you. He's gotten a little lonely. He wants to come here and live with you, but they aren't gonna allow that."

"Are they going to take me back to that school? I won't go."

"I never expected you would."

"Then what's the trap?"

"The folks that took Larry are willing to take a chance on you. They want to have a look at you first. Your Aunt Bess and me went over to see the place on the day we bought the tree. They let me talk to Larry alone."

"Was he okay?"

"He likes those folks. He has his own room and it has bunk beds."

"I want to stay here. Don't you like me here?"

"We all like you, Lenny. But you know they won't let you stay. The state says we harbored you, like they're making you out to be some kind of criminal. We've got to help them get that notion out of their heads."

"I'll run away again."

"You can't cut and run every time things don't suit your fancy. People get you running, they see you like a rabbit and they've got to give chase. Sometimes you have to find a nice, safe hole and hide out until they get tired of digging for you. You understand?"

"I almost jumped off the roof when John Hale came calling." He said the words proudly, as if jumping would have been some kind of heroic thing.

"And that would have been a big mistake. You'd have broken your leg . . . or your neck."

"You said none of us would get hurt falling off that roof. You said the snow bank would make it safe."

"I lied."

Lenny had to think about that for a minute. So did I. We had all heard him tell Mom that the snow bank would make any fall off that roof a minor thing. I had trusted him on that and had settled my cold backside on that roof with all the confidence in the world that I couldn't be hurt if I accidentally slipped.

Pop allowed the shock of the lie to sink in before he continued his negotiation with Lenny. "I know that you're scared, but I have a good feeling about those folks. I thought we'd go over and let you visit with Larry alone for a while. Get him to tell you what it's really like. We'll take your clothes, in case it works out."

"Are you telling the truth or lying again?"

"The truth. If Larry says it's terrible, then we'll put you in the car and I'll bring you back."

"You promise?"

Pop had to consider that carefully. "I'll promise, if you'll make a promise to me first."

"What?"

"That uppity social worker will be there. I don't want you to talk to her or go near her at all. And if she starts to make noises about having me arrested, I want you to keep your mouth shut."

"What if she tries to hogtie me?"

"Even if she were to do that, I don't want you to fight back or cut and run or open your trap and start yapping at her. I want you to promise me that."

"I don't want to go over there."

"I know you don't want to, but sometimes we have to work inside the system to figure out how to get out of it. We have to show up there today or you'll end up back in Philly. You understand?"

"Oh, I understand all right. But I don't like it."

"I'm not asking you to like it. I'm asking you to cooperate."

"I'll talk to Larry. But if it ain't what everybody's sayin', I won't stay."

"Then we'll leave it up to you and Larry. If you can't trust your closest brother, then hell, who can you trust? We'll take your sled along. If you decide to stay, I'll come see you every day the rest of the week and make sure everything's okay."

"You aren't tricking me, are you?"

"No. I'm leaving it up to you. You want to come back, I'll bring you back. Come hell or high water."

Lenny looked to me. "What do you think? Is he telling the truth?"

I had to be honest, and the honest answer was I didn't know.

"Near as I can tell." I looked across the table and met Pop's eyes. "If I was you, I'd trust him."

He turned to Mom. “What do you think? Is he telling the truth?”

Mom looked from Lenny to Pop and back again. “I’d trust him before I’d trust anybody else.”

He emptied his spoon into his mouth. “Pass me some more of that milk, would you? And stop looking at me. I’m going. But I’ll tell you this: first person who mentions Philadelphia sets me on the lam!”

~

Around midmorning, right after Pop and Lenny drove off, Mom ducked her head against the rising wind and walked down the hill toward her new job. She was cleaning houses for folks who still had money. I tried not to think about Marty leaving. It seemed like everybody was going somewhere.

I went into the library and pulled my collection of clippings, pictures, and envelopes from the drawer of blueprints and maps. With all the company over the holiday, I had had no privacy or opportunity to study them. I took them to the rollaway bed vacated by Lillian and settled comfortably onto the bare mattress with my back resting against the wall and my treasures spread out before me.

I picked up a yellowed envelope. The handwriting was not familiar to me but the big looping script spelled out Pop’s name: Sean Victor Branigan. Inside I found two photographs pasted on cardboard and, folded carefully between them, the top half of a newspaper page.

The Jersey City News, October 17, 1918

Two Boys Pulled from Chimney

They wanted to get a glimpse of the new moving pictures, but the two young sons of a city policeman soon found that going down the chimney was not the way to get into the Apollo Theater. When they saw the lights of the projector flickering inside the building chimney, they decided it was a way in to see the cinema. The youngest boy, Sean Branigan, six, shimmied down the brick passage feet first. He was stopped by the closed flue. His brother, Matthew, nine, had stayed atop the roof, and when he realized the plight of Sean, he leaned in and attempted to pull him out. Alas, he fell in after him, headfirst. Solidly stuck, both spent a miserable night, unbeknownst to their recently widowed father.

The mischievous boys were found early Tuesday morning when an employee heard weak cries coming from the theater wall behind the piano. When the man pounded on that wall, he heard the voice of Sean begging for help. They were freed from their cold prison by a group of men using ropes and brute muscle power. The temperature dipped to the midthirties during the night. The boys were dirty, cold, and visibly shaken by their ordeal. Thankfully, the coal heater of the Apollo has not been in use for some time.

The boys' father, George, took custody of his miscreants, offering to pay the city and the theater for any damages they had caused and saying, "It will be a long time before either of them will ever see the inside of one of those movie places. When I get through with them they won't be able to sit for a good long time."

I had believed Matthew died as a teenager. He was three years older than Pop. That meant that, if Pop was eight when he and Mike had taken off on the train, then Matthew was no more than eleven when he died. I wrote in my journal, *Ask Mom about Matthew.*

I ran my hand over a studio photograph. The children—two boys of maybe nine and eleven and a little girl no older than four—were well dressed and posed formally for the camera. The boys appeared stiff and uncomfortable in dark suits and ties. The girl sat in the left front with one leg folded under the other so that her white stockings and black patent leather shoes could speak of good breeding. Her snow-white pinafore revealed no wrinkling or soil. She was smiling widely for the camera. Her eyes twinkled with the excitement little girls exhibit when playing dress-up.

To her right sat a big boy partially obscured by a shadow that made him appear irregular in size and shape. His left eye and cheek seemed to droop slightly. His face was long, as were the fingers of his left hand, which balanced precariously on his right arm. His entire body tilted slightly toward the girl but his dark eyes stared wide open into the camera. I held the photo toward the brighter light pulled in by the three windows that faced the mountain. The shading on the tall boy seemed to be an error of the photographer or a defect in the camera lens.

I turned the cardboard over and found, in the same loopy writing as on the envelope, the date, June 16, 1921, and the names of the children: Michael, Sean, and Mary Margaret Branigan.

Turning the photograph again, I could now see a resemblance to my pop in the other boy, standing in the back. He was stoutly compact, with a shock of bristly hair and a freckled face. His smile was guarded. He stood with both arms held awkwardly at his sides and his hands clenched into sturdy fists. The little girl, dark hair fastened to one side with a silk ribbon, was my Aunt Mary. And the bigger boy in shadow must be Mike, the brother who had done some dastardly deed and died in prison. I studied him closely again. I could see no evil in his eyes or in his smile.

The smaller snapshot was of an older boy dressed in a thick sweater that he had outgrown long before the picture was taken.

His lanky wrists protruded a good three inches from his cuffs and the buttons gaped open over the two-thirds of his chest that the ragged sweater covered. He had made an attempt to hitch up his too-short jeans with a tie of some sort. He had also attempted to comb his hair. His scalp showed cleanly through an irregular part that started about two inches back from his high forehead. The hair had been wetted and pasted to one side as if he had no mirror to check the details. He stood tall and proud outside of a nondescript brick building. His smile was ambiguous, part smart aleck, part relieved, part happy to see the person who held the camera. He stared into the lens with intelligent, alert eyes.

Pop. There was no mistaking that smile or those eyes. I felt sad for him, but curious too. What gave him the courage to smile into the camera like that when he was wearing such poor clothing and obviously had lived a hard life? Who was making him smile?

I heard a noise in the kitchen and, before I could put my stash of history aside, Sally came into the room carrying a hand mirror and a hairbrush.

"I'm trying something new with my hair," she said. "I used my new rubber rollers instead of bobby pins. What do you think?"

Her hair hung straight down the sides of her face and curled smoothly under her chin at the ends.

"It's a pageboy," she said. "Like the English servants. Do you like it?" She held the mirror up and twirled once in a slow circle.

I had always envied Sally's hair. It was black and thick like Aunt Mary's, but rather than hiding it in a bun, Sally pulled hers high into a ponytail that swung and bounced gaily as she walked. I had tried to wear mine like that but I was too impatient to brush out snarls or wait for pin curls to dry.

Her new style interested me. "Yes, I do like it. Could you do that to my hair?"

"Sure."

I moved my pile of papers to one side so she could sit beside me.

"What is this stuff?" she asked.

"Research."

"Research? What kind of research is a kid like you doing?"

"About family. These pictures from the old suitcase."

She picked up the pictures and the clipping. "Oh, yeah. I've seen this before. Pop and Uncle Mike and Aunt Mary." She shuffled the snapshot of the ruffian boy to the top and waved it toward me. Her fingernails were painted pink pearl to match her lipstick.

"Pop's Aunt Maura took this one when he was in Kis-Lyn and she went to spring him out. Right after she took this picture he ran through the woods and hopped into her friend's car. The authorities never did catch him again." She lowered her voice to a whisper and said, "He's still a fugitive."

"What does that mean?"

"It means if they ever catch him, they'll throw him in jail."

"They wouldn't take him away after all these years. Would they?"

"Mom says that he never did anything really bad but he has to keep his nose clean anyway because if he did do something bad they could look up his record and throw the book at him."

I breathed a sigh of relief. I had nothing to worry about. Pop would never do anything worthy of arrest.

She dropped the picture in her lap and went back to the formal photograph. "That's Mike." She pointed to the slightly off-kilter boy.

"I thought Mike was younger than Pop."

"He was. But he was real tall and skinny so he looked older."

"He looks weird."

"Cerebral palsy. Mom said he was born like that. Limped and dragged his arm and leg. He didn't smile right either."

"Is that why he had fits?"

"I guess so."

"Did you know him?"

"I don't think so. Mom says that he used to come play with us, before we moved to the place in Back Mountain."

"What was he like?"

"Mom says he was funny. I think he had a hard time talking, so he talked with his hands and laughed a lot. Marty kind of remembers that he was around when we lived in the house by the railroad tracks."

"I remember a house with no doorknobs. Is that the one?"

"Nope. That was the one in Back Mountain."

"When did we move there?" I needed dates for my newspaper search or I was going to be chained to a cold city library chair forever.

She shrugged. "I was a baby. I think somebody from Pop's work rented us the place."

"When?"

"It must have been 1937. Why do you care?" She picked up the stack of pictures and let them fall.

"I was wondering."

"Why?" She laughed and shook her hair.

"I think it's interesting. Mom said we had an Uncle Ira who killed himself. I wonder why."

"You should talk to Marty. He knew the famous Uncle Ira."

"What was he famous for?"

"I don't know. That's what Iris always says: 'the famous Uncle Ira.'"

"I never heard of him before."

"Just because you're famous, doesn't mean everybody knows you. I don't think many people really liked Uncle Ira. Marty sure didn't."

"How come?"

She shrugged. "He just didn't. He used to have nightmares about him and wake up the whole house. Then Pop or Mom would have to rock him back to sleep. He was a pretty big boy to be rocked to sleep, but that's what it took." She leaned against the wall and retrieved her mirror.

"I had a nightmare once," I said. "When I was real little. I dreamed that a couple of men had a fight in the upstairs hallway and one of them got beat with a spindle from the banister."

"That wasn't a nightmare. That was Pop and Iris's husband Jake. They were having a knock-down, drag-out fight about the house."

"About what house?"

"This house. Nobody thought Pop should have got this place. Lillian said that if Old Charlie and Granny Sue willed the house to Pop, no one had anything to say about it. Pop said he didn't want any goddamned house. Jake said he was lying." She stared at herself in the mirror and then handed it to me. "Take a look," she said. "I think you need me to cut your hair."

I took the mirror from her but held it in my lap. "For crying out loud," I said. "Tell me what happened."

She stared at me. "Jake called Uncle Mike a bad name."

"And?"

"Pop told him to go to hell and said he was going to bed. When he started coming up the stairs, Jake grabbed him and socked him a hard one." She sat up straight as if she could see the fight. As if the memory excited her. "Pop got knocked down, and next thing you know he grabs the banister spindle and pulls it out and whammo! Down the stairs goes Jake!"

"Was I here?"

"We all were. We were supposed to be sleeping but when Marty heard the noise he opened the door."

"Were we in my room?"

"Yeah. But it wasn't your room then. It was Old Charlie's empty room and he was already dead. There was so much company for Granny Sue's funeral we all had to sleep in one bed."

"I thought I'd had a nightmare."

"You were little."

"Was Uncle Ira here?"

"Nope. He was already dead too."

"How did Old Charlie die?"

"Another fight."

Now, I sat up straighter. "With who?"

"Granny Sue."

"You're kidding!"

"Nope. She pushed him and he tripped over the coal bucket. He fell against the stove and it killed him."

This was really getting interesting. I always imagined that Granny Sue was a gentle soul. In the family photograph on the wall she was much smaller than Charlie. Now, not only had she hit the family picture with a broom but she had caused the death of her own husband.

"Why'd she push him?"

"She was mad."

"About what?"

"I don't know." Sally was getting tired of my questions. She took her hand mirror back and studied her hair again.

I couldn't let her stop. "Come on, tell me."

She stood and walked to the windows. "Something about Uncle Ira, I think."

"Who said?"

"Iris told me."

Iris seemed to have answers to a lot of things. I was sorry that I never talked to her.

"Were we here when he fell?"

"Nope. Nobody was here." She turned and started toward the second parlor.

"Then how did Iris know what happened?" I laid my envelope and its contents on the bed and followed her from the room.

"She said that Granny Sue called her to help get Old Charlie off the floor, but she couldn't lift him so she called Mom. We all came and ended up staying, because old Charlie was hurt bad. After the funeral we went back home. Ask Mom. She'll tell you." She went to the front windows and stared off down the road.

"Was I born then?"

"Nope."

"So whose house is this?"

"I don't know. Pop said he didn't want it, but we stayed, and now everybody is mad at us."

"This is a strange family."

She shrugged. "No different than anybody else's. Janet and her family don't even have a pop anymore."

"And what's worse, they've got Iris."

Sally laughed. "Iris is okay."

"She makes Pop nervous."

She swung her short hair back and forth across her face. "She likes him."

"I don't think he likes her."

"No. But he's at least nice to her. You don't even talk to her."

"I don't like to talk to grown-ups."

"Can I tell you a secret?"

"About Iris?"

"No. About me." She stopped talking and sighed. "I have a boyfriend." She flopped into the overstuffed chair.

"You do?"

"Well, I kind of do. His name is Jack and he's one of Lillian's renters. He has an upstairs room and he's older."

"How old?"

"Twenty-two."

"I don't think Mom would like him."

"Why?"

"Because twenty-two is awfully old."

"He's really handsome. And he wears a suit to work. And he always polishes his shoes."

Pop put a lot of emphasis on the need for a man to keep his shoes polished. Now Sally was using the trait to measure a boy's worth.

"Is he nice?"

"Really nice. He lets Janet and me have drinks when Lillian isn't around."

"I don't think Mom would like that at all."

She picked up my warning tone. "Remember. This is a secret."

"You didn't make me promise not to tell."

"Promise me now. Promise me you won't tell."

"Too late."

"If you don't promise, I won't do your hair."

I had never cared about my hair before and I wasn't really sure why I was interested now, but I was. I surprised myself by how much I was interested.

"Okay. I promise."

We were at the supper table when Pop came in. The wind had changed direction, bringing the scent of a southeasterly through the door with him. He hung his coat to dry on the drain valve of the water boiler. He was talkative and full of good news.

"Lenny took to that family like a duck to water. They liked him right away. That snippy social worker was ready for a fight, but she gave in pretty quick when she saw how happy the two boys were to be together."

"I'm so glad. I hope he behaves himself," Mom said.

"I stayed and watched while I had a few beers with the dad. When I was ready to leave, Lenny walked up to me and shook my hand. 'Thank you, Uncle Sean,' he said. He was so darned serious, I would have laughed if things weren't so tense."

I giggled.

Pop gave his head a tiny shake and smiled. "When I drove up the road behind the monastery I saw some guys shoveling dirt around the berm where that pool of water collects in the field. I stopped and asked them what they were doing. Guess what?"

"What?" Mom asked.

"They were from the VFW and they were making a skating pond for the kids."

I clapped my hands.

"Somebody donated a load of dry logs for fires. The light company put in a flood lamp on the nearest power pole. Now that it's raining, that pond will fill right up. Then," he looked down the table at me, "all you need to do is wait for the mercury to drop and you'll get to try out those new skates."

I couldn't speak.

"It's too bad Lenny and Larry couldn't go skating too," Mom said.

"Well, maybe I can pick them up some day and they can. But for now, I think I need a nap." He went upstairs without eating.

Sally moved to the parlor and pulled the telephone after her. As she sat in the darkened room, hoping for a call from her new boyfriend, I thought about how everything was changing and how much I wanted it to stay the same. The house was too quiet with everyone gone, and soon Marty would be leaving again.

Mom sipped the last of her coffee as I washed the dishes. Her face was drawn. She appeared older than her thirty-eight years. I thought of her living in our house as a young girl, probably drying the same dishes as she talked to her Aunt Faye or Uncle Arlie. She had been here when they died. I selfishly had never thought of her life before I came along.

I turned and spoke what was on my mind. "Mom?"

"What?"

"How come you tell us all those stories about the Wyoming Massacre and how Queen Esther took our ancestors to her rock and killed them and how some of the family escaped up Giant's Despair but you hardly ever talk about Faye or Arlie?"

She straightened in her chair, emptied her cup, and handed it to me. "Now, what brought that on?"

I plunged the cup into the basin of warm water. "Because I was looking at the pictures in the suitcase and I realized that I don't know anything about the people who actually lived in this house."

"You know as much as you need to know."

"Sally says that Granny Sue pushed Old Charlie over that coal bucket, right there, and he hit his head on the stove right here." I flicked the dish towel so its edge touched the chrome trim on the firebox of the stove. "You never told me that."

"Sally talks too much."

"Is she right?"

"No. She's wrong." She stood and touched the stove at the damper drawer. "Old Charlie hit his head here."

"And Granny Sue pushed him?"

"She had a temper. She was hard to live with sometimes. But then, so was Old Charlie. It was an accident."

"Did he get a cut on his head?"

She stared at the spot on the stove. "No. He didn't have a bump at all. John Hale says he might have had another stroke and it probably wasn't actually the fall that killed him. He said the accident was a blessing in disguise because Charlie was never the kind of man who liked to depend on other people."

"Did Granny Sue feel terrible about it?"

"I'm sure she did. She said she had a warning. She had a gift, you know. She could hear the dead speaking."

"Did she hear Old Charlie?"

"I don't know. When he died, she sent everyone away. She wouldn't talk to anyone except John Hale. He came up every Saturday. If she needed anything, he let us know."

"Did she say she talked to Faye?"

"She never said she did. She separated herself from Faye long before Faye died. After losing Bernie and Silas, I don't think she could bear the death of another child, so she pretended it wasn't happening. She told everyone that Faye would get better, but she left most of her care to Fern and me. John Hale said it was because she wanted us to learn how to care for sick people—and we did learn. If I hadn't learned that, you might not have gotten better when you had pneumonia and Pop might not be walking now."

"Does she ever talk to you, now that she's dead?"

Mom's hand went to her throat. "Heavens, no! Why would you think that?"

"Because sometimes I think she talks to me."

"Oh, Molly. You don't really believe that, do you?"

I nodded slowly. "Sometimes when I'm looking at the pictures in the suitcase, I know who they are and I never saw them before in my life. I think she's telling me who they are."

"Do you hear voices?"

Now I had really scared her. I talked fast so she wouldn't look so worried. "No. No voices. It's a feeling and a thought, like 'That's Faye' or 'That was when Bernie had that dog named Blacky.'"

"Now who told you that? Bernie did have a dog named Blacky."

I shrugged because I couldn't remember anyone alive ever telling me that. "I think Granny Sue tells me."

"What else do you think she tells you?"

She stood and came to the sink. I turned to the cupboard and began to dry the plates in earnest.

"What else?" Mom plunged her hands into the soapy water.

"About the bedpan. You hated that bedpan and you made Fern empty it all the time."

Mom laughed. "You must have heard me say that. Fern and I did fight over that. If she emptied the bedpan, I'd take out the spit pan. One was as bad, if not worse, than the other. Anything else?"

"I think Granny Sue feels really bad about the way Faye died."

Mom turned on the hot water, rinsed a handful of silverware, and dumped it noisily onto the drainboard. Three forks fell on the floor.

"She should feel bad about that! They left Fern and me here in this house all alone on the day Faye died. When Faye started coughing, I held the spit pan for her. She couldn't breathe and she fought me. I think she wanted to get to the window for some air."

My eyes must have gotten big, because she stopped talking, patted my arm, and pointed to the forks on the linoleum. I bent and picked them up.

"Now I've done it," she laughed as she plunged them back into the soapy water. "Three fallen forks, three visitors to come soon. At least we know they won't be bill collectors."

I couldn't let her change the subject. "Was the spit pan bloody?"

She turned and looked fully on me. "Yes, that's what tuberculosis does. It makes people cough up their lungs."

I felt my own blood drain from my brain. I reached out and steadied myself against the cupboard.

She turned back to the pots in the sink. "Who told you that?"

"About the blood?"

"Yes."

In truth I saw blood whenever I looked into the small basin, and I had begun to worry that I was hallucinating, but I couldn't tell her that.

"Maybe I heard you say it, or else I guessed."

"Well, you guessed right. When Faye was dying, she didn't just cough. She was sick to her stomach too. She filled that basin up."

"What did you do?"

"Fern and me tried to get her to the window, but she couldn't make it. She collapsed and we laid her on the floor and she was gone."

"I would have been scared to death."

"Well, I was, but I wasn't so bad off as Fern. Faye was her mother and, oh . . ."

Mom stopped washing dishes and stared off through the dark window above the sink. She took in a lungful of air, put her hands back into the pan, and swirled the water until she made a small whirlpool.

"Fern threw herself on the floor and hugged her mother and cried. Oh, how she cried."

"What did you do?"

"I ran to the front porch and shouted out to the Donals'. My Uncle Arlie had gone over there to visit Tom. They were good friends. Tom ran down the road and got John Hale, and Uncle Arlie came over and helped me put Faye back in her bed. She was light as a feather."

"What about Fern?"

"We had to pull her away from her mother. She was covered in blood. I took her upstairs to the big tub and helped her bathe."

"How did you know what to do?"

"I didn't. We were all in shock, but Fern was the worst. She shivered and shook and kept moaning 'Mother. My God. My God.' She was never the same after that. She never got over it."

Mom emptied the basin of water and took my cloth to wipe it dry.

"John Hale pronounced Faye dead and cleaned up the mess. He loved her, you know. I think he cried as hard as Fern."

"Is that why Fern never comes to visit?"

"I suppose so. At the funeral she talked to a friend of her mother's from upriver. She collected her clothes and left. She hasn't had anything to do with this family since."

"But you said you were like sisters."

She began to dry the last of the pots. "And I still miss her," she said. "I'll always miss her." She closed the cupboard. As we walked through the door she turned out the kitchen light to signal that our conversation was over.

"I'm very tired," she said. "I think I'll go to bed." She climbed slowly up the stairs.

I went into the parlor and gazed out the front windows. I couldn't get the picture of the two girls and dying Faye out of my head. Lights glowed in the windows of Mrs. Donal's house. I closed my eyes and tried to picture a teenaged Tom running full tilt down Giant's Despair Road to find John Hale.

I had only known an older Tom, who came back from the war and built a new house for his mother. I had helped him plant the Colorado blue spruce tree that now decorated the wide front lawn. I could remember standing next to him as he wet the tree's roots from a series of connected hoses that he called a birth cord because the end attached to a spigot at his mother's old place. Now he had been dead for more than a year and I realized that, in all the years we had lived across the street from him, I never really knew him or the part he played in Mom's early life.

And that told me that most of the people I believed I knew well, I didn't really know at all. Maybe they were all like the underground mine fire that steamed away on the mountainside, only a small part of them showing to the world and the rest of them kept secret, smoldering silently, until something unpredictable fired them up and caused them to burn hot enough to give off warning waves of blue.

That thought caused me to shiver. I moved into the library, opened the drawer of blueprints, lifted my notebook from its hiding place, and opened it to Ira.

I had neatly copied his self-removal line from the family Bible, added that he had been with Bernie when he drowned, which probably had made him sad, and that he had helped Lillian during her divorce. Now I wrote: *Sally says family didn't like him and he gave Marty nightmares.* That was all I knew.

I wished that I could ask Marty about his nightmares, but he was spending most of his time with his girlfriend or working on his car with Pop. If I nosed around too much, Mom would get suspicious and I might have to tell her about the diary. I didn't want that to happen until I solved the mystery. I needed to put faces with the dates and learn why Ira's suicide made everyone reluctant to talk about him. I was fascinated with Ira.

CHAPTER TWELVE

The morning of December 31, 1955, dawned cold and clear. Mom packed last-minute cookies and fried chicken into the top of Marty's duffel bag. We all gathered around him in the front hallway. Mom began to cry, and that made Sally and me cry too.

"Mom," Marty said in a voice as deep as Pop's, "it's not like there's a war on or anything. I'm going to basic and to mechanic school and then I'll be home on leave. I'll be back to visit before you know it."

Mom kept one hand on his back while he hugged the rest of us. We followed him out. Sally skipped down the porch stairs as if her suitcase were light as a feather. She would be taking the Laurel Line back to Scranton and her boyfriend Jack. She climbed into the back seat of the car. Marty rolled down his window.

"Don't look back, Marty," Mom shouted. "You keep your eyes ahead or you'll take a chance on never coming home again."

He shook his head as if disbelieving, but he turned away too slowly for me to miss him dabbing his eyes.

Mom wrung her hands together and then began to sob loudly into her apron. The car moved down the hill. Mrs. Donal stood beside the blue spruce tree and waved. Marty waved in her direction. He didn't look back. Mom stayed in the cold and stared down the hill long after Pop's car had disappeared.

When she came inside, she made a surprise announcement: she wasn't going to stay and watch the New Year come in with Pop and his sister Mary Margaret.

"Mary and Pop have something important to discuss and I don't expect they need me here. I'm going to spend the night with Mrs. Donal so she won't be so alone. Do you want to come with me?"

I hesitated.

"Hurry up and make up your mind," she said.

I barely knew my Aunt Mary Margaret, even though she lived only a few miles up the mountain. She visited with Pop every December 31 to see the New Year in and she spoke to Mom on the phone a few times a month, but otherwise she had little contact with our family. Mom said it was because she had five kids and, like most women in the valley at that time, didn't drive.

"I think I'll stay."

"Okay. But I'll tell you this: Aunt Mary Margaret wants to have a talk with Pop. Don't you let on to him unless you want to spend the New Year alone with your aunt."

As soon as they were gone, I went into the library and laid out everything I had on Aunt Mary Margaret. It wasn't much—the photograph of her with Pop and Mike, a Catholic medal with a broken chain that Aunt Mary Margaret had given to Sally on her eighth birthday, and my parents' wedding announcement, dated February 1932.

> Bess Marcy and Sean Branigan Marry
> Bess Marcy of Giant's Despair wed Sean Branigan of Wilkes-Barre in Saint Ignatius Parrish House, Kingston, February 17. The bride is the daughter of Lillian Marcy of Scranton and Ralph Marcy of New York City. Iris Lukash, cousin of the bride, and Mike Branigan, brother of the groom, stood up for the couple. Maura Hanlon of Myers Court and Mary Branigan of Nanticoke attended the ceremony.

Aunt Mary Margaret probably attended only because of her Catholic expectations. All of Mom's Protestant family, except Iris, probably stayed away because of their dislike for heathen Catholics. I knew that Pop was brave, but marrying Mom against her family's wishes was probably the bravest thing he'd ever done.

I pulled my notebook from the drawer and started a new page and a new outline:

(1) When their mother died, Mary Margaret was a baby, so their father brought her to a relative in Wilkes-Barre to be raised.

(2) She was raised strictly Catholic and always wanted to be a nun, but she met her husband and "gave herself up to her earthly needs"—her exact words.

(3) Her choice made her feel guilty and caused her to be constantly involved in the church to "atone for her sins of the flesh"—Mom's words.

(4) She believes that converting her only brother's children to the Catholic faith is her life's work—Mom's words.

(5) She only gives presents that are religious in nature.

(6) She doesn't ever notice the wink that Pop sends to Mom whenever she brings up his need to attend Mass.

(7) She never brings her family with her when she visits, and she only visits on New Year's Eve.

(8) She shares Pop's love for the hymn "Ave Maria."

I picked up the medal that Sally had once worn to the Protestant church. Its clasp was broken because our Sunday school teacher had torn it from my sister's neck and screamed that she would burn in hell for worshipping idols. I had witnessed the entire event and thought that when the teacher hissed those words she looked more like Iris than a woman of God. I had grasped Sally's hand and dragged her from the church. We held hands and cried all the way home. When we told Mom what happened, she stormed out of the house and headed to the church. That was the last time we attended Sunday school.

I poked holes through some red construction paper, threaded the chain through to the backside, and secured it with tape. The medal stood alone on the front of the red page. Red like the blood of Jesus, I decided, and placed the page in my notebook, along with the envelope of photographs. I replaced the thickening book in the drawer and began to search Pop's record collection for "Ave Maria."

When he hadn't returned by six o'clock, I called Mom. "What should I do?"

"He's probably at the tavern," she said. "I'll call and tell him to get on home. You send him to bed so he's at least halfway sober when Mary gets there."

Ten minutes later, Pop drove up and went directly to bed. When Mary arrived, he was still sleeping.

"I'll go wake him," I said.

"No, let him sleep a while longer. I've been so busy all day. I'll rest a bit before we visit." She fidgeted with her skirt and straightened the collar of her blouse.

I sat crosswise in the overstuffed chair so I could talk to her as she settled on the sofa.

She was tall for a woman, rawboned, and with thick black hair that she pulled back so severely from her alabaster forehead that it made her blue eyes appear wide open in a persistent startle. When she sat, she kept her chin tucked and her back ramrod straight in the way that Pop sometimes instructed me to sit.

"You've grown, Sally," she said.

"I'm Molly."

"Oh, of course." She took a handkerchief from her purse and dabbed her forehead and chin. "I always get you girls mixed up. You look so much alike."

I didn't look at all like my sister.

"Would you like some tea?" I asked.

"Yes. With milk and sugar, please."

As I waited for the water to boil, I went upstairs and tried to wake Pop. It was no use. He mumbled a few words and pulled the covers over his head. I went back to the kitchen, finished making the tea, carried the tray into the living room, and filled two cups.

"Can I ask you something, Aunt Mary Margaret?"

"Yes," she murmured, but I wasn't sure she had heard me. Her hands were folded in prayer.

"I found a newspaper clipping about Pop and I wonder if you could tell me about it."

"Well, of course."

I went into the library and brought back the clipping about the two boys in the chimney. She took it in both hands and held it away from herself like it was some unidentifiable object, foreign and confusing.

"Read it," I prompted.

"Who gave you this?"

"I found it. In the library."

"It was Aunt Maura's."

"Is it true?"

"Yes, of course it's true."

"It's about my pop?"

"Yes." She touched the flat of her hand to her slicked-back hair. "Sean and Matthew." She handed the clipping back.

I smoothed the paper over my knee. "I never knew you and Pop had a brother named Matthew."

She made the sign of the cross and refolded her hands. Her unpolished fingernails were carefully filed and shaped. "May he rest in peace, God bless his soul."

"How did he die?"

"Oh, dear, don't talk to your father about this. It will upset him. I can't have him upset tonight." She lowered her voice to a whisper. "Matthew died as a result of the pneumonia he caught in the chimney. He was upside down all night, you know. He was very ill. Your pop has never gotten over that." She wrung her hands and moved her face closer to mine. "You must never bring this up to him. Never."

Her intensity frightened me. "I won't," I said. "I won't ever ask him. Never."

"Good."

I needed to change the subject. "You know Marty left this morning?"

"I had forgotten that. Your mother told me he was going to basic training. Oh, my. This is probably not a good day for your pop."

"Mom cried the most."

"Mothers are like that."

I could think of nothing else to say. "Should I go get Pop now?"

"Yes. Wake him. Tell him I'm here."

This time he raised himself and went into the bathroom. I decided I'd better brew some coffee.

From the kitchen, I heard him greet Aunt Mary Margaret. I brought a tray with cookies and the pot of coffee into the parlor. Pop had turned on the television. The picture was faded and the announcer's voice sounded like it was coming from a radio a little off its station mark. The camera showed the crowds in Times Square and the lighted ball on top of a high building. This year the ball would be televised for the first time. I wanted to see that ball drop.

Pop waved away the coffee. "Beer," he said. "A nice cold beer, please, Molly."

I carried the coffee back to the kitchen and brought him a glass of beer. I settled behind them on the small sofa, where I had a good view of the television.

Pop didn't drape his arm across Mary's shoulder the way he would have with Mom or us kids. His voice was lower too and, as their conversation mingled with the voices on the TV, I was reminded of my old Sunday school class mumbling prayers that we were only pretending to know.

Pop lit a cigarette. The smoke trailed toward the ceiling. From their backs, with the dim light of the TV as a backdrop, the two adults appeared to be trapped, vacuum-packed spirits in a hazy space.

Mary sipped her tea. Her voice was low and clipped.

When I saw Pop stiffen and lean away from her, I sat forward on my seat in order to better hear.

"You should pray about that, Sean."

Pop mumbled a comment.

"I'm sure God has forgiven you. You have asked for forgiveness, haven't you?"

Pop's head moved slightly, but he didn't reply.

"The sins of the father . . . not the son. None of it was your fault." Mary again raised her hands into prayer position.

Pop turned fully toward her. Now I could hear him clearly.

"There's isn't a day that goes by that I don't think of our brothers, Mary, but you barely knew them. Why are they on your mind now?" He turned to me and said, "Molly, bring me another beer, would you?"

I carried his empty glass into the kitchen.

Mary had a lot to say, but I couldn't hear any of it until I placed the glass in Pop's hand.

"You can't change history. You did the best you could. No one could ask for more. Not even God," she said.

Pop was trying to be nice. "But you have to ask yourself, Mary, why them? What did they ever do to cause such punishment to be placed on them? And what about Mike? How could God allow him into this world so maimed and weak? Why were we born whole, and not Mike?"

"God rules the womb. It is his will. It's dangerous to question him."

I went back to my seat.

"It was my act of stupidity that caused Matthew to sicken and my will that failed Mike. I made promises that I didn't keep." Pop drank his beer straight down.

"Your promise to Matthew was made by a seven-year-old child. No one would expect you could fulfill it. Only promises to God are inviolate." Mary Margaret refilled her cup from the teapot.

"I believe that if Matthew had lived, things would have been much different. He was the strongest of us all."

"God takes the best first. He needs them as angels."

"Has he no power over the devils then? Why does he allow our wicked old man to continue to walk on this earth?"

I realized that he was talking about his father, and that was something I'd never heard from him before. Only Mom had ever mentioned George in our house. I lost all interest in the television.

"Forgiveness is a gift." Her hand, resting on the back of the couch, clenched into a fist. "As much as you have asked for forgiveness, you must also forgive."

Pop's head came up fast and his voice was very loud. "Have you forgiven him, Mary?"

Her hand flew open. She lowered her voice. "I have nothing to forgive." Wherever she was leading, she knew he didn't want to go.

He continued in a loud voice. "He did right by you, taking you to the Garritys'. He should have let Aunt Maura have us."

"I was a baby. The Garritys had a proper home for an infant."

"Aunt Maura wanted to help. He wouldn't let her. Everything could have been different."

"Aunt Maura was a sinner. God rest her soul." Her shoulders moved as her hand made the sign of the cross. "She knew nothing about children."

Magee always said that Aunt Maura was a saint of a woman. I decided that Aunt Mary Margaret must have judged Maura against her own strict rules of life.

"She always cared for us. She never turned us away."

"But what a place! It wasn't the proper place for children!"

"It was a better place than we had ever known. She taught us the things we needed to know—manners and social ways that boys never learned on the road. She taught us how to be normal."

"But she kidnapped you. She took that train to Jersey City and led you away. That was against the law."

Now Aunt Maura was not only a sinner, she was a kidnapper too. Aunt Maura was becoming very interesting.

Pop's voice rose above the muffled cheers of the crowds on the television. "And the old man *was* the law! He brought his cronies from the Wilkes-Barre police and they drug us away. The old man took us back to Jersey on the train."

"He was a man alone. He made mistakes."

"Hah! As soon as he got us back in that Jersey room, he beat the living crap out of us. To teach us not to leave with her again."

"He was weak and afraid."

"He was strong as a bull."

"Was it so bad, Sean? You were young. Your memories could be wrong."

Now she had really riled him. He sat up straight, upended his glass to get the very last few drops from it, and slammed the empty vessel onto the coffee table.

"We lived like wild Indians. Roamed the streets looking for handouts. Dressed in rags. No food. No heat."

"It was hard for a man alone to raise three boys."

Mary's singsong voice was beginning to annoy me. I couldn't understand why she was being so persistent. If Mom were home, she would interrupt them, say something funny or offer some food. I stood, collected Pop's empty glass, and offered Aunt Mary more tea. She waved me away.

My interruption didn't slow either of them. Pop moved to sit on the very edge of the couch and said, "He never tried to raise us. We didn't see him for days on end."

"I'm sure he did the best he could. You need to forgive him, Sean."

"Forgive him? Forgive him for what? For his being a bully and a drunk? Forgive him for calling Aunt Maura a whore?"

"You don't need to use that language with me, Sean. I have to admit, he was right about her. I mean," Mary Margaret put her hand to her forehead, "about that business."

"Oh, for God's sake. He didn't give a hill of beans that she ran a cathouse. He couldn't stand the fact that she defied him. Nobody defied George Branigan."

A cathouse! Even I knew what that was. I had always pictured Aunt Maura looking a lot like Mom—wearing an apron, cooking at the stove, blowing her breath through pursed lips to cool her rosy cheeks, waving chubby arms before she bent to hug a child. Now I learned that she had been more like Aunt Iris and that all of Pop's reminders to us about good manners, proper etiquette, neatness in dressing—all the things he learned from Maura and passed on to us—were suddenly not so nice. He had learned them in one of those places. He had even slept in one of those places.

Mary Margaret forgot to speak quietly. "Sean! Please stop using such vile language."

"Why, Mary? Is it offensive to your delicate ears? Do you think telling the truth will make a good woman evil? Maura didn't have any choices in this world. I don't care what she did to survive."

"If our mother had lived, things would have been different."

"Different? Different how? George was beating her long before he started beating us. You were a baby. I was five. I remember all of it. Like it was yesterday."

"You should try to forgive. If you could forgive, you would forget. Pray about it, Sean. God hears all prayers. Pray that you can forgive him."

"I know what I saw, and I'll never forgive him."

"It makes you bitter."

"It keeps me sane."

"Sean, I have to tell you something and I need you to stay calm."

I thought she had already said enough. Pop was more riled than I'd ever seen him. His breath came in deep sighs, his face had grown red and puffy, and his eyes glared in the light from the television.

I glanced at the screen. The lighted ball of New York's New Year had reached the ground. Outside, explosions of fireworks and gunshots echoed off the mountains as our neighbors celebrated. Inside our house the air felt as thick as jelly.

"I've prayed for hours about this, Sean, and the Lord hath said that I must reach you." She took in a great gulp of air. "I've heard through Father Cavanaugh that our father has requested a meeting with us. I'm going to see him, Sean."

Pop's head and shoulders jerked and twisted. He jumped to his feet and strode a few steps toward the dining room, stopped, and turned to face his sister.

"The bastard!" he said. "And you! I can't believe you would dare to speak to him."

"Father Cavanaugh says he's old, Sean. And sick. He thinks it would be good for all of us to put a proper end to things."

"He deserves to be sick! Let him stay sick and die!"

"He's asking to talk to us."

"Never! I don't want him within a mile of here! I'm warning you, Mary. If he comes near me, I swear I'll kill the bastard with my own bare hands!"

He strode into the dining room and slammed his fist on the table. Dishes and silverware set out for the next day's dinner startled and shook. He raised one hand dismissively, turned, and stomped up the stairs.

His bedroom door slammed closed with enough force to shake the pictures on the parlor wall.

Mary stood, moved slowly across the room, and picked up the telephone. I slipped into the kitchen and looked back at her face. She was not crying. Her lips were pulled into a tight line and her eyes were wide and alert. Her voice was determined as she spoke to her husband.

"Yes," she said, "I need you to pick me up. No, he did not agree." She looked over at me as if suddenly remembering my presence. "I'll talk to you when you get here," she said to the telephone.

To me, she said, "Happy New Year, Sally. I hope this is the best year for you ever."

"Molly," I corrected her. "Happy New Year to you too."

She helped me pick up and wash the few dishes before we walked to the porch stairs. As she climbed into her husband's car, fireworks brightened the valley along the river. A few frightened dogs howled into the night. Too late, I remembered the music I was supposed to play. I went into the house, turned down the volume knob of the record player, and placed the needle on the record. As "Ave Maria" began to play, I turned off the lights and climbed the stairs. There was no light showing under Pop's door.

Tomorrow I would add to Maura's page in my notebook and would start one for George. Of Pop's family, only Mike had been on the diary's list. Now I would add more. I felt strangely sorry for George.

~

Mom returned near noon of New Year's Day. Pop had come into the kitchen earlier, refused coffee, and driven off without a good-bye. As soon as Mom walked through the door, I told her about the disagreement between Pop and his sister.

"I feel bad for Pop's father," I said. "He must be sincere if he asked that priest to help."

"Molly, if you knew everything about George, you would understand why your pop hates him. The last thing he deserves is your sympathy. He's not someone to be trusted."

"But Aunt Mary said that he's sick and old."

"And that's what's so bad about the whole deal. He's lived to be an old man and his two sons died because of his bullying. Don't waste any feelings on that man."

I had questions about Mike, but before I could ask even one, she cut me off. "I don't want to talk about this any more," she said. "I wish Mary had minded her own business and that she would stop interfering in ours."

"Can't I ask one question?"

"No. Not even one."

When Pop failed to return by late afternoon, Mom and I started packing Christmas away. We put all the small things into boxes but needed Pop to help with the platform and to unwind the strings of lights from the skeleton of the tree. When he didn't show up by eleven that night, Mom sent me to bed. I heard her follow a short time later.

~

Something stirred me awake. I lay in the darkness and listened to the sounds of the night house: the hum of gathered wind-voices wheezing around door frames, under the eaves, down through the cellar, and Mom's even breathing sighing through her open door.

I stared into the hallway. The colored lights from the Christmas tree glowed through the darkness. The soprano notes of "Ave Maria" lifted softly through the stairwell, along with the chug of the model train. I pulled on my robe and tiptoed halfway down the stairs. Pop's cigarette glowed above the overstuffed chair.

"What are you doing?" I whispered.

His voice came softly out of the gloom. "Playing with the train."

I descended the remaining stairs and stood in the arched doorway of the parlor. His face showed red and green in the glow of the tree lights. I sidled up to him. "But you're a grown-up."

He reached out and drew me onto his lap. I felt dwarfed by his size. He wrapped his arms around my midsection and rested his cheek against the top of my head. I leaned against his flannel shirt and sighed as the familiar feeling of safety settled over me.

"I never had a train when I was a kid." His breath was full of booze. "Never had a sled or skates or skis or a real Christmas tree." His voice was as lost and sad as Lenny's had been when he made the same kind of pronouncement while we had worked the puzzle.

A rush of pity filled my heart. "Never?" I whispered.

"Absolutely never. I sure rode on a lot of those damned trains though. I did more than my fair share of riding."

I sat up and asked him straight out, "Why'd you ride the trains, Pop?"

"I was running away."

"Why?"

"Well, maybe not so much running away as I was running toward."

"Toward what?"

"A place where I belonged. A place to call home. My Aunt Maura's place." He reached out and tapped one of the dark lights on the tree. It flickered green and went off again. "When that didn't work out, I had to ride to stay alive."

"Was someone going to kill you?"

He laughed. "No. But a boy has to eat to live. You've seen how much Marty, Lenny, and Larry can eat."

When Mom watched those boys eat, she sometimes asked them which leg they planned to fill first. That thought tickled my funny bone. I laughed too. "You didn't have any money?"

"Nope. Seemed like nobody had money then."

"Mom says you had lots of different jobs. Couldn't you have stayed at one of them?"

"They weren't those kinds of jobs. We got paid with food, and maybe a roof over our heads. Sometimes, if no one could give us work, we had to steal to eat."

"The Bible says, 'Thou shalt not steal.'"

"But whoever wrote that thing should have added '. . . unless you're starving.'"

"Were you starving?"

"Sometimes. Not too often. Once in a while we'd end up in a place where folks were worse off than us. That's when we'd high-tail it away and go on to the next place. By the time we got somewhere good, we'd be pretty well starved."

"What did you steal?"

"Eggs. Fruit from trees. Watermelon from fields. About anything to fill our stomachs. Once my brother even pretended to have a fit, so the cops carried him to the hospital at suppertime and they gave him a meal. I snuck in and shared it with him and we both snuck back out and took the next train away."

"They didn't ever catch you?"

"Hardly ever. Most times we got clean away."

"Mom says you stopped riding when you met her and got a good job."

"That's true. It wasn't until Mr. Roosevelt and the war came along that things started to look up."

"Iris said that even after you met Mom, you still wanted to go on the trains."

"Well, it does get in your blood. Pretty soon you're riding because it's what you've always done. Gets to be a bad habit, like smoking or drinking."

"Why'd you decide to stop?"

"I dunno. I guess I wanted to have Christmas." He grinned when he said that. He was teasing me.

"That's too easy. Anybody can have Christmas."

"Not if they never learned how. It was your mom who taught me Christmas."

I didn't know what to say. I studied the lights on the tree, watched the train take a few turns on the track.

"Your mom made me cut a tree the first year we were married. We didn't have a nickel to our names, but she begged or borrowed some lights and we hung colored paper chains on the thing."

"Did you like it?"

"Ho, yes! I thought it was gorrr-geous!"

I giggled and poked him gently with my elbow. "Pop!"

"You see that train? When I was twenty-five years old, your mom gave me that train. Some relative gave it to her and she wrapped it up with paper and ribbons—every car in a separate package. Every three pieces of track tied with a fancy ribbon. She said it needed to be a better train than any I had ever hopped, because I was never going to ride away on a train again. And I agreed with her, and here I am."

"Is that why you wanted all of us to have a good Christmas this year?"

"Partly."

"What's the other part?"

"It's been a hell of a year. I guess I wanted to be like Mr. Roosevelt and give everybody a reason to celebrate."

"It worked."

"Yep. Nothing like a little money and a good holiday to break up a bad streak."

"Mom said you got married in the winter."

"We certainly did. February 17, 1932. One of the best days of my life."

That made me smile. "Why are you sad now?"

"I'm not."

"Yes, you are."

"Okay, maybe a little bit." The train derailed around a curve. He leaned to one side and righted the engine back on its track. When he tried to make it start again, several of the cars went catawampus on the platform. He carefully set them right. This time the train began to move smoothly around the tracks.

"Because of Aunt Mary Margaret?"

He settled back in the chair with a sigh. "Not because of her, but because of the message she had."

"About George?"

"Yep."

"Is that why you ran away today?"

He thought about that for a few seconds. "I didn't run away. I went over and saw Lenny and Larry. Then I went to the cemetery and said Happy New Year to all my dead relatives."

"I was worried about you."

"I didn't mean to make you worry."

"I couldn't help it."

He sat me up and put his hands squarely on my shoulders. "I'm the father here. I'm the one who does the worrying. That's my job. What are you trying to do, take away my job?"

I giggled again. "No."

"Well, you never have to worry about me. I'm not going anywhere."

"What about New Jersey?"

He paused for a long while, let out another big sigh, and hugged me to him. "Well now, that's another story. That's not really a going away. Let's call it a necessary evil. Somebody has to put bread on the table. It isn't going to show up out of nowhere."

"Are we all moving?" My voice trembled, but he didn't seem to notice.

"Maybe. Maybe not. It's too soon to tell."

I didn't know what else to say. No one would give me an answer about New Jersey.

"I don't want you to go alone. I don't want you to be alone ever again."

"Are you worried about that?" he asked.

"A little." I decided to be totally honest. "A lot."

"Have I ever let you down?"

"No."

"Well, here's my New Year's resolution. I will try to never, ever let you down. Can you believe that?"

"Yep."

"Good. Now will you go to bed and dream sweet dreams?"

"Are you mad at Aunt Mary Margaret?"

I felt him stiffen. "Aunt Mary? Mad at Aunt Mary?"

If I let him off the hook, he would evade answering. "Are you?"

"Well, okay, I might be a little mad. But I'll get over it."

"Are you sure?"

He didn't answer. He lifted me effortlessly from his lap and headed me toward the stairs.

"You let me worry about that. You take that busy little head of yours and put it to rest. Go."

He was a pop who always listened, always cared, and who gave his love freely without restraint. Too much was happening, and too fast. All my worries for 1956 were about him. As I climbed the stairs I could hear the faint chug-a chug-a chug-a of the train. I couldn't shake the worry that his drinking could cause him to derail as easily as that toy train. It was a worry he couldn't take away with words.

CHAPTER THIRTEEN

Another cold snap, clear and windless, settled over the valley in mid-January. The moon became a pale white slash in the sky. The earth beneath my feet became rock hard and without give. Trees stood rigid, their trunks shining and unmoving. On the mountainside behind the house, the mine fire vented steam into flat lines that hugged the ground in faded crystal-blue clouds. The chimney gave off lazy ribbons that melted the sky in undulating waves.

Mom kept the fires low, hung blankets over windows, rolled rag carpets against the outside doors, and once again emptied the closets of old coats to be used as blankets. We kept most inside doors closed to hold as much heat in the interior halls as possible. Despite our efforts, a palling cold settled in. I found an extra long, mouton lamb coat at the very back of the hall closet. One morning I pulled it off my bed and wore it as a bathrobe. Mom startled when I walked into the kitchen.

"That coat belonged to my Uncle Ira," she said. "You shouldn't be wearing it. If you want to use it, keep it in your room."

I looked at the coat with new interest. "Where's Pop?"

"He's helping to close down the factory. They're in a rush to finish up the orders they have. They won't be taking any more."

"More work is good though, isn't it?" I took a piece of toast from the table and turned to go.

"Well, he'll be back on the swing shift starting tomorrow, but the hours will be uneven—sometimes six, sometimes three."

"Can we make it?"

"We'll figure it out. At least I don't have those loans hanging over me anymore."

"The wood's almost gone. Can we buy coal?"

"We'll buy it in single bags for a while."

That evening, as soon as supper was done, my friend Connie and I threw our skates over our shoulders and hiked down to the skating pond. We walked straight out on dry pavement to keep the penetrating cold from numbing our toes and curled our gloved fingers snugly into our coat pockets. Ice soon stiffened the scarves around our mouths and noses. At the top of Monastery Hill we caught glimpses of the pond centered in the open field. A solitary lamp transformed wood smoke into a yellowish haze that reflected off the ice and created a fairyland of frozen ochre and pinks. Black stick figures cast moving shadows that melded with the ice like the petals of breeze-tossed flowers. The smoky musk of winter saturated the air.

We ran the rest of the way. Chuck was there, but he was not alone. He spun around the pond with Jennifer Nevil, the willowy brunette with large brown eyes and perfect teeth who had nearly drowned me. His smile when she took his hand squeezed my jealous heart. But jealousy couldn't squelch my youthful enthusiasm. I tied up my new skates and hit the ice from a running start. I showed off with precision turns and showered cascades of splintered ice along the edges of the crowd. I weaved between slower-moving bodies or turned completely around to wave at kids I knew.

I caught Chuck watching me, but he turned to Jen whenever I looked their way. She skated slowly, matching him glide for glide, holding his bare hand in her warm angora mittens and his complete attention with her generous smile.

On our climb back up the hill we stopped at Edward's store. Chuck lived only a few houses down the side alley from the place. Maybe he would walk through the door.

I sipped my cocoa slowly. Too soon we stepped back out into the cold to finish our hike without speaking. Back home, I sank exhausted into my ice-cold bed and slept like a baby lamb under Ira's coat.

~

January turned to February without any letup in the cold. The air became metallic, leaving a bitter taste when breathed through our mouths. The ice fog from the underground mine fire flowed toward the valley, coating shrubs and trees until they crackled with the slightest breeze. The winter sun did its best to melt the offending layers, but each night the ice returned a bit thicker than the day before and became hazardous frozen puddles in the darkness.

Now we didn't speak at all on our nightly forays to the pond. We kept our eyes on the ground and at times crept sideways, crablike, with our hands free to soften our falls.

Without an insulating layer of snow, the deepest waterlines began to freeze and burst. Up and down the hilly streets, men lay on their stomachs on bare ground, leaning into holes pickaxed out of the frozen earth and running torches over metal pipes to keep the water flowing. Evenings, Connie and I walked in the middle of the streets to avoid the open pits and patches of ice. Each time a car passed we clung to each other as we were forced onto glare ice on the roadside. We never thought to give up skating.

One night, with the temperature at four degrees below zero, I skated across the ice, my head craned over my shoulder in search of Chuck, and did a full body slam into Ronald Miller. Protected by layers of clothing and wraps, neither of us was hurt. At first, our close posture, with him sprawled out on top of me, didn't seem like closeness, but when he repositioned his body and began to smile, I pushed him away.

"Jerk," I shouted with more moxie than I felt. "Big fat jerk!"

When I was finally able to slide out from under him, I was so flustered I didn't recognize Chuck standing over us.

He reached out and pulled me to my feet. "You all right?"

"Sure," I answered. But I wasn't sure, especially with his hand holding mine.

He awkwardly brushed ice from my coat. Ronald laughed, punched Chuck on his arm, and skated away. I felt my cold cheeks grow hot. I skated quickly toward the fire without thanking Chuck. I had sensed a danger that I didn't understand. I found Connie.

"I've got a dime," I said. "If we leave right now we can make it to Edward's store before it closes."

She searched the faces of kids around the fire, didn't find anyone interesting, and shrugged. "Sure," she said. "Let's go."

As we moved into the dark field, I heard dragging footsteps behind. A waft of cigarette smoke blew past as we began to climb the long hill. I turned and walked backward for a few steps. Ronald Miller was strolling close behind.

I turned back and took Connie by the arm. "Go faster."

"What's your hurry?"

"I'm cold. Come on!" I dragged her into a near trot.

By the time we reached the store, my heart was beating out of my chest and my lungs hurt from the cold. We ducked inside. I turned to face the door. Ronald strolled past, peered in through the window, and turned down his street. I grabbed Connie's sleeve and yanked her from the store.

"I don't want hot cocoa after all," I said. "But I'll give you my dime if you want it." She happily took the coin.

The next evening, I refused to go to the pond. I sat in the warm kitchen and caught up on homework. Pop had stayed home too. His asthma had begun to flare. He wheezed with every breath as he emptied bagged coal into the coal bucket, and he paused three times as he shook the dying embers of the stove into the ash pit. Mom made him sit at the table while she poured boiling water into a basin. As he breathed in the rising mist, the vapors of menthol mixed with the rotten egg stench of blackdamp and filled the air with the unmistakable scent of a sickroom.

The next night, Connie's pleading worked. We descended to the nearly deserted pond. A rowdy group of skaters was playing Crack the Whip. I tied my skates, rushed out, and grabbed the hand of the last person on the whip. It was Ronald Miller. We flew across the ice at top speed. The strong point man planted his skates and threw the whip so well that half of us couldn't make the turn. I pried my hand from Ronald's and was thrown up over the edge beyond the light. I could hear screams of laughter as others skidded out of control. Their cries faded and became muffled as they moved away.

I gained my footing and began to brush snow from my clothing. I was not alone. Ronald stood between the pond and me. He didn't speak as he shoved me into deeper darkness. The blades of my skates caught on the uneven ground. His wet lips against my cold face reeked of cigarettes and beer. I twisted, pushed both hands against his chest, and kicked at him with one skate. He wrapped his arms around me and dragged me toward the blackest part of the field.

When the heat of his breath touched my earlobe, I thought of all those dead dogs with a hole right there—behind the ear. Fear filled my mouth with dry hay. His mouth covered mine. His tongue pushed against my clenched teeth. The stale taste of cigarette filtered across my tongue and caused me to gag.

I tried to slide down into my coat but he came with me, angling my body back until I felt my skates slide out from under me. My gloved hands could get no leverage against his nylon coat. As my back hit the frozen ground, a sharp pain took my breath away. Ronald staggered sideways, off balance because of my sudden drop. I rolled onto my stomach, scrambled onto all fours, bruised my knees as I tried to lift the toe picks of my skates high enough to crawl away. Ronald grabbed my trailing scarf and cut off my screams with one hard tug.

"Molly Branigan," someone called into the darkness.

I twisted, rolled over, and pulled against the scarf with both hands. I dug the blades of my skates into the hard ground and was able to push myself backward a few feet. The scarf pulled tighter around my neck. I yanked with all my strength and slid back a few more inches. Ronald momentarily lost his grip on the scarf.

That's when I saw Chuck bumping toward us on the uneven ground. He stopped as he recognized Ronald hovering in the darkness. I leveraged myself upright, stood still, and waited for someone to move. The dry taste in my mouth thickened. Chuck was no match for Ronald.

"Molly," Chuck said softly, "your father's here, looking for you."

Ronald glanced toward the ice.

"He's really here," Chuck said directly to Ronald.

Ronald backed up a few feet. "If you tell your pop about this, I'll kill you."

I played my only card. "I'll tell him. You bet I will. If you ever do that again, I'll tell him. And then he'll kill *you.*"

As I pushed my skates against the frozen ground, I stumbled and nearly fell. Chuck righted me. I clambered up to the pond and sure enough, there was Pop, big and tall, waiting.

"Where've you been," he asked.

"I got swung out by the whip," I said. "Chuck helped me up."

Pop smiled at Chuck and shook his hand. "Thanks," he said.

Chuck mumbled a response and skated off. Ronald did not come out.

Pop reached out his hand to gather me in. "I had to leave work early. I'm still kind of sick. I thought I'd stop and give you girls a ride home."

I called to Connie, tucked myself snugly beneath Pop's arm, and wrapped both my arms around his heavy coat.

"Thanks," he said as his boots skidded on the ice. "I'd fall flat on my rear if you didn't hold me up."

Once home, I stood by the coal stove, held my hands over its rising heat, and tried to force out a deep cold that caused me to shiver uncontrollably in the warm room. I had never been kissed by a boy. I had thought about it often and was sure that I would like it. Now I was shocked that I didn't like it at all. Ronald's interest in me was not normal. I wondered who I could tell, or if telling would make me seem a silly snitch.

As I caught sight of the unlatched cellar door, a feeling of déjà vu washed over me. I reached out and banged it shut.

Mom glanced up from her needlework. "You afraid of those cellar spirits, Molly?" When she caught full sight of my face, she stuck her finger. "Goodness. You look like you've seen a ghost. Are you all right?"

"I think I fell a little too hard on the ice," I said.

"You'll have to work on being a little less of a showoff with those new skates."

"I guess so."

She shot me another worried look and was about to say something more when Pop's loud cough echoed from the upstairs hall.

"Dampen down the fire, would you?" she said. "I've got to see to your father." She hurried to the stairs.

For the first time in my life I went through the house and made sure every door was shut tight. I had to tell Pop about Ronald. I knocked on their bedroom door. It flew open immediately. In the light of one bare bulb, Pop's face was pale blue and bathed in sweat. His breath squealed with tight, terrifying wheezes. I went to him and touched his hand. It was colder than mine.

"I need to get him down to the sickroom, where it's warmer," Mom said.

I helped her move him to the stairs. She cried out as his legs gave way. He grabbed hold of the stair rail. Pop and I crept down the stairs, one foot at a time, like two toddlers learning to navigate steep places. Mom went before us. I counted every stair and breathed deeply to keep myself calm. When I felt Pop patting my back, I realized he was as scared as me.

He sank gratefully onto the library chair as we prepared the rollaway bed.

"I need lots of pillows to prop him up," Mom said.

I scurried back to their room, pulled the pillows off their bed, and carried them down the stairs. When I came into the library Pop was leaning forward in that posture of struggle that I knew so well. Mom piled pillows into a stack.

"You need to be in bed, Sean, with your feet up. That floor's too cold. We've got to get you warm."

While she fussed with him, I went into the kitchen and added coal to the fire. Through the open door I could see the covers of Pop's bed quivering. I hurried back into the room.

"Why's he shaking so bad?" I asked.

"Malaria," Mom answered.

"Malaria! How can it be malaria? Malaria only happens down by the equator."

"He caught it when he was hopping freights. Once you get it, it stays in your system forever. He's chilling because his resistance is down and the germ has come alive."

"What can we do?"

"We've got to warm him up. The chills are taking too much of his energy. I've never seen his breathing this bad."

I found the rubber water bottles in the storage closet, filled them with hot water from the boiler, and watched as Mom laid them next to his body.

"I need more blankets," she said.

I went upstairs and pulled the fur coat from my bed.

Mom lifted the top covers so I could lay the coat upside down over Pop's feet and lower body. She retucked the blanket closely around him.

His nervous fingers picked at the wide pelts of lamb's wool.

"Ira's," he mumbled, "old coat." His eyes opened wide and filled with panic. He pulled at the coat. "Get it out of here!"

"He's out of his mind," Mom said as she fought his grasping hands.

But he wouldn't be stopped. The effort of fighting weakened him.

I pulled the offensive coat away and tossed it into the storage closet.

"I've called Doc Rosen. He's on his way. You go to bed, Molly. I can take care of your pop."

"I can help."

"I said go!"

The anguished whine of Pop's breathing seemed to fill every corner of the house. I couldn't think of sleep. I wrapped myself in blankets and knelt before the window. There was not another light in any house that I could see. I lowered my head and began to pray. When I opened my eyes, a pair of headlights was moving uphill from low in the valley. I watched those lights until Doc Rosen reached our house.

I stayed on my knees and made deals with God. If he would save my pop, I would become a Catholic and go to Mass every week with my Aunt Mary Margaret or, if he preferred, I would become a devout Protestant and go back to Sunday school. I would join Christian Endeavor and never miss a meeting. I would even forgive Ronald Miller for his sins and pray for his evil soul. I don't know which of the deals God accepted, but in the morning Pop was still breathing.

Mom was too tired to argue when I refused to go to school. I crept into the library and peeked over the layered blankets. Pop's eyes were closed. His breathing was a little less labored, but his face and fingers had taken on the same color as the ashes we emptied from the kitchen stove. When I whispered to him, he didn't move.

Mom came to the doorway. "Leave him be, Molly. He needs to sleep."

I curled up on the library sofa and pretended to read. I was afraid that he would get too tired to breathe.

Midmorning, Mom hurried John Hale into the room. He leaned over, pressed his ear to Pop's flailing chest, and said, "Sounds pretty bad. The only thing to do is sassafras-and-willow tea, but the mine fire has dried up all the trees."

"Doc Rosen gave him a shot of penicillin and some pills, and a prescription for a powder that will open up his lungs," Mom said, "but Mr. Lewis in the drugstore won't give credit."

I dug my fingers into the groove behind the sofa cushion and came up with bumble gum wrappers and some dirt. It was a hopeless search. Not a penny escaped our eyes.

John pulled a worn wallet from his back pocket and searched through it until he found one dollar. He held it out to Mom.

"No, John," she said. "You'll need that yourself."

"I want you to have it."

"I can't, John. I'll find some. Don't worry."

I would have suggested she call Lillian, but I knew we were behind on the bills again.

"I can help him clear his lungs by clapping his chest. Do you want me to try?" John slid the dollar back into his wallet.

"Yes. Anything."

As he and Mom set to work, I went into the kitchen and stood before the coal stove. I could hear the thump of John Hale's hands on Pop's barrel chest and Pop's intermittent strangled cough. I began to match his loud breathing, breath for breath, until my head became fuzzy and the room began to spin. When I reached out to steady myself on a chair, I couldn't feel my fingertips. I felt myself falling.

John Hale's voice filled the kitchen. "Bess, I need a paper bag."

Mom pulled used bags from the cellarway. John chose a lunch bag and held it over my nose and mouth. It crinkled and filled, emptied and filled, until I imagined that I was breathing for Pop—that I could fill his lungs like I could fill the paper bag. In a few minutes my dizziness subsided and the feeling came back into my hands.

"You're scared to death," Mom said. "I want you to go upstairs and rest. That's an order."

I was madder at her with each step, but after I pulled the covers over my head I fell into a deep sleep.

The slam of the front door woke me. John Hale had brought us Pop's medicine.

It took the three of us and two pages of directions to figure out the whistlelike asthma pump. When I finally volunteered to try it out, the sucked-in medicine caused my heart to race and my breathing to speed up.

"It works," I said. Its effect frightened me.

Pop was too weak to inhale the drug. I wedged myself between him and the bed. Mom pinched his nose. John held the pump into his mouth and instructed him, "Big breath in."

On his first try, his intake of breath wasn't strong enough to tap the metal ball against the capsule. The second time, he took a deeper breath and got some of the medicine into his lungs. The third time, he got most of the medicine in. The final time, he got a good jolt of it.

The effect was immediate. His lungs stopped their melodic wheezing and his face became less pale. He leaned back onto the pillows, smiled, and relaxed into a deep sleep. We three anxiously watched every breath he took.

The next evening Mom scooted me out of the house as soon as supper was done. I headed for the skating pond.

I caught sight of Chuck standing by the fire. Jen had broken up with him. She was used to being taken to the movies and into Wilkes-Barre for sundaes at the Boston Kitchen. She didn't like being out in the cold every night and she had begun going to dances with a local radio personality. Ronald Miller and other boys from Chuck's neighborhood had a stash of beer in a car parked near the edge of the lot. Before long they were speed skating across the pond, careening carelessly into others and knocking some of the smaller kids onto the ice. A fight started. The younger kids left.

I called to Connie. "I think we should go."

"If you want to leave, go ahead," she said. "I'm sick of leaving early."

"Please," I begged. "I'm afraid to walk home alone."

She pushed past me and went chasing after one of the wilder boys.

I moved to the fire, found a comfortable log, and watched as the boys became louder and more out of control. Connie laughed good-naturedly when Ronald knocked into her. She didn't seem to be afraid of him. Soon after, Ronald and some of the guys drove off and the ice quieted.

"What are you doing? Hiding?" Chuck's deep voice startled me. He sat beside me.

"Why would I do that?" I kept my eyes on the fire.

"Because you're smart enough to stay away from Ronald."

"He doesn't bother me."

"He's got his eye on you. You should be bothered."

He turned away and studied the few skaters remaining on the ice. "Do you want to skate a little?"

He took my breath away. I looked at my feet and turned the toe of one skate in the partially frozen mud on the edge of the roaring fire.

"Well, do you or don't you?"

I stood. "Yes, I do."

He took my hand and led me to the ice. We pushed off and glided hand in hand around the outer curves of the pond.

The beer had loosened his tongue. "I tried out for the basketball team but I wasn't tall enough. I go to all the games anyway. Sometime you should come too."

"I don't know anything about basketball."

"But you're smart in school. Everybody says that."

"Yeah." I turned and skated backward so I could see his face. "But that's because I like libraries, not because I'm so smart." I didn't think boys found smart girls attractive. I wanted him to look at me the way he looked at Jen.

"I wouldn't mind going to college." He reached out and took my other hand. "I doubt I'll ever get the money or grades to go."

"I won't have money either, but Mom keeps saying I could get a scholarship. You could do that too."

"Nah. It's too late now. This is my last year. I'll probably end up end up looking for a factory job. I don't think I'd like digging in the mines like my pop and uncles."

I didn't know what to say, so I kept quiet while we made another full circle of the pond. I had never skated with a boy before. I was surprised how easy it was and how much I liked the feel of my hand in his as our skates glided in an easy rhythm.

"Jen will be going to college," he said. "She already has a couple of offers. I'll probably never see her again."

I was about to tell him that I was sorry for him when the carload of boys pulled into their parking spot. They came loudly out of the darkness holding two quarts of beer high in the air.

Chuck released my hands. "You and Connie better go home," he said, "if you know what's good for you."

Connie hadn't seen me skating with Chuck. I had a lovely secret of my own.

~

Pop was sitting up in bed when I got home, reading the paper by the light of a small lamp. His breathing was fast but quieter than earlier. He smiled and put his paper down.

"Going to snow," he said. "I can smell it on the air you brought with you."

"That's probably beer fumes," I said.

"Beer? Where'd you have beer?"

"Not me," I giggled. "Some of the boys. You know how they are."

"I could use a glass or two myself," he said. "Your mother has me on the wagon."

I smiled. That was a good thing.

"I'm coasting on empty and she's in the driver's seat." His hands shook as he picked up the newspaper. I thought it was from his new medicine.

~

The next morning, as soon as I opened my eyes, I knew that something was different. The light in the room was dimmer than usual and had a yellowish cast. I hurried to the window and pulled the shade so recklessly that the mechanism jammed. I reached up and removed the blind from the hanger. Snow was piled up against the window. I wiped a hand across the glass.

The land had been transformed. A light wind blew pellets of ice onto mounding drifts as smooth and round as the glossy meringue topping on one of Mom's lemon pies. There would be no school. I dressed as fast as I could and took the stairs two at a time.

The kitchen was empty. The usual roaring coal fire was stone cold out. I could hear voices coming from the sickroom. I hurried through the library door. The room had the acetone smell of nail polish remover. Pop was in his underwear, swinging his arms wildly and swatting at the shelved books with his folded newspaper. Mom hung on his arm as she begged him to get back into bed.

I ran to them. "Pop! What are you doing?"

"Killing the little buggers," he said. He continued to swat something on the shelves.

Mom let go of his arm and turned to me. "It's the shakes," she said.

"The malaria?"

"No. The shakes. He's coming off the booze. D.T.'s. He's out of his mind."

He did appear to be a little crazy.

"What's he doing?"

"He's seeing things. Bugs. He's trying to kill them."

"I don't see anything."

"Of course you don't. There's nothing there."

"Pop! Stop it!"

"When I'm damned good and ready," he said. "I won't allow critters in my house. I'll kill every damned one of them."

I looked to Mom. "Can't you do something?"

"Doc Rosen said to give him some of that paraldehyde that was in the cupboard. I tried, but he spit it all over me."

"Is that what that smell is?"

She nodded. "Can't say I blame him for not drinking it. But I don't know that booze tastes much better. He can sure get enough of that down his gullet."

"Isn't there anything you can do?"

"Hair of the dog. But no liquor store will be open with all this snow, and there's no money anyway."

"Can't you borrow some beer from somebody?"

"It'll take more than a few beers. And besides, I'm not going to advertise to the whole town that your pop is a such a bad boozer that he gets the shakes as soon as he's short a few."

"Can't you borrow some whiskey?"

"This is the kind of thing this town loves to talk about. The church members would have a heyday."

"So what?"

"So your pop would never forgive me."

Pop climbed up on the sofa and began swatting at the brass chandelier that hung from the ceiling by a chain and one electric wire. It swung dangerously back and forth. He tried to grab hold of it with his hands but lost his balance and stumbled back to the carpeted floor. Mom pushed him. He fell hard onto the bed.

She instantly lay over him and shouted, "Come help me tie him down."

I couldn't tie up my own father.

"Come on, hurry up," she commanded. "Grab hold of one end of that sheet and I'll show you how."

She was serious. And she had planned ahead. She had laid several sheets, doubled and fan-folded loosely across the bed. I stepped forward and pulled the edge of one sheet loose.

"Give it to me!" She thrust one arm across his neck and grabbed the corner of the sheet I held out to her. She doubled the end of the material around her small fist and with the other hand pulled the sheet across his body. "Here," she said. "Help me."

With one hand, she pushed Pop toward me. I helped her roll him. She still had that one end firmly in her hand. The sheet pulled tight. She pulled her end up and over his shoulder and tied the ends together.

"Quick. Grab the other sheet and give me a corner." She repeated the procedure, rolling him and the sheet as one. He became a mummy even as he struggled against her. Once she had his arms pinned, he kicked out his feet. She wrapped his lower torso and legs into a thin blanket. Now only his head and toes moved. He began to laugh in a rollicking way.

"I've seen him like this before," she said. "He won't hurt anybody. He's confused and he'll swat those damned bugs all day if we let him."

"Does he have to stay like that?"

"I suppose so. There's nothing to do but let him dry out and make sure he doesn't hurt himself."

I was embarrassed for him. He looked foolish and cowed. His head swung wildly back and forth as his eyes followed those imaginary bugs.

"There!" he said. "There's one, Toots! Swat it!"

"He'll get loose if he can," she said. "We'll need to put more sheets across him and tuck them way under the mattress."

As I helped her restrain him further, a deep sadness overwhelmed me. I did not like seeing him diminished to the role of a child. I would rather see him drink. I knew where I could get some hair of the dog without having someone broadcast his weakness all over Creation.

I walked back to the kitchen and pulled my coat and boots from the cellarway. I closed the back door quietly behind me.

Bright sunlight greeted me. The snow had weighed down the mock orange and lilac bushes lining the path to form the graceful arches of a heavenly cathedral. I ducked my head and threaded my way though their tunnel of intermittent shadow and light. In the northwestern sky scudding clouds promised more snow before the storm was done.

I couldn't stop to marvel at the changed world. I plowed through the drifts and down the street to Mrs. Donal's house. She opened the door at once. I stomped my feet on the doormat on the covered porch, removed my boots, and tiptoed across the cold cement floor to the open doorway.

I told her everything, even that I knew where she kept her bottles of liquor because I had seen her pour drinks for her occasional male friends.

She threw open the highest door of her cupboard. "What kind do you want?"

"Something strong. He usually drinks a shot and a beer. What do you think?"

She took a full bottle of amber whiskey from the shelf and unfolded a paper bag from under the sink. She handed me the neat package with a smile.

"Tom had the shakes when he first came home from the war," she said. "He kept trying to stop drinking. He went a little crazy. Have your mom mix two shots with a glass of water, wait an hour, then give him more. He'll gradually come around. The water is important because he's probably a little low on fluids."

"Pop never drinks water. He says it will rust his pipes."

"Don't worry. He'll take it this time. And tell your mom that I won't tell a soul. I have a lot of respect for your pop. He's an outsider in this town. There's no need to make things worse for him."

"I'll pay you back," I said.

She laughed. "We'll talk about that another time. Go and help your pop."

I concealed my treasure beneath my coat and hurried back across the road.

Mom took care of the rest.

CHAPTER FOURTEEN

March arrived with gusty winds and drowning rains. One last big snow melted into rivulets that bubbled quietly beneath the glaze of ice and carried off the last of winter. The Susquehanna River became a steel-colored loop of wire that strained the levees in its attempt to snare the buildings of Wilkes-Barre.

Pop did not remember that I had helped tie him down. The ice rink returned to a small swamp. Visits to the city library resumed as I searched for more information on the diary deaths. Silas's run-in with the train was a nonevent when news of World War I battles dominated the newspaper. His death was as unimportant to the citizens of the valley as the deaths of miners had been to the coal companies. But I did strike pay dirt with Faye's and Arlie's 1931 obituaries.

MRS. FAYE CONROY, aged 36 years, daughter of Charles and Sue Ellen Beckerman, died yesterday morning following a long illness due to her care of soldiers as a Red Cross nurse in the war in Europe. Deceased was the widow of Michael Conroy, of Tunkhannock. Mr. Conroy was a valiant soldier who died of wounds suffered in battle in France. She was a woman of splendid character who endeared herself to all with whom she came in contact. She leaves one daughter: Fern Conroy. The funeral will be held Thursday afternoon at two o'clock from the home on Fitch Lane. Serving as pallbearers: Tom Donal, John Hale, Ira Reece, and Jacob Lukash.

ARLEN ASA BECKERMAN, aged 25 years, son of Mr. and Mrs. Charles Beckerman, 42 Fitch Lane, Giant's Despair, died of Bright's disease following a swift decline.

> Preceeded in death by his sister Mrs. Faye Conroy by little more than one week and by two brothers, Burton and Silas. Two sisters survive him: Mrs. Lillian Marcy of Scranton and Iris Beckerman of the home. The funeral will take place on Monday from the home at nine o'clock. Serving as pall-bearers: Tom Donal, John Hale, Ira Reece, and Jacob Lukash.

The massive dictionary defined Bright's disease as a kidney inflammation characterized by the presence of albumin in the urine. That seemed a huge difference from leukemia. The only common denominators in the deaths seemed to be the men who had served as pallbearers: self-removed Ira, war hero Tom, family deserter Jacob, and family friend John. I needed an opportunity to speak to John Hale alone.

Even when I had bus fare, I trudged up the mountain, hoping with each footstep that Chuck would miraculously appear. It didn't happen. I feared I would never skate with him again.

~

The second Saturday of spring break, I bolted down the stairs to answer the phone.

Lillian was frantic. "Get your mom and find your pop. I need someone to come right now and bring Sally home."

I did as I was told.

We drove through rain, thick fog, and slushy piles of snow that at times caused the Chevy's bald tires to slide precariously toward one curb or another. My parents barely spoke during the eighteen-mile trip. As soon as Pop parked the car, I ran through the rain and pushed open the door of the Scranton Hotel, where Lillian rented out airless single rooms.

In the previous century, the Lackawanna Railroad had squeezed the hotel between the fashionable Globe department store and the fabulous Hotel German that was one block from the now abandoned Scranton train depot. Only a newly numbered door and one clean window revealed that any life remained behind its brick facade. The door opened onto a concrete floor and a flight of metal stairs that climbed through four landings. On each landing a heavy metal door allowed access to a single hallway lined with rental rooms. The four floors had been converted to lease-holdings managed by landlords. Lillian leased the second floor. Her single rooms were filled with the same sparse furniture originally installed for overnight travelers who couldn't afford the luxury of the grand hotel next door.

As I barreled through the main door, I startled a tall woman sitting on the bottom stair. She stood, turned, and scrambled up the steps. She was dressed exactly as Sally might dress—in a full skirt, cancan slip, and a Ban-Lon sweater set. I paused to listen as her footfalls climbed each level. One flight. Two flights. A door squeaked open and slammed shut. A boarder from the second floor, most likely.

I ran up to Lillian's floor. The entry door was unlocked. Without pausing I hurried down the dark hallway to the windowless bedroom that Janet and Sally shared. Sally was lying facedown on one of the twin beds.

"Sally?"

She moaned and shook her head.

Pop came in behind me. "Sally?"

On hearing his voice, she scrambled from her bed, fell into his arms, and began to sob. He looked over her shoulder and jerked his head to tell me I should leave quietly. As I squeezed past Mom, she patted me lightly on the back and closed the door.

I was sure Sally had gotten herself pregnant. What else would a girl as pretty as her have to cry about?

I sauntered back down the dark hall to the room that served as Lillian's parlor. The door was open and Lillian was sitting on her couch. I had rarely been alone with her. Shyness sent me to the front window to stare out at the line of cars that passed continuously on the street below. When the silence became uncomfortable, I turned toward Lillian.

"Where are Janet and the boys?" I asked.

"They've moved in with Iris."

"Where?"

"Into a nice walk-up apartment, a block up the street."

"Are Lenny and Larry there too?"

She caught my expectant look and answered quickly. "No. No, not yet. It's going to take some time for Iris to get on her feet and prove to the state that's she's changed. She won't be able to have all of the kids until she's stable."

And that could be never.

"Boy," I said. "By the way everyone is acting, you would think somebody died."

She smiled. "It isn't that bad."

"You've seen a lot of dead people, huh?" I twisted the window lever until the window opened a crack.

"Quite a few. You can't get to be sixty and not have lost family and friends."

My family's voices hurried me back to the hall. Mom held Sally's hand while Pop opened the heavy entrance door and ushered them out. Not one of them noticed me. Their footfalls echoed up the stairs to the next floor and disappeared with the slamming of the landing door. I went back into the parlor and stood at one end of the couch.

"Where are they going?" I asked.

"Upstairs."

"Why?"

"To speak with a man who rooms up there."

"Jack?"

"Yes. He's a friend of Sally."

"Boyfriend," I corrected.

She smiled. "Oh, I doubt that."

She patted the couch next to her. I sat down.

I decided not to give away Sally's secret. "Who was the worst person you ever saw dead?" I asked. I was thinking of the worst as the nastiest, like maybe Silas, but she thought I meant the worst for her to bear.

"Bernie," she said without hesitation.

"The boy who drowned?"

"Yes, he's the one."

"Did you cry a lot?"

"Yes. We all cried a lot. He was so young. It's hard to lose a young person."

"Your oldest brother?"

She nodded.

"I would be really sad if Marty drowned."

"It's something you never get over."

"Do you have nightmares about it?"

"No. It's not like that."

"What is it like?"

"Oh, sweetie, you'll learn that soon enough. There's no use talking about it now."

"Did your brother look like Marty?"

"No. Marty looks like your pop. Bernie looked like my pop."

"Like an old man?"

She laughed. "No, like my pop when he was young. I have a picture of them. Let me look."

She went to her desk and pulled out a box of pictures and papers. I felt her warmth as she returned to the couch. We had never been that close before.

I studied the picture as she held it loosely in her open palms. There was the tall Bernie from the photograph on the library wall. He wore the same rumpled suit and appeared as uncomfortable as he did in the other photograph. His eyes, dulled by the camera lens, did not smile. His face wore a rather perplexed, uncertain expression, as if he were studying the camera and wondering what in the world he was doing standing there, one hand lightly touching a chair back, the other clenched into a fist at his side. He appeared tall and fit and did not seem at all the kind of boy who could succumb to the mysterious forces of a small mountain lake. Behind him, a balding, mustached man peered into the camera.

"I don't think they look that much alike," I said.

"Maybe they weren't physically alike, but their personalities were the same."

"Bernie doesn't look like someone who could drown."

She rubbed her hand tenderly across the picture. "His drowning was a terrible thing. My father was never the same."

"Did you see him drown?"

"No. I was expecting at the time."

"With Mom?"

"Yes. That's why we weren't at the lake. In those days, pregnant women didn't go out unnecessarily. It was shameful to be seen in public."

"That's weird."

She laughed. "Yes, it would seem weird to you, but back then it was unseemly to show yourself when you were in the family way."

"Did they think it was a sin even if you were married?"

She put the photograph aside and patted my knee. "Yes, that's probably what they thought."

"What was the cabin like?"

"It was made of logs cut green from the property. In the summer the logs sweated pitch and made the place smell woodsy and clean. Every night the frogs on the lake sang songs and sometimes a bear would cut through the woods in the back."

"Did they let girls swim in the lake?"

"Yes. The water was awfully cold, but so clear that when we floated on the top we could see fish on the bottom. Our porch jutted over the water. When the lake was full of spring runoff, the men could dive from the rail."

"Is that what Bernie did?"

"I don't know, but I would guess not. It was midsummer when he drowned. The lake wouldn't have been high enough for diving."

"Sally likes to dive. If she were there, I bet she would have dived off the rail. How old were you?"

"Twenty."

"Sally is almost twenty," I said.

"Sally is eighteen."

"Mom was eighteen when she had Sally."

Lillian went on as if she hadn't heard my hint for more information about my sister.

"It seemed like every girl in the house was having a baby that July. My father said it was because there was going to be a war and the human race had to multiply quickly or become extinct. He believed that if most of the babies were born boys, it would be a terrible war."

I could picture the balding man in the picture saying that.

"Was there a war?"

"Yes, and it was terrible, but not because of the babies. All the babies birthed in our family that year were girls, like your mother."

"What other girls were born?" I asked.

"Well, there was your mother and her cousin Fern, and Iris."

"Wow!"

"That's why we were all staying at Mother's house. She was the midwife for the town. She was going to do the birth for me and for my sister Faye. Faye was Fern's mom."

"So who had Iris?" I asked.

"My mother had Iris."

"No, I mean who was expecting Iris?"

She smiled. "My mother, your Granny Sue, was expecting Iris. Back then, lots of mothers were still giving birth when their daughters were old enough to have babies. My mother was fifteen when she married my father."

My eyes must have gotten really big, because Lillian began laughing before I even said, "But that's only a little older than me." Now I was positive that Sally was expecting and that's what all the fuss was about. "So the boys escaped to the lake?"

"Yes. Ira suggested that he and Bernie take the two younger boys to the cabin and get them out from under our feet."

I sat forward. "Was Ira your brother?"

"No, he was Mother's brother and my uncle, but he was only a year older than me. He took a room with us because his parents—my grandparents—had died."

"Which room?"

I felt her stiffen at my straightforwardness and decided I'd better control my curiosity.

She paused and looked toward the hall as if she'd heard someone coming. I looked too, but no one was there.

"Mother converted the second parlor—the one you use for storage now—into a room for him. My father put the French doors in the library and the front hall so he could have privacy."

"He must have liked being so close to the library."

She had to think about that. "No, I don't think he was much of a reader. He was busy with church and did a lot of visiting. He liked cars. No, I'm sure he didn't spend much time in the library."

"Did you like him?"

She didn't answer for herself. "Mother worshiped the ground he walked on. He was such a big help with the boys. When he suggested the lake, she was overjoyed. She had him carry out all the summer supplies so the cabin would be ready in late August, when the new babies would need to be protected from the threat of polio. It was safer for little babies to be away from the city then."

"Was Ira rich?"

"No. The cabin was his, but the whole family used it. That summer he had spent most of his money on a new car. He was eager to try it out on the mountain roads."

"Did you like living with him?"

"I hardly ever saw him. He and Bernie were great pals." She stared at the wall for a few minutes and then began to talk in a rush. "Where was I? Oh, I remember. Once the car was packed, Ira told Bernie he could drive. That's the last time I saw my brother alive. He waved and laughed as he drove away in that open car." She took out her handkerchief. "The next morning, we were all on the back porch when the news came that he was dead."

"And that's when Granny Sue started speaking to spirits?" I had heard this story from Mom, but I wanted to hear it from someone who was there.

"Yes."

"Were you there when she talked to him?" I asked.

"We were all right there, on that porch."

"So you heard him too?"

"No. No one else heard a thing. Only Mother. We had been helping her clear out the icebox that stood on the porch, because the iceman was coming. He always hurried to make deliveries in the early morning because he had to worry about the ice melting. We had gathered on the steps so that he could turn his big horse and buggy around in the driveway without trampling anyone."

"Did he have a nice horse?"

"Yes, and a sturdy wagon with a big icebox on it and two sets of iron tongs hanging on the side. They clanged together constantly and let us know he was on the way."

"What were the tongs for?"

"He used them to heft the ice from the wagon to the porch. He'd dump a huge block of it over the banister then he would run up the stairs and use the tongs again to lift the block into our icebox. He moved fast, so we all stayed out of his way."

"I think ice would be fun."

"It wasn't fun," Lillian said. "It was a lot of work. We had to empty all the food out of the box every week so the man could deliver the new ice."

"And that's what you were doing that day?"

"Yes. I was replacing the milk and butter into the lower rack when Mother suddenly stopped dead still in the middle of the porch and called out, 'What, Bernie? What is it?'"

"Did you think she was crazy?"

Lillian gave a little laugh. "Yes, I thought that the heat had gotten to her, especially when she dropped the rest of the previous week's ice on the porch floor and fell to her knees. The ice broke and Mother knelt right in the middle of it and began the most awful moaning."

"What did you do?" I asked.

"I was afraid for her unborn child, but I was too big to pick her up. I tried to coax her into the shade. She hit at me—batted me away. 'Bernie's dying,' she sobbed. 'He's calling to me! I hear him! I hear him!' We couldn't make her listen to reason. When she wouldn't move, I picked up a piece of ice and tried to cool her skin. It seemed to bring her to her senses. In the end, poor Faye hiked up the mountain and got Father from the mill. When they arrived home, all Mother would say was, 'Bernie's dead. Oh, Charlie, our boy is dead.'"

"And it was true?"

"Yes. The next afternoon they brought his body home."

"Did he hit his head or get a cramp or what?"

"I don't know." She shrugged her shoulders. "Uncle Ira said that he and Bernie had decided to take an early morning swim across the lake. They left Silas and Arlie in the cabin. Ira said he was already near the far shore when he looked back expecting to see Bernie close behind, but he wasn't. He decided my brother had angled off and taken to the shore to play a joke. He waited for nearly an hour but Bernie never showed up."

"How did they find him?"

"A group of men organized at one end of the lake and began searching. They found Bernie's body much closer to the cabin than they expected. They thought he might have tried to get to shore but didn't make it. The younger boys thought they heard someone call out, but in the end, neither of them were sure they had heard anything."

"Was your uncle sad?"

"Oh! Ira was a broken man! He locked himself in his room and wouldn't talk to anyone during the viewing. He pulled himself together enough to serve as pallbearer and spent weeks afterward walking and talking with my young brothers. They all cried constantly. He tried to help them understand."

Maybe that's what Old Charlie's list meant. Maybe he was planning his children's funerals. Maybe Ira was such a good pallbearer, Old Charlie wanted to ask him to carry Pop's brother's casket too. Maybe Ira felt like forever the bridesmaid, never the bride. I bet he was thinking "Always the pallbearer, never the pall."

Lillian wiped away her tears and pulled a card from the papers on her lap. "And then we got this." She handed me a black-and-white postcard of a uniformed Salvation Army band. It was yellow with age. I turned it over and read the fading message.

Dear Bernie,
How does it feel to live without God? Before long you will surely know. I think I can help. You must talk to me.

It was unsigned, addressed to Master Burton Beckerman, and dated July 2, 1915.

"Who sent it?" I asked.

"I don't know. It arrived after Bernie's funeral and upset Mother so much I took it away. None of us ever mentioned it again."

"Maybe if you asked, somebody would say they sent it."

"It's too late for that. For a time, I thought the writing might be Ira's, but it's not. Whoever sent it didn't know Bernie. He always lived with God."

I studied the postcard. "Do you know anybody in the picture?"

"Not a single soul. I haven't looked at it in years. Would you like to keep it?"

"Could I?"

"I don't know why you'd be interested in the old thing, but if you are, you may as well have it. I've no use for it."

I slipped the card into my back jeans pocket.

"Well," she said, "I think that's enough sad stories for one day. A cup of tea would be nice, don't you think?"

I followed her down the hallway of closed doors and waited while she unlocked the kitchen. All the answers to my diary questions might be in her head. If I told her how I had found it and where, she might know what those last scrawled words about the cabin and the car meant. I thought of telling her, as she pushed open the kitchen door.

"If you put out the cups and saucers, I'll put the pot on to boil." She turned to fill the kettle.

I was pulling cups from the cupboard when Mom and Pop came in.

"Where's Sally?" I asked.

"She's in her room collecting her things," Mom said.

I set the cups on the table and started for the hall.

"Don't you upset her more," Mom said.

"Tell her we're going to sit down and have a nice dinner before you all head back," Lillian called after me.

Sally was sitting on one side of her bed, stuffing clothing into a shopping bag. Her face was swollen and her eyes were reddened from crying.

"Lillian says that we should all sit down and have a nice dinner before we start for home," I said.

She shook her head. "Go away. I want to be alone."

I returned to the cheery kitchen and watched as Lillian and Mom prepared steak with gravy and mashed potatoes. Despite the personal catastrophe in my sister's life, I ate heartily. If she had lost her virginity it had nothing to do with me.

As we got ready to leave, Lillian slipped me a can of coconut macaroon cookies from the deli.

"Share these on the drive home," she said. "And when you think of it, say a little prayer for Bernie."

"Do you pray for him?"

"I haven't in years, but I think I should begin again."

In the car on the way home, Sally wouldn't talk, but when she caught me studying her flat stomach she swatted me good-naturedly on the arm and said, "No, I'm not pregnant!"

I shared the cookies with her. She ate three.

~

"Let her be," Pop said when Sally had gone upstairs to move into her old bedroom. "She needs some time to think. When she's ready to talk, she will. Until then, I don't want anybody to bring the subject up."

"Can't you tell me?"

"No. It's Sally's business. If she wants to tell you, she will."

It was too hard for me to hold my tongue, so I went into the library and pulled my notebook from the drawer. I wrote down every word Lillian had spoken about her brother's death before I fitted the postcard between the next pages. I wanted my journal to be more helpful to future generations than Old Charlie's diary was to me.

CHAPTER FIFTEEN

April, and the roads were finally clear enough for us to take the trip to have a look at New Jersey. Pop picked up Lenny from his foster family so he could go with us. Larry had become interested in some girl and stayed behind. Although it had been only three months since I'd seen him, Lenny had grown taller.

"It's because he's had food on a regular basis," Pop said.

"It's too bad it didn't help his mood," I said.

"He has a right to be a little surly."

Lenny and I sat in the parlor waiting for everyone to be ready. I tried to draw him out.

"Pop says this is going to be a real adventure. We're driving over the mountains and across the entire state of New Jersey. He said we might see the ocean."

Lenny didn't respond.

"I've never been anywhere farther than Lillian's," I tried. "That's only eighteen miles. Today we're going maybe two hundred and fifty miles. That's a long way."

"So what? I've been all the way to Philadelphia. And nobody helped me get back. I did that all on my own."

"And in winter," I said to pump him up.

He nodded. "It'll be nothing in your pop's car, now that it's spring."

"It could change back to winter in a flash. And the Chevy's tires are worn bald."

"But your mom can do the worrying about that." He laughed and kicked his heels against the floor. "That's what she's best at."

"Says who?"

"Iris says it all the time."

I would have retorted, but Sally shouted from the front door, "We're ready to go. Dibs on a back window!"

Before I had time to think, Lenny shouted, "Dibs on the other one!"

I kicked the hassock. Now I'd have to sit in the middle, on the drive shaft hump, for three hours each way.

My heart raced as the overloaded car chugged slowly up Giant's Despair Road, past Prospect Rock and the marker that celebrated General Sullivan's march. As we rolled along the two-lane highway through the Poconos, Mom retold the story of Sullivan's march from New York state.

"If he hadn't cleared the way, none of us would be living in this valley today," she said. "We're following that very same trail. The only difference now is that it's wider and asphalt paved."

She had spent her entire life among these tree-covered hills. I knew she didn't want to leave them, but I hoped she would. I didn't want Pop to live alone in New Jersey.

We'd been on the road about an hour when I spotted the sign and arrow. "Look!" I shouted. "The road to Crystal Lake."

Pop didn't slow.

"Lillian said that's where the family cabin used to be."

"And probably still is," Mom said.

In the rearview mirror, I saw Pop's brow furrow and his eyes narrow.

"Can we go look? Lillian told me all about it. I want to see it. Can't we stop?" I turned around in my seat and stared at the road behind us. "Please, Pop. Can we go look?"

"No," he said with a rare sharpness in his voice.

"Why not? It's not that far, is it?"

"Your father said no," Mom warned. "When he says no, he means no."

I wasn't to be put off that easily. "I want to see it. Can we stop on the way back? I want to look at the cabin."

Pop's eyes met mine in the mirror. "I won't go there," he said, "no matter how much you want to see it. So you can stop asking."

Mom stared at him with a look of surprise and disapproval. She turned her head back to watch the road again.

No one spoke again until we reached the top of Effort Mountain, where Pop pulled to the side so we could stretch our legs and look over the panorama before us. He pointed east.

"Now we start across the Endless Mountains and then we'll begin to cross the broad part of New Jersey," he said. "It's mostly flatlands from there, and wider highways. When we get to the new factory we'll have plenty of time to walk through it and maybe look at some houses that the company has listed for rent."

"Do you know what the place is called that we're heading into right now, Sean?" Mom asked.

"No. What's it called?"

"The Shades of Death. It's all drained with canals now, but when my ancestors came through, it was a horrible swamp." Then she surprised everyone by bursting into tears.

Sally, who was still in her funk, squeezed her eyes shut. Tears flooded between her lashes. I twisted my neck scarf into a tight knot. Lenny picked up some stones and tossed them hard over the mountainside.

"Toots. Toots," Pop murmured. He draped one arm over Mom's shoulder. "That was over two hundred years ago."

"But once I pass this place, I might never feel at home again." She turned and climbed into the car.

Pop started out again. He turned the radio on, but there was no signal. The silence became unbearable. He began to sing "Brother, Can You Spare a Dime?".

I tried to sing along, but I didn't know the words. Sally began to giggle.

Mom gave a long look over at Pop. "I know a better one. Let's try 'Side by Side.'" She broke into song. We all knew that one.

We descended through woods and sparsely populated rolling hills. As much of the sunlight shaded away, the air became damp and cold.

The car began to backfire. The engine sputtered as if Pop had turned it off. I thought he was teasing and began to laugh.

Mom's anxious voice silenced me. "What do you think it could be, Sean? Are we low on gas?"

He leaned forward and took a tighter hold on the wheel. "Dunno."

Sally rolled down her window. The rotting dampness of swampland filled my nostrils.

Pop pushed in the clutch. The backfiring stopped and was replaced by the click of tires sucking up tar from the black road. As we picked up speed, the engine began to whine.

"Start, you damned car. Start!" Pop shouted as he popped the clutch.

A tremendous backfire exploded beneath my feet as we all jerked backward in our seats. I heard the clutch pedal hit the floorboard again. We rolled freely into a dip. My stomach rose up and then fell as the back bumper dragged the pavement. Coming up the other side, the car slowed. Pop steered onto the narrow shoulder and stopped. The ripe odor of blacktop mixed with gasoline settled over us.

"Better get out," he said. He pointed to some trees surrounding a clearing ten feet above the road. "That looks like dry land. Grab the food and cooler. If we're going to be stuck, you kids can eat."

He lifted his heavy toolbox from the trunk. We pulled out the food box and began to hike up to the spot. The ground squished underfoot as we broke a path through a tangle of brush. My shoes and socks were soaked before we'd gone ten feet. Lenny carried the ceramic jug of punch. Sally carried the old quilt kept in the trunk for emergencies.

The small knoll was dry and high enough to catch a little sun. Sally helped me spread the cover over the cold ground. Lenny placed the cooler on a nearby outcropping of rock. Mom handed him tin cups. He promptly filled one and drank it down.

On the road below, Pop bent over the engine compartment and tapped with the handle of a screwdriver.

"Hey, Len, come down here, would you?" he called. "I need you to turn the starter over."

"I'm going to eat before I do anything," Lenny shouted back. He reached into a box and pulled out a sandwich.

Mom began to cry again. Sally hugged her quickly. "Don't worry. Pop will fix it."

"It's not that. It's this feeling that we're being forced to go somewhere that we'd never choose. Everything we need is back home. New Jersey will be a lonely place of new folks. I won't know a soul."

"Aunt Mary will be there," Sally said. "She and Uncle Ralph are moving. She told me so."

"I don't want to live somewhere where your Aunt Mary Margaret is my only relative and my only friend."

"We're only going to have a look. Pop says he hasn't made up his mind," I tried.

"There's no other way. He has to go," Mom said.

"Something could still come up." There had to be another way. "Somebody could still call him with a job."

"Oh, Molly, there's no chance of that now. Only one of seventy-five men has found work. That guy's ten years younger than Pop."

Lenny made no move toward the car. I pushed past him and hurried down the wet hill.

"Get in and turn on the key, then push on the starter," Pop said. "Stop when I raise my hand."

I pushed my foot on the starter. It whined for a second, clicked, and silenced. He held up his hand. I climbed out and stood beside him.

"Do you know what it is?"

"Generator. I'll have to pull it."

"Sean, come on and have something to eat," Mom called. "Then you can worry about the car."

"I've got it figured out," he shouted back. "I'm going to take out the generator." In a low voice he added, "Where in the hell I'm going to find another one in this Godforsaken place is another question."

He worked quickly. He let out a ragged grunt as he used both hands to lift the heavy generator out and lay it on the ground. Mom called again.

"Sean, I don't care what it is. You come eat."

We climbed the hill together.

He took a sandwich from Sally and partially unwrapped it so waxed paper protected the white bread from his greasy hands.

"I'll have to hike to the next town. See if there's a parts place open."

"It's Sunday. There'll be nothing open." Mom's voice trembled.

"We crossed the border. Jersey doesn't have blue laws. I hear the place is godless enough to have everything open on Sunday. Even the beer joints."

I felt the same alarm that Mom registered with her eyes.

"I'll go with you," she said.

"You need to stay with the kids. I'll take Lenny."

"I ain't walking nowhere," Lenny said.

"I'll go," I said. I didn't say what was on my mind—that I was afraid he might stop in one of those beer joints and never come back.

"I'm in a big hurry," he warned. "I won't have time for whining."

"I'm one of the best runners in school. I'm even faster than some of the boys."

"Okay. But don't say I didn't warn you."

At the bottom of the hill he picked up the generator with one hand and started off. We waved good-bye to the huddled group and began to climb. A brand new Chevy came flying down the highway. It didn't slow for the dip behind us. Pop's thumb came up and out. I never saw his arm move. The car passed. Pop didn't look up or slow his pace.

I lengthened my stride to match his. His breathing began to make a wheezing noise but he didn't seem to notice.

"Did you used to walk like this with Mike?" I asked.

"I did." He glanced down at me and smiled. "You move a heck of a lot faster than he ever did."

"I told you I could do it." The sun broke through the clouds and steam began to rise from the pavement ahead.

"We could be in for a long walk. Town's at least six miles as the crow flies."

"Somebody might give us a ride."

"If they do, I want you to sit in the front and I'll sit in the back. Or else we'll both sit in the back."

"Why?" I turned around and walked backward up the steep hill.

"That's the safest way. Let me do all the talking."

"Did you ever have anything bad happen when you were walking with Mike?"

"No. Not once in all those years of hitching rides and hopping freights. But it's good to be ready just in case."

I turned back around because he was getting a little ahead of me.

"You've got to expect the best in people," he said. "But if it's not there, you don't want to be the one that's surprised."

"How do you know when someone's bad?" I was thinking of Ronald Miller.

"You never know. That's why you have to pay attention."

"What if you think they're bad and they're not?"

"That's why you keep your mouth shut. If you listen long enough you'll get a feel for the person. You have to let your gut do the talking."

"Guts can't talk." I thought he was pulling my leg.

"Exactly." He laughed merrily.

When I finally got the joke, I laughed too.

In our valley, even in the dead of winter, this kind of exercise would have warmed me. On this eastern side of the mountains, cold dampness seeped through my jacket. Pop noticed the difference too. He pulled a big workman's handkerchief from his back pocket, wrapped it around the generator, pulled his cuffs over his hands, and cradled the grease-covered cylinder as if it was a baby. I hadn't seen anyone pull their hands into their cuffs since Magee last visited and the two men had sat too long on the porch.

Thinking of Pop's hobo friend made me smile. "You do that just like Magee," I said.

"Yes, I guess I do. Old habits are hard to break."

"Too bad we both don't have a long coat like his. It's cold."

"You're not going to start to whine, are you?"

"Nope. I was thinking about Magee. He always wears that big long coat, so he looks lots bigger than he is."

"He's a pretty skinny guy."

"The first time I ever saw him he was asleep on the ground, back behind the garden. Do you remember that?"

"I believe I do."

"I didn't see him in the dead grass until he moved."

"Did he scare you?"

"No. He was pulled into his coat so that only his nose stuck out of the collar. When he popped his head out, he winked at me."

Pop laughed. "A big coat like that serves a lot of purposes on the road. You can stuff the inside pockets full and still have your hands free. A guy can carry a lot of stuff that way. And at night you can double it up around yourself and stay plenty warm even if you're caught out in the open. Magee never goes anywhere without his coat. I'm surprised you weren't afraid of him. You were pretty young."

"But I remember exactly what he said."

"What was that?"

"He said, 'Good morning, Molly. Is your daddy home?' I thought he was a talking butterfly cocoon—because you had read me *Alice in Wonderland*." We walked on a bit farther, and then I said, "Pop?"

"Yeah?"

"Do you think Magee will come visit us soon?"

"When he gets a mind to. He won't be up this way yet. Not for a couple of weeks."

"He always goes where it's warm in the winter?"

"Always."

"I was never scared of Magee, even when he was asleep in the yard that time. I always knew he was good. Was that my guts talking?"

He made the happy chuckling noise that seemed to always accompany talk of Magee. "Yes, that's probably what it was."

"Did you know that about Magee too? When you and Mike first met him?"

He looked way off down the road as if he was seeing something I couldn't see. It was a long time before he said anything. Finally, he answered, "Sometimes it's better to be lucky than anything else. We didn't think about him being good or bad. We were just happy he'd come along."

"How come he never lives in a house?"

"I'd like him to live in our house, but I doubt he ever will. He's happiest when he's moving around the country. He's never settled in for very long."

"Are you sorry *you* did?"

"Did what?"

"Settled in."

We were climbing up a long hill that took his breath away. I stopped, bent over, and untied my shoe. I took my time retying it. He stopped, laid the generator on the ground, pulled his asthma pump from his inside pocket, and sucked in some medicine.

When he finally could answer, he said, "No. I'm not sorry. I've never been sorry. I can't imagine being anywhere else." He picked up the generator and we started out again.

"Not even in New Jersey?"

"Especially not in New Jersey."

"If Magee doesn't show up this year and we move, how will he find us?"

"We won't be moving anytime soon."

"But isn't that why we're going to look? Because we'll be moving?"

"That's how it started out. But now that we're on the road, I've decided to think about it some more."

A thrill of hope filled me. It must have showed on my face, because he stopped in his tracks and stared down at me. We had crested the hill. Ahead, a long downhill stretch of road waited for us.

"I mean that I don't expect we'll *all* be moving to Jersey. I think I might have to go by myself."

I started to whine. I couldn't help it. "But, Pop, you can't go alone."

"Your mom has been crying on and off since we left the valley. I can't live with twenty years of tears. We'll go have a look, but if Jersey is anything like it was, I won't have you kids living there. Besides, I don't think you'll like it anyway. The winters aren't cold enough for ice skating."

He heard the car before I did. His thumb came out and up.

The car slowed to a stop and a boy not much older than me spoke through the open passenger window. "Need a ride?"

Pop leaned in. "Going to Bound Brook?" he asked.

"Yup. I can get you there. Looks like you had a little car trouble. I saw your family back by the road. Your boy said you was out walking."

Pop opened the back door and we both climbed in. "It's this generator, I think." He laid the cylinder across his knees.

"Not much open on a Sunday. I know a junkyard on the other side of town. They might have one."

"If you get me to a phone, I'll start calling."

"No phones except at the diner. I got nothing to do. I'll run you out to the junkyard."

"I'd be much obliged." He offered his hand across the seat back. "Sean," he said. "And this is my daughter, Molly."

The boy took Pop's hand and said, "Mike. Nice to meet you." The words came out all stiff and formal.

Pop was quick to make him comfortable. "Nice car you got."

"Fixed it up myself," he said.

"You did a real nice job."

"Stripped it. Primed it. Painted it."

"You got a spray painter?"

"Nah. Wish I did. I borrowed one from a buddy. Put on three coats."

"I can tell you took your time with it. You from this area?"

"Yeah. Live back there, on that road that cuts in near the top of the hill. I plan to get out, though. Plan to go to school or maybe join up."

Pop nodded and rolled down his window. He let the wind blow on his face. Except when we went to the plant picnic, and once when we visited Iris at the detention center, I'd never ridden with him as a passenger before. I put my hand on the seat and smiled at him. His answering smile was quick. He reached out and patted my hand.

The junkyard was a low-slung shack surrounded by piles of rusting hulks and cut through with narrow dirt roadways. I waited in the car while the boy and Pop scanned down the rows for a Chevy like ours. I watched them walk and talk together as if they'd known each other forever. When I saw their pace pick up I knew they had spotted a compatible car.

Mike threw up the hood of a black shell without wheels or windows. The two of them bent over its fenders and began passing Mike's tools back and forth. When they finally lifted the generator out, they did a little dance with their feet and turned back toward the shack. I'd only seen Pop do that little dance with Magee. I wondered if I would ever be able to bond so easily with an absolute stranger.

The junkyard owner came out from the shack. I could see Pop fidget with his wallet, count out some bills, and hand them to the man. He checked his billfold once more before slipping it into his back pocket. His shoulders rose and fell before he shook the owner's hand. All three wiped their hands on a communal rag.

We were back on the road again when something tugged at my soul. Maybe it was the movement of the car across new pavement, or the open landscape that lacked tall trees, or the scent of the lowlands blowing through the open windows.

I suddenly understood Pop's and Magee's easy smiles and loose-jointed swaying strides. I wanted to hear more of their stories. I wanted to ask them questions. And even as I thought those thoughts I realized that they would never tell me how it really was. They would hold most of the secrets of their lives as closely as every other man who's felt the freedom of the open road. I sank back into the upholstered seat of that stranger's car and knew that someday I could know that feeling too.

Mike returned us to our car, where he and Pop bolted the generator back into place. Pop offered him a buck, but he declined. He asked him to have some lunch, but he said no to that too. The two shook hands. Mike waited in his car while we cleared up the picnic things and repacked the car.

"The Kool-Aid's all gone," Lenny complained, "and I'm still thirsty."

"We'll stop at the nearest gas station and get some water," Pop said.

Mike lined up his bumper and gave us a push to the top of the hill. Pop jump-started the car on the way down the grade. Mike gave a cheery wave. Pop tooted the horn.

We continued on and hit the flatlands, where the sun beat down without mercy to cook the marshy air into a witch's brew of salt, sweat, and the spent gasoline fumes of many cars. We rolled down the windows. There was no relief from the stagnant heat.

Pop pulled into a service station. While the attendant filled the tank, Pop filled the empty cooler from a hose. When the man gave him change he held the coins in his hand and counted them carefully.

Mom poured each of us a cup of water. The warm liquid reeked of chlorine and decaying vegetation. She took one sip and dumped hers.

"I'll never learn to drink this," she said. Her damp hair framed a face filled with sadness. "I can't live here."

I felt my heart contract.

Pop climbed behind the wheel, took a sip from his cup, and made a face. "Pretty bad," he said.

"I can't do it, Sean."

"I know."

"Can we go home now?"

"We'll have to. The generator cost more than I thought. I spent my last buck for gas. We'll have barely enough to make it back."

I couldn't believe we would turn around. "But I want to see the place. I want to see the new factory. I want to see the ocean. Can't we go and look?"

Sally pulled on my sleeve. "Shut up, Molly."

I pulled away.

Sally stared silently out at the mass of cars speeding by on the four-lane interstate.

Pop had the final say. "I'm sorry, kids. We have no choice. We have to go back."

CHAPTER SIXTEEN

In May the Mountaineer began peeling back deeper layers of rock, slate, gravel, and coal. In the middle of the mountain the streams disappeared into steaming fissures that spewed familiar yellow sulfur. On rainy days, clouds of blackdamp hung low over the valley. The maples on the fringes of the hill dropped their bark like the shedding skin of snakes and became a stand of ghostly trunks with the smooth gray patina of well-polished furniture. Their limbs dropped one by one until their massive trunks gave way, exposed bare roots, and fell into the dry creek bed. I began to have dreams of Granny Sue's clawing hands reaching from the creek bottom to pull her shrubs and trees into the smoking sinkhole of her grave.

Now, with more information and more opportunity to search the library archives, I quickly found more obituaries.

> September 12, 1939
> CHARLES BECKERMAN, aged 77 years, former councilman, died yesterday afternoon at his home, 42 Fitch Lane, Giant's Despair, as the result of a fall and apoplexy. He had been in declining health. Mr. Beckerman, who was foreman of Oliver's Powder Mill for most of his life, was well known for his efforts to obliterate the Red Ash underground mine fire. He served on the Giant's Despair council and was a member of the Giant's Despair United Church. Besides his wife, Sue Ellen, he is survived by two daughters: Mrs. Lillian Marcy of Scranton and Mrs. Iris Lukash of Wilkes-Barre; also five grandchildren. One daughter and three sons preceded him in death. Funeral will be held from the home.

And Ira. A clipping dated 1937.

Death of Ira Reece, forty-three years old, found drowned in Crystal Lake near his summer cabin, Monday. The deceased was born in Tunkhannock and resided in Giant's Despair with his sister and her husband, Sue Ellen and Charles Beckerman. His parents were Mr. and Mrs. Alford Reece, among the earliest residents of Crystal Lake, both long deceased. The dead man enjoyed a large circle of friends. He possessed an excellent character and was a most valuable citizen of the community. His loss will be a severe one to parishioners of the Giant's Despair United Church where he was a trustee. He took an active part in carrying out the details of the church work. The younger members will greatly miss his Christian character and friendly ways. Mr. Reece was never married. His sister, Sue Ellen Beckerman, survives him. The funeral will be held from the home.

~

One morning I climbed the horse chestnut tree to watch for Magee. Raspy sections of bark scattered onto the ground. Something wasn't right. No leaf buds showed on its sickly gray limbs. I stopped and studied each cascading branch. Most had lost their tips. I climbed higher into what should have been a pale green canopy. The knobby leaf buds were stiff and shrunken.

I knocked off several small limbs as I descended, then ran into the kitchen.

"The chestnut tree is dead," I announced.

Mom turned from the stove. "What?"

"The tree is dead."

"It probably froze in the late storm. It'll come back."

"It can't come back. It's dead, I'm telling you. Dead as a doornail."

Pop put his newspaper down and stood. "I'll get my jacket and have a look."

"See?" We circled the tree.

He sifted handfuls of rotting bark through his fingers. "Could be blight of some kind."

"Will it fall down?"

"Yes, I think it will. Unless we cut it."

"Please don't cut it."

"We might have to. I'll need to take off a couple of small limbs to see if there's any life at all."

"You're sure that won't hurt it more?"

"It looks like a goner. I'll have the county agent take a look before I do anything." He peered up at the line of smoke from the underground fire and then at the Mountaineer. His brow furrowed.

"Don't climb it again," he warned. "That rotten limb's about to come down."

I went to the porch and pumped the swing as high as it would go. That's when I saw the man starting up Fitch Lane. He was tall and skinny and wore the same kind of loose-fitting clothing that Magee wore. His coat folded and unfolded around his limbs like leaves caught in the ripples of a creek. I watched for a minute before I leaped off the swing in mid-arc and ran into the house.

"Father Cavanaugh is coming," I shouted in my best stage whisper. "He's already halfway up the hill."

"As if Pop doesn't have enough problems!" Mom turned toward the library to find him.

During the winter, when I had read aloud from the Molly Maguire book, I learned that Mom had no more love for the Catholics than she did for the Protestants. She practically spit venom when I came to the part about the Church's involvement.

"The piss-poor Irish miners trapped in the patches complained to the coal companies about their pay and living conditions," she said. "The companies answered by giving their jobs to the Welsh and Polish immigrants who would work for even less pay. So the men began to organize against the companies. That's when the railroad police and local constables rounded up their leaders, accused them of dire crimes, and legally hanged the whole lot."

"What does that have to do with the Catholics?" I asked.

"Well, that's when the Catholic Church drew up sides with the railroad and mining tycoons, because their pockets were deeper and could fill the collection plates. It was the priests in the pulpits who dropped the handkerchief on the Irish miners. The holy fathers branded the organizers cruel and lawless hooligans. Their lace-curtain-Irish parishioners, who had come here first, looked down their noses at their late-arriving countrymen. They swallowed every word spoken from the silk-covered podiums. Men of the cloth don't lie."

"So Pop's great-grandfather was a good guy?"

"Heavens, no. Everybody knew that Pat Branigan was no angel. He was a womanizer and a heavy drinker, and the rumors about him being a headman for the Ancient Order of Hibernians were true. He did use his beer joint as a meeting place, but . . ." She looked to the ceiling and rolled her eyes. "Oh, this is what really gets my goat. On the night he was supposed to have murdered that mine foreman, he was behind the bar, serving up beer and whiskey."

"Didn't anybody tell the judge that?"

"It wouldn't have mattered. The priests preached that the companies had a holy right to the coal. They helped the powerful big shot coal barons overrun the entire valley."

"But, if he was innocent, what about the rest of the guys who got hung?"

"Hah! Most valley folks would never admit that the fast living, storytelling Irishmen might actually have been innocent. But," she pounded her small fist on the table, "this is the very worst part. Even though Pop's great-grandfather was found guilty and hanged, he never gave up being Catholic. And right down to this generation of Pop and Mary Margaret, they're still devout!"

Now here came Father Cavanaugh climbing up the hill with his chains of medals hanging out in full view for the entire town to see—and on a Sunday, no less. I moved to one side of the bay window, where I could watch him. At the front door, he stood for a minute, robed and collared and quietly talking to himself, as if, like Mom, he had some grievances to air. He raised his arm and knocked.

Pop, running his hands over his thinning hair to straighten the graying strands on his temples, rushed from the second parlor. He was composed and sure of himself when he opened the door.

"Well, look who's graced my door. Good morning, Father Cavanaugh. What a fine morning for a walk. Are you playing hooky?"

The priest took his outstretched hand and smiled slightly. "Looking for strays," he said.

Pop led him away from the entry and onto the swing that was still swaying from my quick retreat. Mom didn't call me from my hiding place beside the windows. I decided it was because she was as interested as I in what the holy father had to say. She shut the kitchen door.

On the porch, the priest hesitated. His tone changed to a gentle prodding.

"I haven't seen you at Mass, Sean."

"No, I haven't been, Father."

"And you haven't confessed in some time."

"Not in a while." I could see a small smile break across Pop's face.

"But you intend to?"

"Sooner or later, Father."

"I'd prefer sooner." Even when the swing moved forward, Father Cavanaugh was in too much shade for me to see his face.

"I was burned, Father."

"I heard about that. Last year, wasn't it?"

"A man loses track of time. Did you hear they're about to move the wire plant?"

"I did."

"Jersey, Father. We can barely make ends meet here, where we have no rent to pay." Pop's forehead creased into several lines.

"You could sell the place."

"And who would be fool enough to buy it with a mine fire licking at its back? I tell you, Father, I'm at my wits' end."

"And hitting the bottle a little?"

"There can be a lot of strife in a man's life that even a priest can't understand."

"And that's when your faith can do the most good."

"For sure." Pop nodded slowly.

"You have a good wife, Sean Branigan. A heathen wife, but not sinful."

"Don't give her names, Father." There was warning in Pop's voice. If the priest heeded it, Pop would stay and talk. If he didn't, the conversation would be short-lived.

"It's the truth, Sean. Your wife is heathen in the eyes of the Church, and well you know it. You made a promise to the Lord when you married. You took an oath, the both of you. She would take instructions. She would convert and be baptized in the Holy Church, and all the children after her. They would be raised to honor the sacraments. You haven't fulfilled that vow."

"We tried, Father. She took the instructions. It wasn't right for her."

"The Church is not concerned with heathens, son. Her soul is lost. But the children—until they've been touched by the holy water, they're illegitimate in the eyes of the Church."

Father Cavanaugh didn't know Pop very well. He should have stopped right there, but he continued in his rushing voice, hurrying as if all the saints were upon him.

"No wonder you're having problems, Sean. You haven't kept your promises to God."

"I made those promises to you, Father, not to God. We told you how it was: Her family up in arms, disowning her, not believing we would make a go of it. Mary Margaret on her knees in the church all day. We had to end the fighting. We said, 'Okay, God, we'll leave it up to you. If you make this first child a girl, we'll baptize them all like their mom. If you make it a boy, they'll all follow their pop to his church.'"

"And you had a son."

"And then we decided it wasn't right."

"That's blasphemy, Sean! Only a man of the cloth can speak directly to God. If you continue on like this, you and all your children will burn in hellfire's damnation."

"I hear you, Father. But for now I'll have to take that chance. I know you mean well, but it's not a matter of what I want."

"Well, there's another thing I've come about."

"There's more?"

"Your very own father, Sean. He's come to know the error of his ways. He begs forgiveness. He's a broken man."

Pop gave the porch floor a kick so hard Father Cavanaugh nearly fell from his seat. He grabbed the swing's chain to regain his balance.

"So you and Mary are in cahoots."

The priest squared his shoulders and turned as a whole toward Pop. Now I could see his face.

"Mary didn't start this. George came to see me. He asked me to intervene. To act as peacemaker, if you will."

Pop kicked the floor again. This time, Father was ready. He held tight as Pop shouted, "Peacemaker? There'll never be a peace made between him and me."

"He's asking for what any decent man would honor. A meeting, Sean. A chance to talk."

Pop's boots slapped against the boards of the porch, loud and fierce as a clap of thunder.

"You dare to come here and threaten my children with hellfire's damnation and in the very same breath ask me to forgive the son of the devil himself?

"Sean!"

"If hellfire's damnation is worse than this hell on earth, I'll be surprised, Father! I'll ask you to leave my house now. If there's any true bastard on the face of this earth, it's George. You tell him to stay away."

They both stood up. Without laying a hand on him, Pop began backing Father Cavanaugh toward the stairs. The veins in his neck swelled with rage. His eyes opened wide and glared fiercely from the twisted face I had seen on the man who hit Iris's husband with the banister spindle so many years ago.

"I have three God-fearing kids who didn't do a damned thing to earn a walk in hell. If they're bastards in the eyes of your church, your church can close its eyes and forget there's any Branigans living on this hill. You'd better get off my porch, Father, before I let my temper go and throw you off!"

Now he'd done it. Made all of us bastards and got us barred from heaven in one fell swoop.

Father Cavanaugh raised one hand in the air as if he was going to give a blessing. He looked long into Pop's face and finally seemed to understand. It was too late. He'd gone too far.

Pop turned away and said it again. "There's nothing here for you, Father. No man, no wife, and not one of my children."

"Sean, please," Father Cavanaugh whispered.

Pop didn't soften. "I said get off my porch!"

This time the priest turned and walked slowly down the stairs.

But my father—my normally soft-spoken, self-contained father—didn't seem to be too pleased with himself. He threw back his head as if to ask the heavens for some advice. He went back to the swing and rocked back and forth, his boots smacking down so hard on the porch floor that I thought the boards might splinter apart. Finally, he stood and walked into the house.

I counted to four hundred, taking a big breath between every number, before I followed him into the library. He was bent over a new jigsaw puzzle. "Ave Maria" played on the Victrola. I stood by his side and watched him work for a few minutes.

He spoke without looking up. "Did your little ears hear enough?" he asked.

I felt my face grow hot.

He pushed a chair out from the table. "Come help me," he said.

I shook my head. "I don't like puzzles that have a lot of people in them."

"Why not?"

"They're too hard."

"Only if you make them seem that way. If you're patient and persistent, nothing in this life is too hard."

"I didn't know I was a bastard."

He laughed. "Only in the eyes of the Church. Like justice, those eyes are mostly blind."

"Aren't you afraid of God?"

"No, I'm not. Are you?"

"They said in Sunday school that you should never question God."

"And you shouldn't. And if I thought I was talking to God and not a priest, maybe I would have been more careful about what I said."

"You cursed."

"I did."

"You said we shouldn't ever curse."

"I did."

"Then why'd you curse?"

"Because I wanted Father Cavanaugh to know that I thought he was only a man in a robe and that he didn't scare me."

"Is that what you think?"

"Yes. That's what I believe."

"Because of what they did to the Mollies?"

He laughed heartily but kept his eyes on the puzzle board. "I don't give a damn what they did to the Mollies. That's the bailiwick of your mother. She cares about all that old stuff. I've got my hands full right here with new stuff."

"Do you think God will punish you?"

He reached out and gestured with his hand that I should come to him. I slid under his arm.

"If I believed that God punishes people for things they have no control over," he said, "then I would spend all my time like those priests and Aunt Mary Margaret, on my knees in the church. I don't believe in a God like that. I'm not even sure I believe in any God. But I do know that the rules those churches and priests make for the rest of us are not necessarily in our best interests.

They're to serve themselves and their network of churches. That doesn't mean they're bad. They're a little shortsighted."

"What do you believe in?"

"You. Me. Your mother. Your sister. Your brother. And Magee."

"Do you think Magee will come this year?"

"Any day now. You keep watching." He laughed again. "And let me know if you see any more priests coming up this way. I'll go hide in the woods."

I decided he was smarter than any old priest. I sat in the chair he had pulled out and began to work on the puzzle.

Three days later, Magee came walking up the new mining road below the Red Ash culm banks. He wore the same oversized coat, new brown boots, and a Scotsman's wool cap pulled over his eyes, and he carried the same old canvas and wood-framed back-pack stuffed with everything necessary for him to live.

Mom saw him coming and let out a yell that brought all of us to the basket of wet wash she had been hanging on the clothesline.

Pop was the first to get to him. He pulled the pack from the old man's narrow shoulders and hefted it over one arm as if it were light as a feather. The two of them sent waves of laughter ahead as they ducked their heads under the blossoming chokecherry trees.

I liked to watch Pop with Magee. He saved up a lot of laugh-ter for his friend, and he became more lively and lighter in spirit. Even levelheaded Mom seemed younger and happier when Magee visited. She had already stuffed a couple of chickens and laid them in the roasting pan, and as soon as we were in the house she told me to start peeling potatoes—a whole potful for mashing with garlic and butter. Potatoes were Magee's favorite food. She sent

Sally to the cellar for a three big jars of jelly. She put one on the table for supper, then wiped the dust off the other two and sat them on a corner of the china cabinet. I knew that she would carefully place them into Magee's pack before he left. I also knew that Magee would be off again at first light. He never stayed longer than one overnight. That was his way.

While we cooked, the two men sat on the front porch swing and caught up with all the news of the past year. They drank their coffee straight. Pop had told us that Magee never was much of a boozer because he believed that hopping freights while three sheets to the wind was the surest way for a man to end up legless or dead.

When I was finally relieved of kitchen duties, I went out and sat on the porch stairs. Magee had taken off his coat and slung it over the porch railing. He had lost weight. His Adam's apple stood out from the collar of a worn sweater so oversized that it lay in folds over his chest. As big as it was, though, when he stretched both arms out across the back of the swing it fell to his sides and allowed the outline of his rib bones to show through the woven wool. And his skin was burnished to the color of the bark on the spruce tree down at Mrs. Donal's. When he smiled, his pink gums contrasted sharply with his bronzed lips. He caught me studying him and laughed.

"You look like you seen a ghost," he said.

I was afraid I had.

Mom called us for supper. I watched Magee swirl mashed potatoes and gravy round and round his plate. The good slice of chicken he usually cut up carefully and ate with gusto lay hidden beneath the soggy mound of potatoes. He didn't slather butter and jelly on his slices of bread but picked at the corner of one slice and then folded the jelly to the inside and pocketed the whole thing. He talked really fast to cover up the fact that he wasn't eating.

He pointed his fork at Sally and laughed. "You should have seen your pop the day I first laid eyes on him. Scrawny little kid with long straight hair. And dirty? You should have seen how dirty! He was wearing a pair of pants that were at least two sizes too big and frayed on the ends of both legs."

"Matthew's pants!" Pop interrupted. "The only ones I had that I thought were decent enough to travel in."

Pop had never before allowed stories about himself to be told in his presence. Whenever Mom launched into the past, he would stand, excuse himself, and quickly walk out. Mom's explanation for his behavior had always been that it hurt him to remember. But Magee's stories didn't seem to have the same effect on him. I reasoned that it might be because they had both been there and experienced the events and so Magee might have a right to tell the tale. Whatever the reason, Pop now allowed the telling and I knew my notebook would have a lot of material added before the night was over—hopefully about Mike.

Magee leaned back and stuck his thumbs in the belt of his pants. "So there's this train moving across the Jersey City yard, going back and forth to couple up the freight, and I'm standing out of sight on one of the already-loaded boxcars. There's this one railroad bull in that yard who'd beat a bum's head in as soon as look at him. I'm watching out for him as the train is finally getting on its way, when I see this scrawny kid running alongside the car like he's got riding on his brain. He's so close to the tracks that I think he's going to kill himself. I step up to get a closer look and I see that he's pulling along a bigger but even skinnier kid who can't run so good. The bigger kid is kind of hobbling along, slowing the determined one down. I know that as soon as we get the signal, that sucker of a train is going to take off like a bat outta hell. I lean a little farther out the door and this kid catches my eye. Just glances up and flashes a look. Desperate, this kid is. Running away from something pretty bad.

"Something in the back of my mind says, 'If you don't help this guy, he's gonna die.' So, without thinking about it too much, I step out to the open door and I holler, 'Kid! Here! This way!' And I reach out my hand.

"He ain't asking any questions. He hands off his brother and he keeps pumping those skinny legs while he hangs onto the door slider. I hoist in the taller kid. He's light as a feather. The train is picking up speed and I gotta get the first guy in before we pass that bastard of a railroad dick." Magee wet his lips with a sip of his water.

"He's got a good hold on the door guard and he's running as fast as he can, but the train's moving faster still. I think, 'He's gonna lose a leg. He's gonna fall and fly right onto the tracks.' I seen one of his shoes fall off and I grab hold of his shirt and start to pull. He gets his bare foot over the sill into the car and his brother grabs hold of it. He's stretched halfway in and halfway out. The train is going at a clip now and his free leg is flying out behind him. He can't let go of his hold on the door guard. He's too afraid or too weak to move his hand up.

"I laid down on my belly and leaned out the door to try and pry his hands loose. His brother and me are putting everything we got into the pulling. When he finally decides to let go, he lets loose both hands and we send him flying over me. He lands on the floor by his brother. I say to them, 'We have to get into the corner where nobody can see us,' and your pop starts to cry. It's the saddest sound I've ever heard. We're coming up on a lantern and I know that the railroad bull is going to be there. 'Come on, kid,' I say. 'We have to get outta sight or they're going to get us all.'"

Pop interrupted. "That's the first thing I remember about him." He stamped his foot and laughed. "I can still hear that gravelly voice in the dark car saying, 'Come on, kid, you have to get outta sight or they're going to get us all.'"

"So the three of us crawl into a corner. Your pop's all scraped up and his tears are washing the dirt from his face. When he rubs his eyes, I can see the freckles on his nose and cheeks. He's huffing and puffing, but he looks up at me and he says, sudden and sunny as he could be, 'Hey, mister, thanks!' and I know I got a survivor on my hands. I know he's got what it takes and ain't nothing going to get him down for long.

"Now, the brother—that's another story. The brother's a little slower, a little weaker. I look at them and I say to myself, 'Magee, they got a chance. You help them a little and they got a chance.'"

Mom began slicing into an iced apple cake.

Magee looked at her and then he looked back at Pop. "Did you ever think, then, that you could be sitting at a table like this now?"

Pop let his eyes fall on each of us along the big table. He blessed us with his eyes and for a moment I thought I could see in his face what Magee must have seen.

"Not a chance in hell," he said.

As we girls did the dishes, Magee and Pop went out front to the porch swing with their coffee and cigarettes. Mom took off her apron, reached up into the china cupboard, and took down the box that held Pop's mouth organ. She went to the porch and pretty soon we could hear "Tennessee Waltz" coming through the open front windows. By the time we got out there, the two men were tapping their feet and rolling their eyes as they competed with one another playing "Beer Barrel Polka" and "Pittsburgh, Pennsylvania." As darkness fell, we all leaned back in our places on the porch and listened quietly as the men talked.

"The years have sure been good to you, Sean."

"In lots of ways they have."

"What we would have given in the old days to be able to sit on a covered porch, stomachs full, smoking cigarettes and knowing that we'd both survive with all our God-given parts intact."

"Ah, Magee, we're both lucky we haven't lost a leg or two."

"You did lose your shoes that first day though."

"Shoes? Hell, they were just a couple of soles tied onto my feet with a lace."

"Eight years old and on your own. And with a brother to take care of and no shoes to speak of."

"Wasn't the first time I was barefoot."

"Going to find your Aunt Maura."

"Didn't know what city. Didn't know what state. But we knew it was the train that would take us there."

"She was a fine woman."

"Yeah. Too bad we didn't know our arses from a hole in the ground and were heading in the wrong direction."

They both laughed uproariously. Mom couldn't hold back a smile, even though I knew she'd probably heard the story many times before.

Then Pop's voice saddened a little. "Anywhere was better than where we'd been."

"Your old man was pretty fierce."

"The bastard!"

"Well, you got away."

"We did, didn't we? He never got his grubby paws on us again."

"And look at you now."

"I've been damned lucky."

"Aunt Maura would say you were blessed by God."

"Yes, she would. But if she knew the whole story about Mike, she might say something different. If we were truly blessed by God, we'd have Mike sitting here between us, telling a joke and having a smoke. Maybe drinking a beer or two."

"He did learn to like his beer."

"Too much, some say."

"Yeah, well, you know that was a setup. You know the boy wasn't capable of anything they said. You know that, Sean. Same as I know it. In my heart."

"He worshipped you, Magee," Mom said suddenly from her place in the corner of the porch. "You were his true pop. You were the only father he knew."

"They were both my boys." Magee's voice held a note of pride. "When I saw them huddled in that boxcar corner, I knew God had some purpose for my being there. I took it serious. They never let me down."

"And you never let them down. You and Maura. If it hadn't been for you two, both those boys would have been dead. Starved or killed by a train or worse."

"I did what God expected me to do."

Pop struck a match. As he reached across and lit Magee's cigarette, I could see the look of concern that crossed his face.

"You know, Magee," he said, "you could stay with us for a while. You don't have to be in a hurry to get out West. You could rest awhile, get a couple of good meals under your belt."

"What? You trying to tie an old man down?" Magee laughed and inhaled deeply on the cigarette. "The day I miss that Chicago freight in the spring will be one of my last on earth!"

"Stay with us awhile," Mom said softly. "The kids would like to get to know you better and I'd like to pamper you a bit."

"Ain't you got enough mouths to feed already?"

"One more won't make one bit of difference."

"Ah, Bessie, you know how I am. I haven't spent more than a night in one place in forty years. Staying still makes my legs hurt and my arms jumpy. I got a lot of friends left to see, and as I figure, I ain't got that much time left on this earth to see them."

Pop gave Mom a small smile that meant she'd probably said enough. He leaned his shoulders against the swing and threw his head back so he could see the stars in the heavens.

"I only need to look up at Orion climbing across the sky and I can see you on a freight somewhere, doors open, fresh air flying in, wheels clattering, and you smiling at our friend up there. You used to tell us when we were kids that if we ever got lost from one another we'd need only look up to know we weren't alone."

"And your lovely Aunt Maura said we should listen for our songs and we could be together."

"And, you know, I only need to hear the melody of 'Red Sails in the Sunset' and I can see you and Aunt Maura—how you used to look—the two of you, dancing in your bare feet across her front room. Her in her ruffled dress. You in a clean shirt. Me and Mike sitting on the sofa and laughing whenever you tripped over Maura's tiny feet. Her girls standing in the doorway, giggling. I always remember those days, Magee. And I never forget to say a thanks to you and God."

I ducked my head because I couldn't bear to see Pop's sadness. Mom broke the tension, said we should all go to bed and let the men talk. But even in the deepening darkness I could see that her eyes and cheeks were wet with tears. I got to my feet and hugged both Pop and Magee good night.

I honestly intended to go straight to my bed and fall right off to sleep, but I could hear their deep voices coming off the porch and I wanted to have one more look at Orion and make a pledge that I, too, would always whisper a thanks to Magee.

My windows were open. I knelt and removed a sliding screen, pushed my head out, and craned my neck to locate Orion. The roof overhang blocked my view. When I heard the voices from below and smelled the tang of cigarettes, I lost any inclination I'd had to climb into my bed. I laid my head on the windowsill to listen.

"I keep remembering how you boys talked to one another," Magee said. "How nobody else could understand Mike but you could translate for him as fast as he made the sounds. How much he depended on you."

"Yeah, but after a while you could understand him just as well. The first time you laughed at one of his jokes without me speaking for him, his eyes lit up like a Christmas tree. He was so happy that someone else in the world could hear him."

"I always told Maura that you learned to shut up and listen from taking care of him. That he taught you as much as you taught him."

"We were always in it together. But it was you who saved us from that bastard George. He's back you know."

"George?"

"One and the same. Contacted Mary Margaret and the local priest. Wants to talk to me. Wants to meet my family."

"Holy Christ! What are you gonna do?"

"I ain't going to do anything. The bastard has no business here. He'll stay away if he knows what's good for him."

"Think about what's good for you. You might want to get it off your chest. Let bygones be bygones."

"Never! He's dead to me. He's been dead to me for thirty-six years. He killed Matthew and my ma with his meanness. Me and Mike saw what he did. He hit her until she stayed down and never got up again."

I'd never heard this part of Pop's story before. I was tempted to climb out on the roof to be sure I didn't miss a word, but I knew Magee would hear me. Pop always said that Magee could hear a train whistle a hundred miles away.

"He deserves to rot in the hell of his own making," Magee said. His declaration was followed by a short silence broken only by the gentle creaking of the swing. "Aunt Maura, though. Now there was a gal that never let up. She was a feisty one. She never stopped fighting for you."

"She was our only hope. Came to Jersey right after Ma died. Brought us on the train to Wilkes-Barre. She bought us sandwiches and candy suckers. I had grape. Mike had lemon. Matthew had cherry. We passed them off between us and they lasted the entire trip."

"Mike always did like lemon. Remember when we first landed in Florida and I pulled those lemons off that tree?"

"And you taught us to crack an egg, gulp it down, and follow it with a suck of lemon. 'It's like lemonade,' you said. Jesus, how many times did we get by on stolen eggs and raided lemons?"

"You two remembered all the lessons. Learned them well."

"It don't seem right that Matthew should have died and Mike been killed yet the old man is still walking this earth."

"You gotta let it go, Sean boy. It'll kill you."

"I did let it go. A long time ago. Now he's brought it back."

The night air had turned chilly. I shivered in my sleeveless gown. I crept back to my bed and buried my head under the covers.

~

In the morning I jumped out of bed and dressed as soon as I heard voices. Magee was famous for up and leaving without a trace. I wanted to see him off. He and Pop were in the kitchen, both fully dressed and with their boots on. I don't think they'd slept all night.

Mom was at the sink, already washing up their breakfast dishes. "Pop is going to walk Magee down to the railroad tracks to catch the morning coal train," she said.

"Can I go with them?" I begged.

Magee looked past me to Mom and nodded.

"Okay," she said.

I found my shoes as quickly as I could but I still had to chase after them. The sun was peeking over the mountain and already hot. When I caught up, they were smoking again and not talking. I took Pop's hand and scuffed along on the dusty stripping road, thinking that we were lucky the coal company trucks weren't running on the lower road.

I thought they must be all talked out, but then Magee said, "You know that thing you were telling me about before? The thing what Mike told you before he died?"

Pop looked down at me and answered carefully. "Yeah? What about it?"

"Was that all there was to that?"

They walked along in silence until Pop said, "Little pitchers have big ears."

"Just a yes or no will do."

"No."

"Then there are things you're not telling me?"

"Yes."

"And do you want to tell me now?"

"No."

"Did you ever speak to the uncle about it?"

"I did."

"And did you get an answer?"

"Only lies."

"And did you do anything about those lies?"

Pop looked up at the sun and it seemed like its light must be painful to him. His face scrunched up like Sally's did when she was about to howl. His lips trembled and his cheek twitched. He didn't answer but bent down and laid his hand flat along one rail of the train track.

"Train left the mountain," he said. "It's on its way." They stepped into the middle of the tracks and headed north.

Pop had secrets. Big secrets. And I wanted to know them. I wanted to ask what uncle they were referring to and what that uncle lied about. Were they speaking of the famous Uncle Ira who seemed to be everywhere and nowhere in my family's history?

And what could be so bad in Pop's history that he couldn't tell his best friend Magee the details? Oh, how I wanted answers.

However, I had trouble keeping up because the railroad ties were far between and my legs were still too short to catch each one in the way the two tall men could. At the cut in the hill, where a rock face caused the tracks to narrow around a sharp curve, Pop stuck out his hand. Magee took it in his and held it long and hard.

"You're a good man, Sean Branigan. You've always been a good man and you'll always be a good man. Whatever had to be done, had to be done. Never doubt that, you hear?"

"I hope to God you're right." He reached down and read the rail again. "Coming down the first hill," he said. "You better get against that rock and I'd better get the hell out of here."

Magee smiled and shifted his pack onto his back. He raised one hand, then suddenly bent and kissed me softly on the cheek.

"You watch out for this pop of yours, you hear?" he whispered. "Sometimes he just needs a hand to hold."

I nodded. We turned and hurried back down the tracks and then across the road to the wreck of the old boiler house that had saved Lenny's life during his winter walk. Pop helped me climb to the top of the pile of bricks that covered the ruin and we sat down. A locomotive came into the cut, followed by a pusher car and many carloads of blue coal.

The train screeched and hissed as it strained to slow on the steep grade. I counted fourteen coal cars and six boxcars before Magee jumped. One second he was backed straight up against the slab of rock and the next he was disappearing into a crack of an unlocked boxcar door. He was gone.

We watched the train until the caboose came by and the brakeman waved a cheery hand. I waved with both hands. I hoped that Magee still watched and knew my waving was for him.

My brother and sister had long argued that I was Pop's favorite kid, but the truth was, Pop was my favorite person in the whole world. We thought alike and could give each other quiet spaces when there was some thinking to be done. I sat next to him on that pile of rubble and let him be. He stared off long and hard after the screeching train, then dropped his head into his hands and leaned his elbows on his knees.

I turned and studied the burning mountain. Its treeless white ash slope was split repeatedly by smoking vents that spewed blue haze into the cloudless sky. Only one culm bank capped with dead birches, the smoldering town dump, and a remnant of road separated it from where we stood.

I moved down one side of the brick rubble and into the small entry hole of the boiler house. The dim space was dry. A charred circle told where fires had burned. A stack of dry kindling waited in one corner.

I reached up and removed the loosened brick. The box of safety matches and newspaper squares of dry newspaper jingled with a few coins. I replaced it and moved back outside.

Pop was sitting upright and staring after the long-gone train.

I sat beside him. "Pop, how'd you learn to remember and know so much?"

"Like what?" He turned his full attention to me.

"Like how long it takes for the train to come around the mountain, and where it's easiest to get on board."

"That's no trick. If you hop freights long enough and you want to live and not go to jail, you pick up stuff like that."

"What kind of stuff?"

"Oh, the types of trains, what kind of a load they're carrying, the engineers, the different lines, the railroad bulls. You gotta know where trains slow down to make a grade or change to another track. Those are the places you can get on and off the easiest. But you also gotta know where the railroad bulls are, and who they are, and what their schedules are. If you know when a train is passing a certain spot and who the engineer is, then you know how much he slows down and where he speeds up. And if you can remember what railroad bull is working the line, you are way ahead of the other guys."

"I like the railroad guys. They always wave to me. Did you like them? When you were a kid?"

"When we were kids, some of the bulls turned their backs on us when they knew we were looking to get on or off. But some of them were company men. Those guys would beat the living daylights out of us if they could get their hands on us. Some of them were darned mean. If we were lucky, the jails would already be full and the local authorities would let us go. If we weren't so lucky, they'd throw us in the slammer and let us fend for ourselves. Pretty soon, you either learn or you don't survive."

"Did you ever get caught?"

"Oh, boy, yes. Lots of times. Especially when we were first starting out. We'd end up thrown in an orphanage or a reform school with a lot of other poor kids. They could be pretty bad places. A lot of mean guards watching a lot of mean kids. There was never enough food, and what there was was pretty bad."

"How'd you get out?"

"Usually Aunt Maura would help us there. If we could get word to her, she'd come and try to get us—legal like. But she wasn't our guardian. After a while she had some bigwig in government get her some fake papers that said she was our guardian, but not everybody took those at face value. Sometimes they wouldn't let us out without a judge's ruling, and then we'd have to stay and do their hard work. First chance we got, we'd run away."

"What kind of work did you have to do?"

"Mostly farm stuff. Hoeing and planting and picking. They let Mike sit with the girls and do the cleaning of the vegetables and the canning of the fruits. He always had a way with the girls, even though he was a cripple. He was a handsome fella, but a little slow. Didn't seem to bother the girls though."

"Did you have to do the remembering for him, too?"

"For Mike? Heck no. He was the detail man. He could keep schedules and names in his head like nobody's business. He didn't have much horse sense. He had to have a lot of time to think things out, couldn't think fast enough in a pinch. That was my job. If I said run, he ran. If I said jump, he jumped. But if he said O'Malley was manning the junction between the Pacific Northern and the Kansas Topeka at three in the morning, then I knew not to count on getting off anywhere near there. He was real good with that kind of thing."

"So what was Magee's job?"

"Hah! Magee's job was finding the handout, the food supply, and the job picking melons for all you can eat. Magee knew the farmers and the ranchers and the towns that stuck their hands out and shook on a deal and didn't turn everybody away. He'd say, 'If we hoof it up thisaway for about three mile, we'll find the little town of Salina. Those folks are good folks. If there's a job that needs doing, they'll lead us to it. If there's a church kitchen that has some leftovers, they'll show us where it is. So, come on, boys, let's check it out.'"

"Does he still do that?"

"Yeah, I suppose he does."

"How come he doesn't have any family?"

"He has one brother. He had a wife and baby once, when he was real young. They were killed in a big earthquake out in San Francisco. A lot of buildings collapsed and there were bad fires."

"Do we get earthquakes here?"

"Nah. Nothing like that around here." He looked over his shoulder and pointed his chin at the mountain. "Except for that damned fire."

"Will Magee go see his brother?"

"I dunno. Last I heard he was working a mining claim in Alaska."

"Did you visit him?"

"Heck no. There's no trains go all the way up there. You have to take a boat or swim. And damned if I ever learned to swim."

"Could you walk to Alaska?"

"Couldn't when we was out that way. Now I hear they punched a road all the way up there. Right through Canada they took it during the war. I bet that's where Magee is going. I bet he's going to hitch a ride to Alaska and see his brother."

"Pop?"

"What?"

"Magee looked kind of sick."

"I know."

"Do you think he could make it to Alaska now?"

"No. But I'd like to imagine him doing that."

"I wish he would have stayed."

"He couldn't, Molly. He's lived most of his life sleeping under the stars; he wouldn't be happy sleeping in a house."

"We could have made a bed for him under the porch."

He laughed and ruffled my hair. "He's got a lot of people to see. Maybe he will make it to Alaska and see that brother. Let's believe that's where he goes. How about it? Can you picture him in the land of the midnight sun, talking and talking to his brother? Can you see him doing that?"

I closed my eyes and tried to picture that, but all I could see was that plate of food that stayed uneaten and the bony points of Magee's collarbones. I shook my head.

"Okay," he said. "Maybe I'm asking too much. Let's picture him lying on the wooden floor of a boxcar. The sun is shining through and he's smiling and he pulls himself up so he's sitting with his back against the car. He reaches into his backpack and he pulls out one of Mom's loaves of bread and he breaks off a big hunk and he says 'My goodness, Bessie, that's mighty good bread.'"

I shook my head again, but I smiled because I could almost hear him.

"So, you tell me," he said. "You tell me how you can see Magee."

"I can see him dancing with a lady in a ruffled dress."

"Can you hear the music?"

"Yep."

"What is it?"

"It's 'Red Sails in the Sunset.'"

He stood suddenly and pulled me up by the hand. "Yep," he said. "You got the picture, all right."

~

Sally was sitting alone on the flat rock face that made up the widest part of the trail through the orchard. Pop believed that sad people would ask for company when they were good and ready, but as we neared the spot where the path split, I pulled her way. He released my hand and walked on. I sat beside Sally on the smooth rocks.

"What're you doing?"

"Feeling the sun on my back." A pad of paper and a handful of colored pencils lay on the ground beside her.

"What are you drawing?"

"Cartoons."

"Can I see?"

She had drawn a clown, but with the facial features of a man and the body of a woman. The face had bushy eyebrows and long eyelashes and was surrounded by hair that curled as wildly as mine. Sally had colored the flared poodle skirt bright pink and had filled in the puckish lips with the same color. She had posed high-heeled shoes on thick ankles, but had drawn in dainty hands that drooped from the wrist. A white basket-weave purse dangled from fingers with long, pink-painted nails.

"Does it have a name?" I asked. I held the tablet up and twisted the picture in the air to make it dance.

"Jack."

"Why not Jacqueline?"

"Because it's really Jack." Her tone was more mad than sad. Mom said it was a good sign when sadness turned to anger.

"Jack who?"

"My so-called boyfriend Jack. The one from Scranton."

"Why'd you put a skirt on him?"

"'Cause that's what he liked to wear. He liked to wear my skirts."

"Oh, come on."

"And my shoes and my nylons and my sweater and even my bra." There was no stopping her now. She tore the picture from my hands and jabbed one finger at the clown. "And that's *my* lipstick. And that's *my* mascara. And he curled his hair with *my* rollers. Does that answer all your questions?"

I stared at her, unbelieving.

She tore the picture into tiny pieces and threw them into the air. A slight breeze blew the confetti into the yellow hay of the field.

"Pop said he's a transgrestite, or something like that. A man who likes to dress up in girls' clothing."

"You're kidding."

"No, I'm not. He dressed in my clothes and he went out with other men—on dates!"

"No!"

"Yes, he did. And I thought he was so cute because he liked to look at my clothes and he liked to go shopping with me and Janet and he liked to pick out lipsticks for me. Always pink, even though I like rusty red."

I remembered the girl I had seen crying on Lillian's stairs. I asked her if that was him and she stood up and looked like she wanted to run somewhere, but then she sat back down.

"That was him. Pop had to go up and ask him for my clothes."

That made me laugh, and she snickered a little too. "What did Pop say?"

"He knocked on the door, shook Jack's hand, and said, 'I'm Sean Branigan. I'm Sally's father and I'm here for her clothes.'"

"No!"

"Yep. Like it was as normal as pie for a big, tall boy like Jack to wear a poodle skirt."

"Did he laugh?"

"Who, Pop?"

"Yes. Did Mom laugh?"

"No. Nobody laughed. And I was the only one crying. Mom held my hand tight but didn't say a word. Jack said, 'If you'll hang on a minute, I'll get them for you.' He closed the door and we waited. When he came back he had packed everything nice and neat in a bag. But he still had all his makeup on and his hair curled and his legs were shaved smooth."

"Wow!"

"Don't tell anybody. Please. I liked him. I really did. He was so nice."

"Did you kiss him?"

She studied her hands. "Yes. I even Frenched with him."

"Yuck!" Now I had to stand and move. "Yuck! Yuck! Yuck! How could you?"

"Pop said that he probably likes boys and girls. That he was a sicko."

"Was he mad at you?"

"Pop? No. He wasn't even mad at Jack. He was nice to him. Told him thanks for the clothes and then said that he was taking me home and that he would like it if Jack never came near me again."

"What did you say?"

"I said, 'I'm sorry' and I ran down the stairs."

"No wonder you were crying. I would have cried too. How did you catch him wearing your clothes?"

Sally picked up a stone and threw it into the field. "He didn't know I was back. I looked for him, but he was never around. I thought he had another girlfriend already. Then, I couldn't find some of my clothes and I blamed Janet for taking them. She got really mad."

I sat quietly and waited for her to continue.

"She had already moved in with her mother in the apartment up the street. I went up to say I was sorry for calling her a thief. We were sitting on the building front stoop when I saw Jack's car pull up. I ran down the sidewalk to catch him before he went inside. At first I thought he was a girl and that Jack had liked her enough to let her use his car. But then I realized the girl was wearing my clothes and I got mad. So I went right up and I said, 'Hey! You're wearing my skirt!' And he said, 'Sally! I guess you caught me.' It was so embarrassing. I ran. I told Lillian I wanted to die. I wanted to die! She called Pop."

"I was there when he talked to you."

"I told him something was wrong with my boyfriend. That he liked wearing my nylons. He asked me if I was crying and I said, 'Yes, damn it.' He said, 'You go find Lillian for me, will you?' And I did, even though I was so embarrassed I wanted to fall into a hole and die. I heard Lillian cackling on the phone but then she got serious and she hung up. She said we should sit in the parlor and wait. I said I wanted to go to my room and she said, 'No, your father said you should wait with me in the parlor and that's what we'll do.' But she wanted to laugh, I could tell. She went into the bathroom for a while and then came out and we sat in the parlor and waited."

"I wish I'd looked at him better."

"You saw enough. He was an ugly girl." She started to giggle and so did I. "But this is a secret. You can't tell anyone."

"I won't. Nobody would believe me anyway."

"I have to be sure. You tell me a secret of yours and then I'll know you can't tell anyone else or I'll tell yours."

"I won't tell anyone." I crossed my heart.

"I guess you're too young for secrets."

"I am not."

"Tell me one."

"Remember that big boy, Chuck, that saved me from the river?"

"Yes."

"He likes me. And I like him." It felt good to say that because it made it more real.

"He's too old for you."

"But he likes me, I can tell."

"You're too young for a boy to like you."

"I am not! Ronald Miller likes me too."

"Ronald? What makes you think that?"

"Because he tried to French me when I fell at the pond." Saying that out loud made it too real. I shivered as goose bumps arose on my bare arms.

She sat up straight and stared. "He's a bad boy. You shouldn't have anything to do with him."

"I don't *want* to have anything to do with him."

"You should tell Pop."

"It's okay. Chuck stopped Ronald from bothering me. Chuck held my hand and skated with me."

"And that's all?"

"Of course, that's all. I like him."

"I still think you should tell Pop about Ronald."

"This is a secret, remember? If you tell anyone, I'll blab about Jack all over town and everywhere else."

"Boys like Ronald can do bad things."

"I'm not afraid. I told him if he ever did that again, I'd tell Pop. He won't bother me."

"You never know."

"I know. Pop came to the skating pond that night and Ronald took off. He's as scared of Pop as everybody else around here.

"And Chuck and you skated?"

"And talked."

"Wow! He's a popular boy."

"But he's really nice. And I like him. A lot."

She smiled and picked up her pad of paper. She drew a picture of a boy and girl kissing.

"Here," she said. "This is a remembrance of my dating a transgrestite and you skating with a really nice boy."

"Color it," I said. "Make the boy's hair blond and his eyes blue."

She picked up her pencils and set to work.

~

As the second girl in my family, I received plenty of hand-me-downs but rarely anything new. For my thirteenth birthday, Lillian bought me an entirely new outfit. Mom cut and rolled my bristly hair. Sally applied a few strokes of mascara to my pale eyelashes and some of her pink pearl lipstick to my mouth.

When I looked in the mirror, I saw a pretty stranger with wide eyes, high cheekbones, and a tiny face framed in soft curls. The change made me feel so self-conscious that I ran through the house and out the door as quickly as I could. As I passed Pop on the porch, he let out one of those flirty cat whistles that boys use to call attention to pretty girls. I didn't stop, but I was pleased. I couldn't wait to meet Connie at the corner hangout and see her reaction to my new look.

Halfway down the hill I slowed to watch a big man, chest deep in a four-by-eight-foot trench, sweat and curse as he wrestled with a jackhammer. We had been plagued with low water pressure since the winter freezes and Pop was sure the waterline had broken somewhere on the hill. Next to the hole, on the street level, another man stood with his arms folded over the handle of a shovel. He shouted to make himself heard over the noise of the hammer.

"Nice day, pretty lady."

I ducked my head and hurried past. The jackhammer made a sucking sound as it cut through layers of wet clay and stones. The operator didn't look up.

At the corner of Fitch Lane, I paused. Maybe I wasn't quite ready for Connie to see this change in me.

A sudden pressure dulled all sound and pressed to the center of my skull. A burst of cold air smashed against me from behind. I felt the sting of hail in my hair and a cold wetness coming through the back of my new blouse. I raised one arm to shield my face as I turned.

The man with the shovel was lying on the pavement. Beside him, the thick hose that powered the jackhammer shook and jerked wildly.

Pop was sprinting down the hill. In a trance, I began to walk toward him. Neighbors ran out of their houses. Someone yelled, "Call an ambulance!" A woman screamed.

I felt Pop's shaking arms surround me. He pressed my face into his shirt, lifted me, and carried me Mrs. Donal's porch.

"Keep her here," he said. No one heard. I trailed him back to the hole in the street.

Water bubbled into the pit. The driller lay unmoving next to his wriggling jackhammer. He was making a wet, sucking noise through a mask of blood, hanging skin, and yellow mud. One eye hung down where his cheek should have been.

Pop and another man jumped into the pit. Together they heaved the jackhammer out. It rolled slowly down the incline and then, caught at the end of its tether, careened back and forth like a dog struggling to get loose from a tight leash.

Neighbors dragged the man who had held the shovel out of the way. One man crawled over the equipment trailer, found the control switch, and turned off the compressor. Pop tore off his shirt, lifted the driller's head out of the mud, and wiped at the hole where his mouth should have been. The pit was rapidly filling with water.

He took the man's shoulders while the other guy took his feet and they counted aloud to three. With deep grunts and a mighty heave they slung the bloody body out of the pit. It landed on the pavement with a sharp slurping sound. Pop climbed out of the hole, rolled up his shirt, and put it under the man's head. He pulled off his white undershirt and carefully pushed the dangling eye back into its socket before he wrapped the shirt around the man's head so that it covered both eyes.

As Pop stretched to full height, his head and shoulders loomed over the crowd so that he seemed to me to be that jolly giant on the vegetable cans, except that the wet clay had turned his pants yellow instead of green.

He bent back over the injured man, straightened his arms and legs, took a blanket from someone in the crowd, and covered him. Then he did something I never could have done. He wrapped a corner of that blanket around his finger, gently wiped out the man's mouth, pushed aside the mud where his nose should have been, and carefully pulled on the man's tongue. I heard a gurgle, followed by gasping breaths.

My own gurgling stomach reneged. I threw up all over my new blouse.

An hour later, with my freshly washed hair back to its natural frizz, I sat in the kitchen and watched Mom mix bleach and slivers of soap in a basin of water to soak my soiled clothes. John Hale sat at the table to question me. I felt pretty important as he wrote down my every word.

"How deep would you say they had dug?"

"The man was up to his chest," I said. "I could see the cigarette pack in his pocket."

"And where was the other guy?"

"He was standing next to the hole."

Mom interrupted. "What do you think it was, John?"

"Methane gas," he said. "I think they hit a big pocket not five feet below the surface of the street."

Mom nodded her head. "From one of the old shafts sealed from the mine fire."

"Yep. The poor guy tapped into it, triggered the explosion, and ruptured the water main." He turned back to me. "You're lucky, Molly, that you didn't stop to watch."

"I thought about it."

"Thank heavens, you didn't," Mom said. "You're so small, it might have killed you." She dropped my blouse into the basin and quickly hugged me. "My God, when I think what might have happened."

"But it didn't," I said.

"Luck of the Irish." John winked at me and went back to his report.

"No, it's problem number three for Molly. I can rest easy now, as far as she's concerned."

"Three?" I asked. "Where'd you come up with three?"

"The drowning, the shooting, and now this." As soon as Mom said that she colored red.

John Hale's head came up from his writing. "Shooting? What shooting?"

"Oh, her father was teaching her to use the twenty-two," Mom fibbed.

I don't know if Pop heard that from the porch or if he happened to come in at the right time. "The Bureau of Mines is here," he said.

Mom turned away and busied herself at the sink. I followed Pop and John Hale down the hill, where three men in suits gestured and conversed as they watched a fourth man place sawhorses and warning lanterns around the coffin-shaped opening in the street.

"Is it a major shaft?" Pop asked as he joined the circle of men.

One of the strangers shook his head. "Couldn't be. Might be an old air hole, or maybe a bore pit. No mine shafts under the town."

"There's a shaft up the hill, not fifty yards. Seems logical someone could have extended it."

"Not without asking us," the man puffed up his chest and smiled.

"Can't regulate what you can't see," John Hale said.

The man moved away from the pit toward his shiny black car.

"Lots of subsidence in the last year," Pop said as he followed him to the car. "Makes a man think that the mine fire might be spreading."

The three bureau men exchanged glances before the same guy answered for all of them.

"No. No mine fire here. Stopped years ago, up on the ridge." He opened his car door and put one polished black shoe onto the carpeted floor. "No one needs to worry about the fire. It's under control."

"What do you plan to do with the hole?" John Hale asked. "And the pipe?"

"A crew is on its way to fix the pipe. You'll have water by tonight. Nothing to worry about, trust me. We'll have a truck bring out some rock and fill and it will look as good as new by tomorrow." He swung into the car and pulled the door closed.

"That methane wasn't here when they put the waterline in, and it shouldn't have been here when they dug it out," Pop said as we watched the car drive off.

"If there's no mine shaft below, then there's no need for an air shaft, is there?"

John tossed a stone into a crack at the center of the hole. It took a long time to reach bottom, and when it did it made the plunking sound of stone on water.

"Bunch of sharks," Pop said. "They'll let the companies burn us out before they'll tell them no."

"I'll look into it, Sean. I'll let you know what I find."

"We'd appreciate that. And John?"

"Yeah?"

"Don't forget the party on the fourth. We'll be tapping a few kegs."

"Wouldn't miss it," John said. "I'll bring the wife."

The next morning we had water again and only a scar of new asphalt showed where the injured men had lain.

That same day the wire factory officially closed its doors. Pop would draw no pay until work began at the Jersey plant in September.

CHAPTER SEVENTEEN

Sally started full time at the shoe factory at the end of June. Marty flew home for leave two days later. He was excited about his first airplane ride, but his girlfriend had split up with him. He moped about the house, sometimes slamming doors loudly, sometimes sitting sullenly on the back porch and chain-smoking. He had no car, he had no girl, and most of his friends were working two jobs. It was Pop who suggested that he get in the Chevy and go swimming. Mom's belief that I was now safe from her superstition about the number three cleared the way for me to go with him. She made me promise that I would remember the previous year's near drowning and not take any foolish chances.

We set off for Solomon's Creek on the opposite side of our mountain. The icy creek started as a spring near Mountain Top, dropped through a gap in the ridge, and flowed rapidly toward the Susquehanna. In the early 1900s the coal companies had used huge sandstones left by ancient glaciers to form a series of narrow pools alternating with rocky falls. The pools provided water for the steam plants that powered the now defunct Ashley rail planes. The smooth, undulating surfaces of the sandstone rocks made sunbathing possible around the pool we called Sandy's.

We drove along an unpaved road that alternately crossed and paralleled the rusting rails left by the planes operation. At times Marty was forced to slow nearly to a stop to navigate the tilting car through old washout pits and over tall clumps of weeds that sprouted from the edges of crumbling railroad ties. White birch saplings provided meager promises of shade as they marched along the edges of barren rock fields and climbed through a landscape cut into crosswise sections by the railed segments of the planes. A thick layer of dust soon collected on the windshield of the car.

"That's how they used to get the coal out of the valley." Marty pointed to a rusting series of gears and wheels perched on a brick square clinging to the mountainside.

"With that box thing?"

"Yep. That's one of the steam plants. It held the engine that powered the cables that pulled the barneys that pushed the coal cars over the mountain." He laughed. "Sounds like one of our grade school songs, eh?"

I hummed the tune and laughed with him.

"They hooked the cable to the barney and pushed a whole string of full coal cars to the end of each set of tracks. At the next segment they hooked on a new barney that pulled it some more. When they finally reached the top, it was downhill all the way to Philadelphia."

"Why didn't they use regular trains?"

"They didn't have locomotives powerful enough to get over the mountain. Before the steam engines and railroad cars, they used to fill boats full of coal and pull them up the rails with mules. When they reached the other side, they slid them into canals and floated them to the city."

"The canals Mom showed us on the way to New Jersey?"

"Yep. Must have been the ones. When steam engines were invented they got rid of the mules, hooked up steam engines to cables, and used counterweights to make the grade. Then they added a whole bunch more of these tracks."

"Why didn't they use the boats and take the coal down the Susquehanna?"

"The river used to be wilder and with lots of falls. It was too dangerous."

"Why don't they do it now?"

"Too shallow. It's full of mine silt. Pop's factory made the big cables they used here."

"And now they don't need them?"

"Nope. That's why the factory is no good anymore. It's too old."

"Because the trains take the coal out?"

"Yep. And there's a lot less coal to be gotten out. I know where some neat old cars are. Do you want to see them?"

"Sure." I wasn't all that interested in the rusting piles of junk we were passing, but I liked that my big brother was talking to me like an adult.

He stopped the car and we walked between tilting coal cars, barnies, and gondola boats that were overturned and rusting out. He helped me up on an old flatbed car and pointed to a low hill where miles of thick wire cables lay in rusting loops.

"Pop probably helped make some of those," he said. "They worked fine for a hundred years, but now they're plain out of date."

I wondered if Pop was feeling out of date too.

When we arrived at the pool Marty abandoned me and went across the creek to where the older guys were hanging out. I waded into the water. My near drowning was still too fresh. I clung to the rocks of the pool edges and went hand over hand until the water reached my chest. After the dusty heat on the dirt road, the cold water felt wonderful. I began a slow dog paddle but couldn't get up the courage to duck my head underwater.

I was studying the crowd on the rocks, hoping to see Chuck, when I became aware of a pair of feet standing on the rock ledge above me. I squinted into the sun and the eyes of Ronald Miller. He squatted, seated himself on the rocky edge, and dangled both legs in the water. I'd have to swim around him—or move hand over hand between his slowly paddling feet.

I maneuvered myself along the wall, away from him, toward the outfall and the deepest part of the pool. The tug of swift water as it rushed to free itself over the fall made my hands shake. A shiver ran through me. I had no choice. I had to go back.

As I reached for the rock nearest Ronald's knees, he pulled the leg of his bathing trunks free and exposed his private parts. Looking up into the stark reality of his anatomy made me forget my fear of drowning. I kicked off the rock wall and swam out into deeper water, toward the spot where I had last seen Marty.

I could have swum over to tell him what Ronald had done but it would have been embarrassing around all those other boys. I turned toward the rocky shore. My teeth chattered as I found a place on the rocks, in the center of some kids I didn't know.

The sun didn't warm me. I looked to my left, where a house-sized boulder had become a graffiti board. Painted in huge red letters were the words "On this rock Ronald M. fucked Andrea G."

I glanced toward Ronald. He had seen me read the rock. He smiled. I felt my face go red. I turned my back to him.

The sun beat down on me for the remainder of the day. I refused to go back into the water. By the time Marty and I started home, I was too sunburned to sit. He laid wet towels on the seat to protect my painful legs and back.

When we arrived home, Mom went into a fit. "Molly, I can't believe you would do this. It's pure carelessness."

My head hurt too much to answer.

"Well, come on. I'll need to sponge you with vinegar water and pray it won't get worse."

Her treatment helped. She gave me aspirin and I went to bed.

The next morning, she came into my room. "You're going to blister."

"It was that jerk Ronald Miller's fault."

"What does he have to do with your carelessness?"

"He was at the swimming hole yesterday. He bugs me."

"You stay away from him!"

"That's what I was doing."

She had other things on her mind. "I'm going to rub your back with cold cream; you'll have to do the rest. I need to go to town to pick up some things for the party tomorrow."

As she closed the clasp on her purse I saw papers from the finance company folded inside.

I used up half a jar of cream before I could pull an oversized cotton T-shirt and loose shorts over my sunburn. Pop was in the backyard with the county agent when I came out. I followed them to the chestnut tree.

The agent poked around in the dirt, studied the dried-up leaves, and screwed a round instrument into the trunk of the tree. He tucked samples into his bag.

"I don't see any evidence of insects or blight," he said. "I think the culprit is up there." He pointed to the smoke on the mountain. "I'll let you know what the core samples show. In the meantime, you need to take the tree down. It'll be a hazard when the wind picks up."

I sat beneath the tree. I had lost a good friend and I hadn't noticed it was dying. The trees, the house, the creek, and the town will all turn into a junk heap like the Ashley planes, I thought, and nobody will do anything about it. I was as fed up as Mom with the coal companies.

I went into the library and worked on my notebook. It was thick with pictures and pages of writing. The answer to the mystery of the diary would come clear soon, and when it did I would show my work proudly to my family.

I heard the agent's car leave and another pull in. I moved to the backyard. Pop and Marty were unloading two kegs of beer into tubs of ice in the shadow of the back porch. Pop smiled and handed me a chunk of ice to rub over my arms and legs. It soothed more of the burning pain.

As soon as the kegs were properly seated, Pop tapped into one. A spray of froth drenched him and Marty in pungent ale. They laughed, each filled a cup, then sat in the shade of the back porch.

By the time Sally arrived home, a small crowd of neighbors and friends had gathered for a communal supper. Most of the men moved into the lower yard to lie in the grass and tell jokes and tall tales. I sat on the porch swing and watched Lillian, Iris, and six kids, including Lenny and Larry, spill out of a packed cab. An empty wine bottle toppled out with them. It rolled down the street and was caught by Pop.

His speech was slurred. "What took you so long? I thought you gals could smell a party from fifty miles out."

Lillian's cackling laughter was their reply.

"Where's your mom?" Iris called to me.

I didn't move from the swing. "She's gone into town."

"Well, you'll do then." She crooked her finger for me to come down.

I did her bidding.

"You can put this stuff away." She pushed a bag of groceries into my burned arms.

We carried everything onto the kitchen: bottles of sauterne wine and vodka, cans of orange juice, a variety of lunch meats, cheeses, breads, mustards, and pickles. A deli bag of cardboard containers filled with potato salad, macaroni salad, and baked beans. Bags of pretzels and licorice sticks, an oversized can of potato chips, and a case of soda. It looked as if all the Fourth of July picnics in the world had been transported to our table.

I began to put the food away while the women carried their personal belongings up the stairs. I could hear their suitcases dropping on the hallway floor above.

Lenny and Larry brought one of the new portable record players and a small case of 45 rpm records.

"I've got some of that new guy's," Lenny said. "Elvis Presley. They're pretty neat, but I can't play them unless Iris says so."

"Sally and me learned to jitterbug. We can teach you."

"Nah," he said. "Jitterbugging is for girls."

The bar for liquor and wine on the sink drainboard was falling over with bottles. I did what Mom would have—collected a shopping bag of full bottles and carried them to the cellar. I would bring them out when supplies were low.

I stood in the cool cellar and breathed in its musty, dirt-floored odor. The moist air soothed my skin.

A string of firecrackers and laughter exploded in the lower yard. Lenny and Larry were stirring things up. I hurried up the cellar steps.

As I came into the kitchen, a group of screaming women ran past, with Lenny and Larry close on their heels. The reason for their flight became obvious when Pop came through the door with the garden hose. Cascades of water flooded the linoleum. The women headed upstairs. Lenny and Larry ran out though the front door. Pop reached the limit of the hose length and retreated.

I took a bowl of coleslaw from the refrigerator and started to make room for the containers Lillian had brought. Lenny and Larry burst through the back door again. This time, a gang of Marty's friends chased closely behind. They jostled me aside and knocked the bowl from my hands. It sailed under the table and made a splintering racket as it smashed against the stove. Slick strips of dressed cabbage and broken yellow glass littered the linoleum. I could hear the chase continuing through the dining room, down the hall, and out the front door.

Lillian pushed through the door. "Bessie's home," she shouted to Iris, who was close behind. They hit the slick floor and slid wildly toward the opposite door, clinging to one another and screaming with laughter.

And there was Mom, standing in the doorway. She took in the broken bowl, wet floor, and her screeching relatives. She didn't say a word but turned and ran upstairs. I followed on shaking legs.

At her open bedroom door she stopped dead still. Lillian's and Iris's clothing was scattered on her bed and furniture. A group of women repaired their hair and makeup before her dressing table mirror. She looked around wildly, like a bird looking for a safe place to light. Her hands went to her face.

"Oh, Sean! Oh, Mother! God damn you, Iris!" she cried.

The hose-dampened women murmured apologies as they hurried through the door. When they had all gone, Mom dropped onto the edge of her bed and covered her face with her hands. I sat beside her.

Lillian came to the door. "Now, Bessie. There's no need to make a federal case out of this. It's all just fun. It's the Fourth of July for gosh sakes."

Mom pulled some things from her dresser and pushed past her mother without speaking. I followed closely behind. She stopped on the stairs and turned to me.

"Molly, I can't stay here. I'm going to spend the holiday in Back Mountain."

I stood speechless at the top of the stairs until I heard the front screen door slam. I had to stop her.

I chased her down Fitch Lane, across Marcy Street, and down Giant's Despair Road. A bus pulled into the turnaround. I wanted to comfort her and to be comforted, but she stood ramrod straight, shopping bag hanging from one hand, her purse from the other, and her face wet with tears.

"I can't stay here and watch their madness," she said as the bus doors opened. "You'll have to trust me, Molly. I'll be fine and you'll be fine."

I followed her onto the bus.

"No," she said, with a firmness that frightened me. "You have to stay here. I need to go alone."

A coal train clattered down the tracks behind us. Its whistle blew a warning at the crossing. I stood between the departing bus and the clanking train and shouted for my mother. The bus disappeared down the hill.

I had never seen my mother throw up her hands in defeat. And never before had she left us. Apprehension filled me. I thought about my last history class and the deceits of the Roman Caesars. I remembered how Nero fiddled while Rome burned and I wondered if this might be the same kind of thing, only with Pop being the fiddler and Mom being all of Rome.

Lillian stood in the bay window and watched me climb the hill. I expected that she would be upset too, but when I walked in she turned, smiled, and moved calmly to the kitchen. She avoided the mess on the floor and went out through the back screen door, calling Iris's name.

My sunburned skin pulled tightly against my chest and back. My legs and arms chafed against my clothing. I ran through the front yard and ducked into the woods on an overgrown path that led to the creek. The air under the trees cooled my face and dried my tears. The creek was low. I waded in. A narrow spot where the rocks were smooth and covered with wet moss provided enough space for me to stretch out on my back and allow coolness to flow over me. The tight sting slowly seeped away. Above, through the trees, the pale sky darkened with twilight.

I wriggled to find the deepest part of the water, until only my upturned face protruded from the stream. Relief from pain and tension eased through me. I stayed until my feet and hands were numb.

When I walked back into the kitchen, Pop was sloshing cold water across the floor in a vain attempt to mop up the mess. He was having trouble standing. Bits of cabbage had piled up against the wainscoting as the mop pushed everything to one side of the room.

"You need hot water and soap," I said.

He laughed, too loudly. "Someone left the hot water run upstairs. The boiler is cold." Without looking up he pointed one shoulder at the stove. "Get that thing going, would you?"

He threw the mop onto the floor and staggered toward the door. He sounded like Aunt Iris.

Now I knew how Mom must feel—keeping everything in order, cleaning, cooking, worrying, as she put everyone else's needs before her own. Hot anger stiffened the back of my neck.

Despite his drunken state he sensed the change in me. He turned, grinned, and winked. I turned away.

"What?" he asked. "What's wrong?"

We stared at each other.

"I won't start the stove or clean up this mess," I said.

He shrugged. "Okay," he said. "I hear you. Go."

Now I also understood why Mom became so nervous when there was booze in the house. This man, whom I had always seen through the eyes of a child, had himself become a child. I felt ashamed and embarrassed for him as he stood wide-legged at the coal stove, trying to steady himself with both hands. I had never been unkind to him because he had never been unkind to me. Now I wanted to strike out, to make him see himself as I was seeing him.

I turned, ran into the second parlor, and looked for a place to hide so he wouldn't see me cry. The storage closet door was open. I burrowed into the coats at the very back. I covered my head with Ira's mouton lamb coat and beat at it with both fists. One glancing blow hit something firm.

Stiffening, I thought—the sturdy material Mom added to lapels and button placards when she sewed. But it was thicker than that and slid around between the silken lining and the thick pelts.

I stopped crying, laid the coat flat on my knees, and pressed my fingertips against hard edges. Something perfectly square was lodged near the breast pocket. I pushed the closet door open and carried the coat into the light.

Part of the pocket lining had been sewn shut with tiny, perfect stitches. I pulled a thread and chewed it between my front teeth until I felt it give. A wallet, I thought, with paper money.

With shaking fingers I pulled the threads free and removed a small packet wrapped in linen. As I turned the package over, photographs, sepia-toned and perfectly square, slid into my lap. Two naked people mated like the dogs I had seen the past summer when Mrs. Donal's bitch came into heat. From the show Ronald Miller had given me, I knew that both people in the picture were men.

Flustered, not wanting to see more and yet fascinated by the prospect of studying those male parts, I glanced around the room before turning over the next picture. A man and a boy, naked, lay together on a bed like two spoons. The man's muscles were outlined clearly, as if he was straining at lifting something very heavy.

I exposed the next card. A young boy looked up at me—a cherub, like one of the marble figures in the ceiling corners of the Miners Bank building, but with everything that should have been ivy-covered showing. He stared at me with eyes that were glazed over and unsure. There was something familiar and painful about his eyes. I didn't want to see more.

As I cast wildly about the room, seeking a place to dump the photographs, Pop staggered in. I looked into his face.

"What have you got there?" he asked.

I couldn't speak. I held the pictures up, silently beseeched him to take them.

He snatched them from my shaking hands. "God damn it!" he shouted. "God damn it!" He held the stack in both hands and twisted the thick cardboard, but when they wouldn't be torn he tossed them on the floor and ground them with the heels of his boots.

"Garbage! Forget you ever saw them! Garbage!" He bent over, tried to scoop them up, dropped them, and began again. When he had them contained in his hands, he turned.

Lillian heard his shouting and came running. "What's wrong? What is it?"

"Nothing," Pop shouted. "A bunch of old trash." He pushed past her. A stove lid clanged open.

"What have you done now?" Lillian demanded as she followed me down the hall. I needed to tell Pop that the pictures weren't mine.

I found him standing over the coal stove, stirring the beginning of a fire with the lid lifter. Lenny and Larry stood beside him, straining to see into the blaze.

"Get out of here," Pop shouted. "Go back outside and play. Get away." He slammed the lid closed, tossed the lifter onto the cool side of the stove, and strode out the door. Lenny stretched up, retrieved the lifter, and reopened the lid. Black smoke billowed from the firebox.

Black as sin, I thought. Black as sin.

Lillian took the lifter from Lenny's hand and shoved him toward the door.

"You heard what he said. Go! Now!"

I watched as Lillian poked the lifter into the fire. She was as curious as the boys, and I was as unclean as the smoke she waved away. I moved to the sink and began to scrub my hands.

"What did he burn?" Lillian asked. "What set him off?"

"I don't know."

"Of course you know. Don't say you don't. Tell me."

"I don't know! Go away! Leave me alone!"

My mother was gone, my father was drunk, and I had seen pictures of things that I wanted to forget. I bolted to my bedroom, slammed the door, and threw myself onto the brass bed. The sulfurous scent of mine fire mingled with the gunpowder tang of spent fireworks and settled thickly over the house.

This must be what hell is like, I thought. I lay wide-eyed and silent through the night.

~

In the morning, through my open windows, I could see several neighborhood men curled up and sleeping on the grass. I studied my sunburn. It had blistered and begun to dry. Most of the intense pain dulled into an annoying tightness. I sponged with vinegar, dressed, and carried the bottle of aspirin to the kitchen.

Pop was already up, or maybe had never gone to bed. I could hear him talking on the back porch.

The telephone rang. When I lifted the receiver Mom's voice gave me a moment of hope.

"How are you? Is your sunburn any better? Is Sally there? Did Marty have a good welcome home party?" Hope died when she asked about Pop. "Is he falling-down drunk?"

I perched on the arm of the chair. "I haven't seen him yet this morning. He was pretty bad last night."

"I'm sorry I had to leave. And I'm sorry how I did it. Are you okay?"

I wasn't okay. I was numb and slow-witted.

"My sunburn's getting better," I said.

"Are you keeping vinegar water on it?"

"Yes."

"Are you taking aspirin?"

There were more important things happening than my sunburn.

"Mom?"

"What?"

"When are you coming home?"

"Not today, Molly. I think it's better for everybody that I stay away. Once your pop gets on a toot like this he'll stay with it until he's too sick to move."

"Is it my fault because I didn't let him go cold turkey last winter?"

"Heavens, no! Don't you even think that."

I didn't want to face Pop.

"Can you come get me?"

"I can't. I'm at the farm by the old house. They're having trouble with their car. This house is small, and fieldworkers are sleeping on the floors."

"I don't mind sleeping on the floor."

"It's all men, Molly. You're better off there. Pop never gets mean. You know that. He'll always look out for you. And Lillian will too. I wouldn't leave you there if I thought you weren't going to be okay. Sally will help."

"Sally is busy with her boyfriend. Everybody's busy."

"Doing what?"

"Boozing. Iris and Lillian brought a lot of liquor." I thought I heard her crying, so I quickly added, "I took a whole bunch of it to the cellar."

I wasn't sure if she was trying to reassure herself or me when she said, "See? You know what to do. I knew you'd be okay."

"Maybe I'll go over to Mrs. Donal's house."

"Good. I'll call over there and make sure it's all right."

"Mom?"

"What?"

"Please don't stay away too long."

"We'll see."

Lillian and Iris had made the kitchen halfway right. Mom's favorite crystal pitcher waited on the table, filled with orange juice. Beside it a half-empty quart of vodka waited. As I made toast, the two women squeezed past me to carry the pitcher and a tray of ice-filled glasses onto the back porch. They let the screen door slam behind them. I listened to the sound of ice tinkling and glasses clinking as the women poured drinks for the men. When they giggled, my grandmother and great aunt sounded exactly like my sister's teenage girlfriends.

I stepped onto the porch. Pop and Marty had hauled three old milk cans up from the cellar and were lining them up on the driveway while the men who had been sleeping on the grass staggered about gathering stones. A small hatchet and slivers of tinder waited on the gravel. Lillian and Iris carried their drinks down the stairs and stood by. I sat on a chair.

John Hale came up the stairs and sat beside me. "Bunch of fools. Playing at making nitroglycerin with their bellies full of booze."

"Can't you stop them?"

"No authority. Private property."

Pop tilted a milk can on the shelf of stones, then stacked and restacked each rock until the angle was perfect. He wriggled the can until it was steady and pointed toward the woods. He placed a handful of wood shavings at its base. His hands shook as he spooned some carbide into the can's open mouth.

"Why do they have to do that? Aren't firecrackers noisy enough?" My head throbbed.

"Tradition. Old Charlie's. He brought the ingredients from the powder mill."

Pop lifted a corked bottle of clear glycerin into the air and circled slowly for his audience. When Iris and Lillian cheered, he bowed toward them and measured a good amount of liquid into the can with a dramatic flourish. He measured another powder, added some water, lofted the lid from the milk can above his head, did a two-step circle dance, bent from the waist, and pounded the lid tightly onto the can with his fist.

"He's going to kill us all," I said.

"It's not that bad. He's measuring." John Hale stood so he could see above the gathering partiers. "The explosion will be small."

Iris wrapped a rag around a broken shovel handle. She dipped it into an open pan of gasoline and leaned the torch toward Pop. He struck a match on his pants, held it to the rag, and then waited for the flame to die down before he touched the flaming tip to the tinder.

The explosion blew the cap about ten feet. The crowd groaned with disappointment.

"Where's your mom," John asked.

"She ran away. To the farm where we used to live."

"Smart woman. Why aren't you with her?"

I touched my shoulder with one finger. "Sunburn. Everybody there is sleeping on the floor. Mom didn't think it was a good idea for me."

"Do you have any aloe vera plants left?"

I hadn't thought of that. "Yes. In the library window."

He smiled. "You know how to use them."

Pop stomped out the fire and pulled a second can into place. This time he spooned in more carbide powder and an unmeasured amount of glycerin.

"Now he's getting into it," John Hale said.

I pressed my hands against my ears as one of the men replenished the tinder. Pop touched the torch to the wood. A tremendous blast sent the cap of the can flying through the air. The crowd cheered. Some men hugged each other. Others pounded their fists against the trees. Summer leaves flitted to the ground like falling kites.

As Pop prepared the third can, John walked to the edge of the porch. I ran to a beer tub, scooped up a chunk of ice, carried it back to the porch, and pressed it to my forehead. As the next volley echoed from the mountainside, I squeezed my eyes closed and rubbed the ice over my forehead.

John Hale returned. "Headache?"

I nodded. "From the sunburn."

"And from dehydration. You need to drink a big glass of orange juice and lots of water."

"I miss my mom."

"Me too. She brings sanity to parties like this. She'll be back. I've known her for a long time. She'll come home."

Pop had tired of the carbide cannons. He handed the bottle of glycerin to Marty and came up the stairs. I could tell by the careful way he walked that he was trying to appear sober for John Hale's benefit. I was grateful not to have to face him alone.

He glanced at me before he swept his arm toward the Mountaineer on the mountainside.

"Have you seen what they're doing, John? What do you think of that thing?"

"I think it'll be putting a lot more men out of work. Might be good thing, though, with all the shortcuts the coal companies have been taking in the underground mines."

"I heard they're laying off again."

"Not laying off. Closing down." When he pulled his head back, I could see the knotted ligaments in John Hale's neck. "Taking away all the jobs underground. No need for strong men when they've got a machine like that and a government that allows them to bring down mountains."

"You know the wire mill has closed."

"Have you decided what you'll do?"

"I'll stay with the job. Don't have much choice. Nothing else available."

Lillian came up the stairs and sat next to John. He took her hand and held it for a moment, then turned back to Pop.

"You were smart never to become a miner. One of the guys, works down at the south slope in the big vein, told me they're scared to death of that damn river. He says the engineers have stopped digging boreholes to measure the rock above the shafts. They don't survey and they aren't doing inspections."

Pop shook his head. "Hah! The inspectors mostly turn their heads anyway. They're as greedy as the owners. Somebody's greasing palms."

"You can't fight city hall." John echoed the pessimism that had filled the valley all spring.

"Can't someone go to the union?" Lillian asked.

John leaned back in his chair. "Ah, Lily! Those guys are as bad as the rest of them. Everybody's in bed together. It's like a hundred years ago. Speak up and get yourself killed in the street. Don't speak up and get yourself killed under a thousand pounds of rock."

"Speaking of getting killed in the street, have you heard anything about those water company guys?" Pop asked.

"Yeah. The guy who was up on the street is doing better. The one from the pit is still hanging on by a thread."

"What about the explosion. Anything about that?"

"Spoke with the Bureau of Mines. Didn't tell me anything I didn't know already. Said that big machine isn't venting any shafts. Said it has nothing to do with that mine fire stoking up, that the Red Ash vein doesn't come near the town."

"My father always said that the mine shafts run right under where we're standing," Lillian said.

"Greedy bastards!" Pop said again. "They're up there scraping off the top of the seam. Getting what they can before anybody tries to stop them."

"I'm glad my father's not here to see it," Lillian said.

"Old Charlie's turning over in his grave. He knew how dangerous the fire is," Pop said.

"Hell, it was him that blasted the tunnels closed and stopped the damned thing for all these years." John Hale stood and peered out over the yard. I wondered if he was looking for blue smoke.

"If he was to go underground now, he'd have something to say," Pop said. "I'll bet they've connected all the tunnels."

"And if they have, it will affect every mine downhill from here. Over at the south slope, they tell me, there's water coming in from other sources." John pointed toward Prospect Rock. "Do you see the creeks running like they used to on this side of the mountain? Barely a trickle comes down from those springs. Everything's going underground. Rushing through the tunnels, right down to the valley. Wilkes-Barre will be one big swamp."

"It started out that way, I suppose it could go back to it," Lillian said.

"And up here the damned fire will burn up the mountain and our houses too. The guys who own that big shovel will say they had nothing to do with it and we'll be left with nothing."

Lillian flashed a smile. "You've still got *me*."

The men laughed. I stared up at the mountain and wondered how long we had before the stoked-up fire got to us.

Lillian and Pop wandered back to the people in the yard. John Hale remained.

"Does your sunburn mean you've been swimming?" he asked me. "That you're not afraid of drowning anymore?"

"I'm still a little scared, but Pop says I'll get over it."

"He should know. He's faced a lot of troubles."

"And now he's got a lot more."

"You're a smart girl. You know that, don't you?"

I nodded.

"You must be lonely here, with your sister working and your brother gone."

"And now Mom's gone too." I squeezed my eyelids together so I wouldn't cry. Self-pity wasn't a sentiment encouraged in my family.

"You'll need to keep yourself busy. Find something interesting to do."

"I already did. I'm doing some stuff for my family history."

"Like what?"

"Like finding out about all the accidents that killed Granny Sue's kids."

"Why would you want to do that?"

I shrugged. "I got interested when I found out about the guy who killed himself."

"Ira?" He sat up straighter in his chair, as if I had hit a nerve. I pretended not to notice.

"He's the one. Did you know him?"

"Yeah, I knew him."

"Was he nice?"

He studied my face with new interest. "There were those who would say he was. A lot of people might say that."

"Can you tell me about him?"

"No. Not really."

"Why not?"

He grinned. "Because I try not to speak ill of the dead. They aren't here to stick up for themselves."

When I laughed it felt both strange and good. I liked John Hale.

"Did you know Silas?"

"Not real good. I was gone a lot of the time he was growing up. Heard he was a little wild."

"Were you here when he got hit by the train?"

He fidgeted in his chair. "Yeah. I was here."

I tried to think of a good question but all I could come up with was, "Was it a really dark night?"

He didn't laugh. He closed his eyes and thought hard. "Yes, if I remember right, it was a black night. No moon."

"My cousin said that Silas was drunk."

"I wouldn't know about that."

"Isn't that why he fell under the train?"

John Hale shrugged. "Don't know. Don't think we'll ever know."

"Mom says that he had Iris with him."

"Yes, she was there."

"Mom says Iris was a flower girl for a wedding and Silas was bringing her home."

"I believe that's right."

"Did you see Ira there?"

He stared at me for a long time. "You sure are curious for a young girl," he finally said.

"I like learning this stuff. Mom told me all about her ancestors—the pioneers and the soldiers. But I think Granny Sue's family is more interesting, don't you?"

He smiled and seemed to decide that my questions were harmless.

I jumped back in. "I was wondering about Ira—because he lived here but nobody ever talks about him, and because he killed himself."

"I didn't really know him that well. He spent a lot of time with Bernie, who was my friend. After Bernie drowned, I stayed away for a long time."

"Why?"

He smiled again. "I don't know. I was young. Young people sometimes blame themselves for everything. Even when it doesn't make sense."

"Mom says that everyone is responsible for themselves and only themselves, and if everyone does the best that they can, everybody comes out ahead."

"That's a good way to look at it."

"What was Bernie like?"

"I'm getting pretty old, you know. It's hard to remember those things. I do remember that he was a hard worker and he was smart in school."

"Did you hang around together?"

"We spent most of our time here. I helped him with some of his work so he could have time for the band."

"You had a band?"

"Not us. The church. We played with the Salvation Army band." He must have thought I would consider that to be dumb, because that's what he said. "Pretty dumb, huh?"

I moved to the edge of my seat and blurted, "You sent him a card, didn't you?"

His eyes registered confusion, then lightened with affirmation. "Yes. I did. But how would you know that?"

"Lillian. She kept the card because she didn't know who sent it. She gave it to me. Because I was interested."

"I'll be darned. Isn't that something."

"What did it mean?"

"What?"

"What you said in the card. That he was living without God and he needed to talk to you."

"Oh. It was nothing really. Kid stuff."

"What kind of kid stuff?"

"Just stuff. He had stopped coming to church. He stopped playing in the band. It seemed like something was bothering him. I guess I thought I could help."

"But you couldn't?"

"He drowned before I could talk to him. Do you still have the card?"

"Yes. Do you want to see it?"

"Sometime. Not right now. But sometime I would."

"Did you like Ira?"

"It doesn't matter if I did or I didn't. He helped your Granny Sue and Charlie. Especially after Charlie had his stroke."

"I don't think my mom liked him."

"That could be. He was a bit of a dandy. Old Charlie once said that he was as worthless as a load of rock. Never lifted a shovel in his entire life. But that was after the stroke too. Charlie was a bitter man by then."

"Because of his boys dying?"

"And because he lost everything in the stock market crash of '29. He had made a lot of money by being careful and investing. That's how they built this house. In the end, this house was the only thing he had to show for all his work."

And he had left the house to Pop, who was almost a complete stranger. No wonder Iris was mad about that. Lillian didn't mind. Maybe because she loved her daughter and was happy Mom and us could live here. I would have asked John Hale about Old Charlie's last wishes, but at the moment I was more interested in what he knew about Ira, so I jumped back in.

"What else did people say about Ira?"

He thought for a long time before he answered. "He was seen in the kind of places most Christian men would not want to be seen."

"What kind of places?"

"Dives." He shifted his gaze to the yard.

"Like the Russian hall?"

He thought that was really funny. When he stopped laughing he said, "The Russian hall was part of the church. That's where the wedding was."

If I had been talking to anyone else but John Hale I would have been embarrassed, but I had often seen Pop and John laughing together over a shared joke and I knew he had the same sly sense of humor as Pop. He was not making fun of me.

"What happened to the hall?"

"It burned to the ground years ago."

"My cousin told me that Silas and Ira had a fight."

"You've been taking a hard look at this, haven't you? If they would let girls do it, you could be a police detective, couldn't you?"

"There are already some girl detectives."

"Only in the movies," he said. He reasoned to himself for a short time before he answered my question. "They said that Silas was mad and refused a ride with Ira. He and Iris walked up the footpath by the borehole. Ira headed up the main road. He said he could see the train stopped above the crossing, so he pulled over and ran up the tracks."

Encouraged, I kept going. "Was anybody else there?"

"A lot of people heard the train's bell and brakes. Some ran out to see what the problem was. They found Iris standing by the tracks."

I felt sudden sorrow for Iris. No wonder she was so messed up.

"So she saw the whole thing?"

"If she did, she doesn't remember it. She was in shock."

"The angels were watching out for me. So says the family."

I had been so interested in John Hale's words that I hadn't seen Iris come up the steps. My face burned hotter than my sunburn.

John smiled at Iris. "And your Uncle Ira was watching too."

I couldn't tell if John Hale's words were genuine or sarcastic.

"I've always wondered what he and Silas fought about."

She sat in the chair vacated by Lillian and crossed her legs. A trail of thin blue veins ran up her shins.

"Ira told my father that Silas wanted to visit a married woman in the Scranton Patch," she said. "He said they argued, and Silas decided to walk me home." She placed a cigarette in her mouth and leaned across so John could light it.

I closed my eyes and held my breath against her exhaled smoke. "Did you see him . . . after the train?"

"Silas?" she asked.

"Yes."

"I saw him. I can remember his legs . . . the boots my father made for him, under the train, in the light of a lantern. And someone crossing the tracks and lifting the rest of his body up. He seemed to be in two parts."

"They kept the casket closed." John said.

"Yes, I remember the casket." Her voice seemed to come from a faraway place. She closed her eyes. When she opened them she said, "My father sat in the parlor in a chair next to that casket and wept."

"He loved his boys. All of them."

"He cried a lot after that, but only when he was alone in the barn. I used to climb up to the hayloft and watch him."

"He lost three boys. All in their prime. Just reaching manhood."

"I sometimes wished that it had been us girls who had gone on, instead of the boys. I don't think my father would have suffered our deaths with as much difficulty."

John Hale reached out and touched her arm. "My dear Iris, what would any of us do without you Beckerman girls? The world would be a drab and boring place."

"You old charmer!" I could tell she was pleased.

"I hear you've moved to Scranton," he said.

"Yes. Lillian is helping me get on my feet." She turned to me. "Molly, get me a drink. A Seven and Seven with a little ice."

I moved reluctantly toward the kitchen door.

"I've got my kids back," I heard her say. "I'll make it."

I let the screen door slam behind me. The liquor bottles in the kitchen were empty. I hurried into the library and slipped Bernie's postcard into my pocket. When I came back out, Iris was alone on the porch.

"Where's John?" I asked.

She shrugged. "He went to the bathroom. Where's my drink?"

"Kitchen's out of booze."

She stood and went to look for herself. I headed toward the lower yard.

Lillian stopped me on the path. "Did I see you carry some of that good liquor to the cellar yesterday?"

"I hid it like Mom does. Do you want me to get it?"

"Yes. Bring it up to the kitchen, please."

I moved through the new cellar entrance in the lower yard and closed the door behind me so no one would see Mom's hiding place. It took a few moments for my eyes to adjust to the darkness. I was about to move forward when the door at the top of the stairs opened, cast a beam of light, and quickly closed. I heard foot scrapes, muffled voices, and the soft clanging together of the cast-iron grills and frying pans that hung on nails against the wall on the landing. I crept closer.

Pop's voice came out of the darkness. "Damn it, Iris. What do you want from me?"

"I want to talk."

"We could do that on the porch."

"I want to talk to you alone." Her voice was thick, but more with crying than with booze.

"You've had too much to drink." His voice was cold.

"I can't stop remembering, Sean."

"Remembering what?"

"That you saved me. That you came to help me."

"For God's sake. Not this again."

"You saved me."

"I didn't save you. Bessie sent me to check on you. You weren't in any danger."

"I'd reached my wits' end. You should have let me do it."

"You weren't going to do anything. I saw you look out the window before I came in. You had only enough time to turn on the gas and stick your head in the oven. You weren't serious."

"I was more serious than I'd ever been in my life."

"You were drunk."

"I drank to get the courage to go through with it."

"And then you called Bess to save you."

She began to sob. "It was a bad time. The worst for me."

"We've all had those."

"She's left you, hasn't she?"

"She'll be back."

"She's left you. Now we can be together."

"You're crazy, Iris. Out of your mind."

I heard the slap, could almost feel the stinging blow. I was sure they heard my sharp intake of breath, but Iris's screeching voice drowned out any noise I might have made.

"You swine! You filthy Irish pig. You had nothing until you tricked my father into signing everything over to you. You stole everything from me." Another slap.

I held my breath until I heard Pop's voice clearly in the darkness.

"Iris. Stop!"

"Hit me, you son of a bitch. If you're not man enough to be with me, see if you're man enough to hit me!"

"You're drunk."

"And you're stupid! You're a stupid, stupid man."

"Why do you do this? Why can't we have a good time? It's a party for Christ's sake."

"I hate parties."

"You shouldn't drink. It turns you ugly."

"Life is ugly."

"Ah Jesus, Iris, I've heard all this before. I know you've had a bad time. There are things we can't change. I'm sorry for you. I'm sorry that you're alone. I can't change that. I've got too much on my own plate. I'm not a saint."

"You're as close to one as I'll ever find." She began to sob loudly. "You are. You are. You don't know."

He soothed her. I could hear him making all the shushing noises he made to us kids when we were hurt. I couldn't see them in the darkness but I knew he was holding her. I closed my eyes until I heard the sobbing stop.

"Come on," he said. "Go up and fix your makeup and come outside. It doesn't do any good to keep looking back, Iris. We can't change the past."

Light filled the stairs as he pushed open the kitchen door. "Come on." The door closed behind them.

I carried the shopping bag of booze to Lillian and went to look for John Hale. I found him in the upstairs hallway, walking not from the bathroom but from the front bedrooms.

"I put one of the aloe plants on your dresser," he said. "And a paring knife to cut some stems. You take care of that burn, you hear me."

I handed him Bernie's card.

As he passed Mom's bedroom door, he smiled at Iris, who was standing at the dresser repairing her makeup.

~

Despite dreams of screeching locomotives and hissing gas stoves, I slept through another night of smothering heat. With the first light of day I stretched and threw my sheet aside. The house was quiet. I sat on the side of my bed, used the knife John Hale had provided to slit a thick stem of aloe vera, and rubbed the liquid onto my arms and shoulders. The cooling gel immediately began to soothe the pain of my sunburn. I gratefully dripped more gel onto my upper legs and knees. I pulled my wastebasket closer and tossed in the spent stem. That's when I saw it—the line of bright wallpaper showing at the top corner and down one side of the hot air vent. It was the same kind of line that showed when I had moved Granny Sue's family picture on the library wall.

I moved closer. One screw was totally in and one was loose. Someone had recently removed the cover from the vent and didn't fix it right. Someone else knew about the diary. That someone might have been the person who received Charlie's last angry lines about the cabin and the car.

I smiled at myself in the mirror. This was becoming like a real mystery story. If the diary message was an innocent thing, no one would have reason to come into my room and search for it. I took the stairs two at a time and hummed a tune as I went into the kitchen where Lillian was clearing up the remains of the two-day party.

"Where is everybody?" I asked.

"Sleeping in," she said. "Seems that only Iris and me have the stamina to keep going." She gave a short hoot of laughter before she pointed to a stack of bags filled with discarded papers. "Take that stuff out to the burn barrel for me, would you? Iris meant to, but she seems to have forgotten."

"Where is she?"

"She headed out through the field toward the creek. Said she needed to sweep the cobwebs from her brain."

As I carried the bundles of paper across the porch I passed Lenny and Larry asleep on quilts. They didn't stir. I grabbed some of their unspent firecrackers from the banister and tossed whole strings of them into the burn barrel. I touched the match to the bottom of the papers and hurried into the woods.

I was so preoccupied that I didn't see Iris sitting on a rock by the side of the creek until she spoke.

"We went to Mrs. Donal's last night," she said. "She showed movies on the side of her garage. You should have come. It was Laurel and Hardy and we laughed so hard I nearly peed my pants."

She had never before bothered to speak to me civilly. My suspicions about her doubled. I dropped down beside her and dangled my sandaled feet into stagnant water.

"I was too tired," I said. "And my sunburn hurt."

"Is it better now?"

"Lots."

"It's best for girls like us to stay out of the sun. Our skin's too fair."

The firecrackers suddenly began to explode in the burn barrel. I could hear the shouts of the twins. I laughed out loud.

So did Iris. "Did you do that?"

I nodded and threw a stone into the mud on the creek edge.

"We used to have such fun here," she said. "Your mother, Fern, and me. My mother would bring her hand sewing and sit where you're sitting so she could keep a close eye on us, and she'd let us swim."

"There's not enough water to swim anymore," I said.

She threw a stone too. "No. Everything has changed."

I screwed up my courage before I asked, "Did you and Mom and Fern used to like each other?"

She lit a cigarette and blew the smoke away from me. "What makes you think we don't now?"

I shrugged and threw another stone. A dragonfly with purple wings skimmed over the mud.

"We haven't liked each other for a long time." She said the words matter-of-factly, like she would say 'Pass me the milk' or 'Have you seen the newspaper?'.

"How come?"

"Did anyone ever tell you that you ask too many questions?"

"Pop says that all the time. He says I'm a chatterbox, like Mom."

"He's right. You're awfully nosy. And awfully messy. Where'd you get that shirt, from the ragman?"

I didn't answer. She hadn't changed after all.

"Little girls are supposed to be pretty and clean."

"I'm not little. I turned thirteen."

"All the more reason you should always look your best. Your hair is a rat's nest."

My hand went to my hair. I wanted to tell her that she might be pretty but she sure wasn't a very nice person.

As if she read my thoughts, she said, "I wasn't always like this. It's life that made me this way." She looked like she was about to cry.

"I'm sorry that you had such a bad time when you were a little girl."

"My entire life has been hard."

"Actually, I think my mom does like you, no matter what you do."

"What makes you think that?"

"Because she went to see you at the workhouse even though she hates all those ladies who yell at her from the windows."

Iris laughed.

"Mom says that Granny Sue loved you best."

"My mother hated me."

"That's not what Mom says."

"Your mom was always jealous of me."

"Why?"

"Because she didn't have a real father and I had a real father and an uncle who was like a second father."

"Uncle Ira?"

"Yes."

"I don't think she liked Uncle Ira."

"Like I said, she was jealous."

"Pop says that you can't change the past if all the saints in heaven are on your side. That you can only make today and the next day better."

"And he would know?"

I shrugged.

"Why don't you go play with the boys."

I decided to be nice, even if she wasn't. "Do you want to walk up to see that big machine? The Mountaineer?" I pointed toward the mountain.

"Oh, for heaven's sake! I have a goddamned headache. Go away."

I stood and brushed the dirt from my shorts. "Okay, then. Bye." I was glad to get away.

As I came closer to the Mountaineer and heard the shouts of the men working it, I lost my courage. I looked a mess. Iris said I did. I couldn't let anyone else see me. I headed back toward the creek.

Lillian was standing in the path. "Did you find Iris?"

I pointed to Iris, who now sat with her face hidden between her upraised knees.

"Iris! What in the world are you doing out here?"

"Trying to think," she mumbled.

"Well, that's a new one."

"I wish I'd never been born."

"Oh, for heaven's sake!" Lillian sat close to her.

Iris's shoulders shook. "What is wrong with me today? Yesterday I felt on top of the world."

"It's the drink. You had too much."

"It's not the drink. It was all that talk about Silas. When John Hale started on about the train, everything came tumbling down. Bad thoughts. Madness."

I sat on my rock. Maybe John Hale had checked off the list in the diary. Maybe he had scrawled the angry note.

"I'm sorry," Lillian said.

"Am I crazy?"

"No, you're not crazy."

"I keep hearing Uncle Ira's voice. 'Close your eyes. Don't look.' But I did look. I remember how Father threw himself on Silas. And how, when John Hale pulled him off, he howled like an animal. He was covered in blood."

"It wasn't your fault, Iris. You were a tiny little girl. It was a horrible accident."

"It was someone's fault. I can't remember seeing the train, but I have this feeling . . . of it coming. Sometimes I think I can reach out and touch it." She reached out one shaking hand and pretended to touch something in the empty air. "It makes me tremble inside."

"Oh, Iris! You're so theatrical!"

"Don't say that! Mother used to say that! 'Oh, Iris you're so dramatic. You've got to stop making up stories.'" Her voice began to rise and become shrill. "She never listened to me."

Lillian's voice was tinged with anger. "Stop it! Stop it now! You were a little girl and it was dark and you have no idea what happened. Don't make things worse!"

"You don't know. You closed your eyes. And so did Father and Mother. When Fern's mom died they wouldn't even look at her."

"The sanitarium sent Faye home to die. Mother wanted to care for her."

"Why do you keep that thought in your head? Mother didn't care for her. Bess and Fern and me cared for her."

"Mother was busy with Arlie. He was sick too."

"He got sick and died in a few days. We cared for Aunt Faye for a whole year."

"Why do you need to blame everybody for doing the best they could? Poor Mother was overwhelmed. What did you want?"

"I wanted you to come and take Bess away. I wanted Fern to die with her mother. I wanted to be the only girl, to have Mother love me."

"Oh, Iris. How many times have I heard this from you? How many times will I have to tell you how horrible you sound when you say such things about the people who love you?"

"There's love and then there's love."

"And you had it all."

"I had nothing." She began to sob.

"You always get like this when you've had too much to drink. Do you know who you remind me of? Mother! You're as high strung as she was."

"I'm not at all like her."

"You should hear yourself. You blame others for everything. We did the best we could."

"It wasn't you. It was Ira. He wedged a rod into this family. Father and Mother fought all the time."

"Father didn't approve of his way of living. Or his holier-than-thou attitude."

"It was more than that."

"What more? Tell me. Explain that to me."

"I don't know what more." She put her hands over her face and let out a keening wail.

"Iris! Look at me! You've got to pull yourself together. You can't go on this way. You have to be strong for your children."

"I can't deal with kids."

"That's your hangover talking. When all the booze is out of your system, you'll think differently."

"So now I'm an old drunk. Go ahead. Call me a drunk!"

Lillian began to giggle. In a singsong little girl's voice she chanted, "Iris is a drunk. Iris is a drunk." Then she put her arms around her sister and helped her to her feet. They walked toward the house with their arms intertwined and with Iris's blond head resting on Lillian's shoulder. I followed behind.

At the house, Iris's kids demanded breakfast. While the two women cooked, I went to the library and retrieved Old Charlie's diary. I had learned so much about Bernie and Silas that I had almost forgotten Arlie. I looked at the list again: "Arlie, November 17, 1931, wasted away/POISON?" And right after that note, "Ira."

I had found only a short obituary for Arlie. I replaced the diary in the drawer and took out my notebook. *Arlie,* I wrote, *died suddenly, not slowly.* When everyone left I would add what John Hale had told me. I left three blank pages for that.

Lillian served breakfast. Iris sat at one end of the table, concentrating hard on painting her fingernails. I watched as she spread thick red polish from the edge of each half-moon cuticle to the nail's point. She curled the loaded brush over the end of each. The result was a slick enamel bed that arose from perfect crescents of white.

"Did my mom call?" I asked.

"No," Lillian answered.

"I guess I'll call her then."

"Don't you touch that phone," Iris muttered. "She's the one who ran away. Leave her be."

"Aren't you worried about her?"

"No need to worry about your mother," Lillian said. "She's always been able to take care of herself."

"And everyone else around here," I said under my breath.

Lenny laughed.

Iris looked up from her nail painting. "What did you say?"

"I didn't say anything."

"Well, you must have said something to make my son laugh."

Lenny pushed his plate aside and ran out the back door. It slammed behind him. Larry swallowed his last piece of bacon and followed his brother.

"I guess you're stuck with the dishes," Iris said. She blew on her nails as she pushed through the screen door backward. "Too bad. If you'd been nicer, I might have helped."

CHAPTER EIGHTEEN

Two days later all the visitors drove away. Pop took over the cooking. He made his favorite hobo dishes: hamburger soup—a little meat, a lot of onions, water, and catsup—and camp bean sandwiches, made by placing an open can of pork and beans on the coal stove and then cutting a stale loaf of bread in half, crosswise. He hollowed out the bread, poured the hot beans in, added catsup, and passed the dry innards as dippers. When the beans were all eaten, the bread crust was soft enough to chew. That was Pop's favorite part. For dessert he made graham crackers spread with his own brand of butter icing—Crisco and white sugar mixed together with a fork. We washed it all down with soda he bought on tick at the rod and gun club. He was spending longer hours at the club, where beer was served early and cold, every day of the week.

I gave all my paint-by-number kits to Sally after I labored over a smeared and fuzzy trio of puppies that in the end looked more like lions than pups. I was lousy at painting. I couldn't make the brush stay within the lines on the printed board. When Sally painted out of the lines, she blended colors together and made it look as if she'd planned it that way. Her paintings made me want to dip my feet into the flowing mountain streams she brought alive with a few movements of her brush.

Besides, she needed more kits because she was trying out a new boyfriend. He visited every Sunday and painted almost as well as she. They sat side by side at the dining room table for hours, barely saying a word as they concentrated on their creations. While they painted, they played footsy, rubbing their calves together and intertwining their ankles under the table. Sometimes they linked their bare toes together, like they were holding hands with their feet.

With Mom gone and Pop often absent, I was too often alone in the big house. Sally understood and offered long evening walks when her shift was done. One afternoon in late July we hiked the hot pavement of Giant's Despair to Prospect Rock. A light breeze blew through the trees and cooled the shaded sides of the massive stones. We climbed to a comfortable perch and stared out over the valley. The setting sun highlighted ribbons of highway, the sluggish river, and the slate roofs of the valley churches.

"If Mom was here, she'd be telling us about the women and kids who died scrambling over these rocks," I said.

Sally laughed. "And she'd say how lucky we are to have the stubborn blood of the Marcies and Fitches running through our veins. Look!" She pointed to the adjacent ridge of mountain where several families, their backs bent to their work, were picking huckleberries along a steep face of rock. "If Mom saw them she'd be singing 'Huckleberry miner, kiss my hiner.' Let's do it!"

"It's not the same if we do it. Only Mom does it right."

She sighed. "Do you miss her like I do?"

"More. At least you have a boyfriend to keep you company."

She rested her back against the rocks and smiled. "That is nice. But don't worry. It won't be long before you have one too. Maybe it will be Chuck."

"No. You were right. He's too old for me. I haven't seen him around for a long time."

"Because he's working."

"Where?"

"His pop got him a job over on the south slope."

My heart turned to lead. "Isn't that dangerous for a boy?"

"Shouldn't be. Not with his pop there to watch out for him. Honest. There's nothing to worry about. His pop's been working that mine for twenty years. He'll teach him the ropes."

"I guess he won't be hanging around the skating pond next year."

"Probably not. But maybe on weekends or something."

"He wants to do something like go to college, but he doesn't know how to get there."

"Did he tell you that?"

"Yes."

"He started working with his pop in April. He dropped out of school."

"Oh." I had the feeling he'd made a bad decision. In the valley, college was a far-off dream for most of us.

"Not everybody is as smart as you."

"I'm not smart. I have a good memory."

"You read too much."

"No, I don't." I was getting mad at her and I didn't know why.

She pointed to a figure making its way between the heaped hills of red slag and the steaming vents of the underground fire a half mile below us. "Who's that?"

I squinted into the bright light. "It must be Ronald Miller. Nobody else would be stupid enough to walk on that part of the mine fire. What's he doing?"

"I think he's looking for something."

The figure crouched and disappeared into a tangle of low-growing vines. When he emerged he was fifty yards closer. He stopped, bent over, dropped to his knees, and leaned onto all fours.

"He's playing seer," I said. "He's breathing in the fumes."

"Well, that's a stupid thing to do. He could get dizzy and fall in."

"Lenny likes to do that. He likes the dizzy part."

"You're kidding."

"Honest. I saw him do it."

"You should have told Iris."

"I only saw him do it once. It was a long time ago."

"You're sure? Only once?"

"Honest."

Ronald Miller rolled over and lay on his back staring at the sky.

"Do you think he's okay?" I asked.

"I don't know. I hope so. Should we go down there?"

I felt a shudder run up my spine. "No way. I'm not going any closer."

Sally laughed. "What are you scared of?"

"Doesn't he scare you?"

"He doesn't have a case on me." She laughed again and nudged me with her shoulder. "It's you he likes."

I wished I could think his interest in me was funny. "Sally?"

"What?"

"I found some pictures in that old fur coat. You know, the one made of lambskin?"

She kept her eyes on Ronald. He was swinging his head in half circles as he lay looking at the sky. "Yeah? What kind of pictures?"

"Naked pictures. Of boys."

She lost all interest in Ronald. "Really? Where are they?"

"Pop burned them."

"Figures." She was disappointed.

"They were doing things, and I wondered if that guy Jack did those things when he went out with other boys."

"What kind of things?"

"Laying together and showing all their privates."

"You saw their privates?"

I nodded. I was too embarrassed to say more, and definitely too embarrassed to tell her that I'd seen Ronald Miller's privates too. "Do you think he liked to do that?"

"Whose pictures were they?"

"I don't know. Pop burned them."

"Wow! Somebody was a pervert."

"Was Jack a pervert?"

"Yes."

"Do you think Ronald Miller is a pervert?"

"Because he has a crush on you?"

I couldn't tell her the truth. I was ashamed of the truth. "Because he shoots animals."

She patted my arm. "No. Shooting dogs doesn't make somebody a pervert. Carrying pictures of naked people around does."

Ronald Miller was back on his feet. He staggered up the path toward us.

"Let's go, before he sees us," I said. I scampered up the rocks and over to the Giant's Despair side. Together we ran full tilt down the steepest part of the hill.

When we reached the house, I slumped onto the couch.

"I miss Mom," Sally said. "It doesn't look like Pop will go and make her come home, so I think we should."

That perked me up.

~

I wore my birthday outfit. We took the bus to Wilkes-Barre, transferred, and took another bus that moved slowly along narrow country roads. Mom wasn't at the farmhouse of the old neighbors in Back Mountain. Her friend Josie said she was working the midday shift at a tavern in Luzerne. Mom hadn't said a word about that. Pop would be mortified. Everybody knew a wife never worked a regular job unless her husband was a ne'er-do-well.

We each spent a quarter for yet another bus.

I hummed Mom's favorite tune.

Sally gave me one of her holier-than-thou looks. "Shut up."

She said that again when I protested creeping up the steps to the tavern door. We stuck our heads into the dim room. A wave of dark odors spilled over us—stale beer, overflowed toilet, and cigarettes. A laughing group of men shoved us inside. Country and western music twanged from a jukebox. I pulled closer to Sally and searched for Mom.

Suddenly she was there, her face highlighted in the rectangle light of the service pass behind the bar. I pushed Sally in that direction. She pushed back. We fell through the swinging kitchen door. A blast of oven-hot air hit me.

Mom wore a long flannel skirt, a cowboy shirt lined with fringe, and black leather boots with heels that clicked back and forth on the tile floor, twice, before she noticed us. She wiped her hands on her soiled apron, stopped still, and smiled. Her face was flushed. Damp ringlets escaped from her red headband. I was so startled by her appearance, I couldn't move.

She banged a huge white plate against the steel countertop and shouted, "Philly steak! Up and over!" The plate went sailing over the scarred shelf that opened into the bar. A pair of hands carried the food away.

"Well, lookie here," she drawled in a fake cowgirl twang. "Look what the dog's drug in."

"Mom!" my sister said. "Talk right!"

"My God!" I breathed.

She pulled two stools from under the long counter. "Sit yourselves over here. I'll rustle you up something to eat."

"Mom!" Sally said in her best grown-up voice. "What are you doing?"

"What does it look like I'm doing? I'm working." She brushed her damp hair from her forehead and grinned. "What are you doing here?"

I let Sally do the talking. "We came to take you home."

"Did Pop send you?"

I shook my head.

"You can't work here!" Sally said.

"Why not? Cooking is what I do best."

I had a one-track mind. "Come home."

She concentrated on the grill and the growing number of paper slips that hung on a small carousel in the window to the bar. She read two slips of paper and threw four hamburgers on the grill. She worked quickly, flipped, dipped, coated, layered on cheese, and hollered out, "Cheeseburger up! Chili burger up!"

She turned back to us. "Sit down! Anyone sees you, we'll all be out on our noses!"

We obeyed.

She continued to work the orders. "You came at our busiest time, so I'm going to have to talk as I go. I'll be off as soon as my relief shows up. I'll make you something to eat. What do you want? Cat got your tongues? Hamburger? Chili? Grilled cheese sandwich?" She took two more slips of paper from the carousel. She definitely enjoyed shocking us.

"Nothing," Sally said.

"Don't you stick your fancy nose up at me, young lady." She continued to read orders and throw food on the grill. "Do you want a grilled cheese?"

I stretched up tall so I could watch her drop breaded chicken pieces into a spattering vat of oil. I wanted her to cook for me.

"A ham sandwich," I said.

"Coming up."

My sister's eyes disapproved, but she agreed. "I want one too."

Mom sent out two orders of chicken, a big basket of French fries, a couple of plates of hamburgers, and one club sandwich before she set perfectly toasted ham sandwiches in front of us. She raised her eyebrows when we both refused soda, but poured orange juice into tall beer glasses and smiled as we drank.

I kicked both feet against the metal of the stool and watched her work. She smiled constantly. "We'll take the bus back to the farm and have a nice visit when I'm done." Her hands moved quickly as she spoke.

An hour later, the relieving cook pushed through a back door. She was dressed like Mom but was skinnier and kept a cigarette between her lips as she talked. Mom led us out to the clean air and quiet night. She was different. She walked fast and straight out, like Pop. I had a hard time keeping up.

She didn't speak again until we climbed onto the bus. Then she put an arm over each of our shoulders as we settled ourselves on the long back seat. "Have I finally shocked you two into silence?"

I nodded so soberly it made her laugh.

"Pop still bombed off his ass?"

She did shock me. I nodded again.

"Lillian and Iris gone for good?"

"And Marty," Sally scolded. "You didn't say good-bye to Marty."

"Yes, I did. He came over a couple of times and we had good visits."

"He never told us."

"Of course he didn't. He couldn't come into the tavern if he had you along."

"Does Pop know about your job?" Sally asked.

"I'm sure Marty told him. But whether he did or didn't isn't important. What I do with my time is my business. What he does with his is his."

"There's no more garden left. It's all turned to weeds and dried out." Too late I realized that I was accusing her of neglect.

"I can't do anything about that."

"Don't you care about home anymore?" I wailed.

She didn't answer. She turned to Sally. "So, Miss Prim, I hear you've spent a good deal of *your* time away too."

Sally blushed. "I stayed awhile at the Donals'. Mrs. Donal has been sick and I helped out."

"And that has nothing to do with her handsome grandson, does it?"

Sally changed the subject. "You've got to come home, Mom. Pop has lost it. You've got to do something."

"Nobody can do anything when your pop goes on one of his toots. He won't stop until he's ready."

"Aren't you worried about him? Aren't you worried about us?" I wanted her to take responsibility for everything.

"I do worry, but I also trust that you can handle yourselves. I'm taking a little breather."

"You left us with Iris." That was a major sin to me.

Mom's laugh had become like Lillian's. "We don't get to choose our families. You're not old enough to understand. Everything will be all right. Aunt Iris is a little misguided."

"How can you say that? She's spent half her life in jail!" Sally said.

"Don't exaggerate. She's doing better."

"You don't know her, Mom!" I was sure that I did.

"Look, girls, this is between your pop and me. It has nothing to do with Iris or you."

"You're making Pop feel bad and now he's snockered all the time." She had to accept the blame; otherwise, who was responsible?

"Don't you dare put this on me, young lady! He's snockered all the time because he chooses to be. Things come up from his past like fat red bobbers on a fishing line. That sadness triggers every ounce of his Irishness. He'll drink until he's had enough, and he won't stop until then."

"It's his pop who's making him sad. And his brother Mike. And Magee being sick, and New Jersey. And Iris."

Her face fell. "Iris? What has she done to upset him?"

I shrugged.

"Tell me, Molly. What has she done?"

"What she always does: sits around and complains about everybody and everything. You know how she is."

"That's all?"

"Yes."

"What does she complain about?"

"I told you. Everything."

She looked out the bus window long and hard.

"Mom?"

"What?"

"Is that why you wouldn't come home—because Iris was there?"

"Partly."

"What's the other part?"

"That's between me and your pop."

I decided that I needed to remind her how much she always liked Pop. "Mom?"

"What?"

"Tell me again how you met Pop."

My sister gave me a look that said I was the stupidest person on two feet.

"Oh, Molly. It's an old story. You've heard it lots of times."

"Tell me anyway."

She sighed deeply. "I met him on the riverbank. That was where everyone went on warm summer nights. Iris and me got all dressed up and took the Laurel Line down to the square. Everybody walked then, and the square and the riverbank park were packed with people."

"And you had a crush on a policeman there, right?"

She laughed. "Well, he was cute. I was trying to impress him. I was only a little older than you girls. You know how you see someone and think they're cute?"

I knew exactly what she meant. I thought of Chuck.

"Pop and his brother were sitting on the grass. They were not the kind of boys anyone approved of."

"What year was that?" I wanted definite dates for my newspaper search.

"1932."

Sally interrupted. "People didn't approve of them because they hopped freights and they were out of work. Pop said he only had one pair of pants and two shirts to his name."

"See. You already know this story, so there's no need for me to tell it again."

"He was going to visit his Aunt Maura, but she had customers, so he came down to the riverbank to wait," I said

"Why couldn't he wait on her porch?" Sally asked.

"She didn't have a porch. She lived on the second floor of a house."

"What kind of customers did she have?" I asked.

"The male kind."

"Hah!" I said. "I knew we didn't know the real story. Aunt Mary Margaret said that Maura ran a cathouse."

"Molly. I'm surprised at you. That isn't nice."

"But it's true, isn't it?"

She thought about that for a while before she spoke. "Yes. I guess I didn't realize you've grown up so much. Are you sure you know what that means?"

"That she slept with men for a price."

"To put it simply, yes. Because she had that place, she wasn't considered a wholesome guardian for the boys and they weren't supposed to go there."

"Why?"

"Politics."

"What kind of politics?"

"The kind that can put you in jail."

"Did Aunt Maura go to jail?"

"When the politics weren't right."

"Did Pop ever go to jail?"

She gave me a long, hard, glazed-over look. "You know what? You're getting awfully snoopy."

My face grew hot. She was on to me.

"Come on, Mom," Sally said. "Ignore her. Finish the story."

Mom stared at me for a long time before she decided to go on. "So we went to the river and as we flirted with the policeman your pop walked by, looked me over, and said, 'Hey, there, Tuffy.' I snatched the policeman's bully club and hit your pop on the head. He says it knocked him silly."

"What did the policeman do?"

"Well, that ended any chance I had with him. At any rate, he really had his eye on Iris."

Mom reached up and pulled the bell cord for the bus to stop. We had to hurry to keep up. I decided that when she and Pop met, she was like Cinderella and Pop had been the prince who saved her. I knew that Pop would slap his knee and roll over laughing if I ever said that out loud, so I kept it to myself.

"Why did you fall for Pop?"

She was silent for a time before she answered. "I guess because he was an enigma."

"An enigma? What's an enigma?"

"Hey, you're the gal who likes to spend all her time in libraries. There's a big dictionary at the city one. Look it up."

The farmhouse was tiny—three unheated bedrooms upstairs and three rooms downstairs. It was a homestead cabin with an original lean-to kitchen and a newer, add-on bathroom. The coal stove in the kitchen was used all day for cooking and canning. Opening every window did nothing to cool the house down, so as soon as supper was done, everyone gathered on the porch. That's where we found Mom's friends. We could hear their chatter long before we came through the pine trees that lined the drive. Sally didn't come with us but continued down the road toward the house with no doorknobs where we'd lived.

A bowl of ripe plums sat at the top of the steps that divided the porch into informal men's and women's areas. Mom's friend sat in a straight-backed kitchen chair. Two empty chairs waited next to her. A bushel basket of green beans lay at her feet. On the longer side, five men leaned back in curved iron outdoor loungers and rested their feet on the porch rail. A cloud of tobacco smoke marked their territory.

Mom went inside to change out of her cowgirl outfit. I sat at the top of the stone stairs, ate a plum, and drank the cold glass of water offered to me.

When Mom came back she looked normal again in a crisp cotton housedress. She tied an apron around her waist, took an empty chair, and began to snap beans to jar-sized lengths. I leaned against the stone column, felt the coolness of the stone diffuse through the muscles and bones of my back, and took another plum. The men drank beer. The women drank iced coffee.

It was too quiet. I stood and began to back across the yard.

"Where are you going?" Mom asked.

"To find Sally," I said.

She waved, said something to the men on the end of the porch, bent down, and pulled another lapful of beans into her apron. When she raised her face to the late afternoon sun, she was radiant, relaxed, and full of life.

That's when it dawned on me: This was who she was. This was where she was happy. When she and Pop first married, this is where they chose to live. She had gone back to the big house to help her family and had gotten stuck.

Here there was no mine fire, no monster machines tearing down the mountain, no trucks grinding up and down the hill, and no Iris. Here there was only the soft calling of the whippoorwill from its hiding place by the creek, the scent of tomatoes ripening on fragrant vines, the sound of laughter coming from folks exhausted after a day of hard work, yet working still.

She was a country girl. She knew that about herself. And then the rest of it came to me: Pop knew that about her too. She had already sacrificed too much. She would wilt and die in the industrial part of New Jersey.

I pushed aside the branches of the pine trees, stepped onto the gravel road, yelled for Sally, and ran as hard as I could toward the house with no doorknobs—for the pure pleasure of feeling the power of my young legs carrying me forward. Sally and I would take the bus back home, but Mom would stay here. I was no longer worried. She would come home when she was good and ready.

CHAPTER NINETEEN

The next morning I decided to try to save the neglected garden. I had watered and weeded half of it when I noticed a stooped man turn off the main road and take the path that would bring him by our house. He stopped on the side of the hill, half turned, and leaned heavily on a walking stick. Behind him a new section of the mountain was being torn away by the chain-clanking Mountaineer. The morning sun caught the man's silhouette against another newly exposed face of gray slate and black coal. He became a round sandstone boulder in a field of rubble. He turned to face our house and seemed to roll very slowly downhill until he came to rest against one of the few surviving maple trees.

He straightened himself, brought his hand to his chest, and coughed. Black lung, I thought. Only a man with damaged lungs needed to stop and rest on a downhill walk.

I wiped my hands on my jeans and went through the house to the front porch. I leaned over the rail until I could see him again.

When he came close enough for me to see his face, I thought I saw a sharp intelligence, but then he reached beneath his vest and pulled out a bottle. He tilted his head, drank deeply from the bottle, and wiped his mouth with a sleeve of his denim jacket. His long arms ended in thick wrists and hammer hands like Pop's.

Someone's grandfather, I decided, out to take a closer look at the Mountaineer. I stepped back and sat on the porch swing. The sun cast his shadow on our front steps. He stepped between the hedges and climbed the first stair.

"Hello," he said. "Is this Sean's house?"

"Sean Branigan?"

"Yes." He came closer.

"He's not home."

"When will he be here?"

I peered in through the window to check the wall clock. "In about an hour. Maybe."

"I'll wait for him."

"You'll find him faster at the rod and gun club."

"I've come a long way and I'm tired." His stick hammered the floorboards as he crossed the porch.

Sally came to the screen door.

"This guy wants to talk to Pop," I said.

"I heard."

As he stood in front of the swaying swing, he grasped its chain and sat beside me.

"I'll wait in this nice shade," he said.

I didn't like being so close to a stranger. I stood and allowed him to sit alone on the swing.

"I can call him," Sally offered from the safety of the front hall. "Who should I say you are?"

"Tell him it's his papa. Tell him his Papa George is here."

I opened the screen door and pushed past my sister.

She followed me into the dining room. We huddled together and whispered.

"What should we do?" I asked.

"Let him wait for Pop," Sally said.

"No."

"Call Mom."

"Lock the doors. Don't let him inside the house." I headed toward the back door.

"He's just an old man." Sally grabbed my shirt and held me still.

"Pop hates him."

"You go keep him on the porch while I call Mom." She pushed me toward the front hallway.

"No, *you* go keep him on the porch and *I'll* call Mom."

She shoved me hard again. "I'm the boss when Mom and Pop are gone. Now do what I say."

As I moved slowly toward the door, she added, "Ask him if he's hungry. Or if he wants a drink."

"He already has a drink. In his pocket." I patted my shirtfront to demonstrate where. She understood.

I stepped onto the porch, leaned against the banister as far away from him as I could, and tried to smile.

"What's your name?" he asked.

"Molly."

He laughed and slapped his knee. "Molly. That's a good one. Named after a bunch of hooligans that was hanged." He reached into his pocket, pulled out the bottle, and held it out to offer me a swig.

My face must have registered both surprise and disgust, because he scowled.

"That couldn't be Branigan blood you got running in your veins. Never knew a Branigan that would turn down good whiskey."

I didn't know what to say.

"Is your Mom home?"

"No."

"It's nice shade you got here. Nice place. I hear your daddy owns it."

"It's my grandmother's. She lets us live here."

"That's not what I heard."

I shrugged. "Do you want some water?"

"Nah. Water would rust my pipes."

I stared at him.

"I hope you're a better kid than your father was. Bunch of real hellions, him and his brothers. Nothing but trouble." He took another deep drink from his brown bottle.

"I'm no trouble."

"You think so, eh? Your daddy probably thought that about himself too. He ran away, you know. Up and took off with his retard brother and became a bum."

I didn't like him.

He kept on. "He blames me for everything. Your pop does. I should let him go to hell. I should wash my hands of him." He looked at me with rheumy eyes.

I was ashamed for him—ashamed that he would lie about my pop.

He pulled himself upright in the swing, hitched up his pants with a little tug, and smiled.

"I'd be takin' somethin' to eat, if you got it. A little sannich or somethin'."

I was glad to escape into the house.

Sally covered the mouthpiece of the phone as I came in.

"I found Mom at the farm. She's coming. She said to call Aunt Mary because she can get here quicker. It's ringing now."

I caught my breath. "I don't like that man. I don't want him to stay here. I'm going to find him something to eat, but I don't want to be on that porch pretending everything is hunky-dory."

"What do you think Pop will do?"

"He'll blow a gasket!"

She took her hand off the mouthpiece and spoke to one of Aunt Mary's kids. "Is your mother home?"

I made a sandwich of store-bought white bread, catsup, and a thick slab of cheese. I put it on a plate and filled a glass with spring water. I hoped it would rust his pipes.

As I came back past Sally she whispered, "Aunt Mary knows. She dropped him off on the main road. She says Pop will be okay, that we should be nice to the old man and make him feel welcome."

"Pop will be mad."

We broke into nervous giggles as she set the phone back on its cradle. She walked with me to the porch.

My grandfather took the sandwich but pushed away the water. He didn't say thank you. We tried our best to make small talk. I asked where he lived. He answered, "Around." Sally asked where he worked. He answered, "Don't much." I asked if he was married. He raised his eyebrows like he'd been stung by a bee and answered, "Would be a cold day in hell."

Time crawled by. It came to a dead stop when Pop's car rattled over the culvert and started up the hill. I watched him pull in by the hedges. I wrapped my fingers around the banister and held my breath while he took the steps two at a time.

"Hello, Sean boy," the old man said.

Pop reeled backward on the stairs. He grabbed the rail with both hands and steadied himself. His head reared up like a rattler about to strike. He surged forward.

"What the hell are you doing here?"

"Can't you say hello to your old pop?"

"You ain't my pop!" His voice was high and childlike.

"Sean boy." George said the name softly, in a begging way.

As the surprise went out of him, Pop became adult again, and sure.

"You are not my pop! Out! Get the hell out of here!"

"I want to talk to you, Sean. Your old man just wants to talk to you."

"You're a vile old man. Now get out!"

"I'm asking forgiveness, Sean. On your mother's soul, before I die. I need forgiveness."

I couldn't stand to hear him. I turned and hurried into the house. Sally followed closely behind. Pop's voice followed us in and filled every space of the narrow hallway.

"Then go find that priest, that Father Cavanaugh," he boomed.

"Will you throw an old man out?"

"I will if he doesn't move on his own!"

"Hear me out, Sean."

My sister took my shaking hand in hers. We held together tightly and peered through the dark screen door.

"You listen to me. I said get out! Move, old man. Get out."

The old man folded his arms and glared with a kind of defiance no one should have dared to show my father. "You'll have to throw me out."

I was afraid Pop was going to do just that. But he turned, flung the screen door open, and nearly knocked Sally and me over as he pushed on through.

Sally shouted after him, "I didn't know what to do, Pop."

"It's not your fault." He threw the words back as he continued on into the kitchen. I could hear him muttering to himself as he approached the back door. "On my mother's soul. On my mother's soul."

The back door slammed behind him. George had not moved. I placed the hook lock into its grommet and pulled Sally away from the door. We leaned against the cool wall of the hall.

"I'm going to call Aunt Mary again," Sally whispered. She headed toward the phone.

George took another swig from his bottle, allowed a small smile to show, leaned back, and closed his eyes. It didn't seem that he planned to go anywhere. I went after Sally.

"Aunt Mary is already on her way. She's bringing Father Cavanaugh," she said.

"Oh, my God! Pop doesn't like *him* either."

The only person who could help was Mom. We both knew that. And then, as if in answer to an unspoken prayer, a car turned up the hill. We ran onto the porch. My vision narrowed until my mother climbing out of that car was all that I could see. We rushed into her waiting arms.

She was dressed for work, cowboy boots and all.

"Where is he?"

"He took off," Sally answered.

"He ran out back," I added.

"George is on the porch," we both said.

"Aunt Mary is on her way with Father Cavanaugh," Sally said.

Mom didn't wait to hear more. She thanked the man driving the car, waved him off down the hill, and hurried around the house. I heard another car rattling over the culvert. We waited on the concrete step as Aunt Mary Margaret and Father Cavanaugh climbed from the priest's car.

George shouted from the swing, "I'm not going anywhere until he hears what I have to say. I'm staying right here."

"Sean owes him that much, Father," Aunt Mary said. She and Father Cavanaugh began to climb the stairs. Sally and I followed.

"That could be, Mary," Father Cavanaugh said, "but Sean's a stubborn man. You may not get a hearing tonight."

"Then I'll wait all night," George shouted. "I'll sit right here and wait."

"And I can see where Sean's stubbornness comes from," Father Cavanaugh said.

"I'm not askin' much, Father. Only the respect any man should get from his only living son."

"You'll get none of that from me, old man!" Pop came around the hedges from the lower yard. He took the steps with three quick moves of his long legs. He stopped in front of the swing and shook his fist at his father. "You'll get no respect and you'll get nothing else."

"Sean," Aunt Mary Margaret begged. As she pushed past Pop, she pressed hard on his menacing arm to lower it, then sat on the swing next to George. She took George's hand in both of hers, looked up, and said, "Hear him out. What can that hurt?"

Father Cavanaugh stood beside the swing. "Sean, before God, as your confessor and your priest, I'm asking that you listen to what he has to say."

"You got one minute, old man. Then you leave."

Mom ran through the lower yard. Her breath came in short gasps. Her face was pale. Her green eyes darted to the men on the porch. She stepped onto the concrete stair and paused to listen.

George leaned forward, folded his hands together, and raised them to his chest. His fingers touched his chin as he began to speak.

"I did wrong. I know I did wrong. But I'm an old man now and I can see my mistakes. I want to be with my grandchildren. I want to die surrounded by family. I don't want to die alone."

"Alone?" Pop's voice was steady. "You're afraid to die alone? Tell me, who was with Matthew when he died? Eh? Were you there? Was a doctor there? Did you sit with him as he turned blue and shook? Did you do anything to help him, old man?"

"I didn't know. I didn't know he was that sick. I thought he was faking so he wouldn't get his punishment for the chim'ley."

"You forget, old man, I took his punishment for the chimney. Don't you remember the beating you gave me? 'For the two of you,' you said. 'So you won't never forget.'" Pop turned away as if it was too painful to look on his father. "I didn't forget. I'll never forget."

"I was on the booze, Sean. It was hard for a man alone. You were hooligans, you boys were. You did what you wanted to do. I couldn't keep a roof over your heads and watch you every minute."

"You were alone because of what you did to Ma. I saw what you did to Ma. And I blame you for what happened to Mike and Aunt Maura in the end. Too many sins, old man. Too many sins to forgive." The starch had gone out of Pop. He looked like he might fall to his knees.

Mom dashed up the stairs. She stood behind him, placed both of her hands flat against his back, elbows bent, her face close to his shoulder blades, as if her mere presence could boost him up.

George unfolded his hands and pointed. "Look at your wife, Sean. Tell me you've never been mad enough to hit her. Say you don't sometimes get so riled you have to take it out on someone. Tell me you're a man like the rest of us."

"Don't you bring my wife into this. I've never laid a hand on her. You sicken me." He stepped forward and loomed over his father. Mom pulled on the back of his shirt, twisted it slightly in both her hands, and held tight. "Get off my porch. Go."

Mary stood. "How can you stand here in front of your children and refuse the last wishes of your own father?"

"If he doesn't go now, my children will see worse. Get him out of here."

"Not until you forgive him."

Suddenly Mom's hands were empty in midair. "No, Sean!" she cried.

Pop grabbed the old man by his lapels and pulled him to his feet. They seemed to take up all the space on the wide porch, to fill the air with their anger, to stand so firmly eye to eye and toe to toe that for a moment they were more huge and powerful than that big Mountaineer that was shoveling away our mountain.

"Off!" Pop said. "Off my porch!" He began using his full weight and his upraised knee to force the man to the stairs.

They thumped down each level, Pop pushing and George resisting, until the old man crumpled and sat down firmly on the lowest step. Pop pulled him up again and tried to drag him into the street. The bottle fell out of George's pocket and smashed on the concrete slab. He reached for it and cut his hand on the broken glass. Blood began to mix with the booze as it ran into the dirt.

"Oh, my God!" Aunt Mary Margaret ran down the stairs and tried to separate the men.

Father Cavanaugh followed. He got his arms around Pop from the back and tried to force him to move away. He was not tall or strong enough.

"Let me go, Father!" Pop warned. "I'm going to kill the bastard!"

The old man looked up. His face became an ugly mask.

"It shoulda been you who died in the loony bin and not that imbecile of a brother of yours. At least *he* was a mistake of God. What excuse do you have?"

"You stinkin' bastard. I can't stand the sight of you!"

Aunt Mary Margaret tried again to pull the old man backward but he stepped toward Pop and jutted his chin defiantly.

"At least I never whored myself like your uppity Aunt Maura. And I wasn't no pervert like your friend Magee. How do you think Mike went wrong? Magee made him the way he was. You can blame yourself and Magee for that!"

Mom tried to jump in front of Pop but she wasn't fast enough. She was caught between the two men. She took the full force of Pop's punch, fell backward, knocked George to the ground, and sent Aunt Mary to her knees. Pop raised his arm again but Sally ran down the stairs and flung herself into the mess. She cried out for Mom and pushed both hands against Pop's chest. I could not move.

For one long, stretched-out instant we all stood still.

Father Cavanaugh moved first. He stepped around Pop and pulled the old man to his feet. He helped Aunt Mary Margaret up. He moved them toward his car. He turned once, as if to speak to Pop, then shook his head and climbed into the driver's seat.

I stood at the top of the stairs and watched as Pop knelt before Mom and helped her sit up. He slumped to the ground with his back against the hedges and pulled her to him.

"Jesus, Toots, I'm sorry. I'm so sorry."

Father Cavanaugh began to pull away. George rolled down his window and shouted, "You'll burn in hell for this, Sean. All the angels and all the saints can't help you now."

"So be it, old man," Pop shouted back.

And then a nervous cackle, the one that was so much like Lillian's, escaped from Mom's chest. Her boots were straight out in front of her in the dirt. Her skirt was above her knees. Her headband had fallen five feet away. The fringes on her shirt began to shake with her laughter.

"I saw stars," she said.

Pop cradled her head to his chest and kissed her forehead.

Still she laughed. "We're even, now," she said. "You can't throw that bully club up to me ever again."

That made Pop laugh, even while he kept saying he was sorry.

"What's so funny?" Sally demanded. "I don't see anything that's funny."

I couldn't see anything funny either, but it didn't matter because, there in the gravel with glass and booze and the old man's blood around them, Mom and Pop were hugging. An understanding had crossed between them, a truth that their shared history allowed only them to understand. They were finally in the same place again. I knew that as surely as I knew my own name and that Magee was no pervert.

Sally ran into the house and came back with a hunk of ice wrapped in a towel. Pop took it from her and placed it gently against Mom's jaw. She relaxed against him, buried her face in his shirt, and wrapped her arms around his torso.

I was embarrassed by their sudden upswelling of affection. I crossed the porch and sat on the swaying swing. Sally came up and sat beside me. We smiled at each other. Sally gave a kick of her foot and sent us swinging. I straightened my legs and pumped to make us go higher. Our parents' voices rose up harmoniously from behind the hedges.

After what seemed like a very long time, Pop called up to us, "We have to go get Mom's stuff at the farm. Do you want to come for the ride?"

I looked at my sister and shook my head. She answered for the both of us.

"No," she said. "We'll wait here."

I heard the car door slam and the engine start up.

"She's going to come home," Sally said.

I nodded.

The sun began to disappear behind the ridge of mountains to the west. Dark figures moved down Giant's Despair. Cheerful voices rang softly through the deepening twilight. The dull thud of full huckleberry cans beat a rhythm with steady footfalls. I took a deep breath and sang out, "Huckleberry miner, kiss my hiner."

The group looked over as one, waved, and laughed. We could hear their laughter long after they were swallowed up by the darkness.

CHAPTER TWENTY

Pop left for New Jersey on Labor Day. He carried his work clothes in a shopping bag, set his steel-toed boots on the floor of the car, waved once, and drove away. He had rented a room in the same boarding house as some of his coworkers, who also left their families behind.

I began to cry long before his car disappeared above Devil's Elbow. I cried all night.

When I walked from my room the next morning, dressed for school, the house was strangely quiet. I sniffed the air for the waft of cigarette smoke that usually drifted up through the spindles of the banister. There was none.

I found Mom in the kitchen. Her eyes were red-rimmed. Her face was pale.

"I can't believe we've been forced to do this," she murmured.

I spooned oatmeal from the pot on the stove and dribbled on some honey. I carried my bowl to the table.

Mom stood staring out the window above the sink. Her shoulders shook.

"Now we're the only ones in this big old house," she said. "No men. Only three lonely girls."

The oatmeal was too thick to swallow. I carried my bowl to the sink, set it on the drainboard, filled a glass of water from the tap, and sipped it.

Mom placed a hand lightly on my arm. "We'll be okay. We'll get used to it. Won't we?"

"I'll never get use to it," I said, and began to cry again.

She inhaled deeply, sighed, and gazed out the window at the empty chair where Pop usually sat to drink his morning coffee.

Sally, who had hoped to stay out of school forever but was made to return by Mom, would now repeat her senior year. She came into the kitchen and wrapped her arms around Mom. It was all too much. I picked up my books, called to Sally, and together we started down Fitch Lane toward the high school bus. I tried to be excited, but everything was wrong. Nothing would ever be the same without my pop.

We were only a few feet away from our house when Sally pointed to the crowd at the bottom of the hill.

"That's not school kids," she said. "Something's wrong."

We began to run toward the red light that rotated slowly in front of Mrs. Donal's house.

An ambulance came clearly into view. Two men lifted a stretcher completely covered with a white sheet into the open vehicle doors. As the ambulance pulled away, the light on its top went off.

We waded into the crowd. John Hale placed a hand on Sally's elbow.

"The paperboy found her dog dead on the inside porch this morning," he said. "When he knocked on the door and no one answered, he ran to the store. Harry and me went in and found her in her bed. She must have died in her sleep."

"From what?" Sally demanded, as if John Hale was to be blamed for something.

Sally was the one of us who always managed to keep her head. She hadn't yet cried about Pop's leaving, at least not out in the open. But Mrs. Donal had been a steady part of her life and this was one loss too many for her. She began to sob, right out there in the open, in the center of the crowd.

John Hale wrapped his arms around her. She cried into his shoulder as I stood by helplessly.

"From what?" Sally demanded again.

"Mine fire," he said. "All the windows were closed. Black-damp filled the house."

The school bus nosed its way through the crowd. John Hale guided us to the side of the street. He stood by the open bus door.

"Everyone go on to school," he said. "Come on, girls. Sally. Molly. You don't want to be late on the first day of school."

I stepped forward and obeyed. Sally broke loose, turned, and ran back up the hill.

~

"The state inspectors have started testing houses. They found methane gas in two on Marcy Street," Mom said as she placed supper on the table. She was interrupted by the ringing telephone. When she came back into the kitchen her hands were shaking.

"Mrs. Wriggs and her boarder were sickened too. They found them unconscious on her parlor floor."

"From the gas?" I asked.

She nodded. "Her boarder is a Mountaineer operator at the stripping hole. His dinner was still on the table and the back door was wide open. They say he must have been carrying Mrs. Wriggs toward the door when they were overcome. They were found in the nick of time. If that door hadn't been open they would have died."

I stood and opened the back door.

"But I do have some good news too," Mom added with a nervous smile. "My cousin Fern will be coming to stay with us for Mrs. Donal's funeral."

"Fern!" My heart jumped.

Mom's smile got bigger. "Yes. She's driving in with Mrs. Donal's daughter. They live in the same town in upstate New York."

"And she's staying here?" Sally asked.

"Yes. Oh, heavens." Mom's eyes were suddenly huge. "I haven't seen her in twenty years. What will she think of all this?"

I wasn't contemplating what Fern might think about anything other than the deaths of her mother Faye and Faye's brother, Arlie.

∾

I cried myself to sleep again but awoke more settled. Pop would never let tough circumstances get him down. He expected us to stand together and be strong.

After school I walked across the town square to the library and opened the big dictionary. I turned the pages carefully, ran my finger down word after word, but I could not find *transgrestite*. The closest word was "transvestite, n., a person who derives sexual pleasure from dressing in the clothes of the opposite sex." That had to be it. I decided that sexual pleasure must be what those photographs were all about.

I'd heard my brother use another word for a guy who was queer. I looked for that word and found "homosexual, adj., of or characterized by sexual desire for those of the same sex; n., a homosexual individual. Opposed to heterosexual." I also found "heterosexual, adj., of or characterized by sexual desire for those of the opposite sex."

The definitions sure seemed to dance around something. Nothing made sense. I decided to look up Mom's word: "enigma, n., a perplexing statement; riddle; hence a perplexing, baffling, or seemingly inexplicable matter, person, etc. SYN, see mystery."

Mom had got that one wrong. Pop was no mystery at all.

The nice librarian walked me to the basement. The air cooled as we descended the stairs. The librarian's heels clicked across the tiled floor. She wished me luck and clicked back up the stairs. Alone in that vault of a room, I began to cry.

"Stop whining," I said. My voice echoed through the hollow space. I knuckled down to the job of finding Mike.

After a summer of talking and listening, I had closer dates for the trouble he had gotten in. I began with the 1937 papers. That was the year everything came to a head for the Beckerman and Branigan families. The newspaper changed from a five-page edition of real news to a three-section tabloid of advertisements and entertainment. The rolled papers were heavy. My eyes strained in the dim light. It took several hours to find the first headline: "Branigan Arrested in Child Case." I read slowly, absorbing the details of every sentence.

> Admits Crime When Confronted by City Firemen.
> An outrageous crime was believed solved last night with the arrest of Michael Branigan, 26, of Myers Place, city, charged with criminally assaulting a Kingston child less than three years old. The child was found under the Market Street Bridge early Saturday night. City police said that in the statement they attributed to Branigan, the latter set forth that he was drunk at the time and that he did not realize what he had done until he read a newspaper account of the abduction. Patrolman Jack Deilsler arrested Branigan at 9:30 last night at Public Square.
>
> Questioned by the chief of police and three detectives, Branigan, according to police, finally admitted that he took the child from the automobile on North Washington Street on Saturday night about 7 p.m. The admission by Branigan, police say, came only after he was confronted by five city firemen from No. 2 engine house, a clerk in a North Washington Street store, and a nine-year-old boy of the same street, all of whom identified Branigan as being on North Washington Street. Four of the firemen positively identified Branigan as the man they saw near the automobile containing the child, around the time of his disappearance.

Branigan's apprehension by Patrolman Deilsler culminated an extensive search for "a man with a limp" who was believed by the authorities to have abducted the child from the automobile in which also sat his sister, aged 4. The parents of the children had left them in their automobile above No. 2 engine house while they went shopping. The child was found Saturday night about 8, when two North Wilkes-Barre youths heard moans coming from under the east side of the river bridge. The youths carried the boy to city police headquarters.

Last night at police headquarters the storekeeper said he was positive that Branigan was the man he saw. The nine-year-old boy also said he was certain that Branigan had approached him on the street early Saturday night. Four of the firemen who viewed Branigan at headquarters last night said they were certain they had seen Branigan loitering near the sedan containing the child.

Confronted by the witnesses, Branigan continued to deny that he abducted the boy. He asserted that he was on North Washington Street on Saturday night but asserted that he was at home before 8. Detectives told him that they had gone to his home after 8 Saturday and that he was not there. According to police, Branigan later volunteered information that he abducted the boy.

Patrolman Deilsler last night said that he had had Branigan under suspicion. He stated that Branigan's description fitted closely that of the man who police believed abducted the child. He said he watched Branigan closely for some time and noticed that the latter seemed to be avoiding policemen. He said that Branigan's actions finally excited his suspicions to such an extent that he decided to arrest him for investigation. When Deilsler brought Branigan into headquarters, the firemen and other persons who had reported they had seen the "man with the limp" acting suspiciously on Saturday night were summoned. One after another pointed out Branigan, the police said. Not one of these persons, however, actually saw the child abducted from the automobile. It was reported yesterday that the firemen from No. 2 saw the child taken from the car, but this was denied last night by the firemen.

Police say that Branigan is an orphan and that he resided with an aunt on Myers Place.

My hands shook as I went backward, day by day, until I found a picture with a crowd of shouting bystanders outside of police headquarters. The caption read, "Wilkes-Barre citizens demand police act quickly to find the man responsible for a three-year-old boy abducted and assaulted last evening." Beside the picture appeared the first article about the crime.

Wilkes-Barre Police Search for a Man With a Limp
An intensive manhunt is underway for a man with a limp who is believed by authorities, on the stories of five firemen from Station No.2, to have abducted a child from his father's automobile on North Washington Street. The boy's sister, aged 4, who was also in the car, was not harmed. The child was found last night by two youths who heard his moans coming from under the Market Street Bridge. The child was brutally assaulted.

A man with a decided limp was reported loitering around the automobile by a storekeeper. A nine-year-old boy described the same man as having stopped him on North Washington Street, but the boy was unable to understand the man's speech. He believed the man was inebriated. Five city firemen also witnessed an intoxicated man with a limp loitering near the area and removing the boy from the car.

I studied the photograph. One of the men standing at the door of the police station seemed vaguely familiar, but I couldn't possibly know anyone in that crowd. I hadn't yet been born.

The following day another article appeared:

Michael Branigan's Aunt Declares His Innocence
Maura Hanlon, a woman with a tarnished reputation in this city, told this reporter that she does not believe her nephew capable of committing the heinous crime of which he is accused. She stated that officials have refused to allow her visitation to the man, saying she will only succeed in agitating him further. Branigan continues to be held in solitary confinement at Eastern State Penitentiary. His aunt, appearing downtrodden and in a state of great agitation, collapsed at the doors of police headquarters this morning. She was taken to Mercy Hospital where she remains at the time of publication.

One day later, another headline on the bottom of the front page appeared:

Another Victim of Branigan Crime
Michael Branigan's heinous crime has taken another victim. While Branigan continued to vehemently deny any participation in the brutal assault of a young child, his only known relative died this morning at Mercy Hospital. Doctors say Maura Hanlon succumbed to a heart seizure. Relatives are being sought.

And yet another headline, the next day.

Branigan Dies at Eastern State Penitentiary
Michael Branigan was discovered in his confinement cell dead of an apparent brain seizure this morning. Punishment for his

brutal acts will be denied the citizenry of this good community. The body will be released to his surviving brother, Sean Branigan of Giant's Despair.

Poor Pop. He had warned me not to look too deep, that I might not like what I found. He was right. Now I understood why he never spoke about Mike's and Aunt Maura's deaths.

I paced the chilly space, trying hard to accept what I had read. None of it seemed right. Mike had had some kind of problem speaking—so much so that it had taken Magee a long time before he could understand the boy. How did all those witnesses and the sheriff so quickly understand what he was saying?

I forced myself to settle down and carefully copy everything onto three loose-leaf pages. I folded the pages into a neat square and slipped them into my skirt pocket. When I searched for coins in the same pocket, I realized I would be walking home.

I smiled to myself. Maybe I would run into Chuck. Maybe he would walk with me awhile.

~

Fern arrived late that evening. She parked her big sedan on the driveway and stared up at the porch, where Mom and I waited. She held the rail as she climbed the stairs, her eyes on Mom and a hesitant smile on her face. Mom opened her arms so wide that Fern couldn't help but fall into them. They hugged until they had to separate to wipe away their tears.

Fern was a tiny woman with raven hair long enough to touch the collar of her perfectly cut black suit. Her eyes contained the sharp greenness that marked Mom's family. I took to her immediately. I carried her suitcase to Marty's vacant room. She and Mom followed me up the stairs. When I started to show her where the bathroom was, Mom laughed.

"Your Aunt Fern has spent more time in that bathroom than you ever will, even if you live to be one hundred years old."

By the time she freshened up and came downstairs, something had changed. She was wary. Mom, too. Some mysterious force had come between them. I decided they were like the two rectangular magnets Pop kept in the drawer of the library table. The energy to connect was there, but the wrong ends were lined up.

Fern went into the kitchen, pulled a glass from the cupboard, and filled it with water from the tap. After a few sips, she said in a formal way, "Yes, this water is as I remembered it. The best water I ever tasted. And so cold."

"It's not from the well anymore, and not from the wood tanks across the highway, either. It's from Crystal Lake, brought in by pipeline to a big metal tank they put in this summer," Mom said.

"Yes, I saw that as we came down the mountain." Fern placed her empty glass next to the sink and peered out the back window. "Oh, goodness! I can't see the trees. Are they gone? Did you cut them?"

"They died," Mom said. She lowered her voice and added, "Sean thinks it's the mine fire."

"So close?"

Mom nodded.

"Oh, Bess!"

They moved into the dining room and sat in chairs across the table from each other. I sat in Pop's chair, spread out the city newspaper as he would have, and pretended to be interested in the funnies.

"When will Sean be back?" Fern asked.

"Friday night. He'll be so surprised to see you. He's staying in a rooming house with some other men, so he's not alone, but this is our first week and it isn't easy."

Fern fidgeted with her pearl necklace. "It must be lonely for both of you. I hear he turned into quite a family man."

Mom smiled. "Yes, he did."

"The Donals kept me up on everything in the town. Mrs. Donal loves . . . loved your daughter. Sally, isn't it?"

Mom nodded. "Sally and I cleaned for her and made sure she had good meals. Some nights Sally stayed over. Thank goodness she had school starting or she might have been in that house when it filled with gas."

"She must be terribly upset. It's so difficult for young people to accept death."

"She's taking it pretty hard. She's there now, helping get the house ready for visitors. They've been told to keep the doors and windows open at all times."

"Mrs. Donal wrote me how pretty your girls are and how well they do in school and how nice they are to be around."

"She told you all that?"

"And about your helping Iris's kids. You and Sean. How you never turn them away, even when you don't have enough for your own family."

"We've always managed."

"Yes, but you can't say it's been a piece of cake."

"Iris has had a hard time."

"I hear she's doing much better. That she's gradually getting her kids back. She's moved to Scranton, hasn't she?"

"Up the street from Lillian. Lillian is helping her find her footing."

"God bless Lillian. She always has been a rock in this family."

Mom laughed. "I've never heard her called a rock before, but I guess that's exactly what she is."

"If it hadn't been for Lillian, Charlie and Granny Sue would have lost this house. It was her working and sending money home that kept everybody afloat. I'm not sure the family realizes that."

Mom ducked her head. "You'll meet Sally later, but Marty is in the Air Force in Colorado."

"My oldest boy thought of the Air Force, but chose the Navy instead."

"At least there's no war going on." Mom picked at the side of the tablecloth, smoothed it with one hand.

"Yes, we're fortunate for that." Fern turned and looked about the room. "It seems so funny," she said, "to be here again. Not much has changed. It's like walking back in time. I wish I could have seen everyone's faces when you showed up married. You always were brave."

The ice was suddenly broken. Mom laughed. "They wouldn't let us see any boys. Iris and me sneaked around and made excuses for each other. I went as often as I could to meet Sean on the riverbank, but I was scared to death when we got married. Sean was the one who was brave. He came with me and held my hand as I told them. Do you know what Granny Sue said? She said, 'You're a Catholic?' and then she turned to me and screamed, 'Bess, are you out of your mind?' It went downhill from there."

"I heard they kicked you out."

"Well, of course they did. She told me to get my things and go. I asked if I could call Lillian and she refused. She said she'd do any calling that had to be done."

"Where did you go?"

"We didn't have a penny to our names. Sean had some friends with an apartment in Wilkes-Barre. They took us in. Mike too. He wouldn't have known what to do without Sean."

"Didn't Charlie stand up for you?"

"He tried. But you know how Granny could be when she lost control. She wasn't listening to anyone, especially not Charlie."

"What about Ira? Was he on your side?"

"He wasn't home at the time. He drove down later and he was civil. He shook Sean's hand. You know how Ira was. He'd pretend everything was hunky-dory if the entire world was on fire."

"Yes," Fern said. "He did know how to turn a head." A shudder sent her hands raking across the table. Her manicured fingernails tore off a corner of my newspaper.

"Fern?" Mom's voice was full of concern.

Fern laughed nervously. "Must have been someone walking across my grave. I'm a little jumpy at times."

"You're okay?"

"Fine. I'm fine."

I looked at Fern with greater interest. I had felt the same kind of cold chill run through me at times when I sat in that chair. I had decided that one of the family ghosts had laid claim to that place at the table and, when it didn't like the conversation, caused a stir.

"You must be tired after that long drive," Mom tried.

Fern appeared not to have heard. "Lots of memories in this house. Good and bad. But it isn't as overwhelming as I've imagined all these years."

"I'm glad you came now."

"It was time."

"Way past due." Mom reached out and took Fern's hand. "Oh, your hand is so cold."

Fern didn't pull away.

"It makes me so sad, Fern."

"What does?"

"Our losing each other. You were more my sister than my cousin, and when you left I cried my heart out. They wouldn't tell me where you went or why. Charlie said you were safe. He said you were with friends. Granny said that you would never be back because you had a choice and you chose another family."

Fern looked over at me. "There were things that happened. I'd like to tell you some day, but not now. It's not the time."

"We've missed so much of each other's lives. I thought and thought about you. But then I was all wrapped up in Sean and, well, you know."

Fern smiled. "Iris knew where I was. She took the Laurel Line all the way up to Pittsfield to tell me that bit of gossip. Finally, you were the bad girl. I think she'd been waiting her entire life for that."

"She never said she talked to you."

"I wrote to you and to her, but you never answered my letters. When Cal and I were planning our wedding, I sent an invitation, but no one showed an interest. I was sure it was because Cal is Jewish."

"I didn't know, Fern. I never saw a letter. I didn't know you were married until Mrs. Donal told John Hale. Oh, I wish I had looked for you. I believed you had deserted me."

Fern placed her free hand over Mom's on the table. "And I thought you didn't care about me. What silly girls we were to lose all those years."

"Well, we won't lose any more."

"I was glad to leave the valley, but I was never as connected with it as you. You did leave for a time though, didn't you?"

Mom nodded. "When Sally was born we had to have our own place. John Hale found us a tiny house down by the railroad. Sean's brother moved in with his Aunt Maura. She wasn't well and he was able to help her. But then there was all that trouble. Sean packed us up and moved us to Back Mountain."

I closed the paper, folded it carefully as Pop would have, and went into the kitchen, but not out of earshot. I now knew about the trouble that sent my parents to the house with no doorknobs and I knew Mom and Fern would not discuss it with me sitting there. I was disappointed when Fern changed the subject. I decided that, during her visit, I would stay as close to the two women as I could. They both had things to say about my mystery.

"Moving away was the smart thing to do," Fern said. "I understand that tempers were running pretty hot."

"It was a terrible time." Mom's voice broke. "Sean had to give up the Conservation Corps and the WPA. In Back Mountain he hired out to the farms for not much pay, but farm people are so good. We always had enough to eat."

"And you came back when Granny needed help."

"I felt obligated. She wouldn't accept our help before then. Even after Charlie had that bad stroke, she'd only allow Ira to care for him. After Ira was gone, she depended on John Hale."

"Do you think she hated me?"

"Oh, Fern, it wasn't that. She was a bit off. She stopped speaking to almost everyone after Charlie's death—even Iris."

"Iris believes that you cheated the whole family out of his house."

"You don't believe that, do you?"

"Heavens, no. She mailed me a copy of Charlie's will. It was clear what he wanted. I had no interest in anything here. You've always had my blessing."

"I put aside some things I thought might be your mother's. I've kept a chest for you in the attic. When Sean comes home, I'll have him climb up and get it."

"Oh, Bess, that is so nice. I'd like to have something of hers."

It was all I could do not to run back into the room and volunteer to climb into the attic. I vowed that I would help bring that chest down when the time came.

~

Friday evening, after the burial, we were obligated to entertain members of the family who had traveled for the funeral. The last vestiges of summer heat wilted the boxwood hedges.

The chairs lined up between the glider and the swing quickly filled with ladies in their best mourning clothes. The black wall of dresses against the light green of the clapboard siding seemed to mirror the rich seam of coal newly exposed on the fading green mountain above.

Lillian brought me a brand-new skirted suit of light blue silk with white trim around the neck and covered white buttons down the front. The skirt flared when I twirled. She also dressed the twins. They were surprisingly handsome in their white shirts and belted black pants. They avoided the kisses and hugs of the many relatives by staying in the library and working on the jigsaw puzzle Pop had laid out on the table. As I peered into the library to check on their progress, I was surprised by their conversation.

"Of all the girls at the church, which one do you think was the prettiest?" Larry asked.

"That's easy," Lenny answered. "Molly."

Larry nodded his bent head.

I smiled all the way across the kitchen.

Lillian had placed two tall bottles of good whiskey on the kitchen table. Mom mixed the liquor with 7-Up in several cut-glass pitchers. I carried a tray of glasses and a bowl of ice to the porch.

Iris smiled when she took her beverage. "Thank you, Molly," she said. "You look very nice."

I nearly dropped the tray.

The pitchers emptied quickly. Mom drank an uncharacteristic two glasses without ice.

When I went into the kitchen to refill a pitcher, Sally handed me a tray of tiny sandwiches and napkins. When I returned to the porch, Mom, who had begun to laugh and talk too loudly, was in the process of excusing herself from her guests. Fern had disappeared.

I placed the tray of sandwiches on the banister and followed Mom into the orchard.

"Fern," I heard her call. "Wait."

Aunt Fern turned. Her face was wet with tears.

"Oh, Fern, I'm so sorry. Did someone say something to upset you? They are all so stuck in their worlds, they sometimes don't consider anyone else's feelings."

"It wasn't anything anyone said. It's this place." She smiled and waved her arm as if to encircle the entire house and mountain. "It's coming back and sitting on the front porch and feeling the evening breezes. I loved this place. I so wish things could have been different."

"Let's walk to the creek."

When Mom took Fern's hand and tugged, she reminded me of Sally—how she always pulled me into things when I was too shy to join on my own. I wondered how I would feel if Sally went away for twenty years. It was probably easier to be the one who left than the one who was left behind. I decided if there was ever a choice, I would be the one leaving.

"Have you been truly happy in New York, Fern?"

"Oh, yes."

Mom's comment was muffled, but when she turned her head toward Fern, I could hear her clearly.

"I sometimes wish I could have made a complete break like you," she said. "Sometimes the self-righteousness of folks gets to me, but I'm happy with Sean and my family."

"The mine fire has to be frightening."

"We've lived with it so long. It was only a nuisance until recently. Now it does make me afraid."

Their dress shoes forced them to weave slowly through the chokecherry trees until they reached the hard-packed path to the creek.

"I'm worried that the Donals will never be able to sell the house. It would be such a shame to have it sit empty," Fern said.

"There's talk of government intervention. Some folks are organizing to demand restitution."

"But won't you have to sacrifice your homes?"

"If they can't find a way to control the fire."

"Charlie and Granny Sue put so much of themselves into this place."

"And never found happiness."

"No. There were too many losses."

"I sometimes feel a restlessness in the house. I used to think it was me—that maybe I couldn't be at peace here. Now I suspect that there are some unhappy spirits hanging about." Mom gave a nervous little laugh. "It's probably bad memories on my part."

"I think I feel it too." Fern glanced toward Mom and also laughed a little too gaily. "I've thought about Granny a lot. I wish I'd had the courage to come back before she died."

"She wasn't the same. She didn't recognize folks. I don't think she even knew who she was. I had hoped she'd be able to answer some questions, but she'd forgotten everything."

"What did you want to ask?"

"What we had done to make her so mean. Why she was so horrible to Charlie."

Fern pulled a small twig from one of the trees and began to peel the bark with her manicured nails. "I think it was the loss of the boys. It drove a wedge between them."

"Half the town lost sons. The wars took their toll on almost every family. Everyone else went on."

"Everyone else didn't have an Uncle Ira."

"Were you afraid of him, Fern?"

They reached the creek. Fern's hand fluttered to her throat. "Goodness. When did the creek dry up?"

"The mining company says they changed its flow. But I believe that fire's causing the water table to drop." Mom settled onto the rocks at the edge of the creek.

Fern gathered her dress around her hips and sat primly beside her. "Yes, I was afraid of Ira. He was the reason I left."

I couldn't hear what she said next. I walked up to sit beside them on the rocks.

Mom motioned me away. "Molly, honey, you don't want to spoil your new suit. Go back to the house, sweetie, and be sure everyone is comfortable, would you?"

I didn't argue. I turned back, circled around, and crossed the dry creek bed. Stickers pulled at the silk of my skirt. I pulled it around my hips as Fern had and stooped low behind a thick patch of bread-and-butter vines, where I could watch them and hear every word they spoke.

Fern sat, her back straight, her legs crossed at the ankles, like she was in one of those group high school pictures in the yearbooks in the library.

Mom leaned toward her. "Did he do something bad to you, Fern?"

"Not to me."

"To anybody that you know of?"

She nodded slightly and turned her face from Mom before she continued. "He scared me."

"Why?"

"I think he knew that I had seen something he did."

"Did you see something?"

Fern lowered her head and covered her face with her hands.

Mom reached out, touched her shoulder. When she didn't move away, Mom wrapped both her arms around her. "Tell me, Fern."

Fern shook her head.

"You have to tell someone."

She raised her chin. "I saw him give Mother a drink from a small bottle. She didn't want to take it and he made her. He spilled it on her nightgown."

"Some medicine?"

"In a green bottle. It was that last day. That horrible last day."

"You came to get me. I was sweeping the chestnut leaves off the front porch."

"It was a warm fall day."

"Like today."

Fern nodded.

"I didn't know Ira was home that day."

"He came in from the woods. I was in the front closet, getting fresh towels for the sickroom. I saw him go by."

"I don't remember seeing him when we went in to your mother."

"He went out the back door. Remember the smell? Almonds?"

"I only remember the horror of not knowing what to do. She was so sick."

"The drink he gave her smelled of almonds. It was all over her nightgown."

"Oh, Fern. Do you think he poisoned her?"

Fern began to sob so hard it hurt to watch. "I asked John Hale if there were any poisons that smelled like almonds. He said, 'Yes, of course. There's cyanide, a quick killer. Why do you ask such a thing?' I didn't tell him why."

"Oh, my God. She was so sick and coughing so hard. I thought it was her lungs. Oh, my God."

The two women rocked and cried together.

Mom regained her composure first. "You didn't tell anybody."

"It got worse."

"Arlie."

Fern nodded. "He was in his bed. He had thrown up. He reeked of almonds."

Mom became as still as the boulder she sat on. She stared into the woods. I thought she had seen me, because when she repeated the words her voice was very low.

"You didn't tell anybody."

"I locked myself in the sewing room. I was afraid to look at Ira. I thought he would read my mind and make me drink that stuff. When he was gone, I searched his room. I searched the house. I looked for the bottle. I never found it."

"I thought you had gone mad with grief. That's what Granny said. 'She's crazy with grief. Leave her be.' I didn't try to help."

"I was afraid to tell anybody at first."

"At first?"

"I told Charlie."

"Did he believe you?"

"I don't think he wanted to. But, for a moment, a look crossed his face. Then he said I must be wrong, that I was seeing things."

"And that's when you left."

"Yes. I was afraid Charlie would say something to Ira and he would get me." She began to sob again. "I was so afraid. Oh, Bess, I was sick with fear."

"And I had no idea. Granny told me to leave you alone. I had no idea, Fern. Oh, my God. How stupid I was."

"I called my mother's friend in Pittsfield. I begged her to come get me. She did. She didn't ask any questions. I worried for you, but I never tried to warn you. I was such a coward."

"A coward? How can you say that? You were so brave, always."

"I looked at your Molly at dinner this afternoon. I saw her innocence, her candor, and I realized that she is almost the age of you and I and Iris when all that happened. We were children, Bess. Just children."

"Even at this age, I don't think I would know what to do."

"Who would have believed a child? Uncle Ira was a pillar of society, for God's sake. He was a trustee in the church. He was a colorful bachelor. All the women were gaga over him. I can imagine what they would have said: 'How dare some kid make such accusations against him!' But you know what was the worst, Bess? The worst was that I really didn't think about that at the time. What I thought about was that Granny Sue would beat me within an inch of my life for saying such a thing. And then Ira would get me. That's why I ran away."

Mom folded her arms across her chest and began to rock, as if she were sitting in a rocking chair holding a child. When she finally spoke, her voice was firm and sure.

"He was a monster, Fern. He tried to do something to Marty."

"Oh, no!"

Mom nodded. "When we were living in the place down by the railroad. The same week Sean's brother was charged with that horrible crime. It was at the time of the flood downriver—the 1937 one."

"Are you sure you want to tell me this?"

"Yes. I've never told anyone and I think now's the time. Do you want to hear it?"

"Yes."

Mom shifted her weight, as if she needed to be as comfortable as possible or she would not be able to talk. She held her head straight ahead. Fern tilted toward her.

I willed my bent knees to not weaken.

"Sean had finally got on with the conservation crew. They sent him downriver to help with the flood cleanup. It was a Saturday and I'd had his brother over for supper because Aunt Maura had a friend visiting. Ira stopped by in the middle of our meal and offered to drive Mike home. He said he'd play with Marty while we finished up. I was grateful for that small bit of help, since Sally was still a baby, and colicky, and I hadn't had much sleep."

"You were alone? How old were the kids?"

"Marty was five. Sally was nine months."

"Granny Sue didn't help you with them?"

"She reluctantly helped with their births and that was that. She was still delivering babies in the town at the time. It would have caused a lot of gossip if she had refused to help me. As it was, she left me in the care of John Hale as soon as the births were done."

"You were awfully young to have all that responsibility."

Mom laughed. "It wasn't so bad. John came by often, and Sean helped, and I had lots of friends. Poor Iris was in worse shape. She already had four—five if you count the one she gave away. Granny wouldn't help her either. She told Mrs. Donal that we girls had made our beds and we could lie in them."

"We were all a disappointment to her."

"Life was a disappointment to her. Her only joy was Ira. She doted on him."

"And he was evil."

"Yes, he fooled everyone." Mom shifted her weight, took a deep breath, and continued her story. "Marty took Ira's hand and went out the door with him. About ten minutes later I heard him crying. Mike went out to see what was wrong. He came running back and was so upset that he couldn't get his words out. I thought something awful must have happened. I flew out of the house. When I rounded the corner, I saw Marty struggling to get out of Ira's arms. He was naked and Ira was touching him, down there."

"Oh, Bess!"

"I nearly lost my mind. I must have started screaming, because Ira turned. As calmly as could be, he said, 'I'm helping him go pee.'"

"What did you do?"

"I grabbed Marty. 'Get out of here,' I screamed. 'Get away from my house!' 'You have a dirty mind,' he said. By then, Mike had come out with Sally, who was also screaming. Mike began running in circles, pulling at his hair with one hand and dangling poor Sally from the other. It was a horrible scene."

"Did Ira go?"

"No. He grabbed my shoulders and began to shake me. 'If you lie about this to Sean, I'll kill you and all your sniveling little bastards,' he said. Mike came between us. I put Marty behind me and took the baby. Ira jumped into his car. Before I could stop him, Mike jumped in too."

It was Fern's turn to soothe Mom. She placed one hand on her arm and said, "My God, Bessie."

"He gunned the engine and stared at me. I ran onto the railroad tracks. I was more afraid of Ira than of being run over by a train. I didn't know what else to do. At first I carried both kids, then I had Marty hold on to my skirt."

"Where'd you go?"

"John Hale's. No one was home. I sat on his porch until I got my wits about me. Here I was, with a naked little boy and a crying baby and nowhere to go. I climbed over the culm banks and walked toward Granny Sue's. Halfway there, I realized it was useless to tell her. She would never have believed me. I was afraid to go back to the house, so I knocked on Mrs. Donal's door. I told her that a bum had come to the house and that Sean was away and I was afraid to spend the night alone. She let me stay. She found some of her grandson's clothes for Marty. I never saw Mike or Ira again."

"Do you think Mike was copying him? When he hurt that little boy?"

"I don't believe Mike had anything to do with that boy. Sean and I both believe that was Ira's doing. It happened within hours of letting Mike drive away with him."

I wanted to jump in and say that I didn't believe Mike was guilty either. That I had read those articles—about how Mike had denied it through all those beatings and how those men had decided he was the one, because a man with a limp was walking on the street. I thought about the slant of the newspaper article and the way the writer seemed to say that, in the end, no one had really seen Mike take the boy from the car.

I wanted to hurry back to our library and read my notes again. If Mom was right, Ira was guilty of both rape and murder. No wonder he had jumped in that lake. He must have realized what a horrible man he was. Somebody needed to tell on him now and clear Mike's and the Branigan name. I forced myself to wait.

"What did the police say?" Fern was asking.

"Oh, the damned police. They made up their minds early on."

"Did you tell them about how you'd caught Ira?"

"I never got a chance. I didn't learn about Mike until Aunt Maura came up on the Laurel Line. She couldn't find Sean's sister, so she came to find me. Luckily, I saw her hurrying across Marcy Street. I called to her. She said the police wouldn't let her see Mike. She needed Sean. We went to Wilkes-Barre and had the CCC director locate him. The kids and me stayed at Aunt Maura's. I was afraid to come back here. So, you see, I ran away too."

"You had no choice."

"But I allowed Mike to go off with him. I blame myself for letting that happen."

"You were smart to get away."

"I wasn't smart. Like you, I was afraid for my life and for my kids. Poor Aunt Maura. She loved her boys. She'd been through so much with them. She knew Mike was innocent."

"What did Sean do?"

"It took the conservation director two days to find him. By then, poor Aunt Maura had collapsed from the horror of the newspaper reports. People were hounding her. When Sean arrived he went to the hospital to see her and then to see Mike. She died a few hours later. At the jail the warden told Sean that Mike had been taken to Eastern Penitentiary. Sean demanded to see him. He was crazy with worry."

"Did they let him?"

"Yes. But he was too late. Poor Mike had been horribly beaten. Sean said he was caked with dried blood. Some of his teeth had been knocked out. He could barely crawl to the door of the dirty little cell. Sean wanted him brought out and cared for, but they said that he was too dangerous to bring into another room. They made Sean talk to him through a small window in the door.

"Mike swore he didn't do it. He told Sean that Ira drove him to a beer joint on North Washington Street, where they had a few shots. He said Ira left him at the bar to use the bathroom. When he didn't come back, Mike went to find him. He said he wandered up and down the street for a long time and when cops started arriving he ducked into an alley and walked to Aunt Maura's."

She looked fully into Fern's eyes. "Both Sean and he were still considered fugitives, you know. They had busted out of some jail and had never been caught."

"So he had reason to run?"

"Yes. He had a genuine fear of the police. Aunt Maura said the cops were knocking on her door right after Mike walked in, but he hid. She said he was so upset he wouldn't talk. He didn't tell her what happened. He was probably too embarrassed."

"Why did the police think he had hurt the little boy?"

"He was a cripple. That made him different. He couldn't make himself understood, so he avoided people, looked away. That made him seem guilty. Sean tried to find a lawyer. He never told Mike about Aunt Maura. But it was too late anyway. Mike died before Sean got back there."

"And Ira?"

"No one knows when Ira drowned himself. He came back up here, probably looking for me, but no one knew I was at Mrs. Donal's. Aunt Maura said he knocked on her door the next day and she told him about the arrest. John Hale reported that Ira was sick with grief when he learned about Mike's crime—that it was probably the final straw for him. Granny Sue told John that Ira was inconsolable when he left for the cabin. I didn't believe any of that. I believe he went to the cabin because he was afraid."

"Afraid they'd learn the truth?"

"Afraid of Sean."

"I wish Sean had gotten his hands on him."

"Poor Sean's hands were full. He came up to our house and got clothes for the kids while I made funeral arrangements for Mike and Maura. He stopped at the church. The priest refused to bury Mike. We put him and Aunt Maura side by side in the cemetery and decided the priest's words would be for both of them. There was no money. Lillian helped."

"And it wasn't long afterward that Charlie died too."

"Well, he'd had a stroke, and everyone's emotions were running pretty high. Granny and he had words and she shoved him. He tripped over the coal bucket and hit the stove. He died the next day."

"And Granny Sue never spoke about any of it again?"

"Never. She cut everybody off. Refused Mrs. Donal's help. Refused to go to church. She stayed in the house by herself. If it hadn't been for John Hale she wouldn't have had any outside contact."

From the house, Lillian called, "Fern! Bess! Some of your guests are ready to say good-bye. Bess!"

"We hear you, Lillian," Mom shouted. "There's no need to tell the whole town."

Too bad, Mom, I thought. The whole town should have been told many things a long time ago.

They stood, brushed unseen dirt from their skirts, and walked hand in hand toward the house. I waited until they reached the chokecherry trees before I followed. My legs quivered, my breath caught. I was thunderstruck by all I had learned.

I shut both doors to the library while the ladies said their good-byes. In my notebook I recopied Old Charlie's list, with some changes of my own.

Burton, aged 18, died July 10, 1915 / Probably drowned by Ira Reece

Silas, aged 20, died September 20, 1920 / Probably pushed under a train by Ira Reece

Faye, aged 34, died November 8, 1931 / Poisoned by Ira Reece

Arlie, aged 25, died November 17, 1931 / Poisoned by Ira Reece

Mike Branigan, aged 23, died July 21, 1937 / Killed in police custody after being falsely accused of rape of a child

Ira Reece, child rapist, aged 39, died July 21, 1937 / Suicide by drowning

That night we lined up on the porch as Pop's car climbed the hill. He took the stairs two at a time. The scent of beer reached us before he did. It didn't matter. He was home.

⁂

The next morning Pop carried the ladder to the attic door to hand down Fern's chest. I climbed the ladder and stuck my head above the floor but could see nothing of interest in the dusty space. It was a different story when Fern opened the chest.

She was shuffling through a stack of papers when she stopped to stare at a photograph. I caught it as it dropped from her shaking hand. The man I had seen in the newspaper archives, the one who was standing in the crowd urging the police to hang the rapist, smiled at me.

"Who is this?" I asked.

Fern looked away. "That's our Uncle Ira." She took the picture from me and tossed it into the bag of burnable papers near the door. I waited until everyone left the room before I pulled him from the trash.

Uncle Ira, I thought, there you are, caught at last.

It seemed a strange thing to do, to take that picture to bed with me, but that's what I did. As the fall chill came in through the open windows, I lay back and stared into the man's direct gaze. He wasn't as tall as I thought he'd be. His face was long and pale over high cheekbones. His smiling lips were thin, his teeth white and even. He wore a white shirt, sleeves pushed up so his starched white cuffs rested just below his elbows, a natty vest that looked like it might be silk, a heavy watch fob that draped perfectly from his waist to the watch pocket of his dark pants, and a Panama-style hat cocked to one side of his head. He stood with one leg up. His black brogue rested on the running board of a shiny sedan.

There was nothing handsome or exceptional about him. How could someone this forgettable be so evil? I decided Pop was right—it was important to not expect evil but to be aware enough to recognize it, should it show up.

I turned out the light, slipped the picture under my bed, and thought about Old Charlie. He would have lain on this very same bed, in this very same darkness, and railed at Ira for the terrible things the man had done, yet he was too handicapped to do anything about it. I thought of him carefully writing out his list of suspicious deaths before he had the stroke. How neatly he had lined out the names, how carefully he had put in the dates. And I thought of him writing that last entry into his diary. Ticking off the names with a pencil and adding Mike's, probably with his left hand as he tried to hold the diary still on some surface in this very room. I thought of the angry slant of the letters: CRYSTAL LAKE CABIN MY CAR GO. The uneven pressure on the lead that tore the paper. And I imagined him struggling to the wall, taking off the vent cover, slipping the diary into the adjustable louvers, and screwing the heavy plate securely back into place.

That's when it came to me. He could not have done that alone. I was young and had both hands working perfectly, but I'd still had trouble replacing the heavy cover of the hot air vent. Old Charlie would have needed help.

I sat up and stared into the darkness while I tried to think of who would have helped him. Not Granny Sue. She would have thrown the diary into the coal stove and watched it become harmless white ash. Who else was here?

I went through a list of family and friends in my head. John Hale and Iris were my only candidates.

~

Fern's visit had filled the vacuum of Pop's absence. When she left, the house became cold and empty once again. For the next several Fridays I lay awake until I was sure Pop was safely home. He arrived later and drunker each week. Most Saturday mornings I would find him at the kitchen table as he drank his first beer of the day. He sat with his head down and complained that the noise from the washing machine gave him a headache.

Mom pretended not to hear, but her anger showed in the way she jammed his clothes into the hot water and slammed the lid on the coal stove as she added more fuel.

He watched TV, chain-smoked, sipped beer, and took frequent inhalations from his asthma pump. If his hangover cleared on Sunday, he might work in the yard or visit some neighbors. Each Monday morning a shopping bag of clean clothes waited for him by the front door. His shirts were starched, ironed, and neatly folded. His lunch was packed into another large bag. His work boots were polished, unlaced, and airing near the radiator in the hall.

He had put up a wall as stout and obvious as the concrete block replacement in the cellar.

CHAPTER TWENTY-ONE

In mid-October John Hale announced that the Bureau of Mines and the coal company wanted to meet with the citizens of Giant's Despair to discuss the mine fire problem-that-was-no-problem. I tagged along with Mom to my old sixth-grade classroom. A threesome of black-suited men, appearing too big and too important for the scarred chairs, sat at the front of the room. They posed, carefully casual, their manicured hands resting palms down on fine wool pants. The student desks filled so quickly with adults that I politely went to the back of the room and stood with the late arrivals.

Mom fidgeted in her chair, whispered to John Hale, who sat by her side, and frequently turned fully to talk to a neighbor or friend.

A restless wave moved across the packed space when the official from the Bureau of Mines stood. I wondered if he was the same official who should be checking conditions in the south slope, where Chuck worked. He introduced the other men—a representative of the coal company and the attorney for the City of Wilkes-Barre. The room quieted as he launched into their agenda.

"I understand that recent events have raised concerns that a hazard exists in the mine fire that burns on the edges of your community," he said.

"More like under it," a man to one side corrected him.

The official leaned sideways and held a whispered conversation with the attorney, who gazed confidently over the crowd. Heads bobbed and dipped.

The attorney did not stand when he spoke. "You have nothing to worry about," he said. "No shafts from this mine run under your homes."

Hoots erupted. "One person and a dog has died," a man said. "Two people were sickened."

The official bent his head toward the other two men and again held a whispered conversation.

"I am assured that neither the death nor the sickness was caused by the underground fire. Experts say that natural pools of methane are present in all coal seams in this region."

The crowd protested with murmurs and shaking heads.

John Hale stood. He waited for the room to become still.

"I'd like to beg your pardon," he said with quiet dignity. "I've lived among these coal fields my entire life. Two generations of my family lived among them before me. Never before has anyone ever heard of methane gas killing people aboveground. We're all aware of the underground threat of methane. It seems to be the venting of the mine fire that has brought the gas aboveground."

The mine official smiled and shook his head. "There is no correlation between the mine fire and the recent death or illnesses." He was so sincere I was beginning to believe him.

John Hale sat down.

Harry the store owner stood. "How do you explain all the settling that's been going on, the sinkholes opening into our yards, and the cracked foundations that need to be shored up?"

The smiling official raised himself until he seemed to float above the sea of common folks. He smiled down on us in the same way the church minister used to smile down on my Sunday school class.

"That's directly the result of underground water," he said. "We all know how many springs and creeks flow out of these mountains. You have to expect subsidence under such conditions."

If I hadn't witnessed the explosion in the waterline pit or heard Mom talk about the shaft that ran under our street or stood on the sealed iron pipe that had been drilled into the mine near my own backyard, I might have been swayed by his pronouncement. As it was, I found myself wanting to shout, like the man who next voiced his opinion, "Lying son of a bitch."

The room erupted in laughter.

The official was not touched. "Our main concern is that we stop the fire before it reaches your community, and that we protect the city of Wilkes-Barre."

"And your own ass," a man shouted. Hoots and hollers rang out louder.

Someone shouted, "Your damned fire's already here."

A man stood and punched the air with a closed fist. "What are you going to do, use that big machine of yours and dig a hole big enough to bury us?"

"Sir. Sir." The company representative tried to be heard above the din. "Sir! We have a century of maps and engineering studies. Not one outlines mine shafts running under your community."

"Liar!" a woman shouted.

The company man sat while the Bureau of Mines official raised his hands to ask for quiet.

John Hale stood again. The room quieted.

"We know we weren't granted mineral rights with our properties," he reasoned. "We know the company has the right to the coal. What we don't know is what you're going to do to keep our town alive. What you're going to do to snuff out that fire."

Mom stood up beside him. "And what you're going to do to stop the coal company from opening more shafts and destroying more land just to let more air into the damn mine," she said. "We all see how much coal they're digging out. They seem to be in a god-awful hurry to get what they can. And because of their greed, they're beginning to burn us out. And what are you telling us tonight? Live with it? Well, sir, we've been living with it and now we're dying with it and we want something done!"

She sat down then popped back up. "And we want the company stopped from more digging. We want them stopped from tearing into the mountain." She swung her arm in a wide arc toward the windows of the room. "Not tomorrow and not the next day. We want the company stopped today."

The room broke into applause.

The mining official looked Mom full in the face.

"Ma'am," he said in perfect Ivy League college English, "if you can find any proof that our shafts are running under your house, we'll certainly want to do something about it. Until then, the company can continue its work. It keeps men in jobs. It keeps your community thriving."

She wasn't to be stopped. "If you look around, sir, I think you'll see there's very few people thriving here."

She sat down with a thud. Her face was flushed red, her breath was coming in short gasps, and her small fists were clenched together so tightly that I thought maybe I should find a paper bag for her to breathe into. She took one deep breath, stood, and walked toward me. One by one, the townspeople stood and followed her. She took my arm and led me from the room.

"Our troubles have begun again, Molly. You'd better start counting to three."

~

The last Friday of October, long after midnight, I heard Pop's car squeal in protest as it began its descent at Prospect Rock. I ran downstairs and onto the front porch. When his car rounded Devil's Elbow, I saw that one of its headlights was out. Metal rattled and the engine whined as the car roared down the hill, across Marcy Street, and up Fitch Lane.

I ran into the street. Leaped back onto the concrete step between the hedges to not be run over. Pop jumped from the car, waved his arms in the air like a basketball player who has made a perfect shot, and shouted, "I took on a tractor trailer. And I won!" He bolted past.

By the light of a big harvest moon I saw the bashed-in passenger side of the car. Two wheels were bent, the tires flat.

I followed him inside. Mom raced down the stairs, pulling on her bathrobe and throwing on lights as she came. She pulled him into the dining room and looked him over.

"Not a scratch," she said. "It must be true that God protects fools and drunks." She led him up the stairs.

~

He came into the kitchen late Saturday morning. He was pale and shaking.

"What did I do?"

Mom turned away, picked up the basket of wet laundry, and walked stiffly down the back steps to the clothesline.

I helped him raise the hood, watched as he climbed under each wheel well, and shook my head as he tried unsuccessfully to turn the steering wheel.

"Totaled," he said. We walked around the house to Mom.

"I'll drive a new car home next week."

She didn't say a word.

"I'll catch a ride with one of the guys from the shop this week. I'll take my toolbox and make sure I get a good one. I'll bring it home in one piece."

"And you'll be sober as a judge, when you do." She didn't look at him.

"Yes. I will."

She had made a mistake. She had not made him say "I promise."

~

The next Friday, while she waited for him on the porch, I waited on my roof. I was sure that if he drove up drunk, she would throw him out. I made myself small against the gable of the house as he parked a big black car next to the hedges. He'd kept his word. He seemed sober as a judge.

"Fifty bucks," he said as he settled onto the swing. "It took most of the week to get it going, but there it is."

"It's an awfully big car, Sean."

"It's got twelve cylinders. Uses a lot of gas, but it's only a '42 and it's a Lincoln."

"Where did you get it?"

"Bought it from a guy who had more money than brains. It's like a tank. Indestructible."

"Well, you're not."

"No," he said. "But I think I've learned my lesson."

"I can't stand by and watch you drink yourself to death. What would we do if something happened to you?"

"Nothing will. I promise."

I smiled as silence descended on the sighing swing. I pressed my back against the gingerbread of the house and waited for them to speak again so I could creep back into my room.

"There's another meeting planned for this week with the Redevelopment Authority. I hear this time they've threatened to condemn our houses and knock them down," Mom said.

I inched toward the window.

"They can't legally do that, can they?" he asked.

"I believe they not only can, they will. This week John heard that they want to buy us out. You know what that means."

"What?"

"It means they'll give us only a quarter of what our houses are worth and wish us luck. I won't go for it."

"What are the neighbors saying?"

"Everyone seems to have a different opinion. Some want to take what they can get and move on. Some say the company will have to bulldoze their house down with them in it. Some want to hire a lawyer and fight. Some believe the fire can be doused and it will all blow over."

"We can't fight city hall, let alone the coal companies. They'll knock this place down in a second to get to the damned coal."

"But why? Mines are shutting down all over the valley."

"That vein under us is thick as they come, and shallow enough to get out on the cheap. If they can make us move, it's all theirs."

Goose bumps rose on my bare arms and legs.

"But where would we go, Sean?"

I didn't hear his comment, but it must have been funny because she laughed.

"Sally will be graduating," she said. "Marty will be gone for four years. But Molly should graduate from high school with her friends. Oh, I don't know, Sean. I just don't know."

Invitingly warm air greeted me as I stooped to climb into my window.

"Sean, I'm going to tell you something that Fern told me when she was here. I'd like to know what you think about it."

I stopped dead still.

"Sounds serious."

"Well, it is serious."

I straightened and waited.

"Is it something she would want me to know?"

"I asked her if I could tell you and she said yes, she'd like to know what you think."

"Well, let's hear it."

She began slowly, reminded him of how she and Fern had cared for Faye and how both Faye and Arlie had died that same month. Then she told him about the liquid that smelled of almonds, how Ira had given it to Faye, and how Arlie had reeked of almonds at his death. She paused after she explained why Fern had moved away so suddenly.

He didn't comment. I counted the soothing passes of the swing below. One. Two. Three. Four.

"I've been thinking about everything Fern told me, Sean, and I wonder, do you think Ira could have poisoned Faye and Arlie?"

He answered in the flat tones of an unrehearsed actor. "He could have."

He knew! He knew what Ira had done!

"Really?" Mom's voice revealed the same shock that coursed through me.

"Yes," he said in the same stiff way. "I believe he could have done that."

Another long silence and one, two, three passes of the swing. I could not breathe.

"Fern said she wished you had caught up with Ira. I told her how fast everything happened. How horrible it was. How you couldn't do anything about Ira—that you had too many other things to take care of. But it made me think, Sean, and I've been wondering ever since."

"Wondering what?"

One. Two.

"I wonder why you didn't chase Ira down. It wasn't like you to hesitate. Why didn't you go after him, Sean?"

One. I heard a deep sigh. Two. A loud asthmatic exhalation of air. Three. Then the words, "I did."

She made not one sound. Spoke not one word. The swing creaked in rhythm with the night, sang its quiet song, sighed on its worn chains. I hoped she was holding him, staring into his eyes, showing her concern for the pain in his voice, but I would never know.

When she finally began to speak, her voice trembled. "Oh, Sean. Did you find him?"

I could picture him looking away, turning his eyes toward the night sky, summoning his courage and thinking carefully of some words to take him away from what he knew he had to say.

"Yes," he finally answered. "Yes, I did."

She waited only long enough to put her next question together in her mind. "How did you know where to look?"

"Old Charlie," he answered. "Old Charlie told me where to go. He gave me his car to drive up to the lake."

"Oh, Pop." I whispered. "Oh, Pop."

I pushed through the open window and buried myself in my bed covers. I was full of shame, not for what I heard but that I had eavesdropped so often that I understood what he had said. The message in the diary, "CRYSTAL LAKE CABIN MY CAR GO," was for Pop. He had come up here in a fit of rage and grief after Mike's and Aunt Maura's deaths. Old Charlie had shown him what Ira had done by ticking off each name on his diary death list. The old man had held the pencil in his hand and had added Mike's name to his list. He not only told Pop where to find Ira but also gave him a car to get to him. It was Pop who helped Charlie hide the diary.

Now I knew why my great-grandfather had left him this house and why he had first refused it. Now I realized that the family legend, the one that said I had received Granny Sue's gift of speaking with the dead, was actually a story of childhood innocence. I had heard Granny Sue thanking the man who had avenged the deaths of her children.

My thoughts raced to the angry push she had given Old Charlie, the one that had caused his death, and I wondered if that was the moment she had learned the truth about her brother Ira. And I wondered if she had isolated herself in a crypt of grief because the truth had been too much to bear. But this much I didn't have to wonder about: She had known who Pop was when she pulled him to her and whispered "Thank you." She had shown, with her words and kisses, that she had both forgiven and blessed him.

It was all too much. I pulled my covers over my head and began, once again, to bargain with God. If he would take away this truth—that my pop, the man who was ever dependable and loving, the man who I believed to be honest and kind and straightforward, was actually a coldblooded killer—I would never again strain my ears to hear what others said.

~

I avoided my family for four days while I tried to come up with arguments to disprove my father's deed. I believe I would have been able to put the matter to rest if I hadn't been thrown off course. On Tuesday of that same week, the Susquehanna River pushed through the fragile wall of the south slope mine, filled the shafts with fetid water, and trapped twenty-seven men in the frigid, airless underground.

I heard the news from Sally as I boarded the bus after school. Two of her classmates had fathers working in the mine. She left me and went to be with them. The house was as cold and empty as my heart when I arrived home. Mom had gone to the church to wait with town families for word of loved ones.

I had to know that Chuck had gotten out. I found his number in the telephone book and dialed. The ringing never stopped.

I walked to the church, found Mom and the list of missing. Chuck and his pop were on the list. I didn't stay. I walked back up the hill and sat in the darkened parlor, waiting.

While the valley concentrated on the search for the trapped men, I grieved alone. Chuck filled my every thought. I read and reread newspaper accounts of the desperate conditions in the mine. On Friday the coal company announced that all hope for the missing miners was gone. They needed to fill the breach and stop the river from flooding every shaft. They were permanently sealing up the mine.

"No!" I screamed to the spirits in the empty house. "They can't leave him down there! No!"

I didn't bother to bargain with God. He wasn't listening.

Sally crept into the darkened library. "I'm sorry about Chuck," she said. "Do you need me to do anything?"

"I need Pop."

Car lights crept up and down Giant's Despair Road. I watched and waited—all night. When he wasn't home by morning, Mom began calling other workers from the plant. He had left the tavern when they did. He was behind them on the road. Yes, he'd had a few, but not too many. He was driving fine.

At noon she called the Pennsylvania state troopers. They knew nothing. New Jersey was better informed. He had been picked up for driving drunk and would spend the weekend in jail. He could make a call on Monday.

That Monday he telephoned while I was at school. He had a fine to pay but they had given back his car. He had to appear in court and could not drive until he did. He would not come home until the next Friday.

Others talked freely about the miners' deaths. Only Sally knew of the special place Chuck had in my heart. I cried into my pillow, walked into the woods and threw rocks at birds, lingered at the town dump, picking up discarded bottles and smashing them on slabs of slate.

A week from Black Friday, I skipped school. I spent the morning sitting on a log in the barren field where once the ice rink had welcomed young skaters. In the afternoon I hovered around Saint John's Monastery, waiting for the memorial service for Chuck and his pop to begin. I knew so little about the Catholic faith, I was afraid to enter the sanctuary.

I was standing on the sidewalk watching people file by when Father Cavanaugh strode across the parking lot. He paused as he opened a side door, then turned and walked over to me.

"You're one of Sean Branigan's girls, aren't you?"

I didn't know how to address him. Pop always called him Father, but Mom called all ministers Reverend. Both were too formal for me. I nodded.

"Are you here for the funeral Mass?"

"I think so."

"What's your name?"

"Molly."

"Were you a friend of Chuck's?"

"Kind of."

A small smile crossed his face. "Did you want to come inside for his Mass?"

"I'm not sure."

"While you make up your mind, come with me. I have a few minutes before we begin. Maybe you can tell me a little more about Chuck. I'm a bit short of information on him."

I hesitated. He turned and walked through the door. I followed.

He led me into a small office and I sat in the chair he offered.

"Didn't Chuck come to this church?" I asked.

"His parents sometimes attended, but not often. I don't remember meeting Chuck."

"He was a good boy."

"From what I've heard, I'm sure that's true. It's always a terrible tragedy when someone so young passes away."

I nodded.

"Tell me about Chuck."

"He saved my life. He helped me sometimes."

"How?"

"By walking me home once and by saving me from another boy who wasn't nice."

"That's how he saved your life?"

I laughed because he seemed so startled by my answer. It felt good to laugh, like a spring inside me was wound up too tight and then suddenly relieved of a little pressure.

"No. He saved me when I almost drowned last year. He dived in the water and got a girl who was scared off my back. After he took her to shore, he came after me and pulled me out of the river. I wasn't breathing. I got sick and had pneumonia."

"Wow! He really did save your life."

"I told you, he was a good boy."

"So you came to pray for his soul?"

"Kind of. I've never been to a Catholic funeral before. I don't know what I'm supposed to do."

"It's really pretty simple. There are no caskets today. You can walk by and pay your respects to Chuck and his pop by stopping at the altar. Then you find a seat. When the people stand, you should stand. When they kneel, you kneel. If you don't know the words of the prayers, listen and let your soul say its own prayer. When the Mass is over, you can light a candle for Chuck and make an offering."

"I only have some pennies."

"God doesn't care what you give, as long as it's from your heart."

"Okay."

"I've known your dad for many years."

"I saw you at the house."

"Is he a good father?"

I couldn't imagine that anyone who knew Pop could think otherwise, and I guess my expression told him the answer before I spoke because he smiled broadly.

"Yes," I said. "I couldn't ask for a better pop."

"Then I don't think he'd mind if I gave you something to remember Chuck. What do you think?"

I didn't know what to say.

"Did you know that there is a saint who carried people across rivers?"

"No."

"Saint Christopher. He was a caretaker of children like Chuck, and a wanderer like your father. I think a Saint Christopher medal would be right. One that you can wear around your neck and keep with you."

"The Protestants don't like medals."

"Are you a Protestant?"

"Not anymore. I'm not anything anymore."

He pulled an envelope from his desk drawer and shook out a small silver medal on a chain.

"It slides apart so you can have it engraved. Someday you can put Chuck's name on it." He held it out toward me.

I allowed it to fall into my hand. It was smaller than the one Sally had lost to the Sunday school teacher.

"It's pretty."

"And you'll take good care of it?"

"Oh, yes. Someday I will put Chuck's name on it."

He stood. "I have to get ready for the Mass. You'll need to walk around and go in through the big doors. Thank you for telling me about Chuck. I'd like to say something about him being a hero, during the service. Will that be okay?"

"Yes. Does it matter when I light the candle? I'd like to do it when there's not so many people around."

He smiled. "There is no time frame in heaven."

I stayed for the service, but was too shy to approach the altar where pictures of Chuck and his pop sat on a table surrounded with flowers. I liked what Father Cavanaugh said about Chuck. I saw his mother smile when she heard the story about him saving me. I believed he had not told her about that day and I wondered if boys didn't talk about stuff like girls did.

As I walked up Giant's Despair, the school bus passed.

Sally waited up for me at the bottom of Fitch Lane. "Did you hear the news?"

For a second, my heart leaped with joy. I thought she would say that by some miracle the miners had been found.

"Ronald Miller was caught robbing copper off the top of the telephone poles to sell. They arrested him and threw him in jail."

I couldn't have cared less.

"They say he fought the police and tried to run off. He got himself in double trouble."

I shrugged and started walking.

"Doesn't anything matter to you anymore? What if I tell Mom that you weren't in school today?"

"Go ahead. I don't care."

She shook her head and walked on alone. I didn't care about that either.

CHAPTER TWENTY-TWO

The next Wednesday the mining official held another town meeting. The Redevelopment Authority presented its plans for the town. I refused to go. Afterward, Mom slammed through the front door.

"They have big plans," she said. "They want to run us out, knock down the houses, and dig a big trench to stop the fire."

"Who?" Sally asked.

"A bunch of smooth-talking lawyers and company people with slick mouths. 'For the good of the community,' they said. For the good of their damned pockets is what I say! They're after the fat seam of coal under this place! 'To save Wilkes-Barre.' Hah! To save themselves the trouble of backfilling and reclaiming. Oh, if only I had the diagrams of that old mine. That would give them a start, wouldn't it?"

I knew from my Latin class that Mom's question was rhetorical, but I answered it anyway.

"I think we have the diagrams, Mom."

"What?"

"In the library. With all the paper rolls of Old Charlie's."

She stared at me blankly.

"In the drawer with the blueprints of the house."

"Show me! Show me!" She moved me into the library.

It took all three of us to hold the rolled papers flat on the puzzle board. There were maps and diagrams, overlays with street names and numbered shafts in broken lines—two copies of each. One dated 1921 and one dated 1928. And on the top of each, the words "Red Ash Mine" and beneath that "Prepared for Charles Beckerman."

Mom rerolled them into two fat tubes, kissed each roll, kissed me, put one roll back into the drawer for safekeeping, and ran to call John Hale.

"We've got them, John!" she shouted into the telephone. "We've got them over a barrel. Old Charlie never threw a thing away. I have all the diagrams of the mine. They show the shafts like you've been saying. Clearly. Clearly. Clearly."

~

I waited on the swing with Mom Friday night and listened as she spoke about the stir the engineering plans had caused.

"They show every mine shaft, Molly, and every air shaft, and every seam of coal in black and white. And they show that the richest, thickest, seam of coal lies right through the middle of Giant's Despair."

I was pleased with the discovery but I was really counting off the minutes until Pop arrived. When he finally drove up he was too drunk to talk.

Mom stood, looked him up and down, and said, "Never any sense to try and talk to a drunk. Don't bother coming upstairs. Sleep in the car for all I care." She climbed the stairs without another word.

I followed closely behind.

~

For Pop, there was no greater punishment than rejection. In the morning, when I saw his tall frame folded on the couch, tears of frustration filled my eyes. Mom noticed and led me into the kitchen.

"He doesn't get like this because he doesn't love us," she said. "It's like he's waving a huge red flag that says he doesn't love himself."

"But why?"

She shrugged her shoulders. "If I knew the answer to that, I'd become a millionaire."

But you do know the answer, I thought. You know but, like Granny Sue before you, there's nothing you can do about it.

She refused to speak to him. He pretended not to mind. He borrowed a neighbor's truck and spent that weekend picking coal that had fallen off the dump trucks from the stripping operation. On Sunday I stood in the library window and watched as he cracked large stones of anthracite into burnable chunks. The jagged stones tore open the skin on his hands. Coal dust clotted drops of blood across his knuckles into shining black pearls. He sensed me watching, stood, tipped back the peak of his cap with his jeweled knuckles, and peered up into the windows.

I tapped against the glass. He nodded his head and bent into his work.

He's like a tall tree, I thought, a tall tree that continues to push on through each season, no matter what goes on around him. I was afraid for him. I had learned that the strongest of trees could be easily toppled by the deeds of man.

Winter arrived on Thanksgiving Day. I stood in the darkness of the cellar, shoveled hunks of cracked coal into the furnace, and spoke to the spirits hovering in the darkness. I cried for them and I cried for Chuck. Twice that week I had spent my money on candles in the monastery. My waking world was dark, cold, and empty. Yet, when I dreamed, I climbed mountains on a sunny day, found stone dolls in fissured seams, followed streams that pooled deeply, ran alone and fast over wooded mountains, and gazed on great waterfalls.

Lillian arrived to celebrate, without Iris. Iris had all her children back and was working in the Globe department store. For the first time ever, Pop was absent too. He had to work a shift on Friday and so stayed in New Jersey. We didn't add the leaves to the dining room table and there was no blessing offered.

On Friday night a storm blew in from the north. At twilight it began dumping freezing rain and snow. By midnight I doubted that Pop would make it home. I stood stubbornly in the library windows and watched for lights on Giant's Despair.

Near four in the morning his car slid around Devil's Elbow. I ran to the front windows, watched him glide the big black car past the water tank. I heard the engine roar as the tires lost their grip on the hill of Fitch Lane.

I opened the door wide and stepped out in my flannel nightgown. The frozen wood of the porch floor crackled under my bare feet. Waves of windblown sleet rattled against the trees. I waited under the shelter of the roof until the car pulled in against the hedges.

He didn't turn the headlights off.

I stepped out into the freezing rain and took one step down.

He didn't open the car door.

I held tightly to the rail to keep from falling on the treacherous ice and made my way down the stairs. My feet slipped on the concrete step. I hugged the hedges and pulled myself upright.

Without warning, the Lincoln roared its engine and shot diagonally down the hill. It slowed slightly as it splintered through Mrs. Donal's white board fence, sprayed a shower of sparks as it bounced over her river rock wall, and let out a victorious squeal as it flattened the blue spruce. When it plunged through the wooden siding of the house, it caused a halo of light to flash across the windshield and reveal Pop's startled face.

I ran across the street, felt icy slush squeeze between my toes and soak the hem of my gown. I ignored the sharp points of rock that cut the flesh of my feet as I stumbled over the crushed wall. I pushed away shards of fence rail that grabbed my gown. I smelled the piney blood of the spruce tree as I stepped over its broken branches to throw open the car door.

He was leaning on the steering wheel, breathing heavily. Behind me I heard the cries of neighbors. I leaned in, touched his shoulder. "Pop?"

Fumes of hard liquor and exhaust saturated the interior air. He raised his head and smiled.

"Give me a minute," he said. "I'll back it out of here."

The engine was still running. He jammed his foot on the gas pedal. The automatic transmission moved the car farther into Mrs. Donal's parlor.

I could hear Mom coming across the road crying, "Oh, my God. Oh, my God."

"Pop," I said, "get out. Let me do it. You're going farther in."

"No." He raised a dismissive hand. "It's fine. I'll back it up." He gunned the engine and moved forward a few more inches. The house creaked in protest.

I had to stop him. I reached across, turned off the engine, and pulled the keys from the ignition.

"Oh, now you've done it," he warned.

"Get out," I screamed above the wind. "Get out."

Spruce needles pierced my bare feet. Arctic air quick-froze my long hair into icy strands that struck at my face in the fierce wind.

"Get out, Sean," Mom begged. "Let Molly do it."

When he looked up at me, his face was full of anger. I knew what to expect. I stepped back, turned, and began to run back toward the house.

"Sean! No!" I heard Mom scream.

He was behind me, breathing heavily and closing fast. I felt his hand grab my gown. I stopped and turned.

"Give me the goddamned keys," he said. "Give them to me."

I shook my head.

His fingers dug into my shoulders. "Now!"

I tried to pull away, felt the flat of his hand smack my face. I slipped in the snow and nearly fell before I flung back my arm and threw the keys into the night. The next blow sent pain through my neck and down my spine. My knees buckled. Something wild and fierce cracked open. I came up screaming, lashed out at him, beat his chest with my fists. When I couldn't hurt him with physical punishment, I turned to words.

"Do you know what you are?You're a liar! A murderer! I know what you did. Do you think I'll ever look at you the same again? You think I'll ever be glad that you're my pop?"The wind carried my words above the storm. "Murderer! Murderer! Murderer!"

Mom came between us. She filled her hand with snow, held it against my jaw, and turned me away from him.

"Don't, Molly," she said.

"Don't what?"

"Don't cry."

But I wasn't crying. It would be a long while before I would cry again

CHAPTER TWENTY-THREE

So began our time of stillness. He had taught me how to bide my time, how to keep secrets, and how to hold my heart still. He had not taught me how to forgive.

I avoided him. I went to bed early on Fridays, woke early on Saturdays, and spent entire days with friends. I walked straight past the parlor with its glowing television and up the stairs when I came home each evening.

Mom said he was sorry, that he had turned over a new leaf, that he had stopped drinking entirely. I paid her not one bit of mind. When he finally had his day in the New Jersey court, they took his driver's license away. He began to ride with coworkers. They dropped him off at the water tank around two in the morning on Saturdays and picked him up in the same spot on Mondays. I skipped out of the house early each Monday morning so that I wouldn't have to tap on his door to tell him good-bye.

For Christmas, Lillian bought him a proper bag to carry his clothes—a brown vinyl valise with thick handgrips. The Christmas tree went up and came down. Iris visited, sober and with all her children. They brought presents and no booze. Mom laughed with her as they sipped coffee at the kitchen table. I locked myself in my room.

Aunt Mary Margaret didn't visit on New Year's Eve. She was living in New Jersey. Her father, George, was living with her.

The second Monday in January, I was home sick with the flu. I peeked out between the blinds of my window and watched Pop walk slowly to the water tank, valise in hand, red plaid coat pulled up around his face, wool cap pulled down to meet his collar. He walked slowly and with a certain melancholy that sent a stab of pity through my heart. He turned before he reached Giant's

Despair Road and half-waved toward my window. I jumped away, even though it was impossible that he had seen me. When I came back to the window, he was gone.

The newspaper that morning warned of a prison break. Ronald Miller had escaped from the city jail with another boy who was guilty of more violent crimes. The two boys were believed to still be in the Wilkes-Barre area. Citizens were cautioned to lock all doors. Our doors had no locks. I went into Sally's room and watched the creek and back woods for movement.

I didn't sleep that night. Sometime before daylight I saw Chuck's face, bodiless and huge, floating on the wall at the foot of my bed. He was smiling. I sat up and reached out a hand. The face remained. Rather than fear, I felt a calm come over me, a relief of tension, a surprising peacefulness. I had forgotten how that felt. I closed my eyes for a few seconds. When I reopened them, his face was gone.

That morning, the paper said that Ronald Miller had been taken back into custody but not before he and his new friend had broken into a home downriver and raped a girl. They were placed in Eastern State Penitentiary. The newspaper said their punishments would be severe. I was sorry for him until I thought of Uncle Ira and the many lives he'd ruined or taken. I began to picture Ronald suffering in a cell like Pop's brother Mike. Better now than twenty years down the road, I thought. Better now.

That Saturday, Pop was waiting for me on the porch. "Stay home for supper tonight," he begged. "It would be good to have you sit with the family again."

I tried to push past him.

He blocked my way, laughed nervously, and asked, "Are you ever going to talk to me again?"

I stepped to the door.

"I'm sorry," he said. "I had too much to drink."

I wouldn't listen to more. I ran into the street. Plywood patches covered the hole in Mrs. Donal's house. Broken lumber and spruce tree bows lay against her fractured rock wall. That evidence of his stupidity was the touchstone for my anger. The empty space, where the tree had been, caused my jaw to clench as I muttered epitaphs against drunks and fools.

Mom tried to reach me. "You'll have to stop this stonewalling, Molly. Unless you want to ruin your entire life for one mistake of Pop's."

I pushed past her. The look on her face said she wanted to slap me as hard as Pop had. I didn't care. My life was already in ruins. There was nothing more anyone could do to make it worse.

Sally came into my bedroom. "You'd better listen, Molly. Your teacher called and said she thinks something is wrong with you. If you want to get one of those scholarships, you'll have to have good grades."

"Don't waste your breath. If I was old enough, I'd get out of here. I don't want to be part of this family anymore."

She slammed my bedroom door after her.

John Hale stopped me on my way to school in February. "The Donals don't intend to repair the house. There's no one wants to live in it after their mom's death. You know, they're not mad at your pop for this," he said. "We all make mistakes."

I shrugged him off. "Doesn't matter. The place would never have been the same anyway. Not with Tom's tree gone." I could feel his eyes on me as I climbed onto the bus.

Another storm blew in that day. School ended early. I ducked my head against the wind as I ran to the idling bus. I hurried into the open door and up the stairs. I put my books on the seat next to me to save it for Sally. The driver climbed into his seat and engaged the transmission. The gears ground together.

"Wait!" I called. "My sister's not here."

He spoke into the rearview mirror. "Not coming," he said. "Going to the movies."

I started to protest but stopped when my books were lifted and Pop dropped into the seat. I was trapped on my own school bus. I wouldn't look at him. The windows fogged in the closed space. I wiped a spot clear with closed fingers.

We turned onto Market Street and headed toward the mountain. Sleet crackled against the glass, melted slightly, then froze into tiny icicles that split and fell with the movement of the bus.

The cracked rivulets of ice reminded me of the last Christmas we had spent at the house with no doorknobs. Pop had found steady work at the factory, bought an old car, and was slowly improving life for all of us. Lillian had planned to visit and bring Christmas. A wicked storm blew in, closing the Laurel Line and major roads. We didn't have a phone, and it was nearly evening before my parents realized that Lillian wouldn't make it. I remembered the panic in their voices as they tried to explain that Christmas might be late, that even Santa Claus couldn't travel in such bad weather.

I wasn't to be fooled. I swore he would come. He would bring presents and decorations for the green pine tree that filled the parlor with woodsy scents. I climbed into bed with Sally and Marty and slept fitfully as the wind howled and snow rattled against the thin siding on the house.

Morning had arrived with icicles on the insides of the windows and my feet so cold I couldn't feel them. I ran down the stairs, through the coal-warmed kitchen, and into the tiny front room. There stood the Christmas tree, as we'd left it—with not one present tucked beneath its branches.

I remembered the disappointment I had felt as I dropped onto the sofa. And I remembered Mom saying, "I'm sure I heard

Santa Claus last night. I know I did. I think we should go outside and have a look."

Pop had come in through the front door. His hat was coated with ice and his nose was bright red. I remembered that he made me giggle by nuzzling my neck with his cold nose while he helped me into my coat. He carried me through deep snow. Mom went first, followed by Marty, then Sally. We stood where the road should have been and faced the house.

Pop pointed. There were sled tracks and boot prints on the rooftop.

"I knew it," Mom said. "I knew I heard him up there. Maybe he'll come back tonight, or tomorrow night."

"But look," Pop said. "His tracks come off the roof and head toward the side of the house. I think we should follow them."

The winter sun had crusted the snow with ice. It crunched underfoot. As we came around to the other side, the older kids let out excited screams.

Santa's boot prints ended at a small, umbrella-shaped tree covered in thick ice. Long icicles hung from its thin branches, caught rays of bright sunlight, and made rainbows on the snow.

"My goodness, Sean. What in the world is that?" Mom asked.

Pop snapped a piece of ice from the tree and touched it to his tongue. "Maple," he said. "I believe Santa left us a Popsicle tree. Our very own maple-flavored Christmas tree."

He held a sliver of ice in his gloved hand. I stuck my tongue out and tasted it carefully. It was very cold and very sweet.

He'd always cared for us, but that year he had cared so much he'd climbed a ladder twice in the storm to make sled prints with a two-by-four and footprints with his leaking boots. And he had carried water from the well, mixed it with sugar, and doused that kid-sized maple tree—so we could have a Christmas.

Remembering the Popsicle tree made me feel ashamed. Tears stung my eyes. I turned to him.

"What are you doing here, Pop?"

"We need to talk. I'm sorry that I had to corner you."

I stared out the window. The bus had begun to climb through the roller coaster humps of Coal Street. It swerved repeatedly as it slowly made the grade.

"I think you know something."

I watched the houses fade away through a curtain of white snow.

"Molly." His voice was gruff.

I half-turned toward him.

"You're a smart girl. I want you to know the truth."

"I already know the truth. You are such a stinking drunk you don't remember any of what you did, do you?"

"I remember that I hit you and I hate myself for that. I vowed I'd never treat my kids the way I was treated, and I didn't hold true to it."

The bus stopped at the traffic light next to the Empire Tavern. I expected him to stand, walk down the narrow aisle, and get off. He stayed in his seat.

The bus started up the last big hill before Giant's Despair. I stretched my neck to peer out the small opening on the ice-coated window. Cars were pulled onto the sidewalk at odd angles. The bus lurched as we entered the curve below the monastery. I felt my heart leap into my throat as we careened sideways. Pop reached out a restraining hand and stopped me from tumbling out of my seat. The impact shook the ice from my window. A power pole held our bus sideways. A pileup of cars blocked the hill.

"Everybody all right?" our driver shouted.

Everybody was.

"This is as far as I'm going today," he said. "You'll all be safer walking. Be careful and go straight home." He opened the door and helped everyone exit the bus.

Pop took my books in one arm and placed his free hand on my elbow as we made some headway up the ice-covered sidewalk.

"I know you're upset with me for the car and the house and for hitting you. But I think there's more to it than that," he said.

"What? You think I care about Uncle Ira? Queer Uncle Ira? I don't care at all about him. He got what he deserved." I reached out with both hands and grasped his coat as I began to slide backward.

He stopped and waited for me to regain my footing. "You *do* know."

I planted my feet and looked up at him. "I found Old Charlie's diary."

"What does that mean?"

Other kids pushed past us, laughing and jostling as they climbed the hill.

"It means I know that you went to find Ira. Why do you think I've been asking so many questions?" I said. "I heard you and Magee talking. And Mom and Fern. And I got some stuff from Lillian and John Hale. And I went to the library and looked up the newspaper stories. And you know what? I feel really sorry for Aunt Iris and all of her kids. And I'm sad for Old Charlie and Granny Sue. And I cry for your brother Mike every time I read the articles about him. But, like I said, I don't give a damn about Uncle Ira."

His breath came in short wheezing gasps. I remembered Doc Rosen saying that extreme cold could trigger asthma. I looked up the hill toward the monastery. I tugged on his coat and pointed. "We can rest in the church."

He didn't hesitate. We turned, climbed the drive, and went in through the front doors. At the end of the long aisle, the altar was backlit with dim lights. Pop dipped his fingers in the font of holy water and crossed himself. He led me to a pew near the back, stopped to genuflect, and stepped aside for me to go first. When I was seated, he pulled the kneeler down and settled on his knees.

I sat behind him and watched as he prayed. His back heaved with the effort of breathing.

He was taking too long. Now that we were finally going to talk, I couldn't wait for his breathing to settle down or his courage to be buoyed up.

I slid off the seat and knelt beside him. I turned toward him and whispered, "Do you really believe in God?"

"I wouldn't be on my knees if I didn't."

That quieted some of my anger. "You want to know why I'm so mad at you?"

"Yes."

"It's because you've changed. Jersey changed you. All you do is watch television. I was scared every weekend when you were driving home, before you lost your license. You wrecked two cars and Mrs. Donal's house. Even Tom Donal's tree."

"Molly, I'm so sorry."

I wasn't going to be stopped. "I'm tired of you always being sick from drink. You leave for Jersey with a hangover on Monday and you come back plastered on Friday night. I can never talk to you. And Chuck died."

"Chuck?"

"The boy from the picnic—the one who saved me. You can't remember that either?"

He ran a hand over his eyes and rubbed his temple. "I remember. Of course I remember. He was with you at the skating pond. I don't think I ever knew his name."

"Well, he died. He is still stuck in that damned south slope. His pop too."

He shook his head. "I am so sorry. I don't know what else to say. I am so sorry."

"I'm sorry too."

He started to lift his arm, to reach out to me, but I pulled away.

"He always watched out for me. He was my friend."

"He saved your life. That makes him more than a friend." He lowered his arm and clasped his hands together on top of the polished pew.

"I really liked him." I could feel hot tears beginning to press against my eyelids.

"And he couldn't help but like you."

"I light candles for him."

"I think it might take more than candles to show him how you cared. I think it might take a whole lifetime of trying your best, so you can live a life that's good enough for both of you."

"Like you did for Mike?"

He shifted his weight off his knees and dropped his forehead on his folded hands. When he spoke I could barely hear him.

"I didn't do too well for him. I let your Mom take on a whole bunch of what I should have done. She was always good to him. And she is always good to you. I'm glad she could help you deal with Chuck's dying."

"I never told her."

"Oh, Molly! Why?"

I shrugged. "You don't tell anybody when *you're* sad."

"I tell your mother things."

"You don't tell her everything. You didn't tell her about Uncle Ira."

"That's different. There was no need to tell anyone else about that. Old Charlie and me were already one too many to keep a secret."

That seemed like an awfully big secret to keep inside.

"Why didn't you call John Hale and have Ira arrested?"

He thought about that for a long time before he finally spoke. "Molly, I'm going to give you this one time to ask all your questions, and I'm going to answer them as honestly as I can. But after today I won't talk to you about it again. I have to have you agree to that before I say another word."

"How honest is 'as honestly as I can'?"

"It's the truth as I know it. There are some things I don't have answers for, and that's all I can say. Do we have a deal?"

"I want the whole truth."

"Okay, but we'll have to talk very quietly. Even the walls have ears. You've proved that to me."

I whispered, "Why didn't you tell John Hale about what Ira did?"

"There was no proof. It would have been my word against Ira's. Who do you think they would believe?"

"If Iris knew, why couldn't she help?"

"I think she's buried everything so deep, she doesn't remember."

"What would she remember?"

"I'm sure she saw Ira push Silas under that train. She threatened to kill herself once and said some things that made me believe she'd seen a lot. It was too late, then."

"What would happen if someone found out now?"

"I could spend the rest of my life in jail. Or they might give me the electric chair."

A tremor ran through me.

"You have to believe me, Molly. I didn't plan any of it. I wanted to help my brother and the rest just happened."

"I read the newspapers about your brother. They said he hurt a little boy."

"He swore to me that he didn't do that. Mike never lied to me."

Suddenly all the sadness I'd felt tried to come out at once. I struggled to hold it in. I kept my head bowed. Tears began to fall to the carpet beneath the kneeler.

"Did Old Charlie know?"

"He suspected. He wrote the dates down, was going to go to the authorities, but he had a stroke before he could. After that he was pretty well at the mercy of Ira."

"So the message in his diary was for you?"

"The message?"

"The one that said, 'Crystal Lake cabin, my car, go.'"

I felt him turn his head, could feel his eyes on me.

"Yes. He told me about his boys and about Faye. He knew where to find Ira. He gave me the keys to the cabin and his car."

"Why did he hide his diary?"

"I guess he didn't want Sue to find it. I guess he wanted to protect me."

"Why didn't you take the thing and burn it?"

"I never gave it another thought. So much happened at once." He shook his head as if to clear his thoughts. "Where did you find it?"

"In the heating vent in my room."

"When?"

"Last year, when I had pneumonia."

"Why didn't you ask me about it?"

"I wanted to have a secret. I wanted to figure out what it meant. I wish I'd never found it."

"That makes two of us."

"Did you shoot Ira?"

"No. It wasn't like that."

"What was it like?"

"It was fast. It happened fast."

A movement at the side of the church caught my eye. A priest was kneeling at the altar while a young boy lit candles.

"Maybe you should have told Father Cavanaugh," I said. "Maybe he could have helped you."

"I did tell him."

I turned and his eyes locked on mine. "You did?"

"I made a confession years ago. When I couldn't keep it bottled up any longer."

"And he didn't help you go to the police?"

"Priests take vows not to tell unless they can prevent something from happening. In my case it was all done. I wasn't about to trust the authorities."

I remembered Father Cavanaugh's question about whether Pop was good to me, and I knew now why he had asked. Maybe he had stayed close to Mary Margaret in case Pop should mess up again.

"Do you think Father Cavanaugh trusts you now?"

"He has no reason not to."

"It's not fair."

"What isn't?"

"That no one would believe you but everyone trusted Ira."

"Nobody ever said life would always be fair," he said. "I can only hope it evens out in heaven." He grinned when he said that, and I felt my heart dance a bit. He hadn't changed completely after all.

"How come nobody else knew about what you did to Ira? How come everybody thought he did himself in?"

"They found a note."

"Did you see the note?"

Pop shook his head. "No. John Hale kept it as evidence."

"Did you write the note?"

He hesitated and his eyes opened wider. "No. I didn't go that far."

"How far did you go?"

"Do you really need to know?"

"Yes. I want to know everything. I want to believe you couldn't help it."

He sighed and sat back on the seat. I sat back too, and I didn't pull away when he draped his arm over my shoulders.

"I drove out to the cabin. I was going to make him talk. I was going to bring him back to Wilkes-Barre and make him confess to the police. When I got there, the cabin was dark, so I used Charlie's key to get in. He was waiting for me. He turned on the light and pretended everything was hunky-dory. He said that he was sorry about Mike, that he felt like a fool for leaving him alone and drunk in that beer joint."

"What did you say?"

"I cursed him. I told him I knew what really happened. That I'd seen Mike and he'd told me the truth and that your mom had told me about Marty."

"Did he say it wasn't true?"

"No. He didn't say anything. He pointed a gun at me."

I caught my breath. "Did you get scared?"

"Hell, yes, I got scared."

"Did he shoot at you?"

"No. Not right away. He started telling me that he couldn't be blamed, that Mike wasn't his responsibility. That if I was any kind of a brother I would never have left him to fend for himself."

"Did that make you mad?"

"I was still too scared to be mad. He was coiled up as tight as one of those big rattlers near Prospect Rock."

"What did you do?"

"I asked him if Charlie had been right—if he had killed the boys and Faye. He said he loved all those boys, that he would never have harmed them. He said he knew what I was thinking and that I was sick if I thought he could perform perverse acts with boys."

"Did you know about those pictures?"

"No. And that's the odd thing. I didn't know about any of that, except that some people said he was strange. He started talking about Bernie and beautiful little Arlie, like he wanted to brag about it all but wasn't sure he should."

I had many more questions, but I had learned to listen well in the past year. I held still and waited.

He didn't seem to realize that he was telling me. It was like he was mulling over it over in his mind for the first time.

"While he was talking, I was thinking, that could have been Marty or baby Sally."

He paused, then began to speak again, very softly and with an unusual uncertainty in his voice. "And he kept talking, like the devil had loosened his tongue. He said he loved my kids like he'd loved Charlie's boys. That it was a pure love, and special. And that if I could feel that kind of love, I would understand."

He closed his eyes and looked like he was about to cry. I couldn't let him do that.

"What did you do?" I said, too loudly. I saw the priest's head tilt to one side, so I repeated my words in a whisper. "What did you do?"

He caught the cue and lowered his voice so low I had to strain to hear him.

"I started to be sick. I couldn't hold back anymore. I think I jumped at him. I heard the bang of the gun. I thought he had hit me. I stopped moving and he started yelling. He said the Mike was a worthless piece of humanity. That he deserved to die. That he was an idiot. He started hopping back and forth like a prizefighter and then he bolted out the door."

I had to ask. "Where was the gun?"

"I don't know. I don't think he'd ever fired one before. I think he dropped it. When I caught up with him on the porch, he didn't have it. Once I hit him, I couldn't stop. I don't know how long I beat him before I realized that he wasn't struggling anymore. I pushed him over the rail and heard him splash into the lake. He was facedown in the water.

"I might have done it on purpose. I stood by the side of the lake and watched him float. I didn't move a finger to help him. I went up on the porch and sat in a chair and I watched his back. I probably watched him until I was sure he wasn't breathing, I went back through the cabin, got in the car, and drove back to Charlie's. That was it."

"You didn't shoot him or stab him or anything?"

"No."

"Good."

"Why is that good?"

"I don't think it would be the same if you did something on purpose."

"I left him in the water on purpose. That doesn't make anything better. That doesn't make it right."

"But he was a terrible man. Somebody had to stop him."

"That's not how the law sees it."

"That's how I see it."

"I wish I could believe everyone would think like you, but I don't. When the papers said it was suicide, Charlie and me decided to let it alone."

"Is that why you get so drunk?"

"I don't know."

"I hate you when you're drunk."

"I've stopped. I made a promise to your mother and myself, and I'll do the same for you if you ask."

"I do ask."

"Right here, I'll get back on my knees, in front of God and the saints.

"Do it," I said.

He pushed forward onto the kneeler. I knelt beside him again.

"Say it," I prompted. "Say 'I promise.'"

"I promise you. I will never drink again."

"Say it to God. Say 'God, I promise right now, with Molly as my witness, that I will never touch a drop of booze again.'"

"That's it? That's all you need?"

"That's it, but you have to say it."

"God, I promise right now, with Molly as my witness, that I will never touch a drop of booze again."

"Okay."

"Now, Molly, I need a promise from you."

"What?"

"I need you to promise you'll never speak to anyone about what I've told you today. Not to your mother, not to your sister, not to a friend, not even to your husband when you get married."

I wondered if I could keep that promise.

"Can you promise me that?"

I took a deep breath and said the words. "I promise. I'll never speak a word to anyone about what you told me today."

"Okay then."

"We should have something to seal it with, something to remind us."

He looked around the sanctuary, searched his pockets.

That's when I remembered the medal. The one Father Cavanaugh had given me. I pulled it from my neck and pressed it into his hand. It seemed tiny when he opened his big palm and studied it.

"It's Saint Christopher," I said. "He's the saint who carried people across the water. Father Cavanaugh gave it to me for Chuck—because he saved me from the river."

Pop smiled a little. "I know about Saint Christopher," he said. "Do you think he's the proper saint for a man with a drinking problem?"

"Father Cavanaugh said he's good for travelers. It's worth a try."

He slipped the bit of silver from its chain and dropped it into the breast pocket of his coat. He patted his chest.

"There," he said. "I feel protected already."

That made me laugh.

He put the chain back around my neck. "I'm trusting you," he said.

"And I'm trusting you."

That might have been the end of it, but I had one more question.

"Pop?"

"What?"

"How come you didn't get rid of the diary?"

"I didn't know where it was. I figured Old Charlie must have gotten rid of it."

"You didn't help him put it in the vent?"

"No."

"You're sure?"

"Of course I'm sure."

"Then who did?"

We stared into each other's eyes for a very long time.

"Did they ever find the gun?" I finally asked.

He shook his head slowly. "No. I don't believe they did."

We said it together: "John Hale." And then we started to laugh so much that the priest turned completely around to look at us.

Pop shook his head again. "All these years," he muttered, "and he never breathed a word."

"Because he's like you."

"Do you think so?"

"Sure. Why do you think I like him so much?"

He made the sign of the cross again, picked up my books, stood, and held out his hand.

"Are you too big to hold your pop's hand in public?"

"Nope. Not yet. But I won't make any promises about next year."

I slipped my hand in his. We walked out into the winter wind and continued on our way up the road called Giant's Despair.

Made in the USA
Lexington, KY
18 December 2013